The Cape Ann Hat

by
Letitia Sweitzer

Also by the Author

The Elephant in the ADHD Room
Absolutely!

As co-author:

Dreams That Come True
Tired of Yelling
Understanding Growth Hormones
The Mulling Factor

Dedication

I dedicate this book to my beloved partner Michael J. Cain, who shared his wisdom and encouraged me in my writing in every way, even when I was difficult.

I also dedicate this book to the memory of my great aunt Letitia Douglas Adams, M.D. She was the surgeon who delivered me, then took care of me in her home on the coast of Massachusetts. As an adult I continued to spend my summers with her in Rockport on Cape Ann, a stone's throw from the fictional town of Stonehaven.

And to the memory of my great aunt Frances Douglas Pidgin, whom friends and family called Our Ma. A widow, she lived with my Aunt Letitia for most of my childhood. I learned to read in her lap.

And to the memory of Mary Baker who, back then, I thought was my third great aunt. Indeed, as the live-in housekeeper in Aunt Letitia's household, she did her share of raising me. Mary encouraged me. "Do what you like and you'll live longer," she often told me.

So I wrote this book!

THE CAPE ANN HAT

BY
Letitia Sweitzer

1

The Crash! The Cash?

Rena plucked the money out of the blueberry bushes as fast as she could. She overtook a twenty dollar bill somersaulting across a flat rock and caught another flapping high through the sumac. As her eyes adjusted to the moonlight, she had little difficulty seeing the bills; their surfaces stood out clearly against the crisscross of bare twigs and moonlit granite beneath her feet. She tried not to look at the bills that got away, tried not to think of them.

The thorns of a wild rose clawed at her legs, her occasional complaint was drowned out by the sea and carried away by a stiff March wind across the point. She pressed her thigh deep into each winter-bared bush, enduring the scratches, then leaned far over its dense network of twigs. She snatched a bill from the thorn of the rose bush and another from the stiff clutches of the blueberry bushes. She stuffed them into a plastic bag. The cadence she had used to pick the wild blueberries themselves in the summers of her childhood sustained her now.

Below, at ocean's edge, she heard the tide suck water from

crevices in the headland rock, guzzle tidepools, slurp seaweed straight. The sea drank up the water, then belched it out again. Each new wave hit the promontory with a deep boom, spray splattering the air.

Rena winced with the crash of every wave. Like birds with broken wing, the bills fluttered across the headlands and down the rock on the other side. They lighted for a moment on a clump of grass, broke loose again, descended. Finally, sodden with spray, they clung, one by one, to crevice edge, clung to one last stroke of moonlight, then succumbed to the sea.

If Rena had not pulled the box by its flimsy top, this wouldn't have happened. If she had only closed one door of Paul's car before she opened the other, the wind would not have whipped through the car, blowing the bills out into the March night. If she could only undo what had happened....

The police had called her; the ring itself had sent her into spasms of adrenaline. The Chairman had been hurt, they said. Please come to the car on the rocks at Boding Point. She pulled on the nearest clothes draped over a chair, grabbed her coat, and drove off into the cold. There was the car, just like the police said. He hadn't made the curve at Boding Point in the dark.

But Paul Lawson could make that curve any day of the week, at any speed, dark or no dark. Like every Stonehaven boy, he'd grown up taking that curve with a beer in his hand, with his arm around a girl, at fifty miles an hour, imagining the police after him. He could take that curve. Something else must have been wrong.

The car's nose was crumpled into a boulder, the hood popped and bent, its windshield shattered, the town seal on the side door bowed in. Rena imagined Paul thrown forward, the steering wheel pressing into his chest, glass flying around him. The cold wind from the east stung as it dried the tears off her face.

Why couldn't they have called her to Paul's hospital bedside in the middle of the night, to take his hand and comfort him? Rena couldn't blame the police though; they had to call someone to get his belongings before the tow truck came.

"We figured you being in charge of Town Hall business and all, you'd know best what to do with it," Chief Giordano had said. "No need to worry Mrs. Lawson about it, poor thing."

Yes, Maureen. Poor thing.

Rena had avoided the side of the car where Paul had so recently sat, as if she would find the heat of his body still there and not be able to bear up. She came to the passenger side instead and, putting her hand to her eyes to cut the glare from the moon, looked in the car window.

There was stuff in the car all right; Paul kept it as a sort of traveling office. Even in the dark, she recognized Paul's accordion file, containing information about everyone he ever knew, lying on its side, knocked off its accustomed place on the hump of the floor of the front seat. The door on the passenger side was crumpled, but it had opened, and the wind pressed it against Rena's back while she retrieved the file. Thank God that file was saved. She had only a small fraction of its contents copied and in her records. Paul's hat, his precious Cape Ann hat, she caught by the brim with the tips of her fingers, pulled it to her and squashed it onto her own head. The familiar hat gave her comfort and strengthened her resolve to make everything right for Paul in this hour of crisis. She turned to carry the file to her car. The door slammed behind her.

She came back for the next load. A cardboard box had been thrown off the back seat. It was crushed out of square and the top was popped open. She opened the back door on the passenger side, reached across the seat and tugged at the box by its top flaps. It was heavy, and she had to work it free, tugging first one side then the other. As she pulled the box up onto the seat, the top tore off in her hand. So she went around to the other side of the car to pull out the box.

The door seemed to bind and Rena had to jerk it hard. Then, as the door sprung open, the wind whipped through the car, chilling her face, flailing her hair. She felt Paul's hat blow off her head, and she grabbed for it in vain. It was gone. Then, like Pandora's box, the car emptied in the gale. Gasoline receipts flew out of the ashtray. An empty dry cleaners bag billowed past her like a ghost. Paper things like a flock of frightened bats, blew out of the torn box, smacked her face, and sailed past her and across the point toward the water on the other side. She turned to run after them, holding her arms out as if to catch them in a giant net.

Finally Rena dropped her hands. Useless. She noticed the dry cleaners bag caught on a bush; she picked it up and tied the bottom closed to make a sack. She looked around at the little fluttering papers, caught one, and held it up to the moonlight. These twenty dollar bills add up. She squinted at it again. No, my God, a hundred dollar bill. A hundred dollar bill and there must have been hundreds of them, a thousand of them in that box. A hundred thousand dollars blowing across the rocky promontory, scuttering, flying, winging in a wind off the open ocean, wheeling and plunging into the great Ipswitch Bay.

What had Paul been doing driving around at two o'clock in the morning with a box of money on the back seat? The question stopped her; she stood quite still. There was no good reason. And what about Paul now? Paul, who was agonizing, muttering or perhaps free from agonizing, unconscious, over in Addison Gilbert Hospital. Rena realized she had to either think or gather the money; she couldn't do both. The weight of her thoughts would hold her back. The money was escaping. Get the money.

Save what I can, Rena said to herself, don't worry about the rest. Save what I can, she repeated, a refrain that kept the import of the night from engulfing her. She reached and picked and stuffed until her hands were numb from the cold. She could no longer feel the texture, feel the thinness of the bills. She thought of the famous shipwrecked Cape Ann fisherman, Howard Blackburn, who rowed his ship's dory for five winter days and five winter nights with his hands frozen to the oars until he found land. Like him, she gave herself over to the rhythms of purpose.

Hunting, chasing, reaching, grabbing and grabbing again kept Rena from knowing what she knew, suspecting what she suspected. She ran, gasped for breath, tripped, banged her shin, got up, pushed on until the exhilaration of struggle became a sort of peace and the bag filled.

If only she could get the rest of the money together in this dry cleaner's bag and get it and the box safely into her car before the tow truck came, it would save a lot of questions. Questions a Town Clerk shouldn't have to answer. If she could avoid the little questions now, maybe the big ones would never come up. For now, hunt, chase, reach, and stuff while she salvaged a treasure of thousands, tens of thousands of dollars blowing over the headlands. *Save what I can. Let the rest go.*

Rena heard a car squeal then suddenly slow by the curve where Paul's car had gone off the road. Not the tow truck. Not yet. Just some teenagers stopping, looking down the point, calling to each other.

"Jeez, man. It's totaled."

"It's the Chairman's car! Look at that Town seal. Oh, man, this is big."

Rena heard their voices over the wind and watched their shadowy forms as they examined the wreckage of Paul's car. Then they returned to their car and drove away, slowly at first. Rena heard them gunning down Bay Road on toward Gloucester. Word would be getting around. Rena didn't have much time to finish her salvage. She turned back frantically to the job, jumping towards this bill and running towards that.

The bag was almost full now. She was retrieving fewer and fewer bills. She knew there were many more, but the hand-over-fist gathering was done for tonight. And here came the tow truck.

Rena ran toward her car, clutching the bag to her body, holding her arm across the top to keep it closed. She heard the tow truck door slam, and she could see the driver making his way precariously over the rocks toward her. She rushed to her car door and set the bag down between her legs and the car, squeezing her knees across the top of the bag.

"Anyone here?" the tow truck driver called from the other side of her car. It was Charlie, the regular Town tow operator.

Rena had her hand on the door handle, her thumb ready to press the button.

"Charlie, I'm here," she called out over the top of her car, hoping her voice would make him look up over the car instead of into it when the interior light would turn on.

"Oh, Ms. Everett," the tow driver said.

Rena pressed the button, pulled the door open, ducked down, grabbed the bag of cash, and stuck it on the floor of the front seat.

She slammed the door just as the bag tipped over, the bills spewed out on the floor, and the light mercifully went out.

"Charlie!" Rena called out again over the top of the car. "I got the Chairman's stuff from his car. Just one more thing and he's ready to go," she forced herself to say cheerfully, too cheerfully, for Charlie was now looking with distress at Paul's car, its nose crumpled into the rock, its doors standing open like wings.

"Is the Chairman all right?"

"Oh. No. He's.... We don't know. All I know is what the police told me. He didn't make the curve. Maybe he fainted or something. You know with all that...you know... a while back, maybe he.... We just don't know." As she stammered, she made one more trip to the Chairman's car, starting and stopping to wait for Charlie, leading him away from her car like a mother bird protecting her nest. She reached the wreck first, pulled out the battered box from the seat, bending its torn sides in at the top to close it in case the wind had failed to set a few remnants of the cash free.

"The police called me to come get Paul's stuff. Well, the Town stuff, some files, papers. Nothing personal," she assured him. "Receipts, you know. A few other.... You can't leave things in a car...might get stolen."

Rena was tossing out phrases to distract Charlie, trying to make sense but trying to say nothing. She was confused; she hoped she'd confused Charlie, too. She didn't want anyone to know more about Paul than she did.

The drive home seemed longer than usual. In the strobes of passing streetlights, the plastic bag of money lying by her feet glowed eerily, like a naked body. The bills that had tumbled out now lay lifeless on the floor. The box yawned open on the seat beside her, its flaps sagging over the money that remained packed too deep to fly in the wind.

She turned in Duncan Lane, the back alley that ran behind her house, eased through the narrow gate in the tall fence made of weathered saplings, and stopped her car beside her back steps instead of putting it in the garage. With the motor running, she got out and closed the door behind her softly, just enough to make the interior light go out. She considered her back yard quite private, but

6

noise and lights in the middle of the night might attract attention. She went around to the other side of the car and opened the door. She gathered up the loose bills and stuffed them back into the almost empty box. She glanced through the apple tree at the neighbors' windows, dark now, then lifted the transparent bag and the cardboard box from the car. She cradled them like twin babies and carried them into the house.

In a moment she came out and got in the car again. She sighed at the wheel. One thing done. Now the harder thing. Go to the hospital. She wondered if the neighbors rolled over in their sleep, disturbed by the sounds of her departure from routine, saw in their dreams that the world was coming apart.

Rena leaned forward over the wheel as the road rose, dipped, and curled from Stonehaven through Lanesville and Annisquam, slicing through rock and circumscribing sandy coves. She drove across the front parking lot of the Addison Gilbert Hospital, past the flagpole, and made the turn into the parking lot in the back a little too fast.

Rena sat a minute in the dark refuge of her car catching her breath. For all who go into the hospital must look at life and death in unblinking brilliance. Rena had known both the comfort and the despair of that bright interior when her own great Aunt Amelia lay failing in this same hospital.

Rena finally got out of the car and hurried in the cold wind to the Fisher Lobby only to find it locked. She peered through the glass where the 350th Gloucester anniversary quilt hung in the half-light of the foyer. Then she noticed the sign on the door: "After midnight use the Emergency Entrance." She walked around to the side where the neon light burned its disturbing reddish-orange color into the white uniforms of three attendants on break, who stood under it, puffing on cigarettes, cupping their hands to shield them from the wind.

The wind blew cold off the cemetery, which lay in wait disconcertingly close to the emergency room. A gurney was readied by the door.

Rena lingered by the entrance till the night receptionist was looking away; then she hurried quietly into the maze of halls that would lead eventually to ICU. It had suddenly hit her that they would not likely let her in to see Paul. Just before the nurses' station at ICU, she leaned her shoulder against the wall and closed her eyes in terror. Surely they would not keep her from him.

A nurse strode out of the unit and Rena opened her eyes and straightened.

"Can I help you?"

"I came to see Paul Lawson."

"Only immediate family allowed. Are you....?"

"Like family," Rena said, nodding and mumbling the "like" so that it was inaudible.

"Excuse me?" the nurse questioned.

"His sister," Rena lied.

"Give the night nurse your name," the nurse said, nodding to the desk.

"Paul Lawson," she said to the night nurse as if she hadn't understood what she had been told to do.

"Room 201." Family, thought Rena, as she took in for the first time what was obvious: of course Paul's family would stay tirelessly by his side. That is not how she had imagined it. She wanted them out.

Rena paused in the doorway so she could see part of the room. She could see Maria, Paul's younger daughter. Maria looked up, recognized Rena and started toward her, then stopped and glanced questioningly to the bedside where Rena knew Paul's wife Maureen would be. Rena waited. Maureen herself came to the door.

Rena hugged her, then said apologetically, "They said family only ."

"You're family. Paul would want you here." *Would want.* That answered Rena's first question. She sank into herself like a candle melted to the point of collapse. Somehow she managed to step into the room.

Paul looked unlike himself. Limp, helpless. Hair, dampened into strands, was stuck to his face. Maybe he always looked like that when he was sleeping. No, Paul would look in charge even in his sleep. She wanted to shake him.

"How is he?"

8

Maureen shrugged, and tears rolled out of her eyes.

"Is he sleeping?"

"They gave him something to make him sleep."

"Oh. So he was conscious."

Maureen shrugged again. "He didn't know where he was. He didn't know where he'd been."

Rena patted her on the shoulder as she began to weep again.

"In the morning, they'll find out what has happened to him. Right?" Rena looked at Maria to encourage her. Maria had been Rena's favorite of Paul's two girls in spite of the fact, perhaps because of the fact, that she had been the "difficult" one growing up.

"They said it might be a bad concussion from the crash. But there wasn't enough of a bump on his head," Maria said, her blue eyes darting from Rena to her mother as if trying to inform one without disturbing the other.

"I'm afraid it's back," Maureen said.

"What's back?" Rena said, although she knew.

"The tumor."

Rena wanted to run to Paul and cry, "No, no!" but she bound up her emotion with an unexpectedly strong will and gathered Maureen and Maria in one embrace.

"Maybe not the tumor," Rena said. "There are a lot of things it could be. They can do something. We'll see to that."

"I just hope he's well by the time of the wedding," Maria said.

Rena sighed. How quickly Maria's mind had jumped from her father's precarious condition to its impact on her own calendar. The initial flash of annoyance Rena felt at Maria's callowness soon gave way to empathy. Rena herself had already ordered the snapdragons she was going to nurture in her garden for the wedding. She had promised Maria lavender, peach, and white snapdragons, tended so they would be specimen blossoms. It was going to be Stonehaven's wedding of the century and, as the closest family friend, Rena planned to be prominently involved. A toned-down wedding in deference to Paul's infirmity was not in her or Maria's plans.

Rena sighed again, annoyed at herself now, as well as at Maria, for trivializing Paul's illness.

"He'll be well, Maria. He will," Rena assured her. "Maureen, call me when he wakes up. Don't worry; I won't tire him; I just want to reassure him, tell him everything is fine at Town Hall. Don't want him to worry."

"I'll call," Maureen said.

Rena raised her eyes to Maria to extract an additional promise, and Maria nodded. If Maureen didn't call, Maria would.

Back at her car, Rena cried. She cried for Paul—as near a perfect man as she had ever known—and for herself. She wanted to touch Paul and feel that her hands could heal. She wanted to be alone with him. She wanted everything back the way it was the day before and all the years of days she had worked as Paul's right hand.

And she wanted some answers.

She wiped her tears and began to get a grip on reality and tidy it up. In a day or in a few days, they would stop medicating Paul, and he would regain full consciousness. Then there would be short periods of time when the family, relieved, would leave Paul alone. Then he would call for her right away because, among other things, he, too, would be eager to settle the matter of the money. There might be some urgency about its disposition, and he would tell her what to do with it and how to answer any questions that might arise. And of course, even if he didn't tell anyone else, he would tell her the whole story of the money. He would dispel her worries.

If Paul didn't have a chance to arrange this private conversation soon, she would offer to stay with him on a Saturday or Sunday to give Maureen a rest. Of course, Leslie would soon be home from grad school to see her father, and she and Maria would be around on the weekends. In that case, Rena would take time off from work to stay with Paul and give Maureen a midweek break.

Planning all this soothed Rena. Nothing was ever as bad as it seemed once she had a chance to put her ducks in a row. Save what I can, let the rest go, Rena said to herself. She was over her crying. Now she was keyed up and restless, and she didn't want to go home. As much as she loved having the house to herself as she had for more than two decades since Aunt Amelia died, there were still times when the silence of the unused rooms and long empty halls were cutting reminders that she had no soulmate to share the nights with.

She drove to the end of the hospital driveway and stopped. Across Route 127, a sign announced, "Great Carnival." She looked across O'Malley School toward the field where earlier that night she knew the great mandala of the Ferris wheel had lifted brave people to the sky and the tilt-a-wheel had whirled them till they could hardly walk. Now all was dark. She did not move.

She thought of the land lying before her like a great map as if on that map she could choose the road to resolution. Resolution to Paul's immediate problem—which she feared was becoming her own—and resolution to vaguer questions that drifted like fog around her life.

To the left lay the road by which she'd come, the quickest way back to Stonehaven, along the coast—the coast which had zigzagged down from New Hampshire, gaped open where the Merrimac River met the sea, dumping its silt at Plum Island, curved into Ipswitch Bay, and then jutted out to the rocky peninsula known as Cape Ann. Stonehaven sat on the Northern tip of Cape Ann, taking the full brunt of the Labrador Current.

The first inhabitants of Cape Ann in the early seventeenth century had to scour the rocks for a few yards of beach on which to make landfall. They lived by the sea and died by the sea, sailing in and out from port to port for the smallest transactions with neighboring towns. A road trailed in one long sea curve from town to town like a dog, left behind, follows his master's ship with doleful eye. It was on this route to the north beside the Ipswitch Bay that something had happened to Paul. Turning her shoulder coldly to that road, Rena took the long way home.

On the southern shore of Cape Ann was the commercial fishing center, the city of Gloucester, where the famous monument of the Gloucester Fisherman in full sou'wester wrestles a ship's wheel through a storm. Rena would not go through town and all those traffic lights. Not even for the comfort of driving by Our Lady of Good Voyage where the sweet Madonna cuddled a ship in her arms like a babe. Instead, Rena took the wide soothing curve around Grant's Rotary, picked up speed towards Blackburn Rotary—the same Howard Blackburn who rowed for dear life with his hands frozen to the oars—and on to the road to Rockport.

Past Calvary Cemetery, the lily pond, and the store with the lawn full of whirligigs, Rena put the pedal to the floor. She hit sixty going into Nugent Stretch, that mile-long sweep of asphalt designed for the free spirit, the troubled spirit, the spirit on the run. The rock wall on one side and the gray woods on the other channeled her into Rockport. She coasted past the visitor center and didn't put on her brakes until High Street. There the road into Rockport narrows and branches out like rivulets of water streaming around wooden houses hunkered on the hill sloping down to the ocean. She turned left and dropped to the shore. She passed by the beaches, Front and Back, and gunned it up Pigeon Hill.

She flew over the bridge at Granite Company Wharf, pulling the wheel wide and away from the granite abutment. Steering was as easy as leaning, for her car seemed to remember the way without her guidance, as a horse knows the way and the pace of its rider on a familiar trail. No, it was not her car that remembered. This car hadn't crossed that bridge on a hundred dark, moody nights. It was her body that retained the movement of the road, that swayed for the wide curves, braced for the change in pavement, anticipated bumps, relaxed for the slow parts, and pressed against the seat for speed.

Rena stopped a short distance beyond the bridge, opening her heart to every favorable sensory sign. Gripped by memory, she backed up almost to the bridge again and nosed steeply down a short road to the wharf. At the bottom of the hill, she turned sharply to the right, passed the peeling hulls of boats beached for the winter, and eased into the murky darkness under Keystone Bridge.

Rena ignored the "Keep Out, Town Property" sign and rocked slowly down the service road. Stiff weeds scrubbed the underside of the car, and bare twigs squeaked against its sides. The car shuddered across a washboard of roots, then squished over a wet spot, now rough, now smooth in a familiar pattern. She picked up speed; her hips twitched from side to side like a horse going around barrels. Her own deftness excited her, and a sensuous exhilaration began to rise with the rhythms of the road. She braced for a bump as she swung to the left.

It was the feel of the quarry road she remembered more than the sight. Thirty years before, she had come here with Billy, not once but many times. She had snuggled out of sight against his shoulder, feeling these same rumbles, dips, bumps, and fast places where the bushes raced by.

She came to a partial clearing and several breaks in the thicket ahead. She chose one and eased into it till the car's nose just emerged at the quarry edge. Early morning light silvered the surface, some grainy, some smooth, as water embraced ice.

She turned out her lights and pulled on the emergency brake with a jarring scrunch. She turned her back into the corner made by the door and the seat and stretched her legs over the hump in the middle of the floor. She knew this motion well, but it was not her motion; it was Billy's. In her fantasy, she played his role, too. She almost reached for a cigarette in her shirt pocket as Billy would have once. She didn't smoke but remembered the smell of cigarettes and the sounds of night that had stirred her desires. She wanted to be with Billy now for the first time in years and years, not the Billy today who managed the chain of building centers his father had founded but Billy as he had been when they last parked in that same break in the bushes.

She asked herself, why be haunted by Billy Elmore, an old boyfriend, on a night when Paul Lawson was so much on her mind? It was crazy. When Paul was being taken from her, why was her mind fleeing back to Billy, to this deserted road, to those courting days so irrelevant now?

Yes, this had been Billy's and her place. Every night sound now was just the same as it had been then. Rena closed her eyes and remembered a light kiss on the lips and a moist kiss on her neck and a slow gentle touch of a hand on her breast. Even though she and Billy had parked dozens, maybe hundreds of times the three years they dated, she always made him begin at the beginning all over again. She made him do a reprise of a whole year's petting before he could take up where they had left off. They moved almost imperceptibly forward, putting off only the great forbidden act.

They never got there. It seemed now such a pity they hadn't.

The memory of Billy leaning back in the corner of his white Ford, inviting her, not rushing her, both tempted and protected her. Light fingering on her breast evolved into the warm pressure of his firmly cupped hand; she felt his lips on her throat. Buttons slid through button holes, and her white bra gleamed small but elegant. A deft thumb peeled aside the bra cup sliding the strap off her shoulder. The cool air caressed her, and her nipples pointed up hard. That first wave of bareness, first sensation of being offered naked to the air, was more sensuous than any touch.

Her body was long and lean without any particular flaws nor any particular charm. And so, through willful imagery, she rounded her hips and blossomed her breasts. She tipped her head far enough back that her short brown hair brushed across her shoulders with a silky caress reminiscent of the kiss of the long and voluptuous hair she had back then.

A tingle flowed down her body, and his hand followed. His fingers slipped under the lace of her panties, dazzling white against her tan thighs. Her thighs were now winter white, but she made them tan in her mind. She admired the white against the tan, the soft matte tan against the sheen of white. Then she raised the white satin to him.

A gust of wind set the bay trees quivering, and juniper fronds broke into a frantic shimmy. The swish of their dance outdid the rhythmic sighs of Rena's breathing.

2

Stonehaven

The next morning Rena got up on time in spite of having had little more than an hour's sleep. She looked out her bedroom window to the northeast, over the rooftops of houses clinging to the rocky shore and out through the mouth of the Ipswitch Bay to the Atlantic.

Her take on the day reflected the tone of the sea or, sometimes she'd thought, the other way around. Today it was gray as a business suit, and the lighthouse on Cormorant Island looked like a pen in its desk set holder. She dressed for the office, eager to put that part of her world back together.

She faced the east wind as it blew tiny dots of snow in her face. She nodded comradely approval at the first blossoms of purple crocus also braving the cold. Her feet crunched more loudly than usual on her gravel driveway, and her keys jangled with special sharpness as if the impact of everything she did was magnified. The steady hum of her Taurus made her feel in charge. The solid sounds of her departure, she thought, should reassure the neighbors that the town was going to continue to be run right even though its longtime and beloved Chairman of the Board of Selectmen, Paul Lawson, was absent.

She backed out onto Duncan Lane behind her house. The hill Rena lived on was called Dory Beach Hill by those who approached by sea; to those who followed the road it was the Bay Road hill: one way to distinguish a waterman from a landlubber. Rena turned inland on Adams Road, turned left on Sinclair and left again onto Bay Road, which soon plunged down to the sea. The road edged closer and closer to the water as it approached Stonehaven proper where a ONE WAY sign marked the edge of what the tourists called The Village. There it narrowed and became Front Street, running parallel to the coast line and fronting the harbor. On the water side, the shops were small, cramped between the street and the rocky descent to the sea.

As she passed, Rena noted each shop. The precision of her inventory heightened as her sense of responsibility to this town grew more tense.

Horton's Drug Store, the first store on the right, was famous for its pastel mint wafers, dipped half-way in thick dark chocolate. The store's array of medicines was usually adequate. In her teen years, Rena was sent to Horton's to pick up any prescription ordered by her household. As she watched the serious Horton brothers dispensing medicines, she listened out for a customer who might give them the Code. The Code was a secret word along with certain numbers that the boys claimed they whispered in order to buy rubbers. Contraceptive devices were illegally sold in Massachusetts then but readily available, the boys said, to those who knew the Code. As attentive as she'd been, Rena had never managed to observe one of these transactions.

Next door to Horton's, a narrow store painted aqua, with five steep steps in front, bore a sign saying simply "Anadama." There townspeople and tourists alike bought the famous bread bearing that name. Next was Oddfellows Hall, locked and bolted except on Wednesday evenings.

Then the newspaper and tobacco store, Artie's. It's cool, grit-worn floor boards creaked with an unforgettable melody. Mrs.

16

Cotsworth, a homely, heavy and lovably outrageous neighbor, used to ask Rena to ride with her to Artie's in the summer to buy her a newspaper because parking was tight. Mrs. C. double parked while Rena ran in for a "Scandal Sheet."

"Which paper is that?" Rena had asked

"They'll know."

And they did: *The Boston Globe*.

Next to Artie's was the handcrafts gallery Billy's mother once owned. Rena used to drop by, drawn by Mrs. Elmore's easy laugh and kindly interest. She now understood it was more likely a mysterious hormonal attraction of a girl to her possible mother-in-law, which lasted as long as Billy's class ring hung around Rena's neck.

The bank, safe and solid as its granite walls, came next and then the A&P, where dewy pickles coated in wax floated in a barrel near the butcher counter.

On the other side of Front Street, the buildings were larger, leaning back into the hill, bracing themselves against a tumble to the sea. The bells of the Congregational Church rang each hour and its voice, as distinctive as a friend's, could be heard all the way over to Pigeon Cove.

The old library—now an annex to the new library—was the granite building on the corner of Gordon Street. Across this side street was the old dry goods store now run by a Jewish family. The Blumenfelds lived over in Marblehead but, in the summer, hauled daily truckloads of enameled pots, porch swing hooks, door stoppers, and job lots of Madras shorts to the store while the morning shadows still covered the street like an awning.

Next door, the Stonehaven Art Association was set back from the street, seemingly to allow for the giant elm which uprooted the pavement for thirty feet around. As a teenager, Rena had posed for artists in the studio for a dollar an hour. She sat perfectly still for three hours at a time, letting the flies walk across her face, taking only two five-minute breaks.

Then Ciardi's Market. This morning Mr. Ciardi and his wife were carrying hanging baskets of an exuberant purple flower and hanging them out under the awning while the sun warded off the frost. It would not be long, Rena thought, before a summer display of melons, Golden Bantam corn, rhubarb, and giant bundles of Swiss chard would spill out onto Ciardi's sidewalk.

Front Street, had it continued straight, would have turned into a little road commonly called "The Lane" and run out onto Spyglass Point, which formed one side of the harbor. Instead it turned sharply east. The wide place in the elbow was called Flakes Square for the rows of "flakes," wooden racks where, decades ago, the split and salted codfish had dried in the sun before being shipped to inland markets. Paul kept one of the last of the Stonehaven flakes in his backyard for old time's sake.

"They complain about the wrecked cars up on Quarry Street in Bay View. Is that any worse junk than Paul's old fish-drying rack in our back yard?" Maureen had exclaimed to Rena.

The harbor side of the Square was lined with galleries of artists who set up easels here in the summer sun but wintered in New York. Among the most prosperous, Henry Cota, painted waves crashing on rocks in a hundred different variations. Popular with tourists, Cota was disdained by his peers because he painted from slides. Rena remembered when, decades before, old Max Kuhne's gallery had dominated the row. He painted clipper ships from the memory of his youth when he had crossed the sea from Germany. And Tod Lindenmuth caught, in almost abstract style, the frenzy, even the sound, it seemed, of gulls' wings beating over open buckets of bait. Now those two artists were listed in the prestigious Directory of American Artists–they were also dead and replaced by a new crop of artists who slathered the same street scenes with their palette knives on canvas and rigged the same harbor craft with wisps of camel's hair brushes.

Dress boutiques and candle-and-card shops lined up like books on a shelf. Weathered wooden steps led up to quaint second-story sandwich shops where guests soon would be eating lobster rolls and looking out over the harbor.

That row of shops parted at Main Wharf to reveal a sliver of open sea shimmering beyond the breakwater. Rena could glance back and see the working-boat side of the harbor, where strings of brightly colored buoys dangled across the weathered siding of fisherman's work shacks. She could see seasoned fishermen standing in their skiffs beside their boats, making arcane adjustments to their lines. She saw them press their rubber-aproned bellies against the gunwales and swing their legs over into the boat. She could see them stack and unstack plastic tubs and empty buckets of water back into the harbor. She could smell the oil rich fuel as a motor started up.

This spate of waterfront curled around a little park on the inside corner of Flakes Square. When Rena was young, the spot was just a vacant lot with foot paths worn powdery among the locust trees. Then the town set out a couple of benches and a trash can, which attracted people and pigeons, and so it became Josiah Lawson Park named for the old sea captain, Paul's ancestor, who once owned the land. But no more. Today the town was building a new community center there with an indoor swimming pool, fitness center, a day care facility, and the health department. Local experts would offer adult education classes in paper making and Excel, in accounting and aikido. The dedication would be in May unless Paul's accident set back the schedule. Rena hoped not. Today she could see the workmen unloading the railing for the front steps.

This venture was the final acknowledgement that Stonehaveners needed spreadsheets more than ship's sextants and had abandoned the widow's walk for aerobic stair-stepping. But the new community center was also a final monument to an old industry that had once rivaled and even surpassed fishing. The center was being built of granite from the town's own quarries, the last public building to be made of the very peninsula on which it stood.

Paul Lawson had been the instigator of this impractical scheme. At first he had intended to reopen the Stonehaven quarries and to crank up the machinery that had fallen into disuse in the 1950s. After all, there was one quarry owner who still quarried for his own occasional use. When told in no uncertain terms that such an undertaking for the community center would entail monumental expense and be virtually impossible, Paul had mounted a campaign to collect rock from the scattered chunks and slabs that had lain about Cape Ann since the granite industry went bust. The rock had waited stoically beside quarry, road, and harbor for a railway car that never came and a barge that never weighed anchor.

As a student of local history, Paul held the Cape Ann granite industry in honor as much as he did the fishing tradition of his own forebears. The Finns and the Swedes had arrived behind the Yankees. They took up their mallets and wedges to split off blocks of the gray rock, grainy with feldspar, glistening with quartz. The granite they quarried had built the bridges as close as Pigeon Cove and as far and famous as the one in Brooklyn. It had even paved the streets of Havana, Cuba. The cast-off surface rock, stained tawny with iron, had served as ballast for the legendary schooners of Cape Ann.

It was these leftover chunks of granite that now served Paul's grand scheme of building the Stonehaven Community Center out of the rock of Cape Ann itself. Most of the rock was found in Stonehaven—by the harbor, around the beach parking lots, at the end of dead end roads. Maureen Lawson made the first symbolic gesture of the campaign by donating the two pieces of granite that marked the entrance to their own driveway. Truthfully, Maureen had twice scraped a fender on one of them and had begged for them to be removed. At last, one of Paul's projects had suited her own needs.

Inspired by the Chairman's wife's generosity, Paul's colleagues around Cape Ann began to contribute to the effort in the name of their constituents. The Town of Rockport would not disturb the artists' favorite quarry scenes, of course, but gave generously from the less picturesque deposits found on Granite Company Wharf. The City of Gloucester spared a considerable number of slabs from Folly Point where the headlands themselves had been quarried out, leaving only a rim to stave off the ocean. The Commonwealth also guarded its landmark quarry at the park on Halibut Point but donated a few chunks of granite among those that dotted the woods. Even the fishermen of Pigeon Cove loaded several of the less essential slabs from their breakwater onto a barge for the project.

Rena had watched Paul's eyes actually fill with tears when the offers came. She was a bit misty herself. All in all there was enough granite donated for the facade and steps of the Community Center that would be as beautiful and substantial as that of Town Hall itself.

Paul Lawson also planned to share with the Town part of his

own personal collection of memorabilia. He had mounted in shadow boxes several pairs of old stone cutters' glasses with metal mesh shields on the sides. He had collected old tools—wedges and "feathers" for cutting dimension stone, huge sledges and small hammers, polishing disks and carving tools. The smaller pieces were arranged on his family room mantel; the larger ones lined the walls, and the largest, a cutting wire wheel, was displayed with the cod-drying flake beside his patio. He also had albums of photographs of the men and their machines and the buildings built from the great rock of Stonehaven. Paul had directed the architect to build display cases in the atrium of the new community center where he would set out his quarrying collection on one side and his schooner models and whaling artifacts on the other for public viewing. Then Maureen would have room for more decorative objects at home.

Paul had even offered to donate his Cape Ann hat to "this modest museum," as he called it. Paul's hat was old and rare and therefore valuable. It was also scruffy and unattractive; it looked dirty, made as it was of homespun canvas waterproofed with fish oil and weathered in salt air for seventy-five years. Paul had a perverse affection for this old hat, keeping it on a brass hook in his office and showing it off as the "real" Cape Ann hat, perhaps the last one held in private ownership. The better known Cape Ann hat was the sou'wester worn by the immortal Fisherman of Gloucester, made famous by its image on the packaging of a certain brand of frozen fish filets. Unlike that Gloucester sou'wester hat, whose brim is very deep in back to keep the water blown in a winter storm from running down the fisherman's neck, the Cape Ann Hat was one more suited for fair sailing. More like a flat derby, its brim curled up all around. To Rena, it looked a bit comical. When Paul put it on his own head, as he did at least weekly, he looked, Rena told him, as if his IQ had been lowered by fifty points.

Rena knew every detail of the hat because no visitor could ever mention "the fisherman's hat," meaning the famous sou'wester without Paul launching into the story of the authentic, much neglected, genuine Cape Ann hat.

"If it's so famous and rare, it should be in a museum, not on a hat rack in your office," Rena had finally suggested. And so Paul had stuffed the hat with tissue paper and laid it in his safe deposit box as in a coffin. But before putting it to rest, Paul had commissioned an aged sailmaker in Marblehead to reproduce the hat in new sail cloth, using antique curved sailmakers needles to give an authentic rather than machine stitched look. Paul had dipped the crisp new hat in canola oil because Maureen had said she would not allow it in the house saturated in whale oil or fish oil of any kind. He'd left the hat out on the clothes line through the first sou'wester of that winter to season it and to christen it with the holy waters of a Cape Ann storm. And now he had one wearable hat for a conversation piece and one mothballed for posterity.

Used to have. Rena had felt an intense stab of regret when the hat, the reproduction hat, the one Paul had actually been wearing lately, had scuttered by, rolling and flopping, across the headlands the night before. She'd had to let the hat go for the sake of grabbing the money.

Rena parked behind Town Hall and unlocked the door. The dark emptiness inside welcomed her. She turned on the lights and looked first at the square on her desk calendar and drew a line across March 26 to divide the day into two parts. "Keep town running," she wrote on the top half of the square. She would use the morning for her regular duties. Right on the noonday line she wrote, "Med," to remind her to meditate and to solve what could be solved and accept what could not.

The church bell began to strike and Rena let it ring six times before she looked up, knowing that before the ninth bell, Gladys O'Malley would put her hand on the brass door handle and begin to lean her way into the work day. The door would creak open an inch, and Gladys would lean in a little more. After several such dramatic increments, the door opening would finally gain momentum, and Gladys would fall in. She would catch herself, her feet splayed north and south and her arms fanning the air to gain her balance. Her opening line was always the same: "Where are all the gallant young men?"

There had been a time when Paul or Tony, the public works director, or whoever was standing nearest had responded to this plaint by springing forward to catch the door, taking Gladys by the arm and dusting her off, but the custom had fallen by the wayside and Gladys now had to dust herself off.

Rena waited through Gladys's morning ritual. Gladys took off her black felt hat with a Boston Celtics pin on its grosgrain ribbon and put it on the highest knob of the brass coat rack, stuffed her black clutch purse in the bottom drawer of her desk, and drew a calculator from the middle drawer. Then she took a No. 4 pencil and a Pentel red pen from the top drawer and laid them to the left of her blotter as precisely as the fish fork, the salad fork and the meat fork beside a plate.

When she was done, Rena said,

"Gladys, something bad has happened to Paul."

Gladys's lower lip turned upside down, and her eyes drooped behind her thick glasses.

"He had some sort of spell, a seizure maybe, and passed out., "Rena Said. "He was driving, ran off the road, but that didn't injure him, they say. He's in Addison Gilbert..."

Gladys sucked in quickly, and Rena could see her gathering breath for a question. "...And we don't know what the outcome will be," Rena finished slowly, emphatically, bobbing her head with each syllable to ward off any further questions.

Gladys hung her head and sighed several long sighs as she sat down to her work.

Gladys was a very slow human computer not easily programmed. But once programmed, she never made a mistake, and she never changed her method. On account of Gladys, there were few irate calls from citizens about water bills. A good number of people came into town hall with cash in hand for their bill. They stood by Gladys's desk while she inscribed the payment on a piece of paper and wrote out a receipt. "Come back soon," she said unnecessarily. To those late in paying, Gladys said, "Ayuh. Ayuh. I'm so sorry. Pay a little bit when you can." And they did their best to settle up with Gladys.

"The day you get a new program for the water bills is the day I'm leaving," Gladys had declared. Gladys could easily be replaced by outsourced services for a fraction of her salary. Rena had suggested this to Paul, but he had countered that Gladys's public relations value in town was enormous–important to him as an elected official. She was the town character. And besides, Paul pointed out, he employed her as a kindness; Gladys needed the job for the health insurance. If she ever lost it, her husband, who'd had a bypass operation, couldn't get coverage.

At quarter after nine, Rena noticed Tony taking a last smoke outside the door. She'd let him have one last moment of peace before he got the news but then found she was too nervous to wait and went to meet him. They stood under the stone arch of the doorway and she told him.

Tony shook his head.

"This is terrible, terrible." Rena thought she saw his eyes moisten, and she felt a sudden rush of closeness to the utilities director that she had never felt before.

Tony pushed his way inside, and on the desk next to Gladys he set his accordion file with oversize papers flopping over the edge, infringing on Gladys's desk. Gladys glared at the offending corner of the file and poked it with a ruler till it was confined entirely in Tony's space.

Tony hung his coat on his chair and then started to the back, drawing Rena along with him with a strong grip on her sleeve. Rena tried to stop at her desk, but Tony pushed on towards Paul's office. Rena found herself pulling away from him to block the door to Paul's office. She had been doorkeeper for twenty-five years; people had come and gone, bidden and unbidden, scrutinized but rarely challenged. Now, however, she was seized by a possessiveness all the more intense because the room was empty. "Excuse me. I've got to get the DEP report forms," Tony said, trying to step around her.

"Not now, Tony. Let's just let Paul's office be for now."

"Good grief, Rena. It's an office not a shrine."

"How can you go on with the DEP reports when Paul could be near death?"

"Rena, I'm really, really, really sorry about Paul. I'm upset. You see I'm upset? But one thing I know Paul would want is for the reports to be in on time. Am I right?"

Rena nodded but didn't move.

"If the reports are late, it goes as a violation. Sure, you can clear the record later, but we've never had a violation since the new plant was stabilized. Paul wouldn't want even a temporary violation."

Rena stood her ground in front of the door.

"So could I get the file?"

It took the will of a psychic bending spoons for Rena to go back and sit down at her desk. She put her head in her hands, listened to Tony flipping through the files, and told herself when to breathe. The front door creaked open. Then silence. Rena peered over her reading glasses without raising her head and saw Charlotte Heath, fresh-faced, sneakered, expectant, ready to bounce toward the first person who looked up. Nobody did. Gladys and Tony were buried in their work as if they had heard nothing. Rena lowered her head closer to her keyboard to wait out the deliberate snubbing she knew was coming. Charlotte's sneaker squeaked toward Gladys.

Gladys acknowledged the intrusion with a sigh.

"Take a break, you guys. It can't be all that serious," Charlotte said. She had a little trill in her voice that Rena had always loved.

"Is the town going broke or something?" Charlotte asked anyone in Town Hall who would listen. "Hey, look, the sun is shining. Brighten up."

Rena wanted to say that Paul was ill, to explain the stony silence. But she didn't have the heart. She knew that the silence was for Charlotte alone, that they would all rush to break the news to anyone else. They would hug and commiserate and comfort. But not with Charlotte.

"I need to put up a new fence and a gate across my driveway," Charlotte said to Gladys, laying down a plat of her lot and drawing a line with her finger on it. "And if I put up a new fence, I want it tall enough—you know, so people can't look over it—but somebody told me the zoning allows nothing over four feet." Gladys stared blankly at her. "So what do I have to do to get a—what do you call it?

Gladys made her search for the word.

"A variance?" Charlotte suggested.

Gladys, expressionless, opened a drawer and fingered some papers. Charlotte pulled a cigarette out of her sports pack and put it between her lips while she rummaged deeper for a lighter, then flicked a couple times.

Gladys pulled a form out of the drawer and let it rest a moment on her belly. Finally she turned to Charlotte and laid the form down. "No smoking," she said. She rolled her eyes up in reproach toward the sign on the wall.

Charlotte removed her cigarette, juggling it and the lighter, and with her free hand took the form.

"What's this?"

"Fill it out and send it back," Gladys told her.

Charlotte looked at both sides of the sheet. "Couldn't I just fill it out right now?"

"As you wish."

"After I fill it out, what happens?"

Gladys pointed to the bulletin board where the variance requests were posted until the Board of Selectmen could vote on them.

Charlotte stared where Gladys was wordlessly pointing, then scowled at the form. She scanned the room for a helpful face and, seeing none, vigorously shouldered the door open and went out.

Rena raised her head and watched as Charlotte stopped just outside the window to light her cigarette. After one long drag, relief smoothed her face.

Rena's face turned hot with shame. Why couldn't she have called out, for old times' sake, "Charlotte, how are you?" Or "Charlotte, let me take care of this for you." She was simply too distraught. Or was it her coworkers who inhibited her, she thought, looking at Gladys with particular resentment.

"Humph. She wants a fence taller than a person," Gladys said loudly. "Why should we make a zoning exception for that?"

By afternoon, word about Paul had gotten around town. Rena posted a bulletin by the front door beside the World War II Honor Roll. People read it and came in to hug Rena and ask if they could do something to help. A reporter for the *Gloucester Daily Times* called, and Rena told him only what she would have known as Town Clerk, not as a friend. It was Maureen's business to tell what she wanted the newspaper to know about Paul's medical condition. By quitting time, Rena was exhausted. The knowledge that she alone was now

26

responsible for what happened at Town Hall made her feel as if she had done the work of two. No time for meditation and finding answers. Disgusted, she took a pencil and crossed through March 26 on the calendar.

She drove directly to Boding Point and parked where she had parked the night before, barely glancing at the fresh scar on the boulder where the road turned back toward land. No people were about, the temperature not being inviting. The wind was shifting around, blowing this way and that. It had swept the rocks clean. She walked the whole headland in a grid, back and forth, up and down, looking for bills caught under skunk cabbage, snagged on thorns. Not a dollar to be seen. It was a relief.

And no hat. The hat was most likely in the water now, down where the lobsters burrow. A fitting place, if it could not be on the head of Paul Lawson himself.

Rena drove home, leaning mentally into the curves, as if she were carving out the road through the granite with a power tool. She was glad to turn off Bay Road toward the sea.

3

The Oldest House

Arriving at home, Rena found she had to pause by her back alley to let a Cape Ann Tours van, one of the first of the season, pull out of the way. She liked to imagine the tourists exclaiming, "Oh, here comes The Owner now," as she turned with modest insouciance into the private drive of The Oldest House in Stonehaven. The great age of Rena's house had only recently been discovered. An archeologist from Boston University, summoned by the Cape Ann Historical Association, had come with maps and old records and had asked to crawl under her house to examine the granite foundation walls and the floor joists. He emerged with dilated pupils to give her the news that her house was really a house within a house. The greater part of the house was a turn-of-the-century addition which had taken The Oldest House under its wing, and the two, feathered the same with new shingles, had become indistinguishable.

"Humph," Rena imagined her great Aunt Amelia would have said if she were alive and weeding the asparagus patch when the archeologist came. The old lady had been short on sentiment. The town, however, was impressed. The news led to an historical marker, and walking tours stopped outside the house in the summer. The buses came from mid-March to mid-November. While proud to be the owner, Rena felt embarrassed that there was nothing really to see.

"Take my word for it," the guide must say, "the oldest house is under there."

The early settler did not build this house on the lower ground at water's edge nor pull in nets a few short strides from home. No, he was not a fisherman but probably a timber cutter or lumber merchant, who cut and loaded onto ships the long planks that had also built Boston. The very first inhabitant of this house, Rena was sure, retained the aloofness of a pioneer, keeping himself apart.

Unlike him, Rena thrived on her job at the center of town, with frequent encounters, hearing requests, and meeting needs. She drew energy from people. But there were times when she was subject to swelling waves of pioneer spirit, the desire to go somewhere new, to do something out of the ordinary, to stand apart, even to be alone.

Rena looked out her window past the substantial new homes on the edge of the seawall as if they were not there. Sometimes being on the second story of her house made her feel in control and happy. She came up here early tonight only as a sign of faith, to open herself to a miracle, some great balm that might in a holy moment sweep off the ocean and envelope her like the fog, cleanse her with grace like a rare moist breeze from the South. Let her look far out to sea and beyond the knowledge of Paul so sick.

But there was no miracle, no grace, no balmy breeze tonight. Rena descended the stairs from the airy upper floor and retreated quickly to her darker, cozier refuge, a small room in a little wing two significant steps down from the rest of The Oldest House.

When Paul's tumor had first been discovered a little over a year before, Rena had claimed this room. Once the bedroom of Mary, Aunt Amelia's housekeeper, more recently it had been a junk room, a repository of the vacuum cleaner, the ironing board, half-used supplies and articles never used but too good to throw away.

When Paul's tumor was discovered, her need for this other bedroom, never occupied by Aunt Amelia, began to overwhelm her. The threat of Paul's tumor required some sort of compensatory shift in her home life, the building of a firmer base under shaky timbers.

The rest of the house she kept as she had inherited it with everything of Aunt Amelia's in place: the silver service on the empire card table, the collection of New England Glass Company antique paperweights on the fireside shelves, the Dedham ware rabbits, the cutwork table scarves on the end tables beside the needlepoint chairs. It was all American; Aunt Amelia had no use for foreign imports.

She told Paul in the hospital, where he was recovering from surgery, "I want a room of my own, something apart from Aunt Amelia."

She did not tell him his illness had triggered her need.

"But Aunt Amelia is dead. The whole house is yours," Paul had said.

"Emotionally it is not mine. I want a room I am in charge of," she insisted.

"You are in charge of the whole house. Hell, you run the whole town. What do you want? The world?"

Rena could not help grinning in pride at his acknowledgement, but went on seriously. "Not the world, Paul. One very small room that expresses who I am."

"Don't you express who you are everywhere?"

Rena sighed. "You see only one layer. Think of your boat, Paul. Think of the layers of paint." She gestured with her hand on her heart. "What you see here is just a top coat, Paul. You don't know what color the primer is."

Strangely, Rena noted, Paul's lack of comprehension had helped make up her mind. With the energy born of clear resolve, she cleared that little room in order to make it fully hers. She found another place under the stairs for the vacuum cleaner. She called a carpenter to build the ironing board into the wall of the kitchen. She organized papers, paints, pans, and all the domestic proliferation that previously defied categorization. She threw out things that before had pleaded to be retained . She never heard a whimper. Soon the room was stripped to old wood, heavy plaster, and a dim light bulb.

When the paper boy came to collect for the month's *Boston Herald*, she pressed him into service. The two of them carried down an antique day bed from the attic. They struggled awkwardly with its weight and length but finally positioned it against the wall in Rena's chosen room. Rena fumbled in her pocketbook and came up with five dollars, two quarters, and a dime to give the boy.

Rena had not seen anything quite like this day bed anywhere else, even at the Society for the Preservation of New England Antiques, where she had once worked in Boston. A man she had dated briefly a decade ago, who knew something about antiques, had said it was a "laying out" bed, a place to put the body of a loved one for viewing in the parlor. Every family needed one sooner or later. So they'd taken to calling this acquisition "the Death Bed." It was a joke but one that had caused Rena to put the piece back in the attic. Now the death bed image had faded along with the boyfriend, and Rena felt that the exotic claw-footed couch had been saved all these years for a reason.

Maureen Lawson, hearing about the "study," had passed on the name of her interior designer and the latest issue of *Studies, Libraries, and Dens* . Rena recoiled at the thought of using the same person who did Maureen and Paul's house, as lively and fashionable as it was. She didn't want to hear about what "worked" in Maureen's house. She wanted her own space to be untouched by the ideas of others. She would create an environment that nurtured her.

She lay on the day bed. What would the poets have called it? A couch. That's it. "For oft when on my couch I lie, in vacant or pensive mood, they flash upon that inward eye which is the bliss of solitude." That inward eye. That was what Rena wanted to live by now.

Hazy thoughts and color had gradually crystallized into details of form and fabric. Soft challis with a field of paisley and borders of arabesque. A tent like Napoleon's battle tent which he had borrowed from the Egyptians, or was it Alexander's borrowed from the Assyrians who came down like a wolf on the fold? No matter. She could picture it. The fabric would peak at the center of the ceiling, gathered in by a brass light fixture. The fabric would float in gently dipping pleats to the walls.

She would paper the walls jewel red with flecks of gold and edge the trim with Mayan hieroglyphs. She would reupholster the day bed with good pieces salvaged from worn Turkish rugs. And she would have a throw of deep mohair to keep off the chill when oft upon her couch she lay. It would be a surfeit of pattern and texture.

Burgeoning excitement exploded. Rena leapt off the couch and drove to Gloucester for material. The fabrics designed in her imagination naturally could not be found.

She went next to the other side of Gloucester where her dear girlfriend from high school, Ada Felton Milani, managed the Cape Ann store, part of the decorative arts business her father had built to prominence in Boston. Ada and her husband Phil lived in Stonehaven, and they both commuted to work in stores in other towns on the North Shore. Rena walked into Felton's Interiors with a self-conscious gait, trying to look as if she had been in an interior design store before.

As close as Rena and Ada were, Rena found herself suddenly awkward with her friend in the store. When it was her turn to be helped, she explained to Ada that she wanted yards and yards of an exotic fabric and wall paper and a border print.

"Coordinated?" Ada asked.

"You mean like matching?" Rena scowled.

"Coordinated. Made by the manufacturer to complement each other."

These phrases didn't sound like the Ada whom Rena often joined for Saturday morning coffee, the Ada still in her nightgown.

"Like a set," Ada persisted.

"No, not like a set," Rena persisted. "I want to pick each one out, sort of paisley here, *fleur de lys* there, Arab arches above, rosettes in the corners. I know it sounds like too much. But I have a special room where I want to have *too much*."

"Maybe the harem look," Ada said, pulling down a book covered by a rich pattern of overlapping fans and labeled in gold calligraphy. In small letters it said, "Come with me to..." and in large

32

swashbuckling letters, "THE KASBAH."

Embarrassed to have this thing named out loud, Rena asked to take the book home for a few days.

Was it really a Kasbah she was creating? She had supposed her romantic desires stemmed from her high school English, trappings from Kubla Kahn's "stately pleasure dome" or the Grecian urn's "leaf-fringed legend." Or maybe it was her college anthropology. In any case, it was probably better to shop for this sort of thing among strangers or at home alone.

She found an ad in the paper that said, "Antiques and oriental goods, quality used furniture, porcelain, cloisonné, antique Korean chests, appraisals, and home cleanouts." She went to the advertised address the next Saturday. She browsed through a whole block of used furniture and antiques stores. Too expensive, she found.

She walked down the narrow aisles of the import shops, squinting at Guatemalan batiks, feeling Chilean cutwork, and spreading out Kenyan cloths. She bought an inexpensive piece of Indian cotton bordered in scrolls, a paisley field sprawling with stylized boughs and tendrils–the Tree of Life, the vendor said– enough to drape a small round table. At the antique store she looked for a brass lamp for the table or something unusual to make a lamp from. Dared she hope to find an actual hookah to electrify?

Rejecting the hackneyed decorator borders named "Kismet" and "Karastan" in Ada's wallpaper book, she went to an art supply store and bought a linoleum block on which she gouged out an Islamic arch. She rolled the linoleum with oil paint and pressed the block along a pencil line she had drawn near the top of the wall. For a week of evenings she rolled and pressed, leaned and stretched from her ladder perch, working by the light of a bare bulb, dancing a pavane of shadows across her work. Try as she would, she could not print the row of arches perfectly straight, but in the end she accepted the imperfections. The hand printed colonnade invoked perfectly the rustic Alhambra of her mind.

At Jennifer's Gifts on The Lane on Spyglass Point, she bought a stained glass disc, a foot in diameter, reminiscent of the rose windows in European cathedrals, and she hung it in the one small window of her room. The stained glass was Gothic, of course, but if

Gothic rubbed cassock with Arab and Turk, and Napoleonic went cheek by jowl with Abyssinian, so be it. The unifying element of the decor was the emotional state it nurtured.

4

The Rubaiyat Summer

In the cocoon of her new room Rena had found comfort when Paul had his battle with cancer. He had gotten through that, the tumor had been excised, the chemo had been endured, and the MRI showed no remaining trace of malignancy. Now that Paul was lying once more in Addison Gilbert Hospital, Rena hoped her fears would again be muffled by the otherworldliness of her paisley canopy. Rena lay on her couch, holding her mohair blanket close to her, staring at the ceiling. Blurred images chased free-rolling verses into the fogbanks of memory as she slipped into a half-sleep.

The next she knew she was awakened by the cold edge of sudden realization: What she had created here was not the stately pleasure dome of Kubla Kahn nor the harem look of Felton's Interiors but the book jacket of *The Rubaiyat of Omar Khayyam*. How could she not have known!

She sat up straight as the greater truth flooded over her: The

Rubaiyat summer! Those memories were not just about Billy; they were even more about Paul and Whit and the gang and the roles they played out together to the rhythms of songs heard and unheard.

Now that Paul was once again in peril, Rena had returned to that other world where today was sure, love was sweet, summers were long, and Omar was their bard.

The *Rubaiyat of Omar Khayyam* had been the gospel of that particular summer. It hovered like the voice of the muezzin in the dappled dawn of thought. It started, Rena remembered, with the first beach party of the season at the end of their junior year. It had been a startlingly clear, warm day in the first week of June. The sand had dazzled and clouds had come up from the South and captured the warmth to heat the night.

Spencer, the fire of his red hair extinguished by darkness and his pale skin illuminated by moonlight, stood ghostlike by the ice chest. The acknowledged intellectual of Stonehaven High's class of 1959, he had read political journals they had never heard of and actually had a letter published in the *New York Times*. He also had endeared himself to the masses by his penchant for drink. Their eyes followed the motion of his arm, as the eyes of the faithful follow the raised communion chalice. He scooped ice in his plastic cup with a decisive crunch and held it aloft, reciting, as if composing from the heart:

> *Come fill the cup and in the fire of spring*
> *Your winter garment of repentance fling.*
> *The bird of time has but a little way to flutter*
> *And the bird is on the wing.*

Whether by the magic of its rhythms, by Spencer's rightness of timing, or by its obsession with strong drink, the Rubaiyat seized their imagination. They learned its lines and dropped them, singly or in unison, into any conversation where a pause cried out for drama. Rena thought it was the most exotic thing she had ever heard, outshining even the work of an opiated Coleridge. When school was out, the kids from the Boston suburbs came down to their family cottages and the group swelled to its summer numbers, providing a worthy audience. Then it was Whit the Irreverent who took the Rubaiyat up in earnest, turning impromptu recitation into an art form.

Rena was taking a pottery class from Mrs. Ingram on The Lane in the early evening. She took pleasure in sliding the template around her pieces to shape them and scraping the excess clay off to thin them. Shape and thin, shape and thin. She was thus engrossed when she heard whoops of "Hallo, Rena."

The boys–Spencer, Whit, Paul, Rod the Non-Verbal, and love-struck Billy were standing outside the picket fence that separated the back porch classroom of the potter, Mrs. Ingram, from the sandal-scrubbed dirt lane where tourists strolled. Rena looked up, embarrassed by their impudent grins and ignorant perusal of the class's coil construction. She prayed there was some way their intentional disruption could look like mere friendliness to Mrs. Ingram. The plump craftswoman, whose hips totally obscured the stool on which she sat, only glanced up with slight amusement and continued drawing out the lip of a pitcher with her thumb.

The boys held on to the pickets of the fence and grinned, and then Whit, in his maiden Khayyam recitation, loudly asked, "Which is the Potter, pray, and Which the Pot?"

The tightly knit group exploded with laughter. Reeling up the street, they careened into tourists. Shards of their mirth ricocheted off the fishermen's shacks-turned gift shops.

From that day on, the boys outdid themselves pulling from the Rubaiyat lines to punctuate their life, each contributing according to his taste and wit, until finally all the useable lines had been used and reused.

They were so quick with their lines because they had acquired their own personal Rubaiyats. Rena bought her tiny copy right there on The Lane at Maude's Miniatures, a shop that specialized in things diminutive. She carried it in her pocket.

Paul borrowed his from the Stonehaven Library, renewing it seven times that first summer. "I like to patronize our public institutions," he said. "It's why we pay our taxes."

Billy borrowed his stern black volume, "*English Poetry 2*, Collins to Fitzgerald," from his parents' six foot shelf of Harvard Classics.

Whit, who boasted of illiteracy as his distinction, it seemed, never showed his copy but evidently had memorized the whole. Ada picked her lines up from Whit's performances. The other girls functioned as an appreciative audience. Rod had the book but never carried it, having distilled the work's philosophy to a single word. Spencer, who started it all, had copied in flowing longhand from a book in his grandfather's library so that his version looked for all the world like the manuscript from Khayyam himself.

They had all grown up a short trot from Stonehaven's Dory Beach. They were the "Dory Beach gang," and there they could be found almost any summer evening until the advent of drivers licenses in their junior year. That summer they had moved a little further towards town, to East Beach where they were not under the porch lights of their own homes, a placr where they could ride by and recognize the cars parked by the gazebo and know who was there.

Rena and Billy were regulars, of course. Their ensemble of plaid blanket, pillow, radio, flashlight, and ice chest was just short of housekeeping. To Rena, as much as she loved being alone with Billy, Saturday night did not begin until Paul and Whit arrived. It was Paul who, because he was the only one who seemed to value planning, proclaimed the time and place of their meetings, designated it a party or not—with liquor it was, without, it was not—and, if so, proclaimed it a big party or a small one. Word would spread accordingly. And Whit would come, loping down Front Street from his grandmother's tall clapboard house where, for some reason, he usually had dinner. When Rena recognized him, she would grin silently. The party could begin.

Whit and Paul would stand amid the flotilla of blankets, Paul playing the straight man to Whit's wisecracks. All around them reclined an appreciative, participating audience: Spencer, the Pale, who could not go to the beach while the sun was out, spread-eagled on his blanket, moon bathing but attentive; Rod, whose staccato laugh and inevitable "f'crissake" spurred on their banter; Ada Felton, only fourteen but so cool she was in thick with the older kids; sweet Lynne, Rena's older friend in the senior class, and her boyfriend Eddie, who had already graduated and worked as a clerk in an auto

38

parts store in Gloucester.

Then there were the summer girls: Susie Higgins, a strawberry blonde from Malden; lively Linda McGill from Leominster; and Tina French from Winchester, who lived with her father and wicked stepmother. At the end of that summer there was the newcomer, the instantly popular Charlotte Heath.

Charlotte had just moved to Stonehaven from Melrose. She appeared on the beach one night in the flickering glow of their fire. They heard a little trill, and then "Hey, guys." Then Charlotte laughed her full-throated laugh and seamlessly joined the gang.

Rena did not like them all uniformly but all together they formed a world where she felt completely happy.

They found a smooth spot on the sand and paired off on blankets.

"Wait. Move it further back, the tide's coming in."

"Has anyone got a church key?"

"Yikes!" Susie would squeal, and the boys rushed to see if there was a crab under her blanket.

Then "Yikes!" again when the hand of one of the searchers pinched Susie's behind through the blanket. Whit's raucous laughter would identify him as the culprit.

And finally, Whit would stand until they got quiet then say, "Ah, my beloved, fill the cup that clears today of past regrets and future fears."

Then beer cans sighed sharply under the opener, and ice rattled in the ice chest as the guys scooped it into paper cups; the Four Roses followed.

When the first round was passed about, Paul, the director, would give a signal to Rod. Rod would shout: "Drink!" It was the only word of the Rubaiyat that Rod knew so Paul encouraged him to get his in when he could. A chorus would finish the line as surely as the priest's "Let us pray" brought "The Lord be with thee."

"Drink!"

"For you know not whence you came nor why," shouted the chorus.

"Drink!"

"For you know not why you go nor where."

Rena didn't drink, at least not at first. And when Billy lit up a Kool, Rena held one between her fingers and sucked the menthol out because she liked the gestures of smoking; she just didn't like the smoke.

"Hey, they treat firemen at the hospital for smoke inhalation. It's a sickness," she explained.

Roger the Disgusting rolled towards her and blew smoke in her face.

"Whoa, I'm really going to flunk Aunt Amelia's sniff test this time," she said, fanning the smoke away.

Cups filled and refilled. Empty Bud bottles clanged into the grocery bag. By ten, Billy and Rena were doing some fairly heavy making out, Roger was lying on top of a waitress from the Sea Captain's Inn, and Tina had gone catatonic after four or five drinks.

"Hey, Tina." When Tina didn't reply, Paul and Whit threw themselves down on the sand next to her and sang close to her face, "Tina, Tina, Tina, Tina, uh ho, uh ho what a dreamer..." She did not react to the Perry Como song, so they laughed and let her be. Whit lay back and stared at the sky and for a while the world was silent.

Then, just as Rena had almost forgotten she and Billy were not alone, Whit broke the silence with the Rubaiyat:

"And that inverted bowl we call the sky...
Whereunder crawling cooped we live and die..."

Rena pulled away from Billy to yell, "Pish!" Eschewing (as she said) four letter words, she found that expletive from the Rubaiyat an agreeable substitute.

And Whit called back to her,

'Tis all a chequerboard of nights and days.
Where destiny with men for pieces plays."

"Oh, *peevish boy!"* she dismissed him, as Omar would, and put her face, chuckling, into the warm corner made by Billy's arm.

Whit then took Tina's vacant stare as permission to ease over to Susie, who was now sharing a beach towel with Linda McGill.

"Really, Whit. There's already two of us on this little towel."

"You can sit here, Whit," said Ada, making him space. Ada was every boy's buddy and nobody's date.

This evening the usual peaceful scene was shaken. Lynne and

Eddie were having a serious talk punctuated with Lynne's hushed but high-pitched protests, and they eventually got up and walked along the water. Rena could see them in the distance, arguing. She winced, for in them she saw herself and Billy a couple years further along, and she wanted them to prove they could work things out. No one in her own family ever had. When Lynne and Eddie came back they were quiet and holding each other tightly. Rena sighed with relief.

Tina had to go home for her 11 o'clock curfew or, she said, her stepmother would kill her. She asked if anyone could give her a ride because she was almost late. Paul said he would. He had his mother's Mercury. Whit said he would go along with Tina.

He doesn't want her alone with Paul, Rena figured.

Then Linda said she was ready to go.

She wants to be with Paul, too, Rena thought. Of course. Linda had looked around and seen the only unattached boys left were Spencer, the Pale and Enigmatic, who did not date or flirt or even say much, and Roger who would be all hands now that the others had gone. No wonder Linda was ready to leave. Cued by the sudden exodus, Ada and Charlotte agreed to walk home together and gathered their stuff. Rena sighed. Whenever Whit and Paul went, the party was over, and the beach was left to the serious drinkers and lovers like Billy and her.

The departing girls shook out their blankets down wind, Whit and Paul picked up an ice chest between them, and the girls put their arms around the boys' necks. The group of them stood bumping each other and shuffling their feet in the sand until Whit whispered something to them.

They giggled and straightened themselves into a chorus line, conferred again, and then recited in unison:

'We are no other than a moving row
Of visionary shapes that come and go…

And they stumbled off the beach in a line, walking crabwise to make their shapes more visionary and giggling all the way to the steps where the line fell apart.

Rena saw Paul bound up the steps and heard him calling from

the car:

> *"The stars are setting and the caravan*
> *Starts for the dawn of nothing.*
> *Oh, make haste."*

How clever, how beloved were the initiates of the Rubaiyat!

5

The Dory Beach Gang

When the sharp September chill drove them from their gathering place, the Dory Beach gang moved directly and without discussion up the hill to Charlotte's house. They rang the bell, spoke politely to Mrs. Heath, and filed up the dark stairs like monks to vespers. They knocked, listened for Charlotte's yell of welcome, then opened her door to a flood of light. They entered to a drum roll. Welcome to Club Charlotte.

Charlotte had a drum set in her bedroom that she played along with Dave Brubaker records, but, when she had her friends around, she played to their conversation. As excitement picked up she would brush a little rhythm. Then at a punch line she would break into a solo. "Go, go, Charlotte," the kids would say, and, if they didn't, she'd say it herself. She had posters of Elvis and James Dean and Sal Mineo. She had written to Marlon Brando to request one of his T-shirts "unwashed, with the smell left in." Brando had not responded. He was one of the few.

Guys from Long Beach in Rockport and from The Fort in

Gloucester came over to Charlotte's house, one after the other. "Oh, I want to marry that guy. I really, really do," she would say, squeezing her shoulders together and squinching her eyes in ecstasy. "Thank God, I'm a virgin," she would add, and eyes would roll.

Each boy lasted several weeks, and then another would replace him. Charlotte wasted no tears on the one that left. She was not indiscriminate, but she discriminated fast.

The boys began to refer to her in front of the girls as Charlotte the H. It took the girls a few days to catch on to the unspoken rhyme and to complain about it.

Charlotte's father traveled and was seldom seen. Her mother, in her whining helpless way, tried to keep order. Then she gave up. She became increasingly hard of hearing and, after a while, she no longer knew when the boys went up the stairs and when they left.

Any time was party time at Club Charlotte. The music was always on, the rug was always rolled back to dance, and Charlotte was always game. Billy and Rena came here for the cheerful good times and for the dancing. They clung breathlessly to each other, swaying almost imperceptibly to *Earth Angel* and Doris Day's old *I'll never stop loving you.* They jitterbugged to *Rockin' Robin* and *Crazy Little Mama* and *Maybelline,* learning each other's moves instinctively as they emerged from some primal choreographer. They knew which turn followed which tug and which catch in the arm would signal a dip, and they flowed and bopped and swung together like jib and mainsail taking the same breeze.

Rena had tutored Charlotte in algebra that winter, painstakingly filling in the things the teachers never said about simultaneous equations.

"See, this equals sign means th-i-s equals th-a-t," Rena began, flipping her finger from one side of the equation to the other with exaggerated rhythm. "So if you change one... little... thing on the left..." She squinched her fingers together tightly to emphasize how little. "Then the left and the right aren't equal anymore and you have messed up the equals. The equal sign is not true anymore." She froze to let the principle of equality sink in. "Whenever you change anything on the left, you have to do the same thing on the right to make the equals still true."

"Oh, yeah!" Charlotte had said, making a drum roll on the desk with two pencils.

Rena was energized by this response, flat out inspired.

She would have liked to have signed up to become Charlotte's mentor on the spot, eventually straightening everything out in Charlotte's life from algebra to the rapid succession of boys. While that was not meant to be, Rena was fond of Charlotte and accepted her promiscuity. But times were changing.

Rena tried to slow the pace of the passing scenes. Wait, wait, hold them on the beach. Don't let them go. She concentrated; she grasped their images, naming them, reviewing their mannerisms.

Rena had thought they would all go on forever as they were that summer. Ada would forever be the buddy you could talk about anything with; Spencer would forever drink, think distant thoughts, remain aloof; Rod would say "F'chrissakes" this and "F'chrissakes" that; Charlotte would always go from one boy to the next, Roger would—well, the less said the better—and Lynne and Eddie would forever be in love. Paul would be the organizer, kind and fair, and the straight man to Whit, who would always quip and tease. Billy would take over his father's building supply business—and would always be with Rena. But they had not all done what she expected. Some had slipped out of reach, some were put aside without regret. Even she had gotten off track.

All the while, she had planned for the kids of Dory Beach to stay the same, to lift their cups forever to the lines of Omar Khayyam, while for herself she had planned to go forth to find a different adventure. She would leave the salt box houses and Cape Ann cottages for onion domes and big cities, to know Aztec calendars as well as she now knew harbor marking buoys. For, as seamlessly as Rena had fit into Stonehaven high school life, a compelling vision of another world promised her a destiny apart.

When her high school English class had to choose and memorize a passage of their choice from *The Merchant of Venice*, twelve in the class, one after another, recited, "The quality of mercy is not strained, it droppeth as a gentle rain from heaven..." Was there not some reason why Rena alone spat out, "Hath not a Jew eyes, hath not a Jew hands?" She wanted to be different. The way Mrs.

Durlin leaned forward in her chair at her recital spurred Rena on. And when she read from Tennyson's *Idylls of the King*, she memorized King Arthur's speech effortlessly, without it being assigned: *"But I was first of all the kings who drew the knighthood errant of this realm and all the realms together under me, their head, in that fair order of my table round."*

While only in such a recitation would modesty allow her to utter the syllables, *"but I was first,"* they set her soul ringing like the Congregational Church steeple bell. She would be first to do something; she didn't yet know what.

6

Off to College

Rena had limited her college search to places with brick walkways and white columns, a criterion she would not discuss with a guidance counselor even if Stonehaven had provided one. She was strongly considering Bard, which Spencer had called "a bastion of liberalism."

"Humph. Never heard of it, "Aunt Amelia said. Aunt Amelia herself had ordered Rena a catalogue from Tufts, her own alma mater, which had enrolled substantial numbers of women in their medical school in the early part of the century. Aunt Amelia's ignorance of Bard was enough to cement it as Rena's choice. Billy chose Williams College for equally compelling reasons. So they prepared to part, declaring their undying love and agreeing, at the same time, that they could date others at college as long as it wasn't secret.

Rena settled into the ivy-covered halls of Bard College amid hundreds of acres of field and forest on the east shore of the Hudson River. She aced the Common Course and took her exploratory classes with great dispatch in a hurry to do what she had come for. Then she prepared herself for a major, "moderated," as they said at Bard, toward anthropology; she was one of only a few students in a field newly added to Bard's social sciences curriculum. She liked being in a close-knit group of pioneers instead of being one of many in an established department of jaded eminence. Someday, she imagined, they would look back and reminisce about "the early days" of some anthropological movement.

In April of her sophomore year, Rena had met a guy with troubling dark eyes, a man more than a boy, Rena thought, comparing him to Billy. She felt the stirrings of love and a week before his graduation, she gave herself fully to him.

Rena had another year at Bard before she too graduated. After the commencement procession had reached the Stone Row lawn where diplomas were awarded and tassels turned, Rena walked back to her dorm with her mother on one side and Aunt Amelia on the other.

"Well, what now?" Aunt Amelia sighed. Rena didn't know if she meant what for lunch or what for life.

Rena spent June and July in Stonehaven, paying some dutiful attention to Aunt Amelia, and working in The Little Red Wagon, a gift shop on The Lane. However, she never felt settled in, and so, near the first of August, thinking she must have outgrown Cape Ann, Rena went to Boston to see what would happen, to find The Adventure that would be advertised in the classifieds of the *Boston Herald*. Rena dismissed the idea of living with her mother in her townhouse near Fenway, partly because Eleanor lived with a man, but mostly because living with a parent would be counter to her quest for adventure. She also declined her mother's offer to give her names of contacts for job interviews. Her mother knew nothing whatever about anthropology.

From the beginning, the fifth story walk-up on Isabella Street delighted her. From her bay window, she felt like Juliet on her balcony or Rapunzel in her tower. Rena especially enjoyed the comings and goings of the Marist Fathers from the dormitories of

Our Lady of Victories across the street. Whenever she noticed one of the Fathers walking below, she stood at the window and watched. One crossed the narrow street every day to stand under the shade of her tree and pick off spent blossoms of her geraniums through a wrought iron railing. The Fathers were elderly or retired and went about without apparent schedule or purpose.

She, on the other hand, established a routine to define her new life: clean the kitchen, make the bed, sweep the living room rug. Get the morning paper. Look at the ads. Look for temporary jobs until she could figure out a career. Make calls about job opportunities. Make a list of everyone she talked to. Keep track. Walk to the grocery store around the corner for food for supper. Make a sandwich and eat it by the window.

She folded her clothes and stacked them close together in neat piles on the floor against the wall, just the way she would have stacked them in a drawer if she'd had one. Chests of drawers were a convention, not a necessity. Her small savings from summer jobs were tapped only for tampons.

She walked across the busy intersection to the A&P on Tremont Street. She spent only the change that she'd left on their dresser each day. It averaged about a dollar and a half, sometimes more, sometimes less. She could buy three-quarters pound of pot roast for fifty cents, three potatoes, a few carrots, and a package of frozen spinach as her pocket change permitted. On weekend walks also, she might stop in the store, and she would ask for five pounds of flour and some shortening. With these provisions she could make biscuits or muffins to fill her every night. She was pleased she could feed herself this way.

She had a sense, a dread of becoming a wife and dependent woman, though she had never actually lived with a man. Aunt Amelia had been the man of her family, and she had gone to the bank twice a month and returned with a great wad of cash, which she peeled off as necessary. Being both the man and the woman of the house, the one to earn the money and spend it must have been a great feeling, Rena thought. You would be in charge of your life, know what you were doing and where you were going. Rena would rather be in complete charge of the small change from the bedside table than in a vaguely understood partnership, so she ate for a dollar and a half a day, give or take, in quarters, dimes, nickels, and pennies. It was a skill in which she took pride.

She imagined her mother also took pride in managing on her own. Rena's father had gone away to the War in Europe and when he came back he was different, that was all Eleanor would say. He had disappeared from their lives before Rena got to know him. Rena had soon been sent to live with Aunt Amelia, "because she wanted you," Eleanor had explained inadequately, and because Aunt Amelia had declared the young mother would not be able to take care of a child by herself. Aunt Amelia, herself, for the first ten years of Rena's stay, until she retired, was doing surgery at the hospital every day, but her doting Irish housekeeper Mary, became, for all intents and purposes, Rena's real mother. It was never intended to be a permanent arrangement, Eleanor told Rena, but somehow it worked out that way.

Rena continued to flip through the classifieds of the *Herald* at the newsstand. Of course, if she found a job opportunity there, she would buy the paper. The classified section was exciting, so much bigger than in the *Gloucester Daily Times*. She looked under accounting, administrator, advertising, alterations, assembly, automotive. Nothing about anthropology. She read it again to be sure. Where else could anthropology be? What was another way to say anthropology? She looked under Education. Teacher, teacher assistant, tutor, but nothing about anthropology. If she saw nothing to pursue, she'd close the paper neatly, evened up its sections, and left it on the rack. They probably don't advertise to the general public, someone suggested. Try the bulletin boards at the Anthropology Department at Boston University or Boston College or Harvard.

So Rena went to Harvard and MIT, to BC and BU and all the other places known by their initials. They were oversupplied with their own anthropology students, it seemed. She next made the rounds of all the same universities but this time looking for editing, clerical, or any kind of work at all because she was comfortable with schools. They smiled and took down her name.

When, at last she landed a job as a receptionist for a nonprofit organization she finally felt comfortable enough to consider herself to be self-sustaining. It was meager, but satisfying.

Then came the call from Aunt Amelia's housekeeper, Mary:. "The Doctor has had a stroke. Please come home."

7

Return to Stonehaven

There was no one at Aunt Amelia's house to come to the train station for Rena. Mary would be waddling, clucking, and wringing her hands helplessly; she could not drive. Should Rena call a taxi to come all the way from Gloucester? No. To feel the whole truth of being home, she wanted to walk. She wanted to feel the bright warm sun on her back, feel the brisk October wind on her face, scuff the sidewalks under her feet, smell the autumn smells, speak to people, call them by their names. The suitcase? Ask Mr. Kennedy, the station master, to let her put it in the station where he could keep an eye on it till she came back with a car.

But the station seemed to be closed up.

"They closed the station about a year ago," another passenger told her.

"But how do you buy tickets?"

"Buy them on the train."

The other passengers scurried to waiting cars and drove off, leaving Rena and her suitcase alone on the platform. Well, she wasn't helpless. She'd do something. Paul's house–his parents' house where he had grown up–was just a half a block away at the corner of Depot and Anderson Avenue. She could carry the suitcase that far. It proved to be more difficult than she thought–the hard brown leather handle bit into her fingers–but by carrying it and setting it down and then carrying it again, she reached the Lawson's house.

She set the suitcase up on the porch. She started to ring the bell, but she could see no one was home and wrote a note to Mrs. Lawson instead, explaining. She tucked it under the handle of the suitcase.

She stepped off the porch and held out her arms to feel the air. The sound of a paint scraper next door, the energetic sound of work that accompanied all clear sunny days in Stonehaven, was familiar music. It was a bit cold about the hands and ears but perfect for walking.

Walking is freedom; walking is power. If you can walk a mile, you can walk two miles. If you can walk two miles, you can walk four. If you can walk four miles, you can walk a township. If you can walk from town to town, you can walk across the country. Rena reveled in her freedom and power.

Where Hill Road met Front Street, the row of shops emanated a bright strangeness along with a perfect familiarity. The church bell gonged three o'clock like a sound effect for a great movie about Rena, pioneer woman. She turned away from the village and started the descent to East Beach looking forward to the effort of climbing Bay Road hill.

Rena found Mary as she expected: bustling about the house, leaning forward as if into the wind. She was ironing linen, bleaching porcelain, scalding milk for custard, punching down bread dough to rise again, readying the house for company. Rena didn't feel she was putting Mary out, for Rena knew Mary was relieved to have someone on whom to lavish her richest domestic talents, pent-up during the months of Aunt Amelia's decline. Aunt Amelia was now in Addison Gilbert Hospital. A neighbor had taken Mary to see her. "The Doctor," as Mary always called her employer, was improving; she was beginning to talk a little but could not walk. Dr. Babson had said she could be home in a day or two but warned, Mary reported, that "it could go either way."

"The poor doctor, the poor doctor," Mary muttered over and over. Rena too mourned the great aunt she had known as powerful but who now had lost her indomitable presence.

Rena went to the hospital and found a creature so small and fragile she didn't know how to act. A whole lifetime of deference to the tough old matriarch did not prepare Rena to assume the role of caregiver. Rena was more afraid of this wrinkled child than she had ever been intimidated by the healthy great aunt. She didn't know how to begin. She felt guilty. Was she incapable of tenderness? She was relieved to leave Aunt Amelia's bedside and go back to her aunt's home where more definable tasks would demand her attention.

Rena began to make calls inquiring about wheel chairs and ambulances and finding out just how one lives as an invalid. She had known nothing of this endeavor but got a surprising satisfaction from making lists and checking them off, learning quickly. She made one call to ask a question, which led to another possibility; she made other calls until she had accomplished her goal or chosen a service. To be indispensable, competent, responsible, had a good feel.

Mary, well into her seventies, left all this to Rena as the superior, counting her own experience as nothing. Such is the mentality of the servant.

When a hospital bed and bulk packages of diapers had been ordered, Rena wondered how she was going to pay for these things. She called the bank in Stonehaven for advice, and Aunt Amelia's banker said to get a power of attorney. Rena called Aunt Amelia's attorney in Boston, a woman as taciturn and cool as Aunt Amelia herself, and arranged for a form to be mailed. When it arrived, Rena took it to the hospital and stood by Aunt Amelia's bedside, holding it in her hand. Rena was afraid Aunt Amelia wouldn't understand what she was being asked to sign. Rena was equally afraid that she would.

Dr. Babson arrived just in time, a lively woman whom Aunt Amelia had trained. She was quite different from Aunt Amelia–jolly, almost, by comparison. Dr. Babson greeted Aunt Amelia with a natural manner and genuine good humor that Rena herself could not muster. Rena took her aside and showed her the power of attorney form, expressing the dilemma with raised eyebrows.

Dr. Babson took the document in to Aunt Amelia and said cheerily, "Doctor, we need you to sign a paper for us here." This younger doctor took a pen from her pocket, set the paper on a clip board and laid it on the bed beside Aunt Amelia. Then she propped the pen in Aunt Amelia's gnarled hand, took the hand firmly in her own, and pushed it through a credible signature: Amelia Douglas, M.D.

"There you go," she said brightly as much to Rena as to Aunt Amelia. Decisiveness was next to godliness, Rena noted.

Aunt Amelia's improvement was dramatic, and she soon came home in the ambulance. Mary and Rena together were quite sufficient to care for her; the only difficult part was lifting her for washing and changing. Mary did the less pleasant chores in addition to taking care of many of Rena's needs as well.

A college friend called Rena to say he missed her, not seeing her every day, eating alone. She suggested that, to pass the time, he go home and visit his parents that weekend. Then he could come to Stonehaven on another weekend. He took her suggestion. She rather enjoyed giving him this direction from afar and wondered if in the void left by Aunt Amelia's decline, she was becoming a bit matriarchal herself.

Rena's mother and Richard came to visit the first weekend they could get away. Mary put rum into the fruit cocktail for them, a sign of their standing as guests. Rena felt an unaccustomed equality with her mother, since she was now the hostess providing the hospitality. It was Aunt Amelia's money, but Rena was signing the checks.

Richard earned his keep by building a ramp up the front stairs and assembled the toilet contraption that Rena had rented with the hope that Aunt Amelia would soon be able to use the bathroom again with minor assistance.

A few weeks passed and Rena was at the point of hiring a practical nurse so she could go back to Boston when Aunt Amelia had another in what was to be a series of debilitating strokes. Finally, she was unable to speak at all except in gibberish. But, with this disability, she took on a new tranquility which was welcome. When she looked perkily up at Mary and stammered a nonsensical stream of syllables, Mary cried out in grief, putting her hands over her face. Finally, Mary became able to bear the utterances, patting her employer on the shoulder and saying, "There, there, doctor."

Rena, on the other hand, tried to assume there was cogent intent behind the invalid's expression and replied seriously, "Aunt Amelia, I can't understand your talking, but I can talk to you."

She told Aunt Amelia about her job and the amusing things people had said. Aunt Amelia looked alert, both pleased and quizzical, not unlike her little Pekingese who likewise cocked her head attentively to Rena's voice.

When subjects waned, Rena talked about the history and the ongoing restoration of the Harrison Gray Otis House and soon found herself giving ready-made material, the docents' speech. "Charles Bulfinch (1763-1844), architect of the Massachusetts State House and the United States Capitol, designed the house for his friend Harry Otis in a style that became synonymous with the Federal era...." She gestured to unseen furnishings. "There on the far wall is a portrait of Mr. Otis' grandfather....Here is a hidden safe where Mr. Otis kept his valuable papers."

Rena talked about her life in Boston. She described the apartment and the comings and goings of the priests across the street. She mentioned again her rides on the swan boats, which she noted graciously, Aunt Amelia had provided for her two decades before on their occasional trips to the big city. She hoped her belated expression of gratitude would seep through. She talked tentatively about her mother and then more boldly about Richard and the interesting source of his charm and how it really wasn't a bad arrangement. There was little concern that Aunt Amelia would ever get a chance to repeat what Rena said.

Aunt Amelia would have appreciated the ease Eleanor had with Richard, Rena thought, if she'd had any understanding of what Rena was saying.

"You know better than anyone how uncomfortable real husbands can be," Rena said.

Of course, when Aunt Amelia was healthy, no one dared speak to Aunt Amelia about her husband—long endured but finally shed. Rena watched her aunt's face as she spoke of him now, but Amelia's expression remained the pleasant childlike full moon of a person with no concerns. No, Aunt Amelia understood nothing, both a disappointment and a comfort for Rena to know.

Finally, one weekend in November, her friend came down to Stonehaven to visit. When he arrived on the earliest Saturday morning train, Rena was waiting on the platform. She bounced as he climbed down the steps, an abbreviation of jumping up and down. When she let him load his bags into the cavernous trunk of Aunt Amelia's gray '55 Oldsmobile, she felt as grown up as she had ever felt, but nothing compared to when she actually slid into the driver's seat. The Olds had quite a few years on it but was little driven. It had all the latest gadgetry for its year: automatic light dimmers and the power steering Aunt Amelia had special-ordered to make driving easier on her arthritic hands. How grand to be at the helm of all this!

It was a dreary day, cold, drizzly, gray, the kind of day where ordinary landscapes fare poorly but Cape Ann takes on a misty romance that is among its main attractions.

They left the station without going into the center of Stonehaven. Rena left the best for last. She took him first to Pigeon Cove Harbor where a row of fishing shacks, brightened with American flags and strings of colorful lobster buoys, offered puttering space to working fishermen. Their boats, the ones that were not at sea, lay at their moorings, scarred and rubbed to the muted colors that distinguish working boats from pleasure craft. Stacks of metal lobster pots honeycombed the wall of rock that curled around the harbor. Metal pots like these were not allowed in Stonehaven; only the traditional wooden ones were permitted in public view, Rena pointed out, but she rather liked the postindustrial composition of green-coated metal grid, looped with ropes and knots on the outside and cats cradles of net within.

"Pigeon Cove residents are keeping traditional ways viable by improving on them," she said, summoning up a concept of cultural survival she'd learned in anthropology class. They passed the site of the Cape Ann Tool Company, now defunct, but once the home of a thundering monster that spewed flames day and night. "It's a noisy noise that annoys an oyster" was a tongue-twister Aunt Amelia sometimes said in one of her rare playful moods, and Rena never passed the metal works without saying or at least thinking about the noise and the oyster, irritated perhaps to the point of making a pearl.

At Rockport Harbor, she drove slowly down Bearskin Neck, which forms the Northern rim of the harbor. The Neck is crowded with little buildings, once homes and fishing shacks, now galleries and gifts shops, mostly closed for the winter. Rena pointed out the sign over the Pewter Shop that portrayed an early settler's encounter with the bear. Then they turned up their collars and braved the wind out on T-Wharf for a closer look at the old fisherman's shack called Motif # 1 because, Rena explained, of all the buildings in the country, it was thought to be the one most often painted by artists. While Stonehaven's smaller shacks made interesting clusters on canvas, Rockport's landmark, standing by itself on the end of the pier, seemed to own the harbor. Moreover, it had first achieved stardom by being transported in one piece to a World's Fair.

Motif # 1 was now streaked with age and occasional patching. Like other artists, Rena knew how to mix a little green with the red on her palette to age the shack almost to brown, to give a hint of algae, and to mute the red that caught the eye of every artist and passerby.

"Why do you call him "Doctor" and her by her first name? Is Marlene some kind of servant?"

"Oh, no. Dr. Grenkoff is a woman, too, and now that you mention it, I don't know why. Aunt Amelia always called her Dr. Grenkoff; you know how doctors are about their title. She's an orthopedic surgeon. And Marlene is a social worker, long blonde curls, dainty as a little girl. Aunt Amelia sometimes called them 'the girls'. I really, really like them."

"Lezzies, I guess."

Rena was annoyed. She'd never thought of this before. "And so what if they are?"

"Nothing."

"While you're campaigning for human rights, you'd better wash that word out of your vocabulary."

Rena had made a good point with him, and she was proud.

They rolled slowly through the artist colony at Rocky Neck where they could see a flotilla of fishing boats moored in Gloucester Harbor. In the city of Gloucester, they got out at St. Peter's for a closer look at the fishing fleet, ice houses, industrial sheds, more stacks of pots, and colored nets thrown over racks in picturesque abandon. They read the inscription on the Fisherman's Memorial in Gloucester, got caught at the draw bridge over The Cut, and made their way back along the west side of the Cape toward Stonehaven. They took a detour through Annisquam, stopped to try out the footbridge over Lobster Cove. A little further Rena wanted to show him "the cutest little harbor" at Lanesville. And so on, all the way back to Stonehaven.

They passed by West Beach, East Beach, and Dory Beach, all sand rimmed coves where the famous beach parties had been held. She hoped he would see, feel, as she did, the idyllic mystique of the town that surpassed the charms of all the others and made it the jewel of the rich trove of Cape Ann. If he did not, she would have to teach him. So, as she drove him down Front Street, Rena pointed out the galleries, gift shops, and restaurants as well as the purveyors of hardware and shoes. She told him the original use of each historic building and the eccentricities of its present tenant.

They parked the car and strolled up The Lane on Spyglass Point, huddled against each other, and peered into shop windows. They chose three lobsters from the tanks of Marley's Lobster Shack even though he was squeamish. While Marley's niece cooked the lobsters in boiling water, they bought "tonic" at The General Store and drank it standing in a sheltered doorway on Watson's Wharf.

"Tonic? What's that, medicine?" he said.

"Oh, I forgot. You guys call it 'soda'. I quit saying 'tonic' at Bard, but I guess I'm going back to my old ways here in Stonehaven."

While they licked their fingers, they watched an old-timer gas up his boat, the Helen D., around the harbor at Lawson's Marine where Paul worked with his father. The Lawson enterprise was the heart of the harbor. Lawson's hauled boats, repaired boats—everything from crane service to bottom painting. "Quicksilver Parts, Accessories and Inflatables, Fiberglass Repair and Refinish, Awlgrip, Imron, and Gelcoat," the harborside sign said. They also sold inboards and outboards. They were pulling out the last boats for the winter now. Most of the pleasure boats were already pulled up on the wharf and covered.

"There's Paul," Rena said pointing to a figure giving direction to the winch operator.

She had not really expected to see Paul there even though he was due to take over the business. Paul was not as mechanically minded as his father; he didn't love engines like some boys do who will lean over an engine to listen to its hum as if it were music. Paul was supposed to bring modern business practices to the company and leave the mechanics to the hired help. For that prospect, he had majored in business. But, if Rena knew Paul, he was spending considerable amounts of his time and energies at Town Hall these days.

The winter before, he had run for a spot on the Board of Selectmen. He won and took office in March. Within six months, when the old Chairman resigned for health reasons, Paul won the Chairmanship over the two older, longtime members and two new young members. Rena had never known Paul to do anything halfway, and she expected he was turning Town Hall upside down with improvements.

"Let's go over there," Rena said and hurried him back to Marley's. She watched Bud Marley wrap the steaming lobsters, blazing red now. She paid him from Aunt Amelia's house money. She tucked the warm brown paper package under her arm where it comforted her against the raw cold.

They walked around the inside of the harbor. The wake of a motor boat slapped kerchunk, kerchunk, against the pilings under the wharf; an engine stuttered then hummed; fittings jangled on masts, all the most masculine sounds on earth, Rena thought.

They ducked into the back door of the Candy Corner where Rena bought three huge chunks of fudge. They unwrapped the candy as they walked along the dock. Just as they sunk their teeth into the soft confection, Paul saw them from the dock and waved. Rena wrapped her fudge and put it in her pocket so they could hurry over.

"You remember Paul," she said when Paul came to greet them.

"Of course. The wedding."

Paul reached out his hand and, as they were linked, Rena's two worlds snapped together like railroad cars. She was glad when they stepped back from each other. She gave Paul the third piece of fudge.

Back at Aunt Amelia's house, he seemed to revel in the linen napkins and grow accustomed to Mary waiting on him. Rena found him unusually energized, and she noted the palpable excitement with which he touched her arm. He wanted to go upstairs.

They were not sleeping together because of Mary, but he could not see why they couldn't use one of their bedrooms just for a little while.

"Not in the middle of the day!" Rena hissed.

At night she crept down the hall to his bed, after messing hers up. They made love. He was comfortable and effusive. She was quiet and inhibited.

When he was ready to leave Sunday night, she realized she felt as if she lived here in Stonehaven. She didn't feel like the one who was away from home. Here Rena had her own childhood back, including Mary, who had cared for her since infancy.

Rena clung to him standing on the platform at the Stonehaven station as if they were standing on a seawall and, if either one of them stepped back, that one would be gone.

The next evening he called to give her a message from the Otis House that a volunteer who had taken her place at the desk had been hired on a temporary basis to fill in for Rena indefinitely. That was a relief.

Rena was awakened the next morning by the light streaming in through gauzy, white curtains. She could hear the bell buoy ringing clear and deep, its loudness rising with the pitch of the waves. She went to the window to look out. The sea was a deep shade of green; viridian, Rena said to herself, naming the oil color she would choose to paint it. The white caps were sharp, flake white, liberally applied.

Cormorant Island, too, seemed close and clear, smack in the way of the boats that came around Halibut Point at the mouth of the Ipswitch Bay. Most people, Rena had observed, assumed that Halibut Point, which marked the corner of the Atlantic and the Bay, was named—as it was spelled—for the prized and tasty Cape Ann fish. Not so. If you watched sail boats appear from behind that point of land, coming North from a day at sea, you could see them flying, usually, with the wind abeam. Then, as sails were trimmed, they jibed sharply and ran before the wind to their home port of Annisquam or Lanesville. When the great ketches and schooners of Cape Ann reached the Point, the watch called out to his mates, "Haul About!" If Rena had her way, it would still be "Haul About Point."

The clarity of the day called Rena to reestablish herself with the lay of this land from the footholds on the rocks to the sandy alleys between its shingled houses. She saw that here reconnecting with people would be secondary to the connection with land and sea.

She dressed with buoyant good spirits, deftly pulling her socks on and tying her sneakers with certainty. She opened the door and went out quickly before the cold might make her change her mind. She pulled the door closed slowly behind her, feeling for the familiar click. She welcomed the sharp wind that swiped the warmth of the house off her cheeks, took satisfaction in the crunching sound of each step on the frost stiffened grass. She put her hand on the top of every post of the fence around the yard next door. She flexed the ice crust on every puddle with her toe till it wheezed and cracked. She walked all the way from Adams Road through the Square and up the long hill toward Rockport to recapture, if only by breathing in the air, the heartbeat of the town. The crisp air in her lungs and the cadence of her march brought a sense of wellbeing.

When she stopped and looked back over the town, however, she could not recreate the ownership of domain she had once felt when she walked the alleys, blanketed the beaches, touched the rocks with toe tips as she ran, and recognized all the cars that

62

passed. It was not the same. Knowing was no longer owning.

Children seem to think that homeowners squat on the land, but the land itself belongs to them. They follow creeks, climb fences, take short cuts across fields with absolute certainty that the land is theirs. Just as explorers who have broken a narrow path through snow to reach a mountain top feel themselves qualified to plant a flag claiming an entire untouched region, so children own the land their feet patter through.

Now Rena recognized that the land was divided into private property and she was just another person following a route. No use to shout, "I grew up here, this is mine." Residence was a concept much valued in a town whose hierarchy divided those who live there year round from those who spend their summers there and those who merely visit for a few days. And Rena had abandoned or forgotten the knack of residence. She wished she could announce to strangers passing, "I may not live here now, but I used to. Longer than you."

She walked back more slowly, pulled off her sneakers on the back porch to air, and went in the door to the kitchen, grateful for the homely comfort of socks on linoleum.

The next morning she again woke hopeful, certain that the bell buoy this time was ringing in a new day when she would reestablish old routines with friends. Connection with the land would follow.

She started a list, lying on her bed, of the friends she wanted to take up with again. She pictured them on their beach blankets, shadowy under the night sky but real as the bedposts in her bedroom this bright morning. She looked at these shadowy figures one by one so she wouldn't forget anyone, and she wrote them down in order:

Lynne: She walked home from school with Rena since first grade. Rena was the first—after Eddie—to know Lynne was pregnant. Rena wasn't sure things would be the same between her and Lynne now though; so much time had passed.

She remembered the first Christmas vacation when she had come home from Bard. She rushed with excitement to see Lynne in her honeymoon apartment in one of the old mill houses. Sure enough Lynne was home, still in her robe. They hugged and Rena cootchie-cooed the baby, then about six months old.

"Let's go to the Red Geranium and act like tourists and have lunch. My treat."

"I can't. I have the baby. But I can fix tuna sandwiches and soup here."

"Can't we take the baby? Don't you have a little seat for him?"

"Yes. I have the jumper seat, but I'll have to feed him or he'll get fussy. Then he needs his nap so we could come home and talk."

"Let's do it!" Rena said, ignoring all the complications.

While Lynne showered, Rena sat uncomfortably on a shabby hand-me-down sofa and watched the baby sitting up straight among toys scattered on the bare floor.

"Aaah!" the baby said sharply.

"Aaah!" Rena repeated the syllable back to him and the baby grinned. Rena was pleased.

"Aaah!" the baby said again, kicking his fat little legs so vigorously that he fell over.

Lynne called to her. Could Rena bring her a towel from the hall closet? Rena got one from the bathroom and handed it to Lynne. The air that rushed out in Rena's face was steamy and acrid.

"What's that in the tub?" Rena asked. The tub Lynne had just stepped out of was full of something foul and swampy.

"It's the baby's diapers," said Lynne. "I was soaking them in the tub so I just took my shower over them. I wash them with my feet. You know, like the French make wine."

"Lynne, drain those diapers and put them in a bucket, and we'll take them to my house."

"No, no, no, it's okay. I'm used to this."

"Lynne, we have a washer and a dryer just sitting there."

Rena wasn't sure what Aunt Amelia would think of this charity, but Mary was enthusiastic.

"Yes, yes, poor child. You two have a good lunch. I'll have them washed and dried by the time you get back." Mary liked doing good with Aunt Amelia's machines.

Now Lynne had her own washing machine and two children. She wouldn't be going out at all. Rena erased Lynne's name from the top of the page and put it lower on the list.

Now who, she pondered, were her other favorites from the Rubaiyat summer?

Ada. High on her list. Ada, who, although a year younger than Rena, had taught her almost everything she knew. Ada had shown her how to use a Tampax so she could swim when she had her period; Ada's big sisters again had put Ada ahead of her peers. Ada had clued Rena in on a number of things.

"You know what I heard?" Ada had said one afternoon when she and Rena and Linda McGill had been dangling their legs off the pier. "I heard that when a woman crosses her legs like this"–Ada threw one leg high over the other–"she might be masturbating."

Linda whooped and lustily crossed her legs, as Ada had, thigh pressed against thigh. Rena did not. She hadn't known that women could masturbate anyway.

"Some people just use a banana," said Ada knowingly.

"Oh, I would use a banana," Linda said, "but I'd be afraid it would break off and then I'd have fruit flies."

Ada rolled over on the wood planking like a bowling pin, laughing convulsively and risking rolling off the pier into the green water below.

Rena was completely delighted by how guilt-free they spun off these novelties, even though she could not. She was mostly an observer in the land of gay abandon.

Rena now found herself actually grinning at the memory. She picked up the phone and dialed Ada's home and got Ada's mother.

Ada was working in her father's store, Mrs. Felton said. Oh, yes, work. Rena had forgot that most people work. Ada had a new apartment in Gloucester, Mrs. Felton said. Maybe they could get together in the evening or for lunch. Rena took down the numbers.

Rena leaned back on the pillow and closed her eyes and conjured up the Dory Beach gang again. There on the beach blanket with the rest was Charlotte. She hadn't heard word one from her since she left for Bard. Put her at the bottom of the list.

And there was Whit. Bless him.

Spencer had gone to New York. He probably never once looked back. No use writing him down.

Paul. Of course she would see him.

Billy. Of course, she wouldn't see him. He was engaged to that Gloucester girl. The worry nagged her that the list was not going to be all that long.

Indeed. As a group, as an idea, as a state of mind, the friends from high school, the children of the Rubaiyat, the guys in the cars, the girls on the beach blankets, were Rena's idea of heaven. As individuals, Rena reluctantly admitted, they had become something less.

She did what she often did when disappointed or bored or scared. She rolled over onto her stomach in the bed, buried her face in her pillow, and fantasized sex. She had come a long way since Ada first shocked her with the idea of what women could do with themselves. She no longer protected herself from these feelings, she welcomed them. She played them out.

Rena cast around for a suitable subject for this fantasy. She settled on a memory from the beginning of the Rubaiyat summer when she and Billy had first gone to third base. She had done this one many times before, and she never tired of it. She imagined every delicious step–and then she added a different ending. Then she slept.

Later in the day Rena got up and called Lynne. Rena promised she would come by one day soon to visit Lynne and the children.

"We have another one on the way," Lynne confided. Rena had trouble acting happy for her. She and Eddie were so poor.

"Do you ever see Charlotte?" Rena ventured.

"Not really,"

"Gosh, I'm surprised. You live so close. I was thinking of calling her."

"Nobody sees Charlotte really. You know."

"Know what?"

"Her reputation."

"You mean, that she was sort of...fickle? That?"

"Well, that and more."

"What?"

"Didn't you hear? First, she had to marry this guy, and she had the baby, and then she ran around on him, and they split up. Then she had a bunch of guys from the Coast Guard Station. She lived with someone in Marblehead for a while. But the worst was, she got into drugs. She got arrested. Then she came back here. She was always high as a kite. I think she's settled down now, but nobody speaks to her anymore. "

"I am really, really sorry. I was thinking about calling her..." Rena said tentatively.

"I wouldn't. Like I said. If you care about your reputation."

Rena felt gutted like a fish.

8

RIP Amelia Douglas

By the end of January, Aunt Amelia was no longer in a wheelchair but in bed all day. She had an infected toe caused by poor circulation, and the doctors were unwilling to put her through the trauma of amputation. Finally, however, the infection crept up in long red streaks like ivy on a tree, and the lower leg had to come off.

"She's resting peacefully," the surgeon said, coming out of the operating room. She'd been resting peacefully for three months, so this was no news.

Amelia Douglas died the next day.

Aunt Amelia had made it plain that she wanted to be cremated and wanted no funeral. Rena would do the first with dispatch. Ashes were the only tolerable form of disposal. The second she could fudge on a little bit: no funeral, all right, because no body and no church, but a memorial service seemed appropriate and would not violate the letter of Aunt Amelia's wishes. Was it just a semantic difference? What would people in town say about her if she didn't have any service at all? Besides, the lawyer was pressuring her for some event for people to come and pay their respects. Rena didn't know who these people were.

Dr. Grenkoff, would come, of course–she'd been the first one Rena called–and her companion Marlene, and Mr. Hodges from next door, who every winter had scraped the snow off Aunt Amelia's driveway. Some friends of Rena's undoubtedly, as the lawyer had said, out of respect. Rena wanted to hold the event in Boston because that's where Aunt Amelia had worked for her entire career. They had moved to Stonehaven when Rena was seven and Aunt Amelia retired. But they settled on a service at the funeral home in Gloucester because Mary wanted visitors afterwards; she wanted to do a proper wake. In the end Rena yielded to all the people with strong opinions and desires; she then turned control of it all to Aunt Amelia's lawyer.

Dr. Grenkoff asked the chaplain from the New England Hospital, Aunt Amelia's hospital, once the New England Hospital for Women and Children, to do the service. Just the basics, Rena told him, because of Aunt Amelia's wish for no fuss.

In the end, it was a full-fledged funeral with a casket covered with a blanket of roses the lawyer had ordered in Rena's name. When Rena first saw this spectacle, a half-hour before the funeral started, she was repulsed. She glared at the roses, wondering if a whole season's roses from Aunt Amelia's arbor could have supplied enough blossoms for that one piece. Roses on the arbor were all Aunt Amelia ever wanted; this she would despise. The more Rena thought of how the order had been made in her name, the more upset she became until tears of outrage rushed to her eyes. Mary, grieving beside her, observed Rena's tears, missed her outrage and, obviously touched, began to weep again herself. Rena was glad for the pious impression she had made. Mary seemed to have all the right feelings at the right times, and Rena envied her.

She and Mary and Rena's mother stood in the upstairs hall of the funeral parlor looking out a tiny front window to the street. It was bitter cold and gray, and the wind rattled the windows. Who would come out on a day like this, especially for the unpleasant and unnecessary task of paying respects?

She was relieved when Paul Lawson's car turned in and she could see Ada in the back seat. She had expected them. Paul always rose to occasions. Besides, she and Ada had by now established a regular morning coffee date on Saturday mornings at Ada's house, and they were up to speed with each other. Nice of them to come. At least there would be someone for this spectacle.

She was surprised to see Billy's mother turn in, too. She would never have expected her. She was puzzled moreover to see a trickle of unfamiliar cars turn in and disappear to the parking lot in the back.

When it was time for the family to come in—just Rena and her mother and Mary—the room was dotted with strangers. Rena intended to breathe deeply and go with the outbreath for the twenty minutes necessary to complete the service. But soon it became evident that the chaplain was going to do the whole nine yards for Dr. Amelia Douglas. He recited her entire resume from graduation from Tufts University medical school through her internship and her surgical training until she became chief of the surgical staff. It was a woman's hospital, Rena thought parenthetically, not quite the same as if she were chief of staff at Mass. General, but still a big deal.

Then the chaplain introduced Dr. Florence Gibson, Dr. Douglas's successor as chief of surgical staff, who without glancing at notes spoke at length:

"Hers was indeed a rare gift, for she was one of those who are naturally so endowed with skill, humanity, and idealism that she was able to care for the whole person. Physicians may profitably copy Dr. Douglas's happy combination of traits; her skillful technique, seasoned with kindness, understanding, and unselfishness."

Rena was close to flabbergasted. Granted they had to say something complimentary about the deceased, but Rena, while admiring Aunt Amelia's achievements, had never noted the slightest warmth and precious little empathy. She had overheard Aunt Amelia complain with disgust about women whimpering in childbirth and men, especially men, flinching while she yanked out stitches. Aunt Amelia was tough.

70

Rena herself had been subject to embarrassing examinations and sharp remarks whenever she had the misfortune to be treated by Aunt Amelia, and so she suffered minor ailments in silence—which may have been Aunt Amelia's aim.

To her, Aunt Amelia was an old woman with a great deal of discipline, who experienced only rare affection, which she showed, as she had to Rena, by a generous support that did not require social exchange. Aunt Amelia's lips were crimped into a dozen vertical lines like a drawstring pulled tight; there was no danger of a smile coming on.

"The rewards of medicine are many," Dr. Gibson went on. "Dr. Amelia Douglas must have treasured the spiritual compensation she has known so well in the physician-patient relationship."

Amelia felt the pinch of guilt for never having suspected anything spiritual had been involved in any of Aunt Amelia's relationships.

When the funeral came to a close, Aunt Amelia's lawyer, now thoroughly in charge, stood and announced, "Dr. Douglas's family would like to extend an invitation to all of you to come to their home in Stonehaven following the service."

The gathering seemed to please Mary no end. She managed to dry her eyes and fill and serve platters. It hit Rena too late that Mary, as the one most overtly aggrieved, should not be serving the food. If Rena had had any idea what this event was going to turn into, she would have asked a friend or hired someone to prepare and serve so that Mary could be treated as one of the bereaved. Rena would apologize later for her insensitivity, but she knew Mary would only protest that all she wanted to do was serve.

The gathering was not the solemn affair she had expected; it was more like a reunion or a wedding, Rena thought. A dozen old hospital friends had come down with the officials, and Rena realized by their presence how revered Aunt Amelia had been as a physician in Boston in her prime. More surprising were the nurses who had worked under her. Rena remembered how Aunt Amelia would refer to them as "My nurses." Rena had taken the term as a patronizing expression such as a slaveholder might use, but now she had to consider the possibility that it might have been a term of affection.

She was almost relieved to overhear a middle-aged woman, say to another woman, a colleague of some sort, "We nurses were, you know...., kind of scared of her."

Rena smiled slightly, knowingly, and moved closer to the conversation.

"I know I was scared," the nurse went on. "I remember one day I was changing the bed of an old man. His body was wasted. He couldn't have weighed more than eighty pounds. He didn't know what was going on. I rolled him over on one side and jerked the sheet out from under him. You know how we did it..."

The nurse made a jerking motion with her hand, as the listeners, nurses themselves, jerked and nodded in sympathy.

"To my horror, the man popped right off the bed and fell on his face on the floor. I was so scared. Just then I saw Dr. Douglas standing in the door. I wanted to die before she murdered me. And do you know what she did?"

Rena was transfixed with suspense.

"She came in and, without a word, picked the man up and put him back on the bed, helped me change the sheet, and walked out. I never heard a word about it–ever. I was so grateful."

Rena understood that these people read kindness and understanding in acts, and again she felt guilty for having needed words and smiles.

One of the younger doctors, Emily Burdick, approached Rena, and shook her hand. Rena still was not used to this adult gesture, especially with women, and she let them do the pumping, which they did with authority.

"I wanted to tell you, Miss Everett, that Dr. Douglas encouraged me to become a physician. She was my inspiration, and she helped me in other ways to get into the profession. It would mean a lot to me to have a memento from Dr. Douglas's office, some small thing you wouldn't value yourself. Is there such a thing?"

"Something medical?"

"It doesn't matter."

"A couple of her medical books?"

"That would be fine. Whatever you are willing to part with."

Rena ran upstairs to the crawl space off the hall and dragged a box of books into the light. She flipped through the first few pages of some of them, looking for inscriptions or notes or something that would make them of value to herself. There were none: no records of gifts or early addresses or anything for sentiment's sake. Rena took the box downstairs to the living room, dug her elbow into her hip to lower it slowly to the firm seat of the sofa beside Dr. Burdick.

"Take your pick."

"Oh, thank you," the young doctor said and plunged with such eagerness into the box, setting aside this one and that one in piles, that Rena was moved to say "Take it all. I'm sure I'll never look at them again." The excitement in Dr. Burdick's eyes as she rushed the box to her car, as if she feared Rena would change her mind, gave Rena a feeling of puzzled satisfaction.

"Wasn't my aunt a bit...stern?" Rena asked her, when she returned.

"She was stern. But that sternness was intense devotion to a cause. She had no time for play. We young doctors didn't exactly love her, but there was no one who went through training at that hospital who did not count Dr. Douglas as a great source of inspiration."

Rena felt ashamed again to have been put off by mere sternness. Moreover, she felt insignificant for having no notion of a career herself.

"How long do you think you'll be here," someone asked Rena after everyone else had left and Mary was washing and drying the dishes vigorously in the kitchen.

"I don't know. I have to figure out this last will and testament thing. And what to do with the house. And a really big issue is Mary. I can't just let her go like that. She cared for me when I was a baby. I can't even think now."

Rena felt unpleasantly pressured that someone had even asked. Couldn't they see there was so much to do that she couldn't possibly know what was involved yet, couldn't possibly say how long it would take?

She had to go to Boston for the reading of the will. It went as she expected, the house and furnishings to Rena, the blue chip stocks to her mother, a little cash and some interest-bearing investments were split between them. Rena felt no recognizable emotion at the reading until the lawyer read the bequest of $10,000 to Mary Geary. Then tears rushed to her eyes.

Mary gasped, "Oh, Lord, Doctor. You shouldn't have done that."

Mary had her hand to her head. Poor Mary had no clear notion of how little or much that money was, the sole windfall of her life. Aunt Amelia, Rena had discovered when she took over the household, had been paying Mary $15 a week plus room and board. That little room was the only place Mary had to herself, right off the kitchen. If she got her morning chores done in time, she could listen to *The Romance of Helen Trent* in her room. Rena had complained to Eleanor about the pittance Mary got when her mother came down to visit during Aunt Amelia's last illness.

"Aunt Amelia always said if Mary had any money she would lose it at the race track."

"What race track?"

"In New Hampshire. Those days when Mary would ask for a day off to go to Boston to see her children, she was really going to the race track."

Rena remembered Mary's eyes lighting up when she was talking about the race horses: "Oh, they are so beautiful!," but Rena, just a child, had never wondered when Mary had a chance to see them. She'd assumed these were memories from some distant past.

"How did Aunt Amelia know?"

"Mary left her racing sheets out one day after she'd supposedly been to Boston."

"Well, she did have to go to Boston to get the train to New Hampshire, didn't she? Not a total lie."

Rena had given Mary a ten dollar raise and the next weekend off. She hoped the old lady still had enough energy to go to the races. After the will was read, Rena took Mary by her apartment..

"This is where I live," she had started to say but didn't.

On her return to Stonehaven, Rena started systematically going through the house to see if there was anything that needed to be disposed of before the appraiser came. She sorted through Aunt Amelia's clothes, saving a sweater or two, putting most out for a clothing drive the churches always seemed to be having. Too bad Mary was too fat to use any of the dresses. She offered her Aunt Amelia's most recent go-to-Boston hat.

"Oh, no. I couldn't wear the Doctor's hat," Mary said.

"You could."

Mary shook her head vigorously.

Rena offered her a nice silk scarf and Sunday gloves. Mary enjoyed dressing for mass on Sunday mornings when her arthritis was not too bad.

"Them things are for you; you're her grandniece. You should have them."

"But I'm not going to use them."

Mary seemed pained by the offer. "They are not for the likes of me."

Rena took the scarf herself and reluctantly laid the gloves on the give-away stack. And every hour or so, she knelt on the oriental rug and, like a praying mantis, pulled her arms up to her chest, pressed her chin into her hands, and squeezed herself as if she could physically squeeze out some plan of action.

To have a paid-up house was the cornerstone of security. To have a small income from a handful of stocks to go with it, while not enough to support her, put her in a position where even an inconsequential job such as she had at the Otis House was a living. This security offered by her inheritance, logic told her, allowed her options; but this security, rooted in the house, as it was, seemed just the opposite. It fixed her in Stonehaven. Think, think! The number of crucial elements in her life had doubled.

Rena started on the attic, laying out the old electric fan and a set of ancient golf clubs to discard. She laid the fur pieces, foxes biting their own tails, in a trunk she silently labeled "keep forever." But where would she keep all this forever? Here in this house? Would the house stay empty while she went back to Boston? Would she rent the house to strangers? The only time it was rentable was in the summer, and that would be the time she would want to use it herself on weekends.

Maybe she should just sell it and forget about Stonehaven. The money from the house, invested, would give her a small income to supplement her other small income. And that would be enough.

Of course, if she were to do something drastic like that, give up Stonehaven forever, she wanted a plan.

Distributing Aunt Amelia's property according to the will would take months. No one could tell Rena to her satisfaction why this was so. Mary suggested Rena go back to Boston. Mary had always been the romantic one, encouraging her with her boyfriends. Rena knew that Mary would love to have the house to herself in the interim. She'd turn on her television programs, eat what she wanted, walk down to the water in the evening and meet the Turner's housekeeper in the big house overlooking the beach. Rena had seen her steal moments like these in the old days when Aunt Amelia spent a day in Boston. Rena would be happy to give Mary some weeks as mistress of the house after all these months by the sickbed.

But Rena was afraid to leave without knowing what she was going to do and then have to come back and go through the decision making process all over again. No, she'd have to dispose of this matter before she could go on with life.

Here in Stonehaven, the tulips were coming up the same as they always had, the robins were arriving on schedule, and she didn't feel as if she lived in a nation in crisis.

Rena had to meet occasionally with appraisers at the house and lawyers in Boston. Most of the time she stayed in Stonehaven, and, with spring coming on, it didn't make sense to be anywhere else. Besides the pure joy of spring in Stonehaven, she had to see about connecting the house to the sewer the city had recently run down the street. It had been a high priority of "that nice Lawson boy," Mary had said. If Aunt Amelia had been well, she would have connected to the sewer when everybody else did. The belated connection would take some time and supervision, as well as an extra fee. Rena would try to get the workers to save the rose garden and arbor which bordered–and secretly benefited from–the overflowing septic tank.

While Rena was dealing with the sewage problem, the days lengthened into summer, Rena moved into Aunt Amelia's large bedroom. She gave up the double bed, which had almost filled her little room, for the twin high posters in the Aunt Amelia's room. She kept the white chenille bedspreads and the puckered white blanket covers. She turned them back at night and hung them over the high posts, just as Aunt Amelia had done, in her nightly ritual.

The room ran from the back of the house to the front, which faced the ocean, and had windows on three sides. She could now wake each morning to a full view of the Ipswitch Bay as it met the ocean, of Halibut Point to the right and Cormorant Island to the left, and in the middle the direct route to Spain. And she could look out the back at the alley and down over the fence into her neighbor's side yard. It was a commanding view.

Aunt Amelia's five-year diary still lay on the desk beside the bed. Rena had opened the diary with trepidation, fearing little notes about how unsatisfactory Rena had been as a ward and only child, so to speak. Secondarily, Rena hoped and feared the diaries would reveal the secrets of what was behind the rock wall of Aunt Amelia's face, but she had been disappointed. The scant inch of space allocated to each day, began with an overlong description of the weather and moved on to a statement of the garden work Aunt Amelia had accomplished and then any sewing chores. Few feelings were recorded, no personal conversations. Few events. And the events that were mentioned were only hinted at. "Went to hospital for meeting of the board. Was very dismayed by what I heard." No explanation followed.

Still, as a bedtime ritual, Rena read from the notations for that date as if from an almanac. Never mind that they were boring and barely legible, there was always the hope that tomorrow there would be some revelation.

That winter Rena's relationship with Ada strengthened. The longstanding trust and assumptions formed earlier launched them into new, grown up conversations without a trial period. Almost immediately they had established a standing Saturday morning meeting at Ada's house for girl-talk while her husband Phil went to Boston for a business course. (Phil and Ada had married quietly and were living in the apartment over her parents' garage while saving for a house.) The hiatus of several years had done the girls' relationship no damage. They would have talked for hours over coffee and toast, but stores opened and errands called.

Sometimes on Friday nights, after Ada's store closed, Rena joined Ada and a girl who worked with her and that girl's fiancé and some friends of his for a beer in Gloucester. It was fun, though the girls were more fun than the boys.

Upon arriving at home from Boston one day, Rena cried till she was exhausted and went to sleep. She woke with eyes almost puffed closed. She didn't get dressed. Mary brought her some broth and homemade bread and clucked around her.

"There. There. It's not my business," she said. Rena knew that was as close as Mary would come to asking the cause of Rena's tears.

Rena slept most of the day.

Indeed, Rena had been raised by her once prominent, and reclusive great Aunt Amelia in whom she had observed the sacrifice of everything else for achievement, the satisfaction of independence along with the sorrow of loneliness. Rena planned to venture as far, farther than her Aunt Amelia, without losing the children of Dory Beach or the chorus of the Rubaiyat.

Rena had certainly had a role model in her great aunt Amelia, now deceased, who had been as nearly a recluse as a person on three quarters of an acre could be. Amelia Douglas, this lean woman, who planted, pruned, weeded and sprayed, had also been known as Dr. Douglas, feminist, surgeon, and saver of blue babies. Stonehaveners nodded out of respect as they passed her, snipping suckers from the apple trees with the confidence with which she once snipped out appendices in the hospital in Boston, or tying up errant tomato plants with the firmness that she gathered up hernias. She lived a disciplined retirement without other self-expression until a stroke brought Rena to live with her again until her death. And still Rena felt her aunt's spirit around her.

Today the demands of citizens and coworkers had drained Rena, and the comfortable aloneness of home had turned into loneliness. The vision of Paul lying in the hospital, cut down at his peak like lilacs severed in full bloom, was full in front of her and she could not turn away from it.

She climbed the stairs, pulling herself by each dark stained post that marked off a square of cream white wall leading to the landing at the top. The hallway was cream, the woodwork and ceiling were white. The bedroom she shared with no one was, cream and white: cream walls, white spreads, white curtains. Aunt Amelia's white. Aunt Amelia had disdained the penchant of some people for color and pattern. Simplicity was virtue; thus cream and white.

Rena looked out her window past the substantial new homes on the edge of the seawall as if they were not there. Sometimes the height of the second story made her feel in control and happy. She came up here early tonight only as a sign of faith, to open herself to a miracle, some great balm that might in a holy moment sweep off the ocean and envelope her like the fog, cleanse her with grace like a rare moist breeze from the South. Let her look far out to sea and beyond the knowledge of Paul so sick.

But there was no miracle, no grace, no balmy breeze tonight. Rena descended the stairs from the airy upper floor and retreated quickly to her darker, cozier refuge, a small room in a little wing two significant steps down from the rest of The Oldest House.

When Paul's tumor had first been discovered a little over a year before, Rena had claimed this room. Once the bedroom of Mary, Aunt Amelia's housekeeper, more recently it had been a junk room, a repository of the vacuum cleaner, the ironing board, half-used supplies and articles never used but too good to throw away.

When Paul's tumor was confirmed, her need for this other bedroom, never occupied by Aunt Amelia, began to overwhelm her. The threat of Paul's tumor required some sort of compensatory shift in her home life, the building of a firmer base under shaky timbers.

The rest of the house she kept as she had inherited it with everything of Aunt Amelia's in place: the silver service on the empire card table, the collection of New England Glass Company antique paperweights on the fireside shelves, the Dedham ware rabbits, the cutwork table scarves on the end tables beside the needlepoint chairs. It was all American; Aunt Amelia had no use for foreign imports.

9

The Class of 1959

Rena woke the following morning to the fog horn, its tone so low it was reassuring, as if it came from a big, faithful guard dog, warding off danger. Rena had never known where or what the horn was, only that when the fog rolled in during the night, the big dog stirred and began to growl. The bell buoy was just a tinkle of dog tags by comparison. She looked out the window and saw nothing but white. Blanketed from the world rather than cut off, she felt almost at peace. She sat down at Aunt Amelia's desk and began to make a list of things to do as the new and apparently permanent owner of the house.

When the new sewer connection was in, Rena began amassing rocks over the spot where the old tank had been next to the roses. She found one rock at a time beside the road or in the woods. Sometimes she asked for them; more often she stole them, but in New England taking rocks was like picking dandelions from a neighbor's lawn—it might be considered cleaning up. Rena carried a board in her trunk to roll rocks into the car. It was difficult to transport them and to maneuver them into place, but the task gave her satisfaction. She didn't care when it was finished. That was not the point. The point was the process. She, Rena Everett, could, all by herself, build a rock garden. If she'd had to hire someone to bring a truck load of rock, what would have been the point?

She consulted Aunt Amelia's diaries to tell her what seeds and plants to order, when to plant, and when to prune.

She had made a rough budget, but bills came in that she had not counted on, for example, homeowner's insurance and car insurance for the Oldsmobile had fallen to Rena along with the furnishings.

As winter came on she tended to stay in bed later on weekdays. She was up early on Saturdays to be with Ada. Beyond that, just maintaining the house kept her busy.

In the winter when Aunt Amelia's old diaries reported no outdoor work, only sewing, knitting, and watching TV, Rena was alarmed to find herself daydreaming to the point of uselessness. She had to make a decision. She roused herself from the day bed and marched resolutely up the stairs. She stood with arms crossed looking out over the sea as if demanding something. The waves were becoming higher and, as the wind shifted, scattered wisps of cloud gathered into formations. Rena washed her face, and put on hose. Within minutes, she found herself parking in front of a granite and wood structure, ignoring the meter as year round residents do, and shouldering the heavy door to Town Hall.

Its interior was not a place with which she was actually familiar. She stood in the hall reading the plaques on the walls like a tourist. There was the World War II Honor Roll, the names told a history of immigration: the English—Gable, Lawson, and Page; the Scots—Harper, Buchanan, and Sinclair; and also the "Scofies," the poor Scottish laborers from Nova Scotia—Fergusson, MacDougall, and Douglas; the Germans—Becker, Rohrbach, and Waldman; the Scandinavians—Thuesen, Holgerson, Vigeland; the Finns—Markkanen and Vuorinen; the Italians—Nardulli, Pellegrino, and Scarselli; the Portuguese—Pintassilgo, Alvarez, and Amado; and the

French Canadians—Poythress, Reynaud, and Thibideau. She knew all the names; she called the Scarselli Brothers for her fuel oil; Kirsten Vigeland did her picture framing; Gable Garage kept her car running; and of course, Paul Lawson ran the town.

Art works from the famous regional artists of the thirties and forties lined the walls, realistic oil paintings of quarry, port, and shore.

Announcements curled on the bulletin board if they weren't tacked down: minutes of committee meetings—The Historic District Committee, The Ambulance Committee, The Conservation Committee, The School Committee, The Recreation Committee, The Cormorant Island Commission—petitions for special permits to operate a restaurant in a nonconforming building, requests for variance to build decks without the required building separation, an ad for a custodian for Town Hall and the public restrooms, and the names of a hundred and seventy-eight people on the waiting list for a mooring in the harbor. The inner workings of the town were laid bare and Rena found the minutia intriguing.

She went slowly down the hall, reading the little signs beside the doors lining the hall: Public Works, Assessors, Town Accountant, Treasurer/Collector. When she saw one saying Office of the Selectmen at the end of the hall, she quickened her pace. She pulled open the heavy door and saw a half darkened room with desks and chairs. Rolls of drawings and in and out baskets appeared to be randomly scattered. Another office brightly lit in the corner was conspicuously marked over the door: "Chairman." Rena made a beeline.

"May I help you?" someone said loudly behind her, and she jumped as a young woman overtook her, a stranger who did not know any better than to present herself as an intermediary between her and Paul. Rena stammered a bit while slipping crabwise to the Chairman's door where she knew he would instantly make it plain that no intermediary was appropriate.

Paul was on the phone, leaning back in his green fake-leather chair, holding the phone between his shoulder and ear, fingers laced behind his head.

Paul saw Rena and smiled. Then he winked. A long, slow, warm wink that puckered lines around his eye. A wink that said, even though I'm on this silly telephone call, I prefer to be with you. Paul waved his hand, and the young receptionist, who had followed Rena protectively to the Chairman's door, faded back to her seat.

"Rena. How are you?" Paul said finally when he had extricated himself from the phone and risen to offer both his hands across the desk. Rena didn't answer, just took his hands. They were warm. She wasn't sure she had ever held his hands in hers before. She sat down in a chair across from him and, looking straight into his eyes, wished he could read her mind.

"Remember the way it used to be?" Rena had finally blurted out.

"Maybe," he said, sitting down and tilting back in the chair again. "Try me."

"Remember when the world was young and I used to be somebody?"

The question wiped the smile off Paul's face. He threw himself forward until his changing center of gravity snapped the chair straight with a thunk.

"Rena, you've always been somebody in my book," he said with furrowed seriousness.

Rena sighed, melting.

"Remember, she said, "how we rid Stonehaven of ragweed one summer by pulling up the most plants of anybody in town and we split the ten dollar prize?"

"We must have spent two whole weeks pulling that stuff. We had mounds of it!"

"Remember how we went to Bunker Hill on our class trip and some people had forgotten to bring subway fare back to where the bus was parked, and you and I had to go to Travelers Aid? I don't know about you, but I felt like a Congresswoman rounding up funds for a military campaign."

Paul laughed.

"And the biggest thing–remember how we put together the rally saving Stonehaven High?"

"Yes," Paul smiled. "Us against the world."

It was the year after it was decided that students couldn't get a good education in little high schools like Rockport and Stonehaven so they would be consolidating those high schools into Gloucester High. The idea had been that Stonehaven High would stay open two more years to let the class of 1958 and Rena's class graduate there. The ninth and tenth grades were sent directly to Gloucester, but they gave students in the oldest two classes the option to stay on or go to Gloucester. As a result, Stonehaven High had ended up with only thirteen seniors and eleven juniors. Consequently, during Rena's entire junior year there was talk of closing the school altogether and sending Rena's class to Gloucester for their senior year in spite of the previous plan. The issue came to a head as the class of 1958 prepared for graduation. People began to call it "what may be the last class to graduate from Stonehaven High."

The class of 1959 felt betrayed. They had in no way prepared themselves to become other than graduates of Stonehaven High. A promise is binding, and the breaking of that understanding would spoil the world as they knew it.

In April, Paul unfolded a plan to the group sitting around a table in the lunch room, eating sandwiches from Ciardi's (because they had stopped food service at the high school for lack of sufficient participants). He told him he was going to the meeting of Selectmen at Town Hall that Thursday to try to get a feeling of who was for closing and who was against and why. When they knew where the votes were, they could plan a campaign.

"Who wants to go to the meeting with me?"

No one did. A meeting sounded pretty boring. Finally Rena said she would, if her aunt would let her, because she should help Paul out.

There was another larger meeting the following Tuesday night in Gloucester to discuss the merging of the schools, and Paul planned to go there, too, and see what the Gloucester people were saying about the influx of students from the smaller towns. Rod and Spencer agreed they'd go to that one. It sounded like a little more of an adventure.

"We will find out what they are saying so we will know what ammunition to gather against it. Or...," Paul gestured with an open hand as if to another speaker, "maybe what they are saying will make sense, and we'll be convinced we should close Stonehaven."

"Leave it to Paul to look at both sides of the question," said Whit. "What fun is that? We want to protest."

"A goddam revolution, f'crissakes," Rod said.

"No matter what the facts, we have the right to choose. Even if we choose what some call wrong, we have the right to be wrong," said Spencer, who had obviously been reading outside the reading list again. "The Commonwealth is based on the independent township."

Paul rolled his eyes. "We have to be informed, that's all."

"Okay, okay. Just give me a sign and tell me where to stand," said Rena. "I'm for us, the kids right here. I don't want us to be split up and lost in the crowd."

In the end, Paul went to the meetings by himself because Aunt Amelia wouldn't let Rena go on a school night, even though she was class vice-president, because the doctor thought "a young lady has no business running around at night making a public scene." Paul came back with several pages of notes and explained what was going on. The *Reader's Digest* version of meetings was perfect for Rena. She just wanted to know what this had to do with her. What they needed to do, Paul concluded, was get the voters interested, not just the Selectmen. Get some pressure from the electorate. He suggested organizing a big reunion and bringing the graduates back to Stonehaven to rekindle their interest in keeping their old school alive for one more critical year.

"The majority of Stonehaven grads are right here in the area, but I bet they haven't set foot on the granite steps since they graduated."

"Yeah, I bet they'd be shocked at how run down the place is," Rod said. "They might say 'Scrap it.'"

Rena was flabbergasted. "What do you mean 'run down'?"

"You want to see run down?" Rod picked up the rod used to open the transoms and led them down the main hall, lined with classrooms. He pointed out broken tiles in the hall, loose doorknobs, missing pieces of molding, light-colored places where something used to hang, and brownish splotches on the ceiling plaster. Rena had often leaned her head back against her chair and looked at the splotches over Mrs. McKinnery's desk and seen clown faces, stalking leopards, and iris blossoms in them and had never once thought the words 'run down'. Besides, who notices these things?

"And the walkway in front of the school is cracking up, and the windows all need to be reglazed, and the bushes aren't bushy...," Rod said in an unaccustomed stream of words prompted apparently by his friends' first foray into his area of concern.

"Okay, here's my idea," Rena interrupted. "We get lots and lots of bedding plants—the usual pansies, petunias, geraniums, zinnias— and we put them in pots all around the building and inside too. Like a Swiss village. Nobody notices the cracks in the plaster of those chalets."

"Where are we going to get the money for the plants?"

"We could borrow plants from Adams Nursery. It would be good publicity for them, wouldn't it?"

"Hey, we could actually sell the bedding plants to the people who came," Paul said. "We would make a profit to use for the prom AND we would hide our cracks. Everyone wins. Great idea, Rena."

Rena glowed. "We could get some of the more interesting plants, too, like portulaca, nicotiana, gypsophilia, hens and chickens..." The others were staring at her so she stopped. There was a certain degree of detail she'd found her friends couldn't tolerate. To her, the detail was the best part.

The reunion was set for Memorial Day weekend with graduation on the Monday holiday. They had only three weeks to pull it together. They divided into committees, which Paul and Rena and Rod headed. Rena got Lili Bethea and Betsy Tarr on hers, Paul took Donna the Diligent, and Rod had Billy and Whit. Paul also took Spencer, nominally, as Spencer wasn't a joiner; no one could organize Spencer, but he'd participate in some way he chose.

"We need some people to help," Paul said. "We need bodies. Get some seniors. Also, there are two people in our class we've left out." Rena winced thinking of the two. One boy was quiet and dull as tidal mud. They called him Zorro. That was sarcasm. Karen Omwek was just dumb. She got Ds because if they gave her Fs they would never get her out of there. If you gave her the simplest instruction like "I'll meet you directly across the street from the A & P," she'd say "Come again?" So that's what they called her behind her back.

"Come Again and Zorro, obviously," Rena said.

"We need to include them."

Rena threw her hip out, rolled her eyes, and grimaced–a triple whammy–at Paul.

"I know, I know. But it's the right thing. I'll tell you what. I'll spend a little time with her and see if I can come up with a role she could play. Then who knows; I'll get her to ask Zorro to help her with it and kill two birds with one stone."

Paul actually took Karen out for a lobster roll lunch at Mimi's Cafe the next Saturday.

"You didn't pay for the lunch, did you?" Rena asked.

"Of course. I asked her to go."

"That's a date. Egad, you had a date with Come Again Karen!"

"No. But so what if I did? She's not a disease. Besides, I found out what I wanted to find out. She has a talent."

Paul pulled a wad of paper napkins from his shirt pocket. He laid them out in a row on the table. Rena looked at them blankly for a second and then looked at Paul. He was looking so smug that she looked again. What was it, the way they were folded, the color, the smudges of mayonnaise?

"The drawings on them."

"Oh! I see now. There are little pencil marks."

She held them in the rectangle of light from the transom until she saw on each one a perfect little miniature. One was a lobster pot set at an angle and some nets draped over a rock. Another was a view of the fisherman's shed on Mackey's Wharf, but not from the side the artists usually did. A third drawing was of a figure at a table, not a person she could recognize but a slouch that communicated deep depression.

"Incredible. Incredible. Come Again did these right before your eyes?"

Paul nodded.

"Can she do that again?"

"Of course. What did you think?"

"Wow." Thanks to Aunt Amelia, Rena had taken art lessons, almost unavoidable with the plethora of artists giving classes in town. She had taken oils, watercolor, drawing, as well as ceramics. She had loved the different media, the concepts, the design, but her hand would not draw what she saw in her mind.

"So she can do posters and things like a real artist," Paul said. "Sensational."

"I feel terrific about this," Paul continued. "Then I asked her to find out what Zorro could do to help. She already knows a lot about him. Funny thing."

"So. Who would ever have guessed. Come Again is an artistic genius."

"Do me a favor. Let's call her Karen, okay?"

Rena's face went hot. It was so great to be in. In with Paul, in with the nicknames, inside the inside jokes. Then suddenly he had pulled a switch, and the nicknames were out, and she was out. She was cruel and mean and out.

"Well, Paul, I have to say I admire you for what you've done with Karen." It wasn't a thing she enjoyed saying even though it was true, but she'd found that, if she made amends quickly, her burning face cooled quickly. If she didn't make amends, the whole mess hung on and later moved down to her stomach. She could never, ever not be all right with Paul.

"You know," Paul said, "Karen should really study art. What she needs is an art teacher. Stonehaven High doesn't have one because we're so small. But Gloucester has several art teachers. It makes you see why a person might want to go to a big school. In fact, Karen might be better off in Gloucester after all."

"Paul!" Rena scolded.

"I hate to say it, but it's true. Maybe some kind art teacher would discover her and take her under his wing."

"Here we are living in a veritable art colony and you're saying she has no one to teach her art except in Gloucester," Rena said. She was ready to follow Paul any way he went, but she wished he'd make up his mind.

"Oh, sure, there are artists here, plenty of art teachers but...Rena, Karen's mother works in the sardine factory, and even then she only has work when the boats come in. Her father is out of the picture. They couldn't hire an art teacher even if they thought of it. That's what public schools are for–to give a well-rounded education to kids of sardine factory workers."

Rena knew the sardine factory well but only from the outside. It was a long, low shed standing on a hundred pilings, like a centipede tethered to the shore of Whale Bone Cove west of town. Its windows were encrusted with salt, the residue of a thousand high tides spattered by a thousand stiff winds against the glass. A whistle blew when the boats came in, and a scattering of women put down their laundry baskets, handed over their babies to grandmothers, and turned the burners under their kettles off. They ran like rain in the gutter, meeting and joining, swelling into a stream that flowed down to the factory to gain their $1.25 an hour for as long as the shiny little silver fish were thrown by the shovelful from the boats through the open doors on the end of the shed and onto the conveyors.

"Okay, so let's get started planning the posters, getting a slogan, making lists of stuff," Paul said.

Rena flipped her blue cloth notebook open and found an unused pink divider on which she wrote SAVE STONEHAVEN HIGH: REUNION in neat capitals. She had just turned to the clean lined paper that followed and poised her pen for her first directive when suddenly she heard a most annoying sound.

"Paw-ul," a high sing song voice said.

There was Come Again out in the hall, peeking her face coyly around the door.

"Uh, hi, Karen," Paul said.

Rena raised one eyebrow at her.

Thus acknowledged, Karen flitted through the door and over to their table.

"May I sit here?" she asked Rena, gingerly putting her hand on the end seat between Rena and Paul.

Rena cleared her sweater and chemistry book off the seat for her.

From then on Karen was in on all their planning sessions, looking adoringly at Paul and inhibiting all their conversations.

Who could blame her? To be taken aside by Paul the Perfect

and asked 'My dear, what is your special talent?' or whatever it was he had asked while looking into her eyes over the crusty, overstuffed lobster rolls. Rena knew what had happened. She knew as surely as she knew what bird made the gull-cry overhead. Paul had winked at Karen.

Rena knew well the power of Paul's wink. She had first experienced it in ninth grade standing outside of home room. Paul was engaged in a knot of boys, and he saw her standing nearby alone. He smiled almost imperceptibly at her and squeezed one eye shut like the squeeze of a hand. One eye chose her out of all the people in the world, and the other eye winked, blinked as the shutter on a camera captures its subject. It meant that he was standing with them but his thoughts were with her. It meant he and Rena shared that secret, and it was a secret worth sharing. Weeks later, when she saw him wink at Lily Bethea, she was chilled by the betrayal. Still every wink he gave Rena lured her back into the melting sunshine.

Once the reunion flyers had gone out with Karen's sketches on the front, the alumni gave their support. They had offered door prizes, advice, and services. Rena's plants were a hit. Rod's arrangements of seating was practical. Spencer was not enthusiastic about the cause himself–neither Stonehaven nor Gloucester High suited him–but Spencer's uncle, who was a photographer, set up a camera and lighting for photos of returning class members and old buddies for a moderate price. They offered homemade cookies and brownies for sale. The drawing for door prizes included an oil change at Otis' Jenny station; a one-size-fits-all, hand-painted, wrap-around skirt from The Green Rooster; and a complimentary fish of two pounds or more from Ernie's Fish Market, species to be determined by Ernie.

Paul addressed the crowd between the drawing for the skirt and the drawing for the fish. He explained the plight of the school and the class of 1959's intense loyalty. He spoke of the individual attention Stonehaven's teachers could give and of the value of community.

"Talk to your Selectmen. Tell them you want to keep Stonehaven High open to honor the town's commitment to the class of 1959. Thank you."

Paul stepped down from Rod's speaker's stand, nodding modestly to hearty applause.

"Spunky kids. They deserve a lot of credit," Rena heard a man say, and she passed him a petition and watched him sign his name with a big C and a big R that trailed off into illegibility.

"That's okay," Paul said later. "The right people in town know that signature. He signs the papers for all the mortgage loans the bank makes. They will listen to him."

How clear it was to Rena that Paul's career in local government had already begun in high school. That was when Paul developed his love of campaigns, the certainty that he would win, and a satisfaction with a leadership role that far outweighed the lure of money. Paul's father had expected him to take over Lawson's Marine, and he did work there part time, but Rena now saw how and why Paul had talked his father into hiring a general manager to help. As part owner, Paul took only his share of the profits and a part time salary, keeping his oars in both waters. When the Selectmen saw how well the town ran with Paul committing the major portion of his time to the Chairmanship, no wonder they voted to buy the town a car with a town seal for Paul to drive on Town business. Paul was never not on Town business. Through that and other arrangements, Paul could support himself and his family while doing what he really felt compelled to do.

Rena wished her own direction had been as clear.

Rena wondered if Maureen completely accepted Paul's ambitions in an area that paid nothing but a tiny stipend. After all, Maureen did not grow up loving this town. His stature among the townspeople would not be quite so meaningful to her. Moreover, she did have a fondness for things that money can buy. Her house was a major preoccupation. She was always repainting, repapering, reupholstering. Rena never drove by their house that there wasn't a truck outside with the name of some home improvement service.

Maureen also was a clothes horse. In fact, Maureen dressed not only well, but one might say stunningly. She wore the latest style before anyone else even knew about it, and she could wear anything well. She had the Jackie hairdo before Kennedy was even inaugurated and a Jackie dress to go with it. Then she would turn around and brush her hair all to one side, leaving the other side sleek and stark in a way that would look ridiculous on anyone else. And she'd put a big comb in it, and she looked fantastic. She could wear a strap on only one side of her dress. The shortest skirts, the longest skirts—she could carry it all off. Rena admired that—not the clothes but the carrying off. Maureen had style.

Rena generally paid little attention to her own clothes, less from indifference than from a fear of caring and failing. Maureen Lawson's easy fashion sense seemed to Rena a gift.

"And then there was the prom, we organized that, Paul. Remember us working together?" This was Rena's resume' she was laying out for Paul, a far more convincing one than the one on paper.

"I don't remember much about the prom," Paul said. "It's all a blur."

Rena remembered everything about the prom.

There had been talk of not having one because of the small numbers, but the students had been adamant. They would not be cheated out of this and soon reserved Legion Hall for the event.

Paul, as class president again, had this notion everyone should go and no one should stay away because they didn't have a date. Of course, Rena would go with Billy. Betsy Tarr and Donna invited their boyfriends from Gloucester High. Rod was taking Lili the Lovely. Spencer declared the whole thing was silly and he might not even come, but Rena knew he would. Whit asked Ada Felton for lack of a better idea.

It made perfect sense that the Undateables, Zorro and Karen, would go together. But then Zorro inexplicably invited some girl from Malden whom he had just met once at a roller skating rink in Lynn when he had been visiting cousins. Why did he have to go out to the Boston suburbs to invite a stranger when he and Karen had shared so many years of being the school outcasts together? Zorro's harebrained move had left Karen out. Paul had not invited a date yet, and Rena knew several Stonehaven girls at Gloucester High were all hoping for an invitation. And it would be good to have any one of them, each a part of the old Stonehaven gang, back where they belonged.

"Karen is the only one in the class without a date," Paul said to Rena one day as if that were news. "So...I was thinking...."

"You wouldn't," said Rena.

"I might."

"Why sacrifice yourself on the most important night of your life?"

"Rena, you're right. It is an important night," Paul said gently. "I really care about everyone going to the prom. It's a matter of pride with me–that I can make it happen. There are many more nights to go out with many more girls. I don't care. I want us all to be at our best this one night. And I don't want Karen to have nothing good to look back at."

Rena sighed. "Knighthood errant.... Years of noble deeds," she thought. Only Tennyson could describe Paul adequately. No use stopping Paul from being Paul.

"Couldn't we do that again?" Rena pleaded.

Paul looked quizzical. "You want to do all that again? Pull ragweed or save Stonehaven High or go to the prom?"

Rena sighed. Did she have to spell it out? "Is there anything I could do at City Hall?" she blurted. "A job, I mean. Keep track of things. Think occasionally. Talk to people."

Paul didn't look away, as many men would look away to the corner of the room, considering the possibilities. Paul looked straight into her eyes. Paul saw possibilities. He cocked his head and smiled. "We can probably work something out." And he winked.

Rena felt truly happy for the first time in weeks.

"I really do need an assistant of my own," Paul went on. "The Board of Selectmen has one–Sheila–you met her just now. I'm afraid I'm running her to death with this school thing on top of everything else. Interesting that you spoke of saving old Stonehaven High. You know we're going to build a new one?"

"I read something about it in the G.D. Times."

One side of Paul's mouth turned up in a smile, and Rena was looking for it. Stonehaveners generally abbreviated the Gloucester Daily Times in this way without drawing any notice. But once, in eighth grade, Paul had said something about the G.D. Times, and Whit, as if he'd never heard the phrase before, had blurted out loudly, "the God Damn Times!" The Dory Beach gang had reveled in Whit's zany wickedness. Forever afterwards, none of them could mention the G.D. Times to Rena without the distracting profanity darting across her mind like an arrow out of Whit's bow. This time the arrow was out of Rena's quiver, and Paul's smile showed her she had hit her mark.

Rena had read about the proposed new high school in the *Gloucester Daily Times* without any particular interest. It's not as if the school were going to have anything to do with her.

"That's exciting. Where's it going to be?"

"Up Carson Road between Alexander's Pond and Kist's Farm. You know where I mean?"

Rena knew it well. She and Billy used to go parking there. There were not many dirt roads or undeveloped sites where she and Billy had not been parking.

"Yes," Rena said. "You and I–the whole class of '59–fought to keep the high school open for one more year, and then it was gone, and now we've grown, and we're fighting to get a new one. We've come full circle." Rena felt a pang at the pronouncement. Ending up where they started out was not what she had intended; it felt disturbingly comfortable.

They had grown up in a lull following the closing of the granite companies and the waning of fortunes of small fishermen. Stonehaven not only had lost its own high school but, for a few years, it had lost the commuter train to Boston. The nearest stop on the Boston & Maine line was Gloucester. But now the train came all the way back to Stonehaven, fill-in development was thriving, and the school age population was on the rise.

"The important thing is to manage growth," Paul said. "We manage it now, or we lose our way of life forever." He leaned back in his chair and mused silently. Then he snapped forward again. "We'll work something out." And he winked.

By January 15, the town, at a specially called Town Meeting, approved Rena's salary, which they were to eke out by cutting garbage pickup from twice to once a week. Rena was soon ensconced in her own fake-leather chair in the center of Town Hall between the doors of the Board's meeting room and the Chairman's office.

10

Town Hall

Rena's first assignment at Town Hall, even before she was introduced to the school development campaign, was to make the change in garbage pickup work smoothly.

"I got the vote I wanted at the Town Meeting ," Paul said, "because I promised them I would make it work. Now what does the town need to make once-a-week collection work?"

"Bigger garbage cans," Rena said.

"Exactly. People put out three or four little ones all spilling over. It looks terrible, and our men have to pick up what falls on the ground. What I need is an ordinance requiring one big can and a top that fits tightly. If you could fool around with something like that to present to the Board, it would get us home free."

Rena knew something about causes, it didn't matter if it was garbage or civil rights. If Paul wanted neat garbage, she'd start turning her wheels toward neat garbage. The ideas flowed.

"Why doesn't the town provide each household with a great big garbage can for free, one like the garbage collectors prefer," Rena asked. "The garbage men will be happy, and the homeowners will feel as if they're getting something in return for less frequent pickup."

"Hmm. Not bad. Very good," Paul said. "And how much will that cost?"

"I have no idea. But, remember, you're saving money by cutting the collection in half."

Paul countered, "And remember, we're paying you out of the savings."

"And worth every penny," Rena quipped.

"I'm sure. Okay, get some prices on some cans. Ask Wally for figures on households."

"I'll also ask him to let me talk to some of the garbage men for their ideas."

Paul stepped back to look her up and down. "Rena, I swear, you were born for this."

"And another thing..." Rena was exhilarated now. "...do you realize how heavy a full garbage can is? You don't have to drag yours uphill when it's full like I do, so you don't know. But a little old lady couldn't carry a week's garbage in one can."

Rena knew because Mary could no longer manage the big garbage can at Aunt Amelia's house, and so she let Rena pull it to the end of the alley behind the house, but not without embarrassment and muttering defensively, "Yes, that's all right. You're young."

"Uh-oh." Paul said. "What's the solution?"

"Wheels. A garbage can with wheels."

"That sounds really expensive."

Rena shrugged. "That sounds like progress to me."

"You're right, progress is never cheap, but it's cost-effective in the long run. Actually, Rena," he said leaning to her ear, "it's obvious you and I are the only truly competent people in the whole town."

Rena had already said the sum total of what she knew about garbage. She didn't want to begin her task by having to ask, "But where do towns buy garbage cans?"

When she had started at the Otis House, answering her questions about how to do things had taken her supervisors longer than doing the job themselves. She knew that. So she'd find a solution herself the same way she had when she had taken over Aunt Amelia's care.

Garbage. There was a guy with Harpo Marx hair at Bard who used to talk to people about the environment and making less garbage. He'd probably know someone who did something right with garbage. She didn't know his name. But she got on the phone and got the secretary of a professor there who knew who she was talking about and what department. She called that department and got someone who knew the guy's name. She called the man, and he didn't know anything about manufacturers of garbage cans, but he said she should call the town hall of any town and ask their solid waste disposal department for suppliers. Her face burned. She *was* Town Hall.

In Stonehaven, solid waste disposal meant Wally. Here she was on the phone long distance with a professor in New York, and Wally was right down the hall. But she didn't want Wally to know she was asking dumb questions, so she called the garbage department of the town of Essex, and they gave her the name of a supplier of work gloves and overalls for garbage collectors and–get this–there was actually an organization of waste disposal industries, companies that made products for dealing with garbage.

By the end of the week, Rena was talking seriously to three manufacturers of garbage cans. She hadn't found exactly what she thought they needed, but she was on the way. When she finally had to go to Wally, he looked at her figures, stared at her, and said it would never work. She was crushed. She admonished herself: A young woman who had read all the English poets, was enthralled by lost civilizations, and whose biggest job until now was showing people around an old house should never be figuring costs of garbage collection for an entire town. The worst thing would be disappointing Paul.

Paul loved the plan. As for Wally's misgivings, he said, "You can find things wrong with any plan. But if it's a good idea, you find a way to make it work."

By summer, the rolling garbage cans were delivered to the households just above West Beach as a trial. On garbage day, you could see where the test area ended and the old way began by the huge difference in the neatness of the garbage on pickup day.

Gunny Saks, who, in the time since he had left Stonehaven High, had graduated from lifting and dumping the garbage to driving the truck, was Rena's market research source. Gunny assured Rena that the test area people were proud of their garbage, and Rena felt vindicated. The program was ready to expand.

Paul gradually gave Rena more and more areas to work on. She worked on grant proposals and the annual report, composed letters, and took calls that used to go to Paul, thereby freeing Paul to spend more time working with the School Development Committee on the construction of the new school complex.

When the high school was complete, Paul and Rena moved on to turning the old high school into a middle school. Rena did the legwork on the issues Paul wanted to dig into, and then she followed up on all the decisions that were made. When Paul decided to computerize, Rena found someone to adapt a basic program for them. When Paul wanted some land on which to put a small pump station, Rena found a willing landowner. It was like school when Paul and Rena had been spoken as one word: Paulandrena.

Of course, there were committees for these areas, and their input was valuable, but they did not put clear, full, to-the-point reports on Paul's desk in three days like Rena did after a question came up. Even with the reports, things dragged on. The committees took the reports home to study, and nothing surfaced again till the next bimonthly meeting. Paul warned her not to bypass the committees, and Rena made a point of knowing all their members. On a good day, she could snap through ten calls an hour.

Paul relished most the progress that had its roots in Stonehaven's tradition: The depot was used as a depot again, modernized. The old library, where Rena had read her Bobbsey Twins and Nancy Drews and Paul had borrowed his Rubaiyat, now housed, thanks to Paul, a special collection of local history, regional writers' works, books on local geology, flora and fauna. Paul had a special love of issues concerning the harbor.

For example, Paul thought the hundred and seventy boats waiting for moorings cried out for solution. The harbor master, Mack Cook–he was an old-timer–managed mooring assignments, filling the occasional space that was abandoned, but where was the improvement? Paul noted that at the turn of the century there were more than a hundred boats moored in Lanesville harbor alone. Now that was a pile of boats in a dinky little harbor. And how did they do it? He studied the old pictures of these harbors and considered the dimensions of the boats and the spacing and type of moorings. Rena wrote to eighteen current harbor masters from Provincetown to Nyack asking for the numbers and classes of craft moored, and Paul compared their mooring figures and configurations with Stonehaven's. Then Rena wrote a report, Paul studied it, and, from that and his own ideas, he drew up recommendations.

He walked down to the Yacht Club to talk about the recommendations with Mack before he turned them over to the Harbor Committee.

"What took you so long?" Rena asked when Paul returned.

"Oh, you know. I had to talk with Mack for an hour before I could bring up the recommendations. You can't rush Mack."

"What did you talk about?"

"About the woman who may or may not have spent the night on Sully Sullivan's yacht, about how many would have survived the Battle for the China Sea if there had been one, and about whether it was a '38 Dodge or a '39 Plymouth that Skeet Duncan drove off the pier at Humphries Cove about forty years ago."

"What did he say about the recommendations?"

"Nothing. Said he'd mull it over."

"I'll give him till next Thursday. Then I'll call and say I'm making copies to distribute to the committee to read over the weekend. If he doesn't object, we'll go on, with or without his input."

"I'll shoot the breeze with him middle of next week to warm him up."

Mack Cook cogitated, and they had to wait three months for the Harbor Committee to be ready to respond.

In the end, some boats tied to swing moorings in the outer harbor were changed to fore-and-aft moorings, anchored at two places. This reduction in swing-space made room in the outer harbor for fifteen more jubilant boat owners who had been, some of them, waiting for a decade for a mooring near their homes. Paul made sure the newspaper noted that the fore-and-aft moored boats were safer in storms than they had been before. You have to offer a benefit to everyone you ask to change, Paul had said. Rena knew better than anyone that Paul was born knowing these things.

And so it went. Progress meant doing what they had always done but better. In the years after Paul was elected Stonehaven's youngest Selectman ever, he shaped the town. Rena could see the town was Paul's first priority, greater than his responsibility to the family marine business, although these two interests blended well.

While Rena opened up Town Hall at 8 a.m., Paul dropped off his morning's catch from his own string of pots at Marley's Lobster Shack. While Rena wrote letters for Paul's signature, Paul consulted with his manager at Lawson Marine about the day's business. Paul was usually at Town Hall by 10 a.m. and then in and out until about five-thirty, when he returned to the store to help his manager close up. Rena always knew where he was. She could reach him whenever she needed him at the Water Works or the new shopping area by the depot or over at the high school. When he left, she pictured his car gliding up Main Street and turning on Depot Road. She knew he'd drive slowly by the house where he'd grown up, then pick up speed. She knew where he'd park. She saw him trot up the steps, and she started dialing.

"He just came in the door," the receptionist would say in surprise as if Rena's timing were coincidence.

11

Passing Years

In 1968, Paul's first baby was born. Paul had expected a boy, it was clear. That was probably all he could readily imagine. But he seemed thrilled with this perfect little girl as any father could be. Although Rena had not taken any particular interest in babies in general, she felt a little jealous. Still she was glad to see Paul happy and proud. The baby was named Leslee Elizabeth Lawson.

"Maureen and I agreed she would name the girls and I would name the boys," Paul explained, Rena thought, with a hint of apology. Rena thought at least Maureen could have been required to spell "Leslie" correctly.

Two years later, a second daughter was born. She was named Maria Sorrell Lawson after Paul's grandmother (although his grandmother had never liked the name Maria because "black Maria" was what people then called a paddy-wagon.) Maria was pronounced Mu-rye-u rather than the Italian way. "We changed the rule," Paul said when Rena recalled that naming the girls was Maureen's bailiwick. "She named the first one, and I get the second. I don't know what we'll do about the third."

Rena warmed to little Maria. She gave her the little silver cup that had been her own. When Maria's parents protested, Rena said, "Well, okay, she can borrow it. If I ever have babies of my own, she can give it back. If not, well,...." She shrugged. The possibility of Rena having babies seemed distant.

In those early years of Rena's career, Paul spearheaded the formation of the joint committees with Gloucester, and Rena got the big picture and the small details of how local government works. One year, they streamlined area ambulance service. Another it was public transportation.

Paul had to win and rewin his seat on the Board of Selectmen every four years and then as Chairman of that Board every year. Most people knew this was the best deal the town could have–an almost full time administrator of unquestioned competence for $1000 a year.

The voters saw things happen in other towns. A low-lying peninsula in Rockport, for example, offered for sale to the town for a pittance, had been ignored because no one thought it could be built on and no one understood its value. The town let the point be sold to outsiders. First thing they knew there were condos on it, not ugly condos really–Rena thought they looked like a flotilla of sails coming about in a regatta–but startling in their identical angles. The condos were out of keeping with the entire coast of Cape Ann otherwise dotted with salt boxes and cottages as individual as their owners. And where were the Rockport zoning and planning committees all this time? The word "Condo" was not even in their bylaws at the time, nor was it put into the bylaws after that loss.

But Paul Lawson took note of things like that and did what was necessary to see that it didn't happen in Stonehaven. He brought the issues before the committees and made them follow through. Once when Teddy Moore, a member of the zoning board, accused Paul of railroading a measure concerning bushes on rights of way through the Board, Paul adopted the metaphor. His campaign sign thereafter featured a locomotive charging across a round railroad crossing sign with a slogan reading, "Paul S. Larson delivers the goods." It was the only campaign sign he ever had, the only formal campaign tactic he ever adopted; for the rest, he just listened to people and looked them straight in the eye.

His face was very expressive. When people told him their troubles, he winced. When they made jokes, he threw his head back to laugh. When people surprised him, his eyes opened wide. He may have, Rena noted, even winked as the occasion demanded.

The passage of time was marked not only by elections and annual reports, but by class reunions. Paul and Rena had organized their tenth Stonehaven High class reunion in '69. It was a hay ride to Benny's barn and a barn dance, the one they referred to as the "horse shit reunion." In 1972, David Munson, the longtime Town Clerk, announced his retirement. Paul dropped David's letter of resignation on Rena's desk. "I'll expect your application ready by zero nine hundred hours tomorrow," he said smiling.

"I'll have to move across the hall," Rena frowned.

"It would be easier to move the Town Clerk sign over here," Paul countered.

The position paid significantly more than her position as Administrative Assistant. She thought she could now replace Aunt Amelia's Oldsmobile.

She joined the Massachusetts Town Clerk's Association before she got the job, and she was three weeks into a course in town administration before the Board of Selectmen voted to give her the job. No sweat. As Town Clerk, she had more official duties, duties more tedious, but in general the job was the interesting one of being Paul Lawson's right hand.

At that time, protecting the watershed that was the back yard of all the towns on Cape Ann was beginning to be a big issue.

"Let's go take a look close up," Paul had said one afternoon. "I haven't been back there since the grass fires last summer." Rena shoved her papers into a folder, and they took the afternoon off.

The watershed encompassed all of the central woods of Cape Ann. They went in at Dogtown.

Here early settlers had built one-room wooden homes around a common grazing area. They cut the tall trees for lumber and dragged them to the sea with oxen. When those trees were gone, they used the rest for firewood.

"In one three-week period," Paul remarked, "five hundred cords of wood were cut and shipped by sloop to Boston."

When the land was timbered out, the settlers went to the shore or turned to farming. They cleared rocks and stacked them in long walls about the place. The soil was poor and hard; the crops were marginal or worse. Most left, renting their tiny houses to the poor, the families of fishermen away at sea, and Revolutionary War widows, who kept numerous dogs for protection. When the widows died, only their dogs were left.

Now there were just the bleak door stones, spotted with lichen, and a few cellar holes among the choke cherries and gray beech. A cistern was almost obscured by sheep laurel and jewelweed.

Nothing seemed inert to Rena, but charged with ions. If she only brushed against these artifacts, a chain reaction would occur, energy would be released, and the tenuous imbalance of time rectified. She was elated by the possibilities.

"It's romantic," Rena said.

"It's spooky," Paul said.

"I wanted to be an archeologist once," Rena said, parting the weeds over the cistern. "I majored in anthropology, you remember. I wanted to go to distant lands and live with primitive tribes. And here's an archeological site right here. I'd forgotten. I wonder if anyone is studying it."

"I think we already know everything there is to know about this place," Paul said.

Rena let go of the weeds, and they settled back over the cistern.

Up ahead, Rena saw a boulder and ran to it. She took her baggy jacket off and tossed it over a protrusion of granite. She lay against the rock, spread her arms out to the side and stretched her head back. Her neck was long and smooth. The breeze lightly ruffled her hair and the sun warmed her face. She closed her eyes.

She could hear Paul's footsteps coming close. She felt his shadow over her, and she waited.

"There's an inscription chiseled into some of these rocks dating from the Great Depression," Paul said, "sort of like the Ten

Commandments."

He walked behind the rock and read, "Get a job."

Rena heard his steps go on. He called back the message from the next boulder, "Help Mother."

Rena slipped down from the rock, put on her jacket, and followed Paul. They tramped along a hard path skirting a glacial moraine toward the Goose Cove reservoir. Paul walked out ahead.

It seemed altogether too soon that Paul and Rena felt called upon to organize the 20th high school reunion in 1979. This time they played it safe and arranged a banquet on the water at The Rudder in East Gloucester. It was a Christmas reunion, as they hoped to attract some people who came home for the holidays.

Only fifteen people came, a little over half the class and their spouses. Spencer didn't come. Neither did Lili Bethea, who had married and moved to California because her husband was in the service, and neither did Karen Omwek nor Zorro. But there were new people–Betsy Tarr had married Rudy Guillermo, and Rod brought Cookie, his constant date for several years, whom Rena assumed he would marry eventually. The wife he married his last year at U. Mass. hadn't worked out. The dilution of the class by spouses and dates changed things, Rena thought. Or maybe Benny's barn was a better place to meet after all.

Something happened later that winter that marked the end of an era more clearly than the twentieth reunion had marked the end of two decades.

12

Fire and Loss

It was about eight o'clock at night, and Rena was bringing a cup
of hot water to boil for tea. Steam had fogged up the kitchen
window, a screen against the night. She heard the fire horn honk but
didn't count the number of honks. When she was away from home,
she counted them, as everyone did, to be sure it wasn't her house on
fire. But this time she was home, so she paid little attention. Within
minutes the phone rang. Paul told her the horn had blown a twenty-
three for North Point and the only thing on North Point to burn
was the Hesperus Inn and he was going. He wanted to pick her up.

When they were teenagers with cars, they tried to go to all the
fires, which occurred most often in the heat of a dry summer. Some
of the teens knew a few of the district numbers, but Paul knew all
the numbers and would relay the location of the fire to his buddies.
They would try to guess what was the source of the fire as they
roared down the back streets to beat the firemen.

But this was no ordinary fire; it was the Big One. How dear of Paul to call her now, how right. She got her hooded coat.

Onlookers had gathered already at the wrought iron gate that marked the entrance to North Point, a peninsula, almost an island. This narrow road through the gate was the only way for a vehicle to get onto the point. Paul parked on the side of the road as close as he could, and they hurried to the gate where the police were stopping onlookers, but Paul of course was allowed through with Rena in tow. The men were struggling with the hoses which had to come from far down on the road. Paul gave them a hand with one of the hoses and then let them go on alone. The hoses wouldn't reach, but it didn't matter. The hotel was totally engulfed, and flames shot up like fireworks. Things exploded, timbers fell, the roof crashed in.

"It's gone. There's nothing they can do. They may as well not try," people said.

The firemen had to at least look as if they were trying, but everyone knew this inn had been living on borrowed time. There was no one in the inn. The sole caretaker had come out to report the blaze. Old inns had a way of burning conveniently in the winter when there were no guests. The chief called the fire fight off and went to a containment plan. The volunteers soaked a semicircle around the building to keep the woods near the inn from catching, but it had been a wet winter and there was not much danger of that.

And so Paul and Rena went back to the road and joined the onlookers. They stood by the rope the firemen had put out as a boundary and watched the conflagration. They heard its roar and reflected on its power, on its beauty even. They named the inns that had gone before and disagreed about the dates of their burning. They remembered the hunks of bubbled glass they had salvaged from other fire sites and which were still sitting on the tops of bookshelves back in their parents' houses.

As the flames died down, so did the excitement, and many of the onlookers trickled away. Paul pulled hoses about and took a turn with the shovels. Rena stood alone musing. North Point had been, even with the inn traffic along the top, the nesting place of many sea birds in the spring, a colony of picnickers on summer days, and a network of lovers' lanes and party-paths on warm summer nights.

She thought also of the Inn itself, of the clink of the silverware in the dining room, of the white curtains blowing into the rooms when the windows were opened to the breeze off the water. Especially she remembered the rocking chairs on the porch. When she and Judy were about nine or ten, they used to climb up the rocks from the ocean's edge and watch the guests—all old people, they thought at the time—rocking the afternoon away. Once, late in the season, when the wind was strong, the girls' heads popped up from behind the rocks to discover the old people turned around backwards in their chairs, facing the wall, their afghans pulled around their knees. The girls slumped back behind the rocks and laughed till their sides hurt.

And tonight, as the Inn burned and the rocking chairs with it, the Point was free to return to the wild. Catbrier and sea roses would soon cover the footprint of the Inn, and the terns would lay eggs in the cool ashes. And other kids, who had never known the Inn, would scout among the rocks and underbrush.

When the bell tolled midnight, Rena went to the Town car to wait for Paul. He might be here for hours. She tilted her seat back and dozed. She didn't know how long it was until his hand on the door handle woke her. She let the seat up slowly as Paul slipped in beside her. He was wide awake and wanted to talk.

At first he talked of the fire, the men, and the action. Then he grew quieter. He put his arm across the back of her seat and searched for words. Rena smiled slightly in encouragement.

"The end of an era..." Paul finally said. "And a lot of those people...," he gestured at the crowd now gone, "...these gawkers don't know what they are seeing."

Rena laid her hand deliberately on the seat between them.

"The last of Stonehaven's old inns...," Paul said.

He drew a line down her hand with his forefinger. The gesture tickled, and the line lingered. She rolled her hand slightly toward him.

"We can come and picnic now on those rocks by the front porch. I always loved those rocks." Paul shook his head. "Better hurry. Now that the Inn is gone, the land will be for sale, and all this wilderness around it is in danger and the little paths and rocks and grassy places...."

"Remember the nights," Rena said, "when we snuck up in the bushes and listened to the people talking on the porch?"

"Yeah, spying, the greatest sport. We were such clever spies, but the conversations we overheard were so completely boring."

Rena laughed with untrammeled pleasure.

Paul covered her hand with his, and Rena gulped down the end of her laugh and stopped breathing.

"I love your laugh," he said.

Rena took a deep breath and tilted her face up towards his.

"You and I have shared a lot," he said.

Rena waited. If anything ever was going to happen, he would have to make the first move. Not her.

Paul was seriously opposed only once as chairman of the Board of Selectman. In 1978 Judy Edson, a bright young woman who, in her second term, decided no one should be so entrenched as Paul. He had retained his position, however, and made it a seemingly permanent part of his life.

Both Paul's parents died the same year. Although his father had been quite a bit older, his mother had been treated for cancer for several years and was not expected to live. As the end came near for her, Paul's father had suddenly and swiftly failed. His mother was too sick to go to the funeral. "It was as if he didn't want to be here without her," Paul said. "When he saw she was really going, he checked out first."

Maureen hadn't wanted to move into the old house, so it was with great sadness that Paul sold it. They needed the money for their daughter's education, he said.

Rena thought of her own mother, who was alone and cheerfully independent. Richard had gone off with a man. Eleanor Everett had an ever-changing circle of friends, all younger than she and getting younger. Her social life seemed a lot more vital than Rena's own. While Rena went up for her mother's birthday and an occasional open house or gallery opening, she did none of the constant checking-in that friends her age seemed to be doing with their parents.

The death of Paul's parents left him in the fullness of who he was, not at a peak, but on a long, lofty plateau. Rena felt, by contrast, that she was wandering at the foot of many plateaus, waiting for someone to reach down and tap her on the shoulder, saying, "Climb this one."

13

The Reunion

It was winter. In the time it took to get from her car to the door of the A&P, the wind numbed Rena's leg between the hem of her Polartec coat and her rubberized L. L. Bean shoes. She stopped just inside the door to let the frigid air dissipate before she fished her grocery list out of her pocket.

"Rena!" a voice said. Rena looked up. It was Betsy Guillermo. Strands of gray that had speckled her dark hair were now tinted reddish brown, Rena noted, and she looked good. They both ducked into the soup aisle to get out of the way of a portly gentleman pushing a grocery cart and mumbling over a grocery list. There by the Lipton's display, Betsy asked Rena if "you two" were busy planning the reunion. Rena's mind raced to figure who "you two" were and what reunion, but, when she did realize it was the big twenty-fifth anniversary of high school graduation coming up, she knew exactly who "you two" were.

"Oh, yes. Well, not exactly. We're getting ready to crank it up. There will be a reunion, you can bet on that."

She took the message back to Paul. There was never any doubt that the two of them were responsible. They needed to do something bigger, they agreed, than the last reunion, which hadn't been well attended or very exciting.

"The first thing to do is get the venue," Rena said, "but they will want to know how many people and so...we need some idea." The plan was tumbling around in her mind.

"Let's have it in Stonehaven again this time," Paul said.

"You know what the problem is—no booze here. When we had it at Benny's barn, we cooled the beer in the horse's water trough. That didn't work very well."

Paul grimaced, and Rena covered her eyes with her hand.

"You know Donna—she's married to Gene Holman."

"They run a restaurant in Gloucester, don't they? Isn't it Captains Courageous?"

"That's what I was thinking."

Rena made the call, got Donna, and somewhere in the conversation she realized that Donna was the obvious one to organize the whole reunion right in her own restaurant. Donna and Gene were professionals at banquets. So any doubts about numbers, what to do about no-shows, all that would be dealt with under one roof. It sure would be simpler. Rena had no sooner thought the thought than she was flooded with pangs of reluctance to let the reunion go. She wanted to do the reunion with Paul, no doubt about it, but she forged ahead with the new plan.

"Donna, would you be willing to be the chairman of the whole reunion?.....oh, you, would. Oh, wonderful. ....Paul and I will give you any help you need....I'm just delighted."

It was decided. She and Paul would sit back and enjoy. For once. She wasn't sure it was the best thing, but it was done. The move she'd made had a meant-to-be feel.

The reunion was in good hands. Donna wasn't Donna the Diligent in high school for nothing. She was known for writing down every blessed word the teachers uttered in handwriting as neat as a monk's. She didn't take notes; she transcribed. Rena took

Donna's obsession as lack of perspective.

But this time Donna turned out to have a few ideas of her own. She quickly expanded the reunion to include not only the class of 1959 but, since they were so few, the last four classes that ever attended Stonehaven High.

"It will be like being seniors again," Donna said.

Rena sighed in disappointment but she had to admit that Donna had good reason.

The reunion took place the first Saturday night in May. The fog had been dense all morning, and Rena had planted peas, carrots, beets, and Swiss chard seeds and set out some onion sets, blanketed in blindness. People talk of "living in the moment," a tiny package of time. Rena felt the contentment of living in a tiny package of visible space.

When the fog turned to drizzle, she came in for a long hot shower. She worked some "level one" hair color into her hair—if Betsy Tarr Guillermo could do it, so could she—powdered her legs with lavender-scented talcum, and did her nails. While she lay on the bed to let them dry, she closed her eyes, and her lips curled slowly into a smile.

By evening, a stiff breeze had blown the moisture out of the air, and it was clear and cool, just right for her to wear Aunt Amelia's short velvet cape on her shoulders. Its cut was vastly out of date, of course, maybe coming back, for all Rena knew. Besides, good fabric never goes out of style, Aunt Amelia had often said.

Donna and Gene were sitting at the table marked "Class of 1959" when Rena came in. Rena hugged Donna and shook hands with Gene. She wiggled her fingers at Ada and Phil over at the 1961 table. She greeted Betsy Guillermo. She spoke to Billy, who'd had to leave his wife at home sick. He just might dance with her, Rena thought, but, even as old as they were, their past seemed more inhibiting than encouraging.

Then she looked around at her own class table to see where she would lay her purse to claim the best vantage point for the evening. A Victorian gold mesh purse already holding a place at the table caught Rena's eye. She herself had one of Aunt Amelia's at home in a drawer, languishing in a stack of elbow length kid gloves, left over from the days Aunt Amelia dressed up for the hospital benefits at the Boston Pops. Just the last weekend Rena had noticed several of that type in the window of The Squirrel's Nest on The Lane.

"Vintage is oh-so-in vogue in New York. Of course, in Europe, it's never been out of vogue," Girard, the proprietor, had said, and Rena had noted the prices.

Who but Maureen would have had such a purse? Rena looked around for her. She saw Rod and Cookie standing at the bar, but neither Maureen nor Paul. Wait and see; the purse's owner would be along soon enough.

Then Billy and Gene went to get drinks, and Rena leaned over to the next table to chitchat with Nancy Waring at the next table, class of 1960. When Paul and Maureen arrived, everyone hugged all over again as if they had not seen each other in years. Rena quickly moved over one chair, making room for them. Maureen set her quilted black evening bag on the table.

On the dance floor already a couple was dancing–not just dancing–discoing, dipping, whirling, lifting, spinning, sliding, gliding. Their feet expressed a life far from Stonehaven, a life of priorities Rena could only dream of. The man, so far as they could tell, was a stranger, a sepia John Travolta dressed in a billowing black shirt. At every leap, the woman stretched her tiny black dress till Rena thought it might split. Her glistening blonde hair was cut short and swirled dramatically, the curl adapting perfectly to the contours of her head. Her skin glowed, cheeks highlighted; her eyes were blue and riveted to Travolta's when they reached out to catch each other's hand.

And, most important, she had on no underwear, at least that's what Paul announced to the table after his studied but discreet inspection. Rena tried to confirm this omission, but just as she focused on where a lingerie line should be, the strong arms of Travolta swept up the underwearless one and spun her out across the floor.

"Wow," said Rod.

"Who is it?" said Rod's wife, Cookie.

"I don't know," said Paul.

"Let's see what class they sit down with," said Donna, pulling her folded list from her purse.

"People like that don't sit," said Rena. "At most, they dip."

The music changed rhythm, and the mystery dancers unwound their arms from each other and headed for a table.

"They're coming this way." Everyone stared.

Paul snapped his fingers.

"What?" Rena asked him.

"It's Karen."

"Karen who?"

"You know, Karen in our class."

"Come again?"

"Karen. The artist. I took her to Senior prom."

"NO!" Rena said throwing her hand over her mouth and staring at the glamorous blonde until they made their way to Rena's table and claimed the chairs reserved by the gold mesh purse.

The others oohed and aahed at Karen and her partner, but Rena's mind scrambled to think of something significant to say.

"Karen, I remember in high school you could draw things that looked exactly like the real ones. It was incredible," Rena said.

"My current work isn't representational," Karen said. "I'm beyond that. Have been for quite a few years."

What does one say in reply? Nothing Rena could think of.

Paul got drinks for himself and Maureen. Gene got Rena a gin and tonic. A little strong at first. Rod and Cookie danced. Gene told the story again about how he and Doris met, and everyone laughed; it was a good story to hear every five years. Paul told Lili Bethea, who had come alone from Connecticut, about how the shopping area out on the road to Gloucester would make the little A&P in Stonehaven fold, and that would make it hard on the hardware store, and he was afraid pretty soon the business of Stonehaven would move to the outskirts of town. Rena hadn't thought about that and didn't want to. She got up and got herself another gin and tonic.

The music, a mixture of the fifties and current music, was a bit of a torment. If she had no one to dance with, she'd rather not even hear it. She watched Paul and Maureen dancing sweetly, his cheek against her hair, dancing with the unthinking smoothness that comes from two decades of familiarity.

Watching them, Rena sighed. All this effort of bringing people together was wasted on Maureen. She didn't care about most of them. Paul should have danced with Karen for old times sake. And if he wouldn't dance with Karen, he should have danced with her. It was Rena who had actually shared Paul's long history with these old friends. She had prior possession–before Maureen.

Rena turned away from the dance floor and was staring at the centerpiece when she felt a touch on her shoulder. She turned to see Buddy Krebs from the class below hers. Little Buddy Krebs, now with a thick neck and the beginnings of a beer gut.

"Dance?"

"Let's."

And they went out on the floor to Doris Day singing "I'll Never Stop Loving You."

Monday morning, the sun flicked fine waves like spilled sugar. Rena was as wide-eyed as the lighthouse lamp. She was eager to see Paul and recap the reunion.

Paul came in a little earlier than usual. He handed her a fistful of letters he'd taken home to sign. Then he stood there silently instead of going into his office. Rena looked up at him.

"What?"

"I've met a very interesting person," Paul said.

"Who?" Paul jerked his head toward his office, and Rena eagerly followed him.

"Who?" she repeated.

"Bright, very attractive, very creative...."

"Who?"

"You know her."

"For crying out loud, who?"

"Karen. Karen Omwek."

"For God's sake, you already knew her."

"But she's a different person now."

"You can say that again."

"It's no joke," Paul said. "I called her."

"I told her it was good to see her Saturday night."

"Yeah?"

"I told her I was glad to see she turned out...so well. Well, I didn't say it like that."

"Why didn't you tell her that Saturday night? That's what reunions are for."

"There were too many people around."

"Mmm," Rena muttered while rolling her eyes.

"Rena, we talked for an hour. About stuff. We talked about how she has...evolved...since high school. I told her about my old house—Mother's house—and how I felt when we sold it."

"You got into everything, didn't you."

"Everything. Rena, when I told her about selling Mother's house...and...you know...all of that, Karen's voice shook, and I asked her what was the matter, and she was crying... I mean, not boo-hooing but...."

"I know, I know."

Rena had got tears in her eyes herself when they sold the old Lawson house, especially when she saw how broken up Paul was about it.

"My own wife says, 'Put it behind you and get on with your life,' or 'It's just a house, Paul. It can't bring your mother back.' And here was this person I hadn't seen in twenty-five years listening to me and crying herself. I said, 'Why are you getting so emotional?' "

"I understand why perfectly," Rena said.

"And I told her about the Giant Tree and the cave under the hedge and the shed out back and how my dog Queenie had her puppies in there.

"I told her all this on and on. Then I would stop and apologize, and she'd be very polite and say 'No, no, go on.' And I'd go on."

Rena nodded. "Apparently you found someone who really listened and cared about your feelings."

"Maybe for the first time."

Rena sighed. "Sometimes," she said, "a person you haven't seen in a long time is easier to talk to than someone you're with all the time."

She herself had often ached for what Paul had tasted today. For her, the yearning for someone to talk to came when she was alone on Saturday night. Five days a week, the stream of people in Town Hall and the partnership with Paul himself had really been enough.

"We're going to have lunch today," Paul said.

"She's still in town?"

"She just lives in Manchester."

"Oh. I thought she said she lived in Arizona."

"She used to live in Arizona in an art colony in the mountains outside of Tucson. For that matter, she used to live in New York."

"New York." Rena thought what irony it was that dumber-than-dirt Karen Omwek ever lived in New York and survived.

"What's she doing back here then?"

"She came to be near her mother. And she can continue her art here. After all, anywhere on Cape Ann is sort of an art colony."

"I suppose. So you're having lunch."

"Yeah."

"Well, I guess you both have to eat."

Rena went back to her desk and began stuffing the letters into envelopes.

On Tuesday, a little after eleven, Paul came and stood in front of Rena as if for inspection.

"I'm going to lunch," he said.

"Mmmm."

He rocked back on his heels as if waiting for something further.

"What?" Rena said.

"I said I'm going for lunch."

"Oooh." Rena said, remembering. "Going to talk about art?"

"Probably not."

"Dancing then?"

"No. But, since you mentioned it, did you know that Karen was a semiprofessional dancer as well as an artist?"

"I could see that. So could her guy."

"Yeah. They compete. His name is Marcello. He's not her boyfriend. He's her dance partner."

"Okay. Any particular place for lunch?"

"The Studio in Rocky Neck."

Rena nodded. Over on the arty side of Gloucester, overlooking Smith Cove. Good for steamers and chowder. There would be a bustle of early tourists and a good chance that no one would know Paul. Not that Paul couldn't have a business lunch with a woman. He could.

Rena had been engrossed for an hour in the figures for the reworked city liability coverage. You'd think you could readily see if the new plan was going to cost more than the old one, but the manner of presentation made comparison almost impossible. She was about to reach for the phone to call their agent to say, "Milton, can you cut through this crap and tell me..." when the phone rang and the city attorney was asking for Paul. Rena tipped back in her chair.

"Jim, he's out for....a late lunch..." Rena looked at her watch. Almost 3:30. She snapped her chair back down. "He must be doing some errands."

It seemed Jim had expected some necessary piece of information from Paul by 2 o'clock.

"I'm sorry. I'm sure he must have got the answer for you. I'll have him call you as soon as I hear from him...No....No..." Rena stood up and paced, stretching the telephone cord to its end almost to the door of Paul's office. "I think he had to...resolve some matter in Gloucester.... Okay. Top priority. I promise."

It was after four when Paul returned. Rena glanced at her watch, then cleared her throat.

"Jim says he needed some info by 2 p.m. Think you can make that?"

"Jim! Oh, crap."

Then Paul seemed to shake off the matter. "We finished lunch over an hour ago. We got up, and I wanted to pay for us both. And she let me."

He stopped speaking as if this small gratification was a revelation of infinite importance. Rena nodded, not quite knowing the significance but wanting to acknowledge she knew there was one.

"We walked to the marine railway. We walked up and down the Neck three, four times. I told her things, she told me stuff...."

Paul stopped and looked at Rena, and Rena knew she was supposed to see what was happening here, but damned if she was

120

going to name it for him. She shrugged broadly and held her palms up.

"So," Paul said.

"So what?"

"So what do you think?"

"Just don't do it again."

14

Concrete and Rock

One morning in late June the door creaked partially open then stopped. Gladys squinted at the gap.

"What is it, Gladys?" Rena asked.

"A bag is coming in the door."

Indeed the bag did enter first, at eye level, followed by Paul shouldering his way in. "I give up. What's that, a pig in a poke?"

"I've got an exciting answer to a thorny problem. Rena, Tony, come out back and let me show you."

Rena and Tony lined up behind him.

"What about me? I could use some excitement," said Gladys.

"You, too, Gladys," Paul conceded apologetically.

In the alley behind the Town Hall, Paul set the bag down. "ConcreteAll" in green letters proclaimed across the unbleached paper bag.

"Tony, bring me the jar of waste on my desk."

Tony hurried to get it.

"Waste, the bane of modern man, the threat to our future," Paul said, taking the jar full of murky black liquid from Tony and holding it aloft. "Waste from the linotype machine factory, full of heavy metals. Hazardous waste. And where do we keep it?"

Paul looked around at the eager faces as if they were school children who do not know the answer to the teacher's question. "Come on, where do we keep it?"

"In a jar on your desk?" Gladys said.

Paul laughed, his pomposity happily punctured, and lowered the jar.

"Yes, Gladys, in a jar on my desk. About a quart. But there are thousands of gallons of this hazardous waste jelling in a holding pond in the woods behind Murdoch's farm, waiting for eternity or the Second Coming, whichever comes first. And this same stuff, give or take a few parts per million of metal, is mucking up the county as ponds fill up, and mills close because they can't dispose of their waste."

He looked around at the group, standing like children waiting for a Christmas present to be unwrapped.

"Well, I think I have a solution." Paul held the bag of concrete mix up to the light to read the directions.

"The solution to the world's waste problems are written in the instructions on the back of a bag of concrete?" Tony said.

Paul laughed. He laughed at himself—Rena loved that in him—he laughed in appreciation at Tony, he laughed because he was about to do mankind some good. She couldn't wait.

Paul jerked the string that opened the bag, first on one end. When that didn't work, he started jerking on the other.

"Get me a paper cup from the washroom, Rena, if you please."

Rena dashed off, hating to miss any of this performance. When she came back, Paul was skinning the bark off a stick with his pocket knife. "Isn't this a little primitive to be the greatest discovery of the modern age, Paul," Rena said, handing him the cup.

"Oh, ye of little faith."

Paul measured out a cupful of the concrete mix and poured it into the murky black wastewater.

"That's one part." He repeated the process. "That's two parts."

He stirred the mixture after each addition until he had the right proportion of the cement and sand mixture to the right amount of wastewater.

"There."

Everybody looked blankly at the jar of dark, wet concrete mix.

"What do we do now, say 'abracadabra'?"

"If you like, you can say 'abracadabra,' or you can say ten hail Marys, or you can do a rain dance, but I'm going to wait..." Paul glanced at the instructions on the bag. "...six to eight hours."

"I get it," said Tony. "You're going to mix cement with the waste and turn the whole pond into concrete."

"And we can go roller skating on it," Rena said.

"Neato," said Tony.

Paul laughed. "Not a bad idea, not a bad idea at all," he said squinting his eyes and rubbing his chin thoughtfully.

"Is that a joke?" asked Gladys.

"I think it was," said Rena,

But she wasn't sure. The plot thickened with the concrete.

"Don't leave before we've had the grand opening," Paul called to them, so at five o'clock they gathered outside his door.

He led them out back where the jar was sitting. He picked it up by the neck, slipped it into a paper bag, and twisted the paper close around the neck.

"When you christen a ship, you break a bottle across the ship's bow. When you christen a bottle, what do you do?"

"Break a ship across..." Gladys said excitedly.

"Yeah, yeah," Tony cut her off.

Paul motioned them back and then smashed the bottle against a metal post that held up the chain link fence. The bottle broke into a thousand pieces. Paul pulled the concrete object from the bag and poked the shards that stuck in the concrete with a stick until they fell off. Then he set the thing down for inspection.

"Well, it needs some work, but here we have a new material that will rid the world of many of its hazardous wastes."

Gladys asked, "What's it used for?"

Challenged, even charmed, it seemed, by Gladys's question,

Paul said, "This is a door stop, used to hold my office door open so every citizen of Stonehaven can feel free to walk in and tell me what's on his mind."

"How many door stops can we use?" Gladys pursued.

"Thousands, maybe millions, Gladys. Every household in the USA could use at least a couple, don't you think?"

Paul, once the straight man, it seemed to Rena, had taken on Whit's irreverent humor and become both the earnest straight man and his own comic foil.

"Seriously, folks," Paul continued. "I've talked with a couple people about this, and they say concrete for roads and construction has certain properties that this stuff may not have. Without a lot of research and development, it could not be used for anything. But here's the beauty of it. Up till now we've had a liquid with undesirable solids. The wastewater treatment people don't want it. But pour some concrete in it until it qualifies as solid waste and we have a lot more options for disposal."

"Great idea," said Rena.

"You mean we're not going to get a skating rink?" said Gladys.

Rena stifled a laugh as she pictured Gladys on skates, a plump myopic figure being pushed out onto the pond like a ship let out of dry-dock and then losing her balance and waving her hands to catch herself. "Where are all the gallant young men?" she'd cry before she went splat.

"It was a joke, Gladys."

As the others gathered their things and left, Paul said to Rena, "I'm going to Essex for a drink after work."

"Fine."

"If anyone asks, say that I had to look at a rust problem on the tank over on Hubbard Road. "

"Why should I say that?"

He answered with a long silence.

"Oh, Paul! It's Karen again."

"Yeah."

She sighed a long sigh and curled her lip.

"Now don't be a mother," Paul said.

"Paul, this changes things."

"It doesn't change anything for me."

"It changes everything for me," Rena persisted.

"I don't see what it changes at all."

Rena scowled, unable to answer him.

"What does it change for you?" he pressed.

Bits of answers careened through her head and tears welled up in her eyes. She fought them and turned away from Paul. To regain control, she changed the subject.

"Just how does Karen earn a living? Surely she can't make a real living being an artist and dancing?"

"She teaches art at Manchester High. And she sells some of her work. Dancing is just a hobby. She's very involved. She has teacher friends and an artist group and a dancing group."

"And now she has a Town Hall group," Rena pouted.

He replied to her sarcasm benignly. "Karen calls it a 'subculture.' The intersection of subcultures is what life is all about."

"Karen said that?"

"Yeah."

A year ago, Rena couldn't have pictured Karen Omwek–plump, pimply, not-too bright–saying anything at all about life. Weight loss and dermabrasion Rena could understand, but the brain transplant she had trouble imagining. It just proved there was hope for all mankind. Rena sighed, slumping into her chair.

Then she pointed her finger at Paul. "What you are doing is very, very dangerous," she said.

Paul pulled up a chair directly in front of her desk and sat down. He put his elbows on the desk and, his chin in his hands, looked up at her so long she was afraid.

Finally, he said, "Did you ever fall in love–with someone you weren't supposed to love?"

Rena breathed in very long breath. Her fear was realized. She went with the outbreath.

"Yes, I think so."

"What did you do?"

"I didn't do much. I didn't flirt. I didn't say anything. I lived through it. I fantasized. And waited for it to pass."

"And did it pass?"

She waited overlong then said, "Never mind me. You're the one who needs to think this thing through.

"I'm taking Karen out in the boat," Paul told Rena the following Tuesday.

Like a boy tells his mother where he's going, Rena thought.

"In your boat?" Rena said, raising one eyebrow. She had often seen Paul's boat at the dock. A working boat, cream and maroon, cluttered with white plastic buckets smelling of the remnants of last week's bait, lines coiled loosely in locations his feet had memorized, sprays of discarded sea weed shriveled dry on the seats. Rena could almost hear him say, "Watch that line," as he guided Karen over the deck by the elbow, brushing the dried seaweed off the seat with his callused hand.

"Yes, in my boat," Paul said, and, conceding to the meaning of her raised eyebrow, he added, "I'll clean it up a bit."

Taking Karen out in his boat was a step to a new plateau, a step not unlike taking a girl home to meet his parents. Rena knew.

And now Paul was going out in his boat with Karen, a place to be private, yes, but much more. They were on the crest of a wave and would not stay poised there for long. For in that boat Karen would be quickly caught up in the wind's will, troughed in the depths of Paul's desire, immersed in the squall that was spinning him like jetsam. And Paul would finally talk, for some mysterious floodgates had opened. Paul would put his fear into words and his desire; he would cry out to her, she would ask of the danger. He would tell her the futility of his oars against the water.

Finally, in the quiet after the storm, he would ship oars and sit beside her, and she would look up at him, her destiny in his strong, callused hands. Rena slipped down into her chair and rested her head on the back. She closed her eyes. Paul would turn to her. She could feel his lips almost touching. He would put his hand in the middle of her back and pull her firmly to him. Their lips would touch; their tongues would melt together.

Rena's mouth opened, her lips searched. A warm mingling ran down her body, spread in all directions. Rena arched her back and raised her breast towards his hand. For the first time she could imagine Paul going on from tenderness to passion. He was no longer chaste.

Suddenly, Rena's reverie ended, and she looked around. The court house was empty now, thank God. The clock said almost four. She put her head on her desk and sighed, then picked up her pocketbook and hurried out.

She didn't notice the beaches, the rock-walled yards flying by, only the passing of time. She left her car in the driveway, not turning it so it was headed out as she usually did. She ran up the back steps, whirling around the posts. She fretted with the key, opened the door and closed it with her whole body, and threw herself on her day bed.

"Where do we keep the key to the padlock on the gate to Humphries Point?" Paul asked one day.

Humphries Point, dividing East Beach from West Beach, was a favorite place for campfires and had been closed since August 1 because the grass was so dry.

"The fire department has the key. Public Works has the key. Why would you want to go there?"

Paul didn't answer. Catching on, Rena rolled her eyes.

"Paul, does this Karen person have a home? I mean why can't you just go to her place? Light a candle, put on a little music, pour a little wine—like grownups do?"

Paul's shoulders sank. "She lives with her mother. You remember the woman who worked at the sardine factory?"

Rena did.

"I admire Karen," Paul went on, "for moving back here to take care of her mother."

"I'll give her points for that. But what will you do in the winter, Paul, if this should last that long? It gets cold outside."

"We'll work that out when the time comes. For now, town property closed to the public fills the bill."

"Paul, this is like high school. Trying to find a place to park."

"So where is the extra key?"

This reminded Rena of how a couple gets stuck forever in the dance that was popular when they got married. Some are stuck in the jitterbug, some in the twist. They never learn another step after the wedding vows. When it came to courtship, Paul was stuck in park.

Rena rummaged through some things in a box on top of the financial file. A metal knob that had fallen off something, a bunch of safety pins left over from a fundraising road race, an old AWWA membership card, an extra key to a truck the city junked two years ago. "You don't need that anymore," she said, tossing the key into the trash can. "Okay, here. It's one of these. I don't know which one. Take them all." She tossed him a ring of keys.

"Thanks."

"Tonight?"

"Right now while it's still light. Maureen has a club meeting, and I'm on my own for dinner. No reason I can't have a picnic."

The evening was warm. No reason Rena shouldn't have a picnic herself.

At quitting time, she locked up and drove to Dory Beach and, instead of parking in the parking lot like a tourist and walking down the concrete walkway, she parked on the street near the other end of the beach where a narrow path, walled in between two eight-foot hedges, led to a cliff overlooking the beach. This dark corridor between the hedges–was it kept open by the shoulders of beach-goers brushing through, Rena wondered, or did the owners of the adjacent homes prune between the hedges to provide a conduit for the rest of the world who did not own oceanfront property? Or would it grow closed one day, capturing a housewife from Saugus in its dense tentacles. As a child, Rena had never thought to ask, only accepted the parting of the hedges as the Hebrews must have accepted the parting of the Dead Sea. Now as Town Clerk she wanted to assign responsibility for everything.

She plunged into the sunless avenue where questions of responsibility melted into shadows. She took her shoes off. Cool, powdery sand sifted between her toes. She did not brush away the veil of gnats that dotted her skin but hurried on to the end where she popped into bright light again as if uncorked.

The gnats drifted back to their stygian corridor. Rena stood for a moment at the overlook and flung her eyes out over the sweep of sea from Humphries Point to Halibut Point. She paused to see if this was a day when Plum Island and even Mt. Agamenticus in Maine were visible. They were not.

She brushed her hand along the metal guard rail just to hear the familiar breathy ringing the gesture would make. For each configuration of sound–a light touch of fingers on metal or a heavy hand leaning for support, terry cloth dragging on wooden steps, canvas bag against wet bathing suit, sandal on concrete footing, flip-flop in sand–could tell even a blind man what kind of people might be pausing there: a fully-equipped Connecticut family on vacation; a white-shinned old man in baggy shorts, stopping to rest on each step; a bathing beauty; a lone child, brown, dripping, sans towel, sans shoes, sans parent, sans all.

Rena scrutinized the rim of grasses clinging to the edge of the cliff. Tough beach grass withstood both the ravages of the nor'easter and the gouging of the most intrusive tourist toes. She waited while an elderly woman clambered up the wooden steps and set her straw basket on the landing to rest. Rena nodded politely. The woman took out a plastic cup with bendable straw and took a drink before making her way into the path where the sun never shone. But Rena did not go down the steps the woman had ascended. These were new steps. She remembered when the Council funded them about fifteen years before. Rena was looking for something else. She quickly found it–a familiar break in the grass. Rena waited till the matron had disappeared between the hedges, then quickly stepped through the break in the grass and dropped over the edge of the cliff.

Rena's feet, pigeon toed, deftly found each rock step of the descent, carved into the cliff who knows when, abandoned since the wood stairs were built. The girlish toes that once knew the location of each gouged step, its size, its slope, were now turned askew from bunions, but they did not forget.

Where the trail of notches in the precipice reached the bottom, Rena turned away from the beach and onto the rocks. The rocks, too, lay exactly as they had since God tossed them there.

The girl-part of Rena, which seemed a separate entity now, wanted to run on them as she once had run in bare feet, glancing off angled surfaces. If one rock tipped under her weight, she was airborne before it mattered, lighting on the next and the next. The girl rushed on now, but the woman made careful choices and planted her feet solidly, a concession to adulthood. It was enough for her soul to be free.

She made her way from the dry rocks to the high tide line where algae made the crossing perilous. She grasped the seaweed on a large rock and inched around it. In its shade she found a tide pool she'd known long ago, paved with black mussels, studded with Chinamen's hats, descendants of the very ones she had poked at thirty years before. A small transparent crab skittered among brown periwinkles along the pool walls. The water rushed in and out without seeming to disturb the tranquil life there. Rena went on. She slipped knee deep into an inlet, wincing as her toes pressed into barnacled rock. She did not mind the strands of podded seaweed lashing her shins. When a rising wave filled the ravine, she gave herself over to it and slipped, fully clothed, into the crystalline water. Its shocking cold brought a familiar rush, and she gulped the feeling of being young and lithe and all powerful. She sank down to bring cold fingers of salt water into her hair, leaving nothing unrefreshed. She floated, face to the sky, water lapping at her ears, while time and space lost all proportion. The world became infinitely large, infinitely small, she could not tell the difference.

She rolled over and caught the current rushing out, used it expertly to carry her to a certain rock—Black Giant, the kids had called it—roughly rectangular like a body sleeping on its side, hip and shoulder covered with barnacles. She pulled herself partly out of the water—with effort where once it had been effortless. She threw her leg up onto the black granite and rolled onto its surface where she lay heavy and safe. She picked her away around to the back of the rock toward open sea.

In the crook of the sleeping giant she sat, laid her head back against the granite and drew her knees up, letting the water drain out of her soggy knit skirt.

Rena could easily see Humphries Point from here, two coves away. She could see the dark seaweed line and the tawny bare rock above. She knew Paul and Karen had picked out a spot there not unlike hers, facing the sea, hidden from the land, a bed of clean, hard stone. But he would have blankets and pillows and wine. Rena had only her imagination.

Paul would lay the blanket carefully, pick up errant rocks that might poke through, and he would deftly skip them across the water. He would put pillows just so and invite her to sit. The same breeze that washed Rena's face would flutter Karen's blonde coif enchantingly. Paul would set the wine in the shade—he would have the advancement of the sun across the sky accounted for. And he would kiss her lightly and then sit back to let her guide him.

15

Crossing the Line

"I've been thinking," Paul said that afternoon, bringing Rena a cup of coffee unbidden and setting it down on the edge of her desk. He went back to get himself one.

Rena glanced around the Town Hall. Gladys had gone home early. Tony was out. The new office girl was running off copies loudly on the machine in the back room. Rena and Paul were alone. She waited in suspense.

"What have you been thinking, Paul?" Since Karen, any revelation of Paul's thoughts had become a stimulant more potent than coffee.

"I've been thinking...a lot...."

"Yes." She leaned closer to him.

"...About how you have to know what you want in life."

"Life?" Rena raised her eyebrows to encompass the breadth of the word.

"And what I want is...."

Paul's pause was so long and titillating that Rena ran through an index of possibilities: breaking up with Karen, divorcing Maureen and marrying Karen, or realizing that his soulmate was neither one of them but....

"I want to make Stonehaven the best run town in America with the best quality of life for a town of its size."

Rena snapped straight up in her chair. She loaded a spoon with Cremora and stirred it vigorously into her coffee.

"If there is an award for it, I'd like to win it," Paul went on, "but even if there isn't, I'd like to know that this town is the closest it possibly can be to the American dream. Not the best resort, not the most charming town, but the best place to live. A balance between a progressive community and an historic town that keeps its dignity. That's the goal. Now, to reach it, I have to lay out some steps."

He pulled out a mechanical pencil from his pocket and pressed the cap so the lead slid out just so. He pulled a piece of paper from Rena's paper recycling basket, turned the blank side up, and began to draw a string of rectangles across it hitched together with ampersands like a train.

"...Here is a sort of time line. And here in this box is where we are now. And here on the end is where we're going: the perfectly balanced town."

"The perfectly balanced town!"

"Of course, there are boxes in between to fill out. That's the main point, but there can also be boxes that drop down from the main line. These are okay, not necessarily bad, but they weigh you down, pull you off track. Then there can be hooks up here, really support systems or outside help or something. Then there's a certain critical point where..."

Rena put her hand over her eyes and let her shoulders go limp.

"You're not interested in this?"

Rena breathed deeply and pulled herself slowly back to an attitude of attention. "I'm interested, Paul. Go ahead."

She had to be interested because with every new project she had to make a shift in prioritizing her time. Paul had so many projects, present and future, that he was working on. Rena wondered how he'd ever manage without her to do the day-to-day running of the city.

One afternoon, Paul called Rena into his office. He sat behind his desk curling the papers in his hand and swatting things absently with them.

"Yes?" Rena asked.

Paul swatted his trash can hard enough to make it reverberate, then said, "I want to be alone with Karen."

"You have been alone with her," Rena said. "In a boat. On Humphries Point. At ..."

"I mean alone alone."

"Oh, that kind of alone," she said, curling the corner of her mouth in disappointment that Paul wouldn't acknowledge to her what they both knew could have, and surely did happen on Humphries Point, however rocky.

"Besides, it's getting cold for boats and rocky promontories."

"Paul. I know you are fully aware. But I've got to say, think about what it means when you cross the line. Really cross the line. Or are even alone enough to cross the line. Because legally I think being alone is the same as crossing the line. Now you and I know that the intimacy you share is more important than what you actually do. You've already crossed the emotional line. You can't help that. But now, Paul, you could really get into trouble."

She waited for Paul to take in her broadside, then she painted a picture. "Think about Maureen and picture her face when she finds out."

Paul nodded. "I've thought about it. I value Maureen. Maybe I still love her in a way, but the person I am with her is a cardboard box. A neat, reasonably strong, safe...container. The person I am with Karen has stepped out of that box. I can't go back."

"And what kind of person is Karen?"

"A person who listens and makes me feel safe to explore some parts of me I never knew existed."

"Yes, yes, but why isn't she pursuing someone she can actually have. Why is she wasting her time...."

Paul looked at Rena sharply. "I don't think you like Karen. You

135

never did. I can accept that... but I make no apologies. No one can ask me not to do this."

He stopped and looked hard at her. "I value your opinion, I value your friendship. I'm sorry you don't approve. I hate it. But I have to do this. It's not what you have always heard about affairs. This is not an affair. This is my life going forward. I ask you to have a little faith in me."

Rena felt inexplicably relieved. If there was anyone walking on this earth in whom she would have had faith, it would be Paul. Faith was the magic word. Faith is a relief. Paul shuffled his feet and idly flipped through a report on the back of the desk.

"How would you feel about Karen and me being in your house on an occasional afternoon?"

"Don't push it."

"Honestly. How about it?"

Rena went through two silent Hail Marys before she answered. She had learned the Hail Mary as a teenager in the way she might learn a song she disliked. She had disliked "Bye-Bye, Love" by the Everly Brothers when it was number one for a whole summer, but when it finally, mercifully, faded to number 8, she found herself humming it. Just so with the Hail Marys. A radio station had run a regular hour long program of nothing by Hail Marys, for the linguistically impaired, she scoffed. While deriding the mindlessness of it, she had memorized it down to the upturn of the second syllable of Je-SUS and the low, quick muttering of the second, "Holy Mary, mother of God..." It differed from going with the outbreath in that it gave you something to do.

"So how do you feel about Karen and me being in your place?"

"Mixed."

"How so?"

"Well, I take a certain interest in your....arrangement, I'll admit. But I don't approve...that is, I don't judge at all so how can I approve. It's one thing for me to observe, another for me to aid and abet."

"You have aided and abetted before."

Rena slumped her shoulders in despair. "Yes, I know that. That still doesn't mean I approve. But in my house, Paul? That's like inviting you."

"No, I invited myself," Paul countered. "I don't want to make you uncomfortable. But I want...it would be nice if I could have a place close to Town Hall. We waste so much time driving to places where people don't know us."

Rena started another file.

"Okay, not in your bedroom. That's maybe too...close. Is there a part of the house that you feel is more...appropriate than the rest? Your study maybe?"

Rena's "study" was her secret joy. Her room in the oldest part of The Oldest House wasn't the secret; no, she'd told everyone she had redone a room into her "study." It was the joy that was secret. She didn't think she wanted Paul and Karen there. Still the dark little room with streams of light coming through stained glass, the deep squashy pillows, the cocoon of fabric seemed ideal for such a tryst. She pictured lying on the day bed, paisley curling across the wall behind, the Tree of Life billowing overhead, enveloped in the warmth of his breath, safe, soft. It was perfect for love.

But might Paul laugh at the excess of her decoration, look down on her presumption of romance? Would he be embarrassed for her, plain Jane, imagining herself in the Kasbah. He'd see it about like a jewel in her belly button. Then she thought of Karen there. Judging the decor. She was an artist, after all.

"No. Not the study."

"Where then?"

"Okay.... I may regret this...and we have to work out the particulars....but in principle, you can use the guest bedroom. You would be guests. What will I tell people?"

"Nothing, I hope."

"Well, people do pay attention. They can't see through the tall fence if you come in by the alley, but people could recognize your cars turning in."

"It's none of their business who turns in."

"Of course not." She was clearly going to be on her own here, but she'd think of something.

Paul and Karen had come once a week to her house all winter.

Karen picked him up and brought him in her car, parking it well down the driveway by the back door. None of her neighbors had mentioned the visitor. Rena had even come to enjoy the periphery of the weekly event. She laid out fresh towels in the guest bath. She pulled out the pieces of dried plants in the vase on the dresser that seemed tired, replacing them with new evergreen fronds or a spray of seed pods or whatever she thought would have a form of interest to the artistic eye.

In the evening of the day of each tryst, Rena observed that the lovers had attempted to put everything to rights again, but they never did it perfectly. She took proprietorial pleasure in evening up the edges of the blanket and noting that the fold marks in the formerly crisp pillow cases were blurred. The wash cloth in the bath was always stiff from drying on the rack instead of her dryer.

June came. The warm sun pulled her outside for hours on weekends, warm but not hot. The garden was fresh with new sprouts and unblemished by spent leaves. She had energy saved up from winter to spray the rose bushes and the fruit trees with vigor. She set the tuberous rooted begonias out in the pots on the front doorstep. They weren't as showy as she would have liked there at the front, but they had been Aunt Amelia's choice, and Rena understood that the final success of the plump blossoms unfolding among the parasol leaves was worth the wait. She'd cut rosy rhubarb stalks for a tangy pie, meaning for it to last a week. And then she'd eat a whole one in a weekend, sliver by sliver.

Lucky for her, she could eat as much as she wanted without fear of middle-aged spread. By chance alone, she'd stayed as slim as a girl. What had been an unremarkable body in her youth had become exceptional in middle age, and she noticed her body now more than she ever did in her prime. She reveled in her energetic pumping of the sprayers. She bounced up and down from her knees as she moved along the rows, digging a groove in the black earth with a stick to bury the seeds. When she showered after her gardening, she wished she had someone to show her lithe body to. The only thing that had changed over the years was that instead of going from the garden to letter writing or reading, she had taken to lying down in her little room "just for a moment's rest" and not infrequently falling asleep.

One day as she was headed for the day bed, she found the mohair throw neatly folded at the end. Now, Rena had a way of tossing it across the bed in an unstudied way that she thought rather artistic. She would never box it up in a perfect square like in a hotel. She threw it off and stared at the bed. She examined the pillow and found a hair. She took it to the light. She tore a hair out of her own head to compare. The one from the bed was definitely lighter. Rena glared at the bed, heat seeking, outlining the pattern of warmth that might still remain.

She sat on the end of the couch and looked at her room through the eyes of the intruders. What did Karen think of the hand-blocked border? Did she notice its slight unevenness and, if so, did she consider it a mistake, or did she recognize it as a desirable sign of handcraftsmanship? And what had Paul made of her whimsy? Had they snickered at her excess?

"Okay, okay, I'm sorry. I didn't know it was such a big deal," Paul had said when she came to work early and confronted him in his office. "It'll never happen again."

"Good," she said, and then shifted to worry that Karen and Paul might think her compulsive or phobic.

But Paul was good as his word and, after that, all evidence of lovemaking was confined to the guest bedroom.

In July, on weekends and in the cool of the day after work, Rena tied up the rambling rose on the arbor and cut off the dead blossoms from the New Dawn. She powdered them for black spot and kept an eye out for Japanese beetles. She wore a wide-brimmed straw hat now against the sun, as Aunt Amelia had, because her once creamy tan skin had a tendency to get spots like the roses. In her sunnier moods, she waved to the people on the tour bus. Mostly she ignored them, engrossed in the more important task of fighting aphids. Her greatest joy was in the weeks when the roses, coral bells, and baby's breath all bloomed together and she could cut bridal bouquets for the dining room and still give some away. She sent several bouquets to Maureen by Paul as this was the one home decorating feat at which she could truly outdo the Chairman's wife.

It seemed there were an unusual number of issues that required

Rena's attention that summer. There was the funding of collective bargaining agreements with various unions of police and of other town employees. There were the permits for the stabilization of Main Wharf. There was the study for controlling storm damage on two of the beaches. On top of that, July presented all the special issues of the summer influx of people. Rena had a system for prioritizing these demands. Paul went with his passion.

Paul had been on the phone with the Harbormaster as there was so much demand in the summer for temporary mooring. The Town could find the money and then recoup it from the mooring fees if they could find the room for short term tie ups.

"You know what I'd like to do?" Paul asked Rena. "I'd like to use my mooring stone, slip an oak tree through the center, and drop it in the outer harbor."

"But that mooring stone is a valuable part of your collection," Rena said. The only other one she had ever seen was lying on display at the park on Halibut Point.

"So put my name on it and drop it in the water. I'd rather see it in its original use than as a planter in my back yard. It's not as if being underwater would hurt it."

Paul put in a call to Carl Nordhelm, the tree cutter, to be on the lookout for a proper oak. Carl came through. He knew of a stand of trees going down on a construction site in Ipswitch. They topped the chosen tree, then they ripped it out of the ground, roots and all, with the bulldozer on the site. Carl agreed to haul it for free, and, with the winch and all the muscle power down at the wharf, together they put the trunk of the tree through the hole in the center of the mooring stone.

They had the tree twirling on the winch before they figured out it would be safer to float the tree and tow it to the mooring location without the stone. They'd carry the stone separately. Then getting the stone over the floating tree trunk without losing it in the water would be the challenge. Paul raced home to look at some of his books of old photographs to see if they could get a hint of how it was done. Rena was in Town Hall, tracking this activity and relaying phone calls.

"Really Paul, you're going to have to get a cellular phone."

When the problem seemed almost solved, Paul called Rena to come down for the launching. "Wait, wait for me to go home for my camera," she said. "You have to document this. Fifty years from now, someone may want to know how it's done. Plus, if you fall in, I definitely want it on film."

By the time Rena got there, a crowd had gathered on the Yacht Club porch and on the wharf. Counting the kibitzers in skiffs, they had all the advice they needed and more. By the end of the day, Stonehaven had an oak tree mooring, limp leaves still clinging, in the protected area of the outer harbor. Rena's photograph of the installation ran in the *Gloucester Daily Times* two days later.

That was not the most exciting day that summer, however. That day came in August.

"I've got to tell you something," Paul said, gesturing toward his door. His eyes were twinkling.

Rena stood impatiently as Paul closed the door and came around his desk. There are so few good surprises in life, and she was ready.

"Sit down."

Rena sat, Paul sat, saying nothing at first, apparently savoring the moment.

"Paul, what is it? Another triumph? Are you torn between modesty and pride?"

Paul smiled and shook his head.

"Is it job or personal?"

"I'll tell you." He rubbed his palms together in pleasure. "This is it: She's pregnant."

Every ounce of flesh on Rena's face headed south. She let her mouth hang open until a reprieve seemed possible.

"Maybe it's just irregularity," she suggested. "You've heard of menopause? She's almost too old to be pregnant. Good God, she must be forty-four, just like the rest of us."

"Confirmed this morning."

"By an actual doctor?"

Paul nodded.

Rena pressed her hand against her forehead and closed her eyes.

"Oh, my God. What are you going to do?" Rena took a deep breath and in the lull without oxygen composed herself. "The moving finger writ," she said softly, "and having writ moves on nor all your piety nor wit can lure it back to cancel half a line, nor all your tears...."

But Paul was evidently not in the mood for the *Rubaiyat*. He jumped to his feet. Rena sucked in hard, almost cowered.

"I don't want to cancel half a line! I don't want to cancel anything!"

"Godawmighty, Paul. You have lost your mind."

"I'm happy as a clam," he shouted, "and I thought you would be, too."

"Paul," she drew the name out in three syllables of despair.

"We'll work it out."

"How? Paul, get a grip on reality. Where's she going to have this baby? At Addison Gilbert? What's she going to put on the birth certificate where it says father's name? Birth certificates are public record, you know, not that the clerks won't have it from the Thacher Light to the New Hampshire line before the reporters at the G.D. Times could sharpen their pencils."

Paul put his hands up in front of his face to ward off Rena's attack.

"And what about child support? And what about Karen's age? A first baby at her age–our age–is high risk, you know."

"Okay. So we haven't got everything worked out. We're doing that. For example, we first went to Beverly Hospital. They have a birthing center and everything. But the more important thing is that we're ready to take responsibility for this. We're not announcing it to the world, no, not right now anyway, but if we get in a tight spot, we're not going to lie. It's a spiritual thing, Rena. It sounds corny, but it's true. We're committed to each other–before the world as necessary, before as few people as possible for now–namely you."

"Oh, lucky me!"

"I thought you'd want to know."

"Well, maybe yes, maybe no, but it's an incredible burden."

"You are the one person I can count on in the world, outside of ...."

"Yes, yes, that's it. I now know something I can't tell anyone. I have to be guarded, worry about everything I say."

"Think of all the things we've been through just like that. Rena, you love secrets, you groove on being the one that's in. And you have never slipped and said something. I trust you completely."

Rena drew in a long breath and during the outbreath she tried to think of nothing. When all the breath was gone she said, "When is it due?"

"First of March."

The phone rang. "More later," Paul said reaching for the phone.

"Much more," said Rena turning toward her desk.

Rena didn't have time to catch her breath until after work. She'd had a grant request that had to be postmarked that day. But, once she was in her car and scooting up Main Street, she began to count backwards from the first of March. By the time she had maneuvered around the one-way portion of Front Street and was gunning up Bay Road hill, she'd figured this baby was conceived around the third week in June. By the time she turned into Duncan Lane behind her house, she had put two and two together.

Rena pulled herself slowly up the back steps, swinging in a wide arc around the corner post on the landing. She let herself in, leaving the keys in the door. She paused at the door of her room, looked at it with new eyes.

She went in and sat down gingerly on the couch, no longer the death bed but the bed of conception still quivering under the Tree of Life. She ran her fingers over the velvet cover; crushed velvet, they had called it in the fabric shop, but now it seemed more crushed than before, bruised by the hot, moist pressure of passion. She spread the mohair throw in her lap, lifting suspicious whorls of nap to the window light as if looking for the stains of fertility. Where first she had felt betrayed by the breach of her privacy, now she felt awe at the result.

Over the weeks that followed, awe turned into vicarious passion as Rena incorporated what must have happened on her day bed into her own fantasies.

The next morning the ocean was glassy. Where it met the sky, the color didn't change; only a passing cloud had wiped the sheen off. Rena dressed and went to work as smoothly as the passing cloud, only to be greeted by Paul, who had come in early, evidently troubled.

"I have a problem, Rena."

"So what else is new?"

Paul sighed reprovingly at her. "My life is joyful, Rena. It has some difficulties, yes, but I am a happy man. I do not consider I have a problem."

"I could have sworn I heard you say you had a problem."

"Forget it," he said, escaping to his office.

"I'm always here for you, Paul," Rena called mockingly after him as she settled into her swivel chair.

She was finishing up the agenda for the upcoming Council meeting to be posted, when Paul called to her. "Okay, Rena, are you ready to be serious?"

"As ever."

He looked at her silently, composing himself, while she tried to hold an expression of deep caring.

"Okay, this is it. I want very, very much to have a son."

"Well, you've taken the first step."

"Yeah, but it might not be a son."

"True."

"I don't want to be this way, but I am desperate for it to be a boy."

"Mmmm."

"I don't want Karen to feel bad if it's not. But I don't think I'll be able to hide my disappointment. I'm not proud of myself about this, but it's a consuming desire."

"Let's see. How did you feel when Maureen was pregnant?" Rena thought the mention of Maureen's name would give Paul pause, but he never seemed to miss a beat.

"I'll admit, I wanted a boy first," Paul said, "but... that was over in an instant when I saw Leslee. She was mine, she was adorable. She was a little doll. Same with Maria. I wanted a boy even a little bit more because that time I already had a girl. But that lasted about ten minutes after I saw her. I was in love with those girls. But..."

"But?"

144

"But after each one, it wasn't like that's the last, I'll never have a son. It turned out we didn't have a son, but there was no big announcement in the sky. Now I want someone to share my life with, a little person to show the things I love, a boy to pass on my lobster territory to..."

"And the girls?" Rena asked.

"The girls...they were the apples of my eye, my sugar dumplings... But now...I can see they're Maureen's girls. She's taken them over. Sure they come up and hug me and give me those little smiles, but it's so short, then they're off."

"Kids are like that. Remember when you were one? It would be the same way if they were boys. Maybe more."

"No, no. That's what I'm getting at. Last night it hit me. Okay, they called 'Hey, Daddy,' when I came in. But then they went on talking with Maureen for an hour. They didn't make any sense. They were laughing and giggling and changing subject so fast I never could get the drift, talking about people I'd never heard of."

"You know, Paul, sometimes a man complains his kids never tell him anything. But I've noticed sometimes a man doesn't ask. A woman asks: What did you do? What did he say? And what happened then? What was she wearing?" Rena herself had pursued many a story with Paul's own girls that she bet he'd never heard.

"If I ask, they say, 'Yes' and 'No'. That's all," Paul almost pouted. "They are my wife's children. Listen to this. Last night. Leslee and Maria came in at nearly the same time. I heard them talking to Maureen. In bed later, I said to Maureen, 'what did the girls say?' She said, 'What do you mean?' Like she didn't understand the question. I said, 'What's going on with them?' She said, 'Nothing.' Just exactly like they would say, 'Nothing, Daddy.'" He imitated their high pitched, coy voices.

"I said to Maureen, 'Well, what were you and the girls talking about?' She said, 'Oh they were talking about the boyfriends they had in junior high.' I never knew they had boyfriends in junior high. I almost yelled, 'Boyfriends!' She said, 'Not serious boyfriends, just guys they liked and wrote notes about and sat with at the movies.' My girls sat with boys at the movies? Why didn't I know about that? She said just what you said: 'Why didn't you ask?' Kelly says she's going to the movies with Kim and Cindy; why should I ask what boy was she going to sit with? She'd call me suspicious and nosy, now wouldn't she?"

"Probably," Rena admitted. "But I'm sure they'd think Maureen was nosy, too."

"I finally said, 'Okay, why were they talking about the boyfriends they had in junior high? It's been six years.' She said, 'No reason. They just got to naming them all. One thing led to another and they started giggling. We had a good time.' Do you see what's wrong here, Rena?"

"You wanted to be in on that conversation. But, really, Paul, would you have sat still for a listing of boyfriends from junior high?"

"No, you're right. I didn't want to hear a list of boyfriends. But, yes, I wanted to be in on that conversation. I wanted to be included. I didn't want them to stop giggling when I came in the room. That's it. That's what happened. They stopped giggling when I came into the room."

Rena saw actual tears in Paul's eyes, and she was shaken. She took in a deep breath and went with the outbreath, and then she said to herself: Rena Everett, you are not responsible for the happiness of Paul Lawson.

"I realize girls are just that way," Paul said. "If they had tried to tell me about the boyfriends they had six years ago—you are right—I would have left in boredom. Or I would have said, 'Why are you talking about old boyfriends? That's over. Talk about something useful.' Maureen hates that. And that's why I want a boy. A baby boy belongs with his mother, of course—and mine has a wonderful mother—but I figure later a boy and his father can kind of relate."

Rena nodded. Paul was right. Women can be apart for years and then finally pick up the phone or meet for lunch and be in the middle of a conversation that had no beginning and no end. One long lifetime conversation. Like hers and Ada's.

"I expect you're right, Paul," Rena said. "Girls talk. But a lot of people say fathers and daughters are closer than daughters and mothers..."

"I want a boy."

"I'll pray for one," Rena said and she meant it.

If Paul did have a boy, he would do all those man-type things that he could fit into his complicated life. Rena could see them all. They would go to sea, Paul would teach him to bait pots, to haul in halibut. He would tell him the stories of Stonehaven and demonstrate the use of each hand tool in his quarrying collection. He would take him to town meetings in Stonehaven and to the State House in Boston and show him the sacred cod mounted on the wall to remind all who pass of the source of Yankee wealth. They would walk the Freedom Trail together, tracing the footsteps of the patriots–all of them men, as they will see but never note–and talk about how to keep our country great. When the boy grew to be a teenager, there would be no hiatus of giggles when Paul came in the room. There would simply be no giggles. For men bond for emergencies. They bond in wars or surrogate wars on playing fields. In the absence of emergency, they stand shoulder to shoulder, silently bonding for the day they will know they can count on each other. In the meantime, what is there to talk about?

And yet, the decades of silence of the heart bring a yearning. Not in Maureen, Rena supposed. Her emotions had flowed out in giggling with the girls, confiding with friends over bridge, choosing fabric and china with merchants. She was probably satisfied. As Paul had been for forty years. For Paul, the basketball, paper route, student government, school consolidation protest, college, the family business, the community organizing, the elections, and North Shore Task Force had been satisfying.

Rena suddenly saw it all now in black and white like the photos in the Stonehaven High yearbook: Paul had organized the dancing in the lunchroom of Stonehaven High, but Paul had not danced. He had set the needle on the records, but he had not reached out to take a girl's hand. The other photos of the year book flipped through Rena's head like those funny action books that made crude moving pictures when you thumbed through them. She saw Paul in charge, Paul arranging, Paul deciding, Paul making something work. But no Paul and Sue or Paul and Linda or Paul and anyone. Maureen had been the first, and so he'd married her.

Dating is like musical chairs. You date and break up, date and break up, and for a long time you are too young to marry, and the music goes on. Then one day the music stops, and you marry the one you're standing beside at the moment. as Rena would have married Billy, if they'd been older. When the music stopped for Rena, all the chairs were taken. When the music stopped for Paul, he was with Maureen.

Now something had breached a dam that had held back all the accumulated need of Paul's heart. And Karen had been there the day the dam began to leak. She had said, by tears in her own eyes, I see the leak; let it go. And Paul had known the joy of emotion flowing untrammeled.

And all the while that Paul was rediscovering a pattern of courtship, his girls were taking up courtship 1980s style. You would think that Paul, in love again, would see their desires in a new light, but no, if anything he was more conservative than ever. Maria had a boyfriend he and Maureen didn't like. He had no respect for authority, Paul said, and persisted in calling for Maria late at night and whenever he pleased even though Paul had once demanded that he limit his calls to the hours between seven and ten.

"Three hours should be enough," he complained.

But the worst was, he was getting too familiar with Maria.

"He actually put his hands under her...." He held his palm up like a scoop.

"Her...?"

"Her butt, as they say these days. Now that may not seem like a big thing to you, but when I see that and when I see she didn't bat an eye, I know they're comfortable with touching—too comfortable—and this has got to stop. I know I can't stop him, so I'm going to have to stop her."

"You can't," Rena said, "It's different these days and not as bad as you think." She recalled not only the old days of sacred (though often broken) rules of the fifties but the decade that followed when "being comfortable with touching" was the ideal.

"The only difference was in the fifties, when you broke a rule, you felt guilty," Rena told him. "Frankly, Paul, I wish I'd broken a few more rules in high school myself. If I were Maria, I would definitely break more rules."

"Just what I needed to hear," Paul grumbled.

148

16

Labor Pains

The winter was cold and long. One snow fell on another and the plows made a wall so high the street signs were covered. A layer of ice glazed the world one day when the sun melted the surface and the next night froze it again. The wind brought tears to eyes and reddened exposed flesh.

And so Rena was surprised to see a surveyor's truck from Beverly parked on Bay Road along the edge of North Point near the old gate. She slowed and watched as a survey crew unloaded equipment from a truck onto a sled. The sewer project would not get that far for a year or more and they had voted down straightening out the curve between Whale Bone Cove and North Point. The curling, plunging road was a big part of the charm of the coastal town. No telling what the surveyor was there for. She'd ask Paul about it.

"Not Town business," Paul had said, but the mention of

surveyors seemed to bother Paul. He didn't like any project going on in town that he didn't know about. He'd check it out.

Paul knew the family that owned the property on North Point where the Hesperus Inn had been until it burned early in 1980. He knew that family had sold it. What was new, he learned, was that the company had in turn just sold an option to a developer. None of this was connected to any local real estate people, but a grand nephew of the original owner was on the Board of Selectmen. In fact, Reg Scott owned a small piece of land across the street and a few yards down from the Linotype factory, right where Boding Cove gouges into the isthmus of North Point. Reg's rental house looked almost directly at what was left of the old gate to Hesperus Inn. Reg admitted he'd heard that the company that optioned the North Point land planned to develop it and, in that case, Reg's rental house could become hot property. He could have a store there—after all, it was zoned for general use—and attract people who paused to come and go from the new development whatever it might be.

Paul had got on the phone with someone he knew on the Metropolitan Areas Planning Council who had a contact at the Department of Environmental Protection and got word that some preliminary inquiries had been made there concerning the Old Hesperus Inn and the steps to take towards getting approval for some waterfront alterations. This was serious business and something to look into, but in the last five years very little change on the waterfront was getting by the scrutiny of the DEP. Very little. You could hardly repair your own wharf if it rotted through. Best to watch the project though.

Eventually the snow evaporated leaving dirty white patches everywhere, and then at last a general thaw set in for a few days and the streets ran with water. The roadside depressions filled to the brim and the potholes slopped with water before the whole thing froze again. Boot marks of mud were preserved on icy surfaces like directions for some complicated dance.

One day in mid-February, Rena stamped her boots extra long at the door and clumped down the hall. She hung up her coat on the wooden coat rack Paul had salvaged from the old high school, and she poked her scarf in its pocket.

"How are we doing?" she asked Paul, holding on to his office doorjamb and leaning deep into the room.

"The doctor says it will be any day. Rena, I'm going to be with her when the baby comes. This is very important to me."

He and Karen, Paul told Rena, had talked about inducing labor some time when he could be there, but realizing the birth itself could not be scheduled, they abandoned the idea.

Paul wanted to set up a signal with Rena. If Karen went into labor during the night, she would call Rena and Rena would call Paul. If Maureen answered the phone, Rena would say, 'The main pump stopped.' That would mean he should come.

"It's safer this way. Maureen might get the phone first. I don't want Karen to have to talk to Maureen. Suppose she had a labor pain while she was talking?"

Rena very reluctantly agreed. Good thing they arranged it because before dawn two days later the phone rang. Rena's adrenaline exploded. She grabbed the phone.

"It's coming. The doctor says it's time to go. Tell Paul I'll be sitting by the door watching out for his car." Karen's voice sounded very close.

Rena made the call to Paul about the pump. "They'll be watching for your car," she said carefully.

She did not sleep again, lying still, excited, watching the sky lighten and listening to the surf. The sounds, unnoticeable in the daytime, became clear at night. She heard each wave advance, break, and withdraw, pulling a train of gravel behind it.

Paul did not come in the office the next morning. Rena shrugged off all inquiries. He had not come in by lunch time, and she hated to go out without hearing from him. She considered calling him at the hospital but thought better of it. At five-thirty she was still waiting and the others had gone home. She was sitting at her desk when Paul came in, a five alarm smile on his face. It was here. It was a boy.

Thank God.

"He's Paul S. Lawson Jr.," said Paul.

"In your mind. What's he really named?"

"Paul S. Lawson, Jr."

"But you can't name him that really. You may as well put an announcement in the paper."

"Look, we have this all planned out."

Rena rolled her eyes and threw out her hands. "Paul, you and Karen must spend all your time planning. Are you sure this whole affair hasn't been for the thrill of the scare? Life has become too tame for a lot of men, so they make excitement—like having babies in secret."

Paul laughed sheepishly. "Just listen: Yes, he'll be Paul S. Jr. but we'll call him P.S. Get it? Paul Sorrell but also P.S. like something written as an afterthought to a letter but very important. He's kind of a post script to my life, isn't he?"

"Cute."

"How we thought of it, actually,...well, I said.... it's kind of corny...but sometimes I said goodbye on the phone to Karen and then I'd say 'P.S. I love you.' That's what made us think of the nickname, when I realized I was saying my own initials."

If Rena had seen in Paul's affair with Karen a passion she had never seen before outside of his civic ambition, she was now seeing an unabashed self-expression, a mushiness that she might have approved in the abstract but which in reality made her uneasy. She felt as if the ground around her had turned to wet sand and the tide was sucking at her feet. She had to pull against the force and scramble for higher ground.

Never did a proud father take such an interest in his child. Paul noted all the milestones. P.S. had rolled over front to back. Three weeks later he rolled over back to front. He began to smile. He began to coo. He slept through the night.

It was on P.S.'s six month birthday that Tony brought in the Boston newspaper and plopped it on Paul's desk. Not that Rena kept time by P.S.'s milestones, she assured herself, it's just that Paul was telling her how P.S. was sitting up by himself exactly on schedule. Paul sat down on the floor to give a demonstration, his knees out to the side. He was sticking out his behind and leaning forward and trying to hold his ankles as the baby did to steady himself.

"He even tries to put his toes in his mouth and that makes him roll over."

At that moment, when Paul was tugging his toes unsuccessfully toward his mouth and Rena was laughing at him, Tony came to the door. Tony made one of his priceless comic expressions. Rena and Paul laughed but they did not offer an explanation. It was clear something intimate was going on between them.

"What you got there, Tony?" Rena said quickly.

Tony flipped the newspaper onto Paul's desk.

"I just thought you'd like to see the latest news on the North Point property."

Paul struggled up from the floor, and Tony showed him the small piece.

"Huh. So the Corps ruled out deepening the cove. Could have told 'em. So much for that plan."

Rena and Paul had a private laugh over their close call after Tony had left. Then Rena got serious.

"Paul, we really should be more careful talking about P.S. around the office. Someone's going to put two and two and your second childhood together."

"Never. It's too improbable," Paul had said. And they laughed some more. As the months passed, P.S. was pulling up on the coffee table. He then stood up holding on to a chair. The next week he let go, and several seconds was 67575standing by himself. Then three steps in a row before he dropped to the ground. Paul would pull Rena into his office and shut the door to tell her each new thing P.S. had done. This private audience occurred so often, with laughter and fond smiles trailing after, that Rena feared the others might think she and Paul were having an affair.

She witnessed Paul's joy and knew it was too big to keep just between him and Karen. Paul had been the one she'd shared her ups and downs with, but she'd never had any one big joy; now his was drowning out her small satisfactions. How could she say, after P.S. had taken his first steps, that she had found a pattern for a rose arbor that met her needs and planned to build it herself? There were days when everything in her life seemed pointless.

When P.S. had his first birthday, Paul invited Rena to the party February 18, 1987. "Not me, I don't belong there," Rena protested.

"Yes, you do. I want you to see him, Rena. Besides I want you to be there for this milestone in my life."

"You have Karen now for that. You two share it. Like married people do." She tried to remember if by any chance she had been at either of Paul's daughters' first birthdays. She thought not.

Afterwards, Paul pulled Rena into his office to see the pictures. There was Paul holding P.S. in his lap in front of the cake lit with one candle. There was Karen, blonde as ever, but older and more ordinary than she had remembered from the reunion, not a beauty but beautiful with contentment, holding P.S. in her lap, then another picture of Paul and P.S. with a present. Rena then realized they had needed her to take pictures of the three of them together; she almost regretted she hadn't been there to do it. But then, in the next picture, there they were, a family portrait.

"Who took this?" Rena asked in alarm.

"Karen's mother. See, she's in one of those pictures. Here..."

"Karen's mother! I just realized she knows about you!"

"Of course. She knows the baby came from somewhere."

"Paul, what does she think about you?"

"She likes me."

"I guess she does. Not many married fathers of unwed mothers show up at their baby's birthday party wearing party hats."

"She really likes me, personally, I mean. And I like..."

"Of course, she does, Paul. Everyone in the world likes you. You're likeable. But what I'm getting at is this baby is no secret. Grandmothers like to brag. I remember when you were sneaking around my house because you couldn't go to Karen's because her mother would see you. Now you're having family portraits together. I wish Karen's mother was somehow out of the picture."

"Karen's mother is an important part of the picture. She keeps the baby while Karen works. I'm just glad P.S. doesn't have to go to day care."

"Well, I wish she were an immigrant who speaks no English or something."

Caroline Kennedy got married that year causing disturbances all over Cape Ann. The wedding of the martyred President's daughter gave Karen what were apparently her first pangs of unwedded blues.

154

She lamented to Paul that she would never have that kind of a wedding. Her chance for a long white dress and a church full of relatives was gone.

"Does a real wedding mean that much to a woman," Paul asked Rena.

"A real marriage does."

"You know I spend as much time with Karen and P.S. as a lot of married fathers do with their families. Caroline Kennedy is the last person I thought would put Karen in a funk."

"Caroline Kennedy is a symbol, Paul, of all Karen is missing."

"What she misses is seeing me when I get up in the morning—which is no great loss."

If he didn't get it on his own, there was no point in Rena explaining further.

The next day Paul said, "Caroline Kennedy's wedding is a symbol all right. Maureen went bananas over the little shamrocks all over the dress and now she's trying to find some material like it. She says it's for Maria's prom dress. Hell, that's a year away. I said, it won't matter what kind of a dress she wears as long as she's dating that creep." Rena knew flocked organza well. Her aunt Amelia had bought some just like it, only sprinkled with roses, not shamrocks, thirty years before. The fabric was breathtakingly ethereal, but then, to Rena's dismay, Aunt Amelia had made it into a frock that was a shepherd's crook away from being Little Bo Peep's.

"No matter how much they say it's only a piece of paper and the wedding itself is just a waste of good money, a big wedding is still a symbol of happy-ever-after," Rena said.

"I thought we were talking about prom dresses."

"No, we were talking about weddings."

As soon as she said it, she wished she hadn't. Karen's funk began to descend over Rena, too.

Only a month or two later, the predictable happened. All the way from her desk, Rena heard Paul cootchie-cooing on the phone and ran in to tell Paul that baby-talk carries and that people down the hall would either realize he had a baby or would think he had gone completely over the edge. In response, Paul handed her the phone and what she heard was "Daddee, Daddee."

"Why don't you put him on the speaker phone so the whole Town Hall can hear him?" Rena said. "It's only a matter of time," she noted under her breath.

What was wrong with Paul that he thought he could get away with this? Paul the Pragmatic, where had he gone?

Rena knew all the cute things that P.S. said that year, followed his growth and his language development, saw the photos and watched them fill up an album and then another, carefully locked in Paul's bottom desk drawer.

And so Rena was more relieved than anything else when Paul asked her to go to lunch with him one drizzly autumn day, saying, "I've come to a decision point and I want to talk to you about it." They drove over to Folly Cove in the welcome rain, the first real rain since June. They pulled up in front of the Folly Cove Inn, an indication of the importance of this little talk, Rena noted. She unfolded her napkin and laid it in her lap, luxuriating in the smooth feel of the linen, stiff with starch and care like Mary's napkins used to be. Then she said, "So what's the decision?"

"Not so fast," Paul said, sliding his fork and knife out of his napkin. He put the napkin in his lap and set the fork and knife far apart and folded his hands on the cleared place.

"I've been trying to put my priorities in order," he announced, pausing for effect. Rena nodded approval. "To focus on my top priority, I have to give up a lot of other things I also care about."

Rena actually felt her eyes moisten because she knew how dear were the things Paul would have to ultimately give up.

"Finally," Rena said, with sorrow and relief.

"What do you mean 'finally'?"

"I mean you can't go on like this. The tension will get to you. It will make you ill. The uncertainty, the...the guilt."

"Rena, I have no guilt. You just think..."

"I'm sorry. I won't say any more. I just worry about you. I walk around on eggshells for you even if you don't." She folded her hands in front of her to show that her composure was restored.

"Now, about my top priority. The main thing is that everything needs to be centered."

"Centered," Rena repeated, thinking the word strange for Paul but intrigued and determined to savor and remember every nuance of this turning point in his life.

"Yes, centered. Stonehaven needs to be centered, too," Paul went on. "We need a focal point at the center of town to replace the summer tourist activity that fades after Labor Day. It has to be a social focal point even more than a business focal point. There was a time when the focal point–both social and business–was the harbor. But we have to face the fact–as painful as it is–that the harbor no longer...."

Rena stared at Paul as if he were a maniac. She made no attempt to follow what he was saying. She felt a sharp edge pressing on her throat and she had to look away from him.

Without her encouragement, he wound down, first subdued, then silent.

They sat in a heavy fog of thought. Her own heart beat grew until it engulfed her.

When the sharp sensation at her throat had softened into a dull ache, Rena stole a glance at Paul. He was folding and unfolding the corners of his napkin, pressing the diagonals in place with doleful precision, staring like a blind man, doing origami by feel.

Then, after a few painful moments, a cheerful look swept over Paul's face like the sun coming out from behind a cloud.

"Well. Let's splurge and get the key lime pie," he said.

Late that afternoon, when Rena's productiveness had waned, she went to Paul's office.

"If you want to tell me about the focal point of the town now, I'm ready," she said contritely.

He rubbed his hands together and began by painting a picture of the early winter scene, when the tourists were gone, leaving shops empty and shutters closed. It was true, he admitted, that year-round residents were relieved at first to find the streets empty, and in September they took long walks to exult in the footspace. But then they drifted. Stonehaven became less a cohesive town than a series of residences strung out along the road to Rockport and the road to Gloucester. A suburb without a center.

"It has a center, Paul. Flakes Square and the harbor have always been the center, always will be."

Paul pointed out what they both knew: since fishing was diminished and pleasure craft now outnumbered working boats, the harbor was mostly quiet from fall to spring. When the owners of the cafes of summer took down their hanging baskets and, like Bedouins, rolled up their awnings and slipped away, nothing seemed to pull the town together.

"And why?" asked Paul rhetorically.

"It's a resort." Rena shrugged. "Swells in summer, shrinks in winter."

"Never mind the tourists. I'm talking about us, Stonehaveners. Why do we not have a focal point?"

"Cars," Rena said, trying to be the good history student. "When boats were king, the harbor was the focal point. Now cars are here and all roads lead to Gloucester and Boston." She stopped and looked at Paul for confirmation just as she used to look to Mrs. Durlin, the English teacher or Mr. Young, the senior year history teacher at Stonehaven High.

"It's because we don't gather anymore," Paul said.

"Town meetings at the high school," Rena consoled.

"Once or twice, okay, three times a year."

"Caroling in the square at Christmas."

"That makes it four. Sure, there's a fried dough breakfast at St. Mark's Church and an aerobics class at St. Anthony's. First here, then there. But there's no place you can always go and know you'll see everyone."

"Like when we were kids, you mean? Like driving by the parking lot at West Beach and knowing everyone will swing through there some time that night?"

"Yeah, like that. For the women, I guess it used to be the old A&P on Front Street but now they go to Gloucester to shop or to the IGA in Rockport."

"Yes, it's time we had a Super Store right here with all the seasoned hummus, the weird mushrooms, and those knobby South American roots, if only to look at."

"No. A Community Center. That's what we need." Paul said it with a flourish as if he were unveiling a statue.

The term named so literally the abstract concept he was

describing that Rena got no additional meaning from the announcement of the thing, as if the art he was unveiling were abstract and incomprehensible. But when she saw him looking expectantly at her, she obliged him by saying, "Aahh."

"It would have to be in the park next to the school."

"The park?"

"It's not much of a park."

"It has trees and...

"Yeah, locust trees. More like weeds."

"Lawson Park, named after your ancestor, the sea captain!"

"We could keep the name, use it for the Community Center maybe," Paul said, waving her remark away with his hand.

"We would build this center out of granite, Stonehaven granite. It would tie the new building in with the other public buildings without being stodgily imitative. It would have a substantial mass with livable features, an interior court yard perhaps and glass walls open to it. Massive and traditional on the outside and contemporary and light on the inside. We would have an architectural competition for the design."

"What about parking? Finding a parking place here is life's most significant uncertainty."

"That's part two of my plan. The landfill has only got a year or so to go before it must be capped. Now that space would make an ideal town parking lot and we already own it."

"Paul, that's too far from the center of town."

"Patience," Paul said, raising his hand to fend off her concerns. "If we had a shuttle bus that ran from the parking lot to the community center every few minutes, it would take people to the center. It would solve that problem, and it would help relieve congestion in the summer, too. We could ban those huge tour buses from the Square altogether and make them let off passengers at the parking lot."

"How much would a shuttle bus system cost with the drivers' salaries and all?"

"That's the next step."

Of course. The next thing Rena knew, she was checking with all the Massachusetts college campuses which had shuttles, and Paul was on the phone to the Metropolitan Area Planning Council.

"Transportation is the MAPC's five-year focus anyway," Paul said. "Stonehaven could be its showcase. There would be grant money and ...."

Rena could see the grant application documents stacking up on her desk. She had begun to fill them out in her sleep.

The rest of that year was focused around the North Shore Task Force, a regional group under the Metropolitan Area Planning Council. Paul had been instrumental in its formation. He could see there were certain issues that could be dealt with better together instead of as individual towns–transportation, emergency services, tourism, for example. Paul was elected by the other town representatives as the Task Force's first chairman. He was clearly happy to expand his influence and, even though his first objective after the Task Force was formed was to get the new shuttle for Stonehaven, Rena saw for the first time that maybe Stonehaven was not big enough a realm for Paul Lawson. Maybe someday he would run for governor. And then what would her new job be? Maybe she would get her own office with carpet on the floor. And keep a tiny apartment in Boston for week nights. She wondered fleetingly if she would be up to a state-level job.

In April, Paul stopped by Rena's desk one morning with something on his mind.

"Maria wants to pierce her ears before the prom," he said quietly.

"Sounds reasonable to me. She must be the last one in her class."

"You sound just like her. But I put my foot down."

"What's wrong with pierced ears?" Rena didn't have them herself but she sometimes wished she did.

Paul ignored the question. "I've said when she's eighteen she can do as she pleases, but she's three months short."

"Is this about age or about authority?"

"It's about values. First, she has pierced ears; the next thing, she will be pregnant."

"That's not how it happens, Paul," Rena laughed.

"This is not funny."

"And what does Maureen say?"

"Maureen encourages her. Clothes, boys, pierced ears, boys. These are all distractions."

"From what?"

"From what she should be thinking about."

"It's your mother, isn't it, Paul? She thought the only people with pierced ears were immigrants, right?"

Rena knew a little bit about this from Aunt Amelia who compassionately doctored the Armenians and the Puerto Ricans but was ever watchful of their ways creeping into her personal world.

"It looks cheap," Paul said.

"Cheap! A nineteen fifties word if I ever heard one. Yesterday's cheap is today's chic, Paul. Get with it."

The next day, Maria stopped by the office on the way home from school. She was leaning all over Rena's desk while she was waiting for her father to get off the phone. She put both her hands on the edge of Rena's desk and lifted herself almost off the ground. She was hard to ignore. Maria was clearly looking for a heart-to-heart so Rena gave in.

"What's up?"

"Dad says I can't have pierced ears."

"I heard."

"What! He told you?"

"You were going to tell me anyway so what's the dif?

"It's not his business anyway."

Rena remembered a time when she had bought herself a two-piece bathing suit with her hard earned summer cash. When it was wet, it pulled down so her belly button showed, a nice neat one that Aunt Amelia herself had tied in the delivery room. Aunt Amelia had objected to her wearing the suit, the neatness of the belly button notwithstanding. Rena, like Maria, had thought it was none of Aunt Amelia's business. But Aunt Amelia countered, "Remember, I have to LIVE in this town. I can't have people talking about my niece." As if every other girl in town did not wear two-piece bathing suits and as if Aunt Amelia ever heard anyone talking anyway.

Rena had slunk away and dragged out an old photo album of

sepia scenes mounted on black paper and dated in the 1920s. She remembered a photograph that had caused her extreme delight, one of Aunt Amelia and her brother and another man, perhaps a beau—was it possible—posing on Crane's Beach. Aunt Amelia had on a black knit bathing suit that came almost to her knees, but more important, it clung to her nipples even dry and it sagged so much at the arm holes that you could see in through the sides all the way to Egypt. Rena presented the picture to her great aunt. No explanation was necessary.

"Hmph." Aunt Amelia said. That meant it was a draw and Rena would hear no more about the matter. She wore the bathing suit, but, out of deference to Aunt Amelia, she put a long shirt over it until she got down the street and she rinsed it out herself and dried it on the towel rack so that Mary would never leave it hanging in full view on the clothes line.

"The point is, Maria, that, with your father, the past is your greatest weapon," Rena concluded. "Now I happen to know that, at the turn of the century, fashionable women had pierced ears. Look in all the estate jewelry shops. They are full of antique Victorian earrings for pierced ears. Now here's what you do."

Rena directed Maria to find a photo of her great, great grandmother Lawson for whom she was named. Rena remembered it well because Paul had put it out on display for the party after Maria's christening.

"I guarantee your great-great-grandmother had pierced ears and I think you will be able to tell by the way the earrings dangle tastefully from her ears. Cameos or elaborate filigree, you'll see."

Maria went directly home, found the picture, and, judging by the results, followed Rena's strategy with admirable skill. Luckily the holes did not get infected, and Paul barely noticed the event. Rena then gave Maria her graduation gift early—some small cubic zirconium studs for the prom.

That whole episode gave Rena a slightly enlarged perception of her own political skill. Maybe she was ready for a state-level job!

An event early that autumn further increased Rena's sense of personal power. A Saturday midday meeting was held of her own neighborhood association at the home of Rick Talbot, a lobsterman in the old tradition. It began with a covered dish dinner. Rena brought a potato, bacon, and bean dish. Rick himself contributed a precious thirteen pounds of lobster salad. Neighbors brought various stick-to-the-ribs casseroles to round out the menu. When the bowls of lobster salad were cleaned down to the last few smudges of mayonnaise and a rim of celery, the meeting was called to order.

The topic of discussion was the poor condition of Dory Beach Road, whose patches and pot holes made a trip along the road an art form of slowing and swerving and speeding up and falling in accompanied by a composition of rattles, squishes and thunks. Rena accepted this performance as normal but was not averse to new pavement either, a fortunate state because she didn't want to be seen as using her position at Town Hall to influence. Some residents insisted they campaign for a new layer of pavement; others said the slowing effect of the disrepair was desirable and that a new surface would only encourage speeding. Those for improvements tended to be on one end of the road and the status quo people were mostly on the other end. And so, in a rare confluence of good sense, they voted to lobby the board for new pavement on the west end of the road only, leaving the others to the charms of the rocky road. So that was that, and Rena was rising out of her seat to go when Mabel Mulligan cleared her throat.

Mabel, a stocky, red-faced woman who did not seem to have enough breath, began, "Some of us feel...," and looked around to identify her constituents with a glance, "...we need to speak out...." She wheezed and began again, "... about something that has been bothering us... for some time."

Between wheezes she explained that the neighborhood had agreed time and time again to standards of yard maintenance, but that one eyesore remained and, worse, it was right on the corner of Dory Beach and Sinclair Road where it was viewed from two directions. The offending structure was the stack of lobster pots in Rick Talbot's front yard.

"It's spoils the image of our neighborhood... to have work equipment... in the front yard. The neighborhood zoning law... says clearly no commercial...."

Rena's heart pounded in dismay. She waited for someone to stop the woman during a wheeze, but no one protested, and Rena began to wonder what the others thought. Her own anger mounted and she found herself rehearsing a bold rebuttal in her head. How dare they...!

When Mabel said, "not in keeping with the neighborhood," Rena exploded.

"You come and eat this man's lobster salad at sixteen dollars a pound and you wipe your mouth on his napkins and you pat your tummy and then you complain about his lobster pots! If anything on earth is in keeping with this town, it's lobster pots. This town lives by its lobster pots."

"But they're metal lobster pots," more than one person cried out. "If they were wooden, it would be okay," another chimed in.

In truth, Stonehaven had an ordinance against having metal lobster pots in view. The metal ones, coated in green plastic, had been relegated by law, from the time of their introduction, to the back yard of commercial establishments in the village area. Only the traditional wooden pots, grayed with use, were allowed in view and these were encouraged, stacked in roughhewn geometry suitable for framing. Residential rules, by contrast, only forbade commercial displays and objects "not in keeping" with the neighborhood.

"The tradition is," Rena said with arched eyebrow, "that we are a lobstering town and we have used metal pots for..., well, many years...." Paul would have known the exact number.

"But it's the wooden ones that are traditional," someone cried out. "That's what you think of when you think of Stonehaven."

"What you think of? You mean the key ring lobster pots? The refrigerator magnet lobster pots? Ha!" Rena cried. "Have you ever noticed the souvenir pots all have the rounded tops of the Maine lobster traps. These are not our pots, never have been. Ours are flat, rectangular, not bowed like in Maine."

Rena adapted Paul's speeches on the regional differences in lobster pot construction as her own. And then she diverged from his.

"Have you ever noticed?" she said, "that what you think of when you think of Stonehaven has never been the reality?"

Rena stopped, shocked at hearing herself, wondering if she could be said to be ranting. But she was into it now. No turning back. So she hurried on to her point.

"Have you seen the thousands of green metal pots and blue and red and yellow floats stacked along Pigeon Cove Harbor? Only three miles away and the tourists flock there and photograph and paint them. Those metal pots are colorful and as interesting in their modern angles as the old wooden ones, and most of all, they are real. We should be proud that the only real lobsterman among us...." She glanced at Rick; he looked embarrassed and she stopped. She almost cowered against the backlash. But there was none.

"That's a good point," someone said as if Rena had made a mild comment.

There was a vote or perhaps there wasn't. Rena didn't hear over her pounding heart. But the matter was somehow dismissed and the empty platters of the feast were wiped clean with paper napkins and carried away without further ado. Rena's heart did not stop racing until she had closed the door of her own house behind her.

Two evenings later, the phone rang and Rena answered. It was Rick Talbot, the lobsterman. Would Rena like to have dinner at his place and watch a video afterwards?

Rena's mental picture of Rick spun into a blur like the blades of his outboard; his sharp nose and ruddy face shaded by his Evinrude cap became ungraspable. When he came back into focus, she wet-combed his usually windblown hair flat, gave him a Lands' End shirt, and put into his callused hands a cracked lobster tail on a plate garnished with lemon and parsley. She quickly conjured up a vision of Rick making sexual overtures, unbuttoning his new shirt down to the chalk white chest. Not that she in any way thought it would come to that, but the image was the acid test just to see if any flicker of interest was remotely possible. No flicker was discernable anywhere on Rena's body, but the call had so taken her by surprise that accepting was the only thing she could do gracefully or at all.

Ada was gleeful, teasing Rena like a teenager. "Call me when you get in. No. That would be too late. I'll call you early in the morning before work and, if you don't answer, I'll know you spent the night!"

"Don't be ridiculous."

Instead of eating at the confluence of long porches where the neighborhood had gathered, Rena and Rick had their meal in a cozy breakfast nook steps away from the stove where Rick had cooked it up with surprising skill. The chowder was delicious, creamy, chunky, well-seasoned; the blueberry muffins were both tangy and sweet; the conversation was stilted as she waited for signs of his making a move. There were none. The movie was satisfying, and the parting awkward.

Rena thanked him profusely as she left, reiterating her compliments about the food.

"Thank YOU," Rick replied.

A feeling of closure warmed Rena as a kiss would not. The invitation was apparently a payback for her public support, pure and simple.

After weeks of taking turns using the one lane around the asphalt truck and the roller, half of Dory Beach Road was resurfaced. The end of the new pavement joined the old pavement right in front of Rena's property. The melody changed. Now the cars rattled up to her house and then went silent, like a dory being pushed off the beach first scrapes then glides soundlessly into the water. It seemed more cars went that way than came back, but the ones that came back were quiet, sneaking up, then suddenly going thunk into the pothole in front of her house. It took some getting used to.

When winter came, the whole score changed with the squeegee sound of tires on wet road, then the jingle of chains, and the crunching of snow. It had taken the paving to bring this euphony into Rena's consciousness and she realized the comings and goings of people, their pace and direction, marked her days at home into manageable units and buoyed her mood. The effect was the difference between a moment of silence in a telephone conversation and a dead phone. Or the difference between being tuned in to the pulse of a town and being lonely.

As the year came to a close, Rena reflected that she had been more satisfied than in previous years. There is with age perhaps a mellowing of desires. She had settled into Paul's dilemma, having given up on his solving it; it was his problem, why should she worry.

In December, the Christmas tree in Flakes Square seemed to glow more deeply with color than ever. Her own white lights in the windows purified the house again, erasing the dust or smudges and worn places in upholstery and transforming it once more into the ideal house she had always supposed it was. The carolers who came along the road from St. Anthony's, as Christmas neared, brought sweetness to the season. She had no Christmas of her own making.

The Saturday before Christmas, she went to an open house at her mother's in Boston—it wasn't as elegant as when Richard was there, but it was different and it was Boston.

At the Stonehaven Town Hall, they decorated the doors and, on Christmas Eve, they closed early and had punch and peanuts and exchanged gifts. Then for Christmas Eve dinner, Rena was invited as always to Paul and Maureen's. She took a present for the family and gave the girls identical small presents to put under the tree and left early so Paul and Maureen could finish their still lavish preparations for the girls' Christmas morning.

Christmas Day, Rena slept as late as she liked. When she awoke, the sea color was deep jewel-like as it should be on such a special day. The waves were choppy, white-capped like snow on a fir tree. She got up with energy and began a project that she had selected for the season—to celebrate having an extra day to herself and to keep her from wondering if it might be more fun to be with family. Her project this year was to transform her glassed porch into a greenhouse. Her Christmas present to herself was a serious set of grow lights and shelving material. By dark that evening she had installed the lights and built one set of shelves for pots and seedling trays. Afterwards, she pampered herself by sitting in hot perfumed water, deep enough to soak her back.

The climax of the season, for several years now, was Doug and Girard's New Year's Eve party on The Lane. All the shopkeepers and artists who were tenants on The Lane on Spyglass Point were automatically invited and, beyond them, to be on Douglas and Girard's guest list was to be truly "in the group." Doug and Girard pulled out all stops. Girard drew each invitation with a new theme, each year wittier than the last. Doug centered the table and surrounded the wassail bowl with a veritable woodland forest. Moss-based compositions of leaves and ferns covered the tables and dripped off the mantel like the furnishings of a fairy lair. Little porcelain squirrels romped through the cones and seed pods.

Among the tendrils of tundra, large dishes steamed. Roasted vegetables, their flavors concentrated, their juices caramelized, nestled around a rosemaried pork roast. Fresh tuna steaks were scored into latticework and Harvard beets were sauced in crimson. Parmesan puffs passed by as often as Rena took a breath.

Doug, red-faced and plump, was the essence of Santa Claus himself; his long time companion, the thin-faced Girard, the length of his face extended by the point of his beard, was wry and witty. It was he who brought out the fiddle, when everyone was mellow with drink, and enticed even the shy into song by the fire. No one represented the spirit of this town more than Doug and Girard, though neither were natives, neither were of the old traditions. Doug was once a carpenter but he preferred cooking; Girard had been an architect but he had an eye for fashion. Five years before, the two of them had opened the all-year-round specialty shop, The Squirrel's Nest, that set a tone of quality for the whole Lane. Their first notable success was the introduction of Icelandic wool sweaters, gray and black and white depending on the sheep. After Doug and Girard came, other shops dared open earlier and stay open longer because Doug and Girard's shop drew a constant trickle of buying customers in all but the most inclement weather. Every resident and shop keeper on the Neck spruced his space up, whether former fishing shack or carriage house, setting out window boxes in spring and miniature fir trees in winter to match Girard's topiaries and garden figures.

When midnight came, there was kissing all around and, demure though his embraces were, Rena got more pleasure from them than she was supposed to. She savored every whisker of it and put the sensations away for long winter fantasies. This year there was an extra one to think about. Rick Talbot's. His lobster shack was on The Lane so he was of course invited, and she couldn't remember if she had ever shared the ritual peck with him in years before or not. This night she gave his kiss extra time, what with her defense of lobster pots and his subsequent expression of gratitude over dinner recalled through the transforming haze of the New Year's wassail. The kiss, along with the archetype of The Lobsterman, would fuel a year's worth of fantasies of love at sea on a small craft although the man in the fantasy would, Rena already knew, bear little resemblance to the real Rick Talbot whom she had planned, if the occasion arose, to reject.

No one left the party until the creme brulee had been served. It was glorious, a pure egg and vanilla custard, rich with a soul-stirring topping that defied description. It was Doug's specialty and no one from Stonehaven would ever touch the dessert anywhere else. One year Doug had been painfully stricken with shingles and lay in bed directing Mildred Huffines from The Knitting Needle in making the concoction. At the crucial matter of the topping, he made Mildred leave the room and pulled himself up to do that sacred part alone. At nearly one o'clock, the crowd dipped their little spoons into their little custard cups and hummed their annual approval.

The carols, candles, tree in the Square, dinner with Paul's family and Doug and Girard's party created all the holiday season Rena ever wanted. More would be surfeit to Rena, after the pub opens and she is shunned, wonders if this means she won't be invited to Doug and Girard's New Year's Eve party Here begins 1989. By early the end of winter, Paul had built clear interest in the community center project over a period of months by speaking to council members and civic groups. Now that the idea had jelled into an expectation in the minds of the town's residents, Paul was beginning to bring the plan one step closer to action. He soon began to solicit formal proposals.

One proposal located the community center on vacant land near the edge of town; a second proposed site was closer to town on a part of the old Draper farm. The third proposal was for a granite building in keeping with the older city buildings and located in the center of town near the Square on the site of Josiah Lawson Park. The first proposal involved buying land; for the second plan, it could probably be arranged for the land to be donated. For the central location, of course, the city already owned the land.

"We have to listen to all sides," Paul said, although Rena knew for a fact he was firmly behind putting the community center in the center of town. The town would hire a consulting engineer to design the project and evaluate the construction bids. Paul wanted to use good old Rod Draper, who now ran his own engineering company, and he alerted Rod to contact the Board, but that's as far as he would go. He stepped out of the meetings every now and then to let the Board discuss the candidates on their own. Paul was scrupulous about choosing people to do the town's work. No influence peddling allowed. Paul had to turn down friends sometimes just because they were friends.

"But Paul, all the best people for the job are really your friends," Rena had said more than once. "It seems unfair in the other direction to have to choose people who are not your friends."

"I have to avoid even the appearance of impropriety," Paul had replied.

"I hope you'll enjoy learning to play the harp," Rena retorted.

"What?"

"Because that's all you're going to be doing in heaven. All the fun is going to be elsewhere."

Rena caught a sheepish grin on Paul's face as he slumped over, deflated.

Rod was hired probably because his was a good firm. But the Board knew what Paul wanted. He didn't have to say anything. The Board knew Paul had to be happy with the engineer.

In March, P.S. turned three. In the pictures, Rena could see the baby fat had gone and the child's legs had skinnied some. She could see Paul's grin on his face in one picture, nothing of him in another. A desire to actually see the child in person came and went. P.S.'s existence was rarely forgotten if sometimes out of mind.

"Let me tell you something funny," Paul said one morning as he signed the letters Rena had typed up the day before. "You know the girl who was eating something and a spider came?"

"Janet?" Janet had replaced Sherry in the tax office. "Janet is phobic about spiders. I don't know the latest. What?"

"No, no, no. In that little rhyme. Miss Somebody.

"I don't know what you're talking about."

"Miss...oh, yes, Miss Muffet. I know you know her."

"Little Miss Muffet? Paul, my mind could not have been farther from Little Miss Muffet. You want to talk about HER?"

"This is so cute. P.S. says 'sat on her tuffet, eating *she's* curds and whey' instead of *'her* curds and whey.' That's so smart, don't you think, understanding the pattern of the possessive and creating her own. Don't you think that's smarter even than saying '*her* curds and whey?' Shows he's really thinking instead of just parroting."

"Yes. Language development is really amazing."

And then Paul started saying, "*We'res*" as in "That boat is just like *we'res*."

"Like what?" Rena had said.

"*We'res*. Remember? It's what P.S. says instead of *ours.*"

Rena felt stingy that she didn't laugh or congratulate him for remembering or something. She didn't know why she couldn't give Paul the satisfaction.

17

Tradition vs Progress

Several years earlier, Trimark, a development company out of California, had bought an option for the thirty-two acres of land on North Point where the old Hesperus Inn had stood until it burned. Spectacular surf pounded the rocks on the east side of the point, toward the ocean, till its tip cowered to the West. This surf over the millennia had carved so deeply into the Point that it was almost an island connected to the mainland by a narrow isthmus of stubborn rock. The west side of North Point was calmer; the point protected North Point Cove where the lithograph machinery factory had operated.

On that same cove, on a small strip of land that was part of the Hesperus Inn property across from the factory, were the fishing shacks of the North Point fishermen, mostly lobstermen who kept their gear in the shacks, moored their lobster boats in the cove and sold their lobsters from the store on the dock. The fishermen were assessed a mooring fee by the Town, the same as any other mooring arrangement. The buildings, which had been put up on the land decades before, were handed down from father to son or, on rare occasion, sold to another fisherman; the land beneath them, owned by the Inn was lease-free. The picturesque goings-on of the fishing business had been an attraction to the Inn's guests; the steep path leading down the rock headland from the Inn was obscured now by sea grape and blue-stemmed grass. But the cove remained a mecca to artists, tourists, and seafood lovers who bought fresh lobster meat right off the dock. The lobster came in one door, swung a few seconds in the iron-gray scales tinged with rust, and went out the other door wrapped in brown paper. Artists from around the world turned their backs on the factory and set up their easels facing the collection of wooden shacks each decked out in buoys identified by their owners colors. Lobster pots were stacked between the shacks, the boats came and went from the harbor, and the fishermen did their jobs in apparent disregard of their own quaintness.

The whole of North Point had long been zoned for general use because of the hotel, the litho factory, the fishing industry and, before that, a quarrying activity from which remained three small quarries now full of water.

The sale of North Point to Trimark was contingent on approval of the Department of Environmental Protection, the Corps of Engineers, and the Municipal Conservation Board of Trimark's plans for a resort on the site, tentatively named Wildwater. Trimark had a string of very successful marina/hotel/condo/ complexes on the California coast, the Gulf of Mexico and elsewhere, based on "small town livability" and "human proportions," Architectural Digest had written. Trimark had recently set up a Boston branch office with the object of getting a toehold on "the other Cape" as Cape Ann boosters called the point of land north of Boston, acknowledging its obscurity in the shadows of the more toney Cape Cod. Cape Ann was "more blue-collar" according to another Boston developer who commented on the difference for the newspaper. Trimark apparently aimed to buy in cheap and then "toney-up" Cape Ann's image.

Wildwater plans included clearing a portion of the shore line of rocks on Trimark property between the fisherman's harbor and the litho factory and hauling in sand for a beach. The rocks would be piled up beyond the harbor to form a small breakwater to partially enclose a new marina. The hotel complex would be built around the largest of the three picturesque quarries. Condos would stagger down the rocks to within licking distance of the highest winter tides.

An environmental impact study had been done. A main

concern of the state and federal environmental protection agencies was always the preservation of the wetlands, especially those grassy tidelands whose black bottoms ooze with clams and eggs and larval forms, "the cradle of the sea." But Trimark's project, perched as it was on the point of rock, disturbed no mud flats. Surface drainage was a concern but Trimark detailed maintenance of areas planted in native plants, buffers, and holding ponds, as well as erosion control during construction. These Trimark people were no amateurs.

The environmental impact study and other investigations had been going on for four years and the newspaper had made note of various steps, impasses, compromises, provisions: No new breakwater could be built for the marina. Motor craft would be restricted to a small portion of the proposed marina area; any other moorings would have to be for sail boats only. No rocks could be removed to make a beach but sand could be brought in to cover the rocks, and so forth. In the end, Trimark had to abandon the idea of a marina because, without a breakwater the water was too rough.

"Ha! I could have told them that," Paul would say upon reading each forced compromise. It was understood that the skirmishes with the regulatory agencies would go on forever like the Hundred Years War.

Then the unexpected happened: The U. S. Army Corps of Engineers and the Massachusetts Department of Environmental Protection, and the other powers that be finally approved a set of plans for the project. The greatest hurdle for the developers had been cleared. Paul got a call within minutes from a colleague in Boston just before the approval became official.

Rena heard Paul slam the phone down and leave his office, and, since he usually told her where he was going, she looked out the window to where his car was parked. She saw him out back, kicking at a hillock of weeds and taking the trunk of a poplar tree and shaking it angrily. He was muttering to himself.

Tony came over to the window to see what Rena was looking at.

"Cussing is what he's doing," Tony said after they had watched a bit.

Paul did not actually tell them the bad news until several hours afterwards.

A full report appeared in the *Gloucester Daily Times* two days later.

"I can't believe it," Paul must have said a dozen times turning the newspaper pages back and forth, reading and rereading. Copies of the official public documents were on the way.

"What are you going to do?" Rena asked Paul.

"Fight it. Here I am trying to pull the people back into town, building with solid granite–symbolic in every way–solidifying our history, our center. Strengthening from within... and here they are, bringing in a carnival from California."

"Well, there was, after all a big hotel there before." Rena tried to console him. "And the factory used to operate day and night. And a trolley ran down the street. In a way, it will be bustling like before."

Paul squinted in pain, and Rena realized that countering his view, even for his own comfort, would not work, so she changed her tack.

"The more centered the town, the more peripheral the resort will be," Rena said, "By building the new community center, you are centering the town as never before." Restating his view had been a mainstay of her support for Paul over the years, but it did not seem to comfort him now in his distress.

"I should have reacted sooner," he grieved, shaking his head so low his chin grazed his shirt.

"I don't know what you could have done. But now Trimark will have to do a presentation at a public hearing–that's fair–we just need to look at the plans for weaknesses."

Within a week, Trimark announced it was exercising its option and buying the land. A closing date was set.

"That kind of investment will make them determined," Paul noted. "Desperate even. We'll have to make it much too much expensive to pursue."

"Can we do that?"

The next morning the sea was the color of the bottom of an aluminum pot poked grainy by the fork of a diligent cook. A pen and ink day if ever there was one. Rena mentally outlined the island with the stroke of a thick-nubbed pen; she made it black where the seaweed lined the shore. She flicked up the side of the light house on Cormorant Island with a finer point; she had mastered its bishop-on-a-chess-set shape when she was a child so that she no longer bothered with real pen and paper. She shaded with tiny dots or deepened the shade with zigzags. She never tired of the seascape, its varied shades and mood. She tried to picture the view that had greeted the guests of the old Hesperus Inn on North Point every morning and would perhaps greet the residents of Wildwater, if that development ever came to pass: a sea like this one, no island like hers, but a view of New Hampshire and even Maine that would be muted by a distance that would require a light wash or smeared charcoal.

At Town Hall, Paul seemed to be his regular calm self, but of course the problem that plagued him hadn't gone.

That afternoon, Paul announced he was going to take a few days off and would begin battle anew on Monday morning. He was going on his annual southern deep sea fishing trip. Every year, he and Rod and Tim, Rod's younger brother, Warren the Evinrude factory rep, and a couple guys from the Yacht Club went to the Gulf of Mexico, wallowed briefly in the body-temperature water by the beach, caught a sleazy show in Panama City, and then headed out to sea where they continued their bonding in the warm, decadent waters of the South. They set out their lines for sea bass, fought the spunky bluefish and gawked at the occasional shark. They had their pictures taken with their catch. They would come home with bass steaks and bluefish filets in an ice chest, a sack of oranges, a red face—for southern sun is a scorching force that takes Yankee skin by stealth—and tales of slow-talking good ol' boys and friendly waitresses.

Even though time was critical, Rena was happy for Paul's plans. The clammy hand of defeat would fall from his shoulders and the southern sun would warm his ego till it rose like bread dough in the window. He would return with renewed energy and faith in the ultimate victory.

A week later, Paul brought in photos of his deep sea fishing trip

176

with the guys to show her. He called her in his office and shut the door. There was the usual snapshot down on the docks with Paul posing with his biggest fish dangling on the hook of the scale. But this time there was something different. There standing in front of his father holding his pudgy hand up to touch the fish's tail was P.S.

"Paul! You took P.S. deep sea fishing! He's only three years old! It's a miracle he didn't fall overboard! Did you tie him to the mast?"

Paul had a ready answer: Karen was there to take care of him. Paul's fishing buddies actually were never there.

"I don't even want to know how you pulled this off," Rena said, throwing her hand up dismissively.

Paul seemed stung. He put his pictures into the drawer without showing her the rest and pushed the drawer shut. He turned his back to her and looked out the window.

Rena had lied when she said she didn't want to know how he pulled this off. She puzzled over it voraciously. Did the fishing buddies go to the Gulf separately? Did he tell them he couldn't make it and risk that the guys might mention to Maureen they were sorry Paul couldn't go with them? Or did he give them some hint they should keep his absence a secret? Each scenario made Rena a bit more anxious so that she had to remind herself several times, during the outbreath, that this was not her responsibility.

She cut her eyes toward the naughty boy who was not her responsibility. He was holding his free hand over his eye, as if blocking his vision on one side, and then again blocking the other, nervously and nonsensically fiddling like a child who has been reprimanded.

"What are you doing?" Rena finally said sharply.

"What do you mean?"

"Why are you covering your eye?"

"Oh. I've been seeing things double lately. I noticed it on the boat in Panama City. Two images of everything. It's annoying, so sometimes I cover up one eye to make the other image go away."

"You probably need glasses," Rena persisted. "When's the last time you had your eyes examined?"

"Never by an eye doctor. Just those charts on the wall in junior high."

"I see two images not quite in the same place, myself, Rena said. "I can't imagine how glasses fix it but they do." She furrowed her brow to help think of everything she had learned about her eye condition. "But covering one eye doesn't help me. Maybe yours is something else. Anyway, you need to see an eye doctor."

"It's about time you had to wear glasses like the rest of us," Rena told him. "We're tired of you looking like Peter Pan."

Later, Rena picked up lunches at Ciardi's and brought them back to the office so they could finish up an information packet and get it out in the two-thirty mail. She put her sack on her desk and handed the other to Paul.

"Here's *you's* lunch," she said, joking to get back on his good side.

Paul grinned. "It's *jou's* lunch though, not *you's*, " Paul said. "The P.S. dialect is a little irregular."

Rena smiled. She really did think that was funny. And then she began to think about the word and couldn't get it out of her head. She went back to her desk and tried to set up some columns on the computer but couldn't concentrate. To get past it, she had to get up and walk into Paul's office.

"It's not irregular, Paul."

"What's not?"Paul sad. "It comes from Would you Did you. Listen: Wouldjou like some carrots? Didjou pick up your ball? It's a perfectly regular word."

Paul grinned and Rena was pleased.

Soon after the environmental plan was approved for the Trimark development, the plans for Wildwater were sent to the Stonehaven Building Inspector, the Planning Board, the Conservation Committee, and the Board of Selectmen. Paul combed through it, marking all the problems he could see, in case the other boards missed any, and calling Rod when he needed an engineer's explanation.

The building inspector found that the architects had generally been meticulous in compliance. The Planning Committee also got a crack at them and made a list of variances needed. There were always variances needed for any construction in Stonehaven; in fact, there were fewer for Wildwater than most developments because of the ample open space and no current building. There were, however, two glaring problems.

One was the fake light house to be erected at one end of the hotel. It would soar 45 feet in the air and was to be the resort's identifying landmark, one that would appear as a logo on the Wildwater sign, letterheads, and promotional material; in fact, such a structure was Trimark's signature, Paul learned not a light house per se but a tall structure "in keeping with the surroundings." In Tucson it was a mission-style campanile; on Vancouver Island, it was a totem. The lighthouse designed for Wildwater was authentic in design.

The other and critical violation was that the roadway including the shoulder into the resort is twenty-seven feet narrower than required for a commercial establishment of its size. The roadway and shoulder would take up the entire isthmus connecting North Point to the mainland. While it was apparent that the cars and even a fire truck could come and go as well as anywhere in town, narrow as its roads were, the roadway did not meet the rules. While many, if not most, successful establishments were "non-compliant," grandfathered in, for them variances were routinely allowed so places of business that had been working for a hundred years might continue in such a way that profit was feasible. New construction was another matter.

The Board of Selectmen also considered the plan. They declared the water storage facilities were not adequate to supply Wildwater and the Town could not be expected to build sewers to the resort. If they had been able to afford sewers, they would have done so for their own residents. They suggested that Trimark would have to have its own sewage treatment plant. Rena drafted a letter to that effect addressed to Mr. Leland Johns, Trimark's executive vice president, who was in charge of the Wildwater project.

Paul signed them and shrugged. "The costs will be prohibitive. Plus there are impossible variances needed. And don't worry, the Conservation Committee will stomp Wildwater flat."

It seemed the spit was barely dry on the stamp, when Mr. Leland Johns was on the phone, cordial as a long-lost cousin. He wanted to talk.

Paul was up for it. Time to draw the line in the sand. Paul girded himself to meet the enemy like a knight riding to the edge of his fiefdom to meet the intruder at the border. And Rena would give him her scarf to wear into battle. No one had actually met the intruder before but his reputation has preceded him. Rena was curious about his face and his size and his manner as well as his facts. Paul was only worried about his power. Rena waited for his return on the castle walls.

"How did it go?" Rena began.

Paul shrugged. "Too soon to tell."

"Was he nice? Was he nasty?"

Paul shrugged again. "Oh, he was nice."

"Wonderful."

"Not wonderful. It was all part of the act. He pretended to listen. He kept saying he understood my concern. He was just trying to get me off my guard."

"What was he like?"

"A son of a bitch."

"How did you know he was a son of a bitch?"

"I just know."

"Well, what else did he say?" Rena wished she had been there. Men didn't seem to be able to report important details. Experiences seemed to bypass their language center, bouncing over whole chunks of brain, to some cerebral bottom line. Rena wanted it synapse by synapse and word for word.

"He said, 'No problem.'"

"Oh, Paul. Maybe there is no problem after all," Rena said. "Maybe this is not such a powerful threat."

"Oh, there's a problem. This Wildwater thing is a whole new town. With a hundred condos and two hundred hotel rooms and I forget how many townhomes, almost five hundred people when full; That's ten percent of our entire population, who care nothing about Stonehaven at all.

"It's bad enough that there are fewer of us each year who actually have roots on Cape Ann, but these people are not even the butcher, the baker, and the candlestick maker–real people– these are

180

tourists and we are Disney World attendants. And now it's not just in summer; it's all year round. What are we becoming?"

"So how did you leave it?"

"I don't know. I think maybe I convinced him it wasn't worth the fight. Only time will tell."

Over the next few days and under gentle prodding, details seeped out of Paul. The enemy was obnoxiously agreeable. He had offered to disguise a water tank. Trimark would build the sewer it needed at its own expense.

Paul had countered that you could not disguise a water tank by painting clouds on it and that the Conservation Committee would never allow excavation for a sewer pipe on the isthmus which was fragile enough as it was. Mr. Johns had promised, nonetheless, to make everything right.

It was several more days before Paul could bring himself to express the final indignity. They had offered him a lifetime parking pass at Wildwater and a slip for his sailing boat.

"As if I would move my boat from the Stonehaven Harbor, where my ancestors docked in 1672, to tie up at his plastic pier! And if I ever park my car on North Point while the smell of his carcass lingers, shoot me."

Rena stood back in fascination.

"Is that what you told him?"

"To that effect."

Well, now she understood that old line: he WAS cute when he was angry. Rena smiled.

He was soon to be even angrier. The very day after the closing of the sale to Trimark, a copy of a letter came over the FAX from the California firm headed "Re: Fishermen squatting on Trimark land." It included a plat of the land with a circle drawn by hand around the strip of land that curled from North Point around the Cove toward the litho factory. It showed little house symbols sitting on this land like the houses and hotels of a Monopoly game which were, coincidentally, almost exactly the architecture of the fisherman's shacks and market that lined the little harbor where the North Point Cove lobster fleet moored.

"In view of the non-contractual status" of the fishermen's

presence there, the letter said, Trimark had no individual to address and therefore had no choice but to make a public declaration that all use of that land and shore to the low tide mark would be subject to rents equal to $325 a month per user. Those seeking a lease agreement should contact Trimark at its Boston office.

Paul went through the roof. Then he called the Town attorney, Jim Cohen. Jim began looking into the matter of rights of long time users. Rockport had been doing the same to keep the Atlantic Path, which crossed private property along the ocean edge, open to hikers, picnickers and birdwatchers who had used the path for over fifty years. Information on the legal issues was just a phone call away. But the fishermen had already sent a letter to the *Gloucester Daily Times* signed only by "the Fishermen of North Point," declaring their rights as users for a hundred years. Their case was not identical to the Atlantic Path issue, for the fishermen of North Point were particular individuals not the public and they had built structures there and were running a thriving business in fishing and selling.

Rena called Rick Talbot to get the scoop on the more repeatable language from the fishermen's rally where the letter was read aloud. It was the first time Rena had actually initiated a call to Rick.

"We'll go to jail before we pay rent to those bottom-feeders," Rick told her. Rena tingled a bit at his bravado. It reminded her of way back when.

The Conservation Committee had several concerns about the Wildwater proposal, even though the DEP has passed on the environmental impact. The biggest problem was the roadway over the isthmus. The Committee was conservative as the name implied. Elaine Alpern, for instance, the previous winter had argued that the Town not be allowed to remove sand—three feet deep—from Bay Road which had washed up during a winter storm. The beach was, Elaine had said, a barrier beach and, sand thrown up by a storm was nature's way of bringing balance: protection along with destruction. The ocean was rising six inches every hundred years, Elaine pointed out, and the land was sinking and we should do nothing to hasten or impede the natural order. The people who lived on Bay Road eventually overruled Elaine so they could get their cars out of their garages and go to work.

The Conservation Committee, however, including Elaine Alpern, was annoyingly sanguine about the resort, saying there were problems but noting how cooperative and nice the Johns fellow was and how he was willing to work with them on the entrance. He had promised to preserve the isthmus, to make sure nothing Trimark did would hasten or slow the natural progress of nature. He hoped, they reported to Town Hall, that the Conservation Committee would support him in preserving the isthmus in its natural state so that he would not have to build any artificial superstructure to widen the road in.

"Seduction instead of rape," Paul scoffed. "The enemy does not want to confront, just weasel in. But we have our laws and town rule and there will be a confrontation. Just wait."

The election of November 1988 was a nonevent as usual. Paul had been a shoo-in since his second election. Paul only gave one speech, as was his tradition, at Legion Hall. Besides the usual pleasantries, he promised to fight the development. This was not the unanimous issue he once thought it was, and the response was divided. Basically, the Square crowd and the folks on The Lane applauded enthusiastically. They didn't want shops and restaurants at the resort to compete with theirs. Also, those who lived on Dory Beach and along the western end of Bay Road were concerned about increased traffic and a changing view of North Point across Boding Cove. Those who lived further from the proposed development and those who had service businesses kept their hands in their laps at Paul's call to arms. They all, nonetheless, gave him a warm round of applause at the end of the speech.

"I'll be reelected, of course," he told Rena, "but there's some apathy about fighting Trimark. I'll have to work on that."

The public hearing was early in December. Rena assumed she would now get to see the infamous Leland Johns, but when they had all assembled, some standing against the wall of Meeting Room A, the largest meeting room in Town Hall, she could not pick him out. "Which one is he?"

"He's not here, the coward. He's sent a representative."

First, a new spokesman for Trimark, a vice president of some sort, gave a nice little opening speech.

Then the California architect in a sea-green slubbed silk shirt rolled open sheets of plans for the project. Everything was outlined in great detail in azure on translucent paper. After offering a glimpse of the drawings, the architect gestured to an assistant and slides appeared on a screen on the back wall. An architect's drawing in color showed the inn buildings in shingles and granite with long driftwood-gray porches. Then a restaurant with outdoor tables and umbrellas by a quarry.

Actually, Rena thought, the place looked like the garden of Eden with hot showers. And just when she was thinking that, the architect said the new project reminded him of the old barn-like wooden hotels that used to stand sentinel on almost every point of the rocky coast and which had all burned decades ago. Wildwater would just replace those massive structures, the lawyer promised.

Boy, he had done his homework! He knew the right buttons to push. Rena looked at Paul, scowling with his fist against his mouth, and cringed because she remembered she had said the very same thing to him about replacing the old hotels. She hoped he didn't remember that. Rena actually had to work to harden her heart against the project by envisioning fat, middle-aged men in yacht captain hats strolling down the Atlantic Path from North Point to town, right in front of her house, and ladies in straw hats with cameras, asking "natives" to pose.

Then the Trimark people began to roll out the winter scenes: Slides showed interior shots of the lobby with ice skaters on the quarry gliding on the ice clearly visible through a glass wall. The vice president stepped in to say that they were in the process of negotiating an agreement with a celebrated figure skating coach to bring his Olympic hopefuls to train here. People could sit and watch the young skaters leap and glide and even fall–an insiders view of future medal winners. Guests of course could skate here when the ice was free. There would be ice shows and a snow queen. And there would be a Christmas ball and a New Year's Eve gala.

Well, she and Paul wouldn't be there, they would be cozy in their cottages treating carolers to hot chocolate in the weeks before Christmas, caroling in the Square on Christmas Eve, and having an intimate New Year's Eve party at Doug and Girard's Squirrel's Nest to which no one from Wildwater would ever be invited.

Then a lawyer in a crisp gray blazer, short black skirt and sheer smoke gray stockings stood up and talked of buffers and erosion control, hidden parking areas paved with a grid of alternating paving blocks and spaces where the grass could grow and water could seep in, and construction material that blended in with the rocky promontory.

When the presentation was all over, Rena felt discomforted by the realization that she had found herself momentarily attracted to the Wildwater project. She would, however, oppose it with every bone in her body for the good of Stonehaven.

The Planning Board was generally negative about the overall impact the development would have on Stonehaven but specifically they could not find much to quarrel with. One member who had moved to town only seven years before (from Texas) saw no problem at all. That was the trouble with these people who moved in; they're full of energy, they want to get involved, but they don't have the same perspective as those who were raised here. Only two out of the five members were originally Stonehaveners. The Board of Selectmen withheld signing off on the plan until the Board of Appeals would have dealt with the variances. The various boards had ninety days from the initial hearing to sign the Universal Permit necessary before building could start.

Early Christmas Eve, before she left for the caroling around the tree in Flakes Square, Rena got a call from Rick Talbot asking if he could take her to Doug and Girard's New Year's Eve party. It seemed silly—she'd see him there anyway and he had to backtrack to pick her up. She said, "Yes...if you want to come all the way over here..."

"It's less than three miles," he said.

They arrived together, shivering and stomping off the snow. Once inside, they were pulled apart by the greetings and beckoning of friends and hardly saw each other again.

The creativity of "the boys'" awed Rena again. The cheer of the guests enveloped her. Basking in the cradle of inclusion and the warmth of the wassail, Rena was perfectly content for hours. Finally, at midnight, Rick found her. His New Year's kiss was sweet and demure as last year and his was not the only kiss of which she partook.

"It doesn't get any better than this," she said to Rick, as they got in line for the serving of the wassail. "Those people over in Wildwater, if they ever get their New Years Eve ball, they'll look down on the twinkling town of Stonehaven and know they are really missing something."

"You'd enjoy gloating," Rick said. "but it'll never happen."

One day early in the New Year, Rena woke and looked out over a dark blue and lively sea; small choppy waves chased with silver from the oblique early light swept in with cheerful energy. But there was something very wrong! Cormorant Island was missing! It was gone. Not there. Not there at all. Erased. Rena was transfixed.

Many a morning she woke to find a fog bank had rolled in during the night and obliterated the island, merged with the water, dissolved the edges of her neighbors' rooftops, and blurred the pussy willows into ghosts lurking at the edge of her yard. Those were days that muted artists' palettes and spooked fishermen. But today was not one of those days. Today the air was clear; each pussy willow twig was sharp against the patches of snow. The houses at water's edge were crisp and clear; the waves were distinct and glittery. There seemed even to be a horizon in the distance where water met air but without a hint of land or a nub of light house. It was as if Rena's house had been lifted up during the night by a great flood and set down in a different place on the shore.

Rena settled on the edge of Aunt Amelia's high poster bed to watch. The silvered waves swept in, oblivious to the ghostly emptiness behind them. Rena never tired of watching waves, swelling here, waning there, catching up and joining, breaking up and disappearing, little waves skittering across bigger ones like playful babies on their mother's back. They came in and broke on the rocks in good humor, without fury; they slipped back without leaving a mark. Somewhere they rejoined the crowd and moved forward again.

Then, behind the panorama of waves, slowly, without motion, a thin dark line developed at the top of the sea. The line thickened. A

186

small stub appeared, visible only to the knowing eye. Then slowly, slowly, a slender tower grew upward from that small foundation. Finally the curtain was entirely lifted and Cormorant Island and lighthouse were unveiled.

Rena would tell no one but Paul about this. "The fog!" the Town Hall crew would blurt out, early in the story, trivializing the experience before she could communicate its magic. Only Paul would listen and comprehend the spirit of the thing.

She hoped he would be in early, but he wasn't, and about ten o'clock, Paul called to say he'd sprained his ankle early that morning and wouldn't be in at all.

"Oh, I'm sorry. Poor baby. Have you seen the doctor? Have you got crutches?"

Paul didn't answer.

"Does it hurt still? I have some Tylenol with codeine left over from when I had the cracked tooth. Codeine is magic. Paul?"

Paul grunted.

"Paul?"

"The worst thing..." His voice quavered.

"Paul! What's the matter?"

"The worst thing is how I fell.

"The ice on the pier. Every year I warn you..."

"No," he said, sighing at her guess, "I just sort of gave way. Rena, I didn't even know what muscle to move to hold myself up. It was weird. It was scary."

Rena held her breath for the rest.

"The doctor wants to do a brain scan."

Rena gasped.

"Just to rule out some things," Paul added.

"Rule out what things?" Rena said. "You mean he really thinks...."

"I don't know," he said cutting her off.

The next few weeks were a jumble, the neurologist in Gloucester, the specialist at the Leahy Clinic, the CAT scan and finally on a Sunday, Paul called her over to his house.

She stood on the doorstep, while the doorbell chimes played, examining the pattern of water stains on the shingles as if she had never seen a weathered shingle before, as if understanding the flow of water down walls and the pooling of drips around doorways would change something. And then Maureen was at the door. Rena looked at Maureen's face as if she'd never seen it before either, and she realized how little she knew Maureen, how really little. Rena hugged Maureen with no feeling and Maureen took her coat. Maureen rotely offered coffee and Rena declined.

Maureen waved her to the den where Rena could see the top of Paul's head over the back of his recliner. She knew he knew she was there but she stood a second trying to put off the moment.

"Paul?"

"Rena, come here."

She could see he was ready, not wanting to wait. She stood in front of him.

"It's a tumor, they said. Probably malignant. I won't tell you the odds that it's malignant. Odds are only odds. So it's surgery. And then....we'll see." The word *malignant* hit Rena like a giant breaker on the back of her neck. She was bowled over by its force, her face pushed down in a blinding turbulence, unable to breathe. As much as she had known of the facts of life, she still had not seen this coming.

When the force released her, sprawling but breathing again, she did not know where to focus, where to reach out her hand and touch. She held out her hand to Paul in his chair as if he were yards not inches away. Not to comfort him but to grasp him, to keep from being pulled back in the undertow. He took her hand and pulled her to him. She knelt by his chair, and they held each other. There was not a thought, not a single thought between them, only aching.

When at last they pulled apart and looked into each other's eyes, they both saw tears. Rena pulled herself together with conscious effort. She would be brave for him. Had to be.

And then Paul blindsided her. He did the one thing that would throw her off balance, strike her in a soft unprotected spot: He winked.

Rena threw herself sobbing onto Paul's knees.

For everyone concerned, it took weeks for the enormity of the diagnosis to break up into smaller, more manageable concerns.

It was clear Paul's strategy would be to move full steam ahead: surgery, radiation, chemo, whatever they said and with whatever time and energy he had left to continue moving through the boxes to his goal. Paul had never been an introspective person; he was a doer. It was his strength. Rena could not say the same for herself.

When Paul went into surgery at Massachusetts General in Boston, Rena went to work to keep things running but she got not one thing done. Phone calls from unknowing people only distressed her.

In the evening she got the word: The surgery, they said, seemed to have got the whole tumor. There was one spot they were not sure of, right on the edge where they couldn't cut any further. The radiation was for that. Soon after the surgery, Paul came home to recuperate. Rena, all the members of the board of selectmen, Tony, all traipsed over to Paul's house to help him continue working.

Gladys had said, "Why don't we just not mention Town business to the poor man."

"Paul lives for Town Business. Without Town business he'd really go bonkers," Tony said.

At Town Hall, Rena did everything dull that had to be done. The Selectmen held one Board Meeting without him. Lyndon Moore took charge, and they put off every vote Paul would have cared about. The one thing they did take to him was the idea of a granite festival to coincide with the groundbreaking for the Community Center. Paul would recruit a committee on the phone from his bed. That should be easy. Who could turn a sick man down?

In February, everything Paul had set into motion the previous year came to fruition. The financing of the Community Center went through, the bonds sold even faster than expected. That was as good a medicine as the doctor could have ordered for Paul. By the end of the month on an unusually mild day, Paul was back in his boat in spite of Maureen begging him not to. He insisted on doing it alone.

"What if you got faint? You could fall in the water!"

"No better way to go," Paul said.

No better way, but no one was ready for it to be anytime soon, so they all held their breath. Rena was relieved every morning when he showed up at Town Hall. Sometimes he asked a few questions and went home. Sometimes he worked till one or two, then went home for a late lunch, and napped in the afternoon. Sometimes he came around again in the late afternoon, stopping in at the store first. Sometimes he didn't.

Radiation followed Paul's surgery and several rounds of chemotherapy were to get any stray cancer cells. The treatments soon made his hair fall out. In fact, it was coming out in such hunks that Rena had to brush strands of it off letters she was sending out and check her coffee cup twice. She wished he'd get the shedding over with, and so she was both relieved and shocked when Paul said, "It's time for the buzz cut," and he headed over to Jimmy Herrick's barber shop.

"Come on over and watch," he called to Tony on his way out. To Rena's surprise, Tony grabbed his coat and went after Paul.

Afterwards, Paul took the rest of the day off, but Tony came back shaking his head in admiration.

"What a great attitude!" Tony said. "He was like the damn Pied Piper."

Paul had gathered people on the way the way to the barber, Tony reported. He'd waved to Charlie Bonneau in his store and Charlie came. He'd rapped on the window of the pharmacy and got one of the Horton brothers and even a customer to come.

"Word got around. There were eight or ten guys standing around laughing like it was their kid's first haircut," Tony said. "It was the funniest damn thing."

The next day, Paul came in the office slick as a butternut squash.

"I gave it the coup de grace. Good bye hair. Get used to it."

"Oh, Paul. It will come back."

"Maybe."

"Oh, it will. And anyway, you don't look so bad. Remember Yul Brynner? He was sexy."

When Rena closed her eyes and listened to Paul's voice, in her mind he still had hair. She wondered if it would grow back before she lost this picture altogether.

The next day Paul wore a hat to work. Not just any hat, but the Cape Ann Hat, the real Cape Ann hat, the hat of which Paul was apparently the world's only connoisseur. Paul came to work on the following day wearing the hat, and he didn't take it off. It had become a part of his head. It was hard for Rena to say if it was an improvement over the bald head, but it did keep his head warm. Its brim also did for his head what elephant ears do for elephants. It was hard to see Paul Lawson, hero, in the comic figure under the curled brim. He seemed an old man, his handsome features the same but harsher without the boyish wisps of hair on the brow. Every line seemed a ditch, the nose and ears seemed enormous.

But what could Rena say? Here was, she supposed, the Essential Paul, unadorned. In a sense, he was heroic. His motto: Don't hide, dramatize.

Each time Paul came in, Rena was eager for him to start talking. She would sit and listen to him until the old familiar voice transcended the new image. On February 20, two days after little P.S. turned four, Paul brought photos from the Quick Photo into Town Hall. There in living color was Paul in his hat beside P.S. and the birthday cake. The glare of the four candles lit up the brim of the hat like a halo. Then, in the next picture, there was P.S. with the hat on his head, pulling the brim down with his hands on both sides and laughing in full abandon. Rena wished the child could laugh like that forever, laugh right through the day that would come sooner or later when the jig was up.

At the end of March, Paul had another scan and the doctors reported nothing negative.

"They don't call it a cure," Maureen said. "They never call it a cure."

"Let's call it remission," Paul said. "Let's live on as if its going to be okay."

18

Groundbreaking

It was after the spring thaw, but there were delays, and they were not ready until summer was almost upon them. The heavy equipment coming and going from the site would be disruptive in the Square and would jeopardize the summer business upon which merchants there depended; so they decided to leave the heavy earthwork for the fall. Some thought the groundbreaking ceremony should proceed in the spring as planned, but Paul wanted the groundbreaking to be the real beginning, not just a symbol.

"I want to turn the first spadefuls," Paul said. "Then I want to see progress every day."

That decided it: Groundbreaking would be late in August. The main foundation work would be done in the warm weather of September, and the granite walls would be mortared on into October, when day time temperatures would often be above the required 40 degrees. Besides, breaking ground in late August allowed them time to plan The Granite Festival to coincide with the arrival of the first chunk of granite to start the foundation. This would be a way of whipping up community enthusiasm for the effort, making residents more tolerant of the annoyances of construction.

In March, the committee for the granite festival met in the Oddfellows Hall because Peter Burbank was on the committee and he had the key to the Hall. Rena attended because she had to be in on everything now, in Paul's place, just in case.

"This is why we need a community center, so we can have a place for a bunch of people to meet," someone said.

Peter pulled out two six packs of cold beer. "Here's a little inspiration to get the ideas flowing."

"Ask Paul, will we be able to have beer in the community center?" They chuckled.

"What we need more than a community center is a bar."

Groans rose from the committee. Stonehaven, like neighboring Rockport, was dry. No liquor, not even beer or wine, was sold in town and of course there were no bars. The urge to drink was satiated only by a determined drive down the back of the Cape to the package store in Gloucester. The towns had been dry since 1856 when Rockport's Hannah Jumper, at age seventy-five, led a barrel-smashing, bottle-breaking crusade of two hundred women to destroy every drop of alcohol within reach of their hard-drinking husbands, brothers, and sons. The hatchet-wielding fury of Mrs. Jumper and friends made a lasting impression on Rockporters and Stonehaveners alike.

The Granite Festival Committee was grateful for the brew imported from Gloucester and to whoever made the run to the package store. Brainstorming required priming. They popped open the tops of their beer cans and reached for the little bags of chips Rena tossed down the table. "So how do you have a granite festival?" someone began.

"The granite for the cornerstone comes down the chute or whatever–how does it come?"

"On a conveyor belt.

"Okay, people gather along the conveyor belt, applauding as the first block comes down. It gets loaded on the boat–what kind of a boat?"

"A barge."

"Okay, the barge is decorated. And all the boats from the harbor are out there to follow the granite from the wharf to the harbor landing."

"Good, good."

"That's it? That's the festival?"

"Well, okay, earlier in the day you have a fair—hot dogs, tonic, arts and crafts...."

"F'crissakes, Stonehaven is a goddam arts and crafts fair three hundred and sixty-five days a year."

"Okay, we have a parade from city hall to Granite Company wharf."

"What do you have in the parade?"

"Floats. A marching band. Miss Stonehaven."

"We don't have a Miss Stonehaven."

"Well, get one. The contest will be part of the buildup."

"We used to have a Labor Day parade, don't you remember, right down Main Street."

"Why don't we have it anymore?"

"We got too sophisticated."

"We got too sophisticated for a parade?"

"You had to see the parade."

"Just for starters, what would a Granite Festival parade have?"

"The Legion Band."

"Of course. But what can we do to make this parade different from all the others?"

"Yeah. Different from the Horribles parade and the Rockport Fourth of July parade."

"We could have an old-timey parade, everything the way it was back in the heyday of granite."

"Paul would like that."

"Yes. Have the first block of granite pulled from the harbor to the construction site in an old wagon by a big work horse."

"Where would we get a work horse?"

"Benny used to have a work horse to bring in his hay. Maybe that horse could pull the wagon."

"That horse'd be dead now. Horses only live about twenty years."

"People could dress in turn-of-the-century clothes or roaring twenties or whenever the hell we are talking about."

"Oh, yes! The museum has pictures of people all dressed up waiting for the trolley. We could look at their clothes."

"Trolley! We could have a trolley–no tracks, of course. We could get the one CATA has, put it in the parade."

"The museum in Gloucester has a real cart they used to haul granite in.

"No, no, no. It's got to be ours."

"Yeah, Stonehaven or nothing. I mean, can't we have a goddam parade without Gloucester?"

"Besides, the museum's cart is too valuable to loan out. But it would be simple to make a replica."

"Okay, okay. Now we're cooking. Rena, write this stuff down. What else?"

The committee was silent a few moments, thinking.

"So. We have a few ideas already, and we can have an old-timers' meeting or something to brainstorm."

"We could have a few old cars. John Rickover's 1929 Chevy, and I see an old Rolls around here a lot. Find out who owns it."

"It's summer people."

"No, no, no summer people."

"If we don't want Gloucester people, we sure don't want Worcester people and New York people, and...

"Where would we be without all those people?"

"We don't need 'em, not for this."

"Hey, hey, hey, guys. I have an idea. How about if we have the festival in September instead of August, right after Labor Day. How much difference could that make to the schedule? The weather's still good but the summer people have gone home."

"If any summer people are willing to stay or to come back for the festival, they qualify as Stonehaveners and we welcome them. Okay?"

"Okay."

In early April, Paul's monthly scan was clear. Paul had won

against overwhelming odds, an outcome Paul divulged only now that two consecutive scans had shown him cancer-free.

His new image of seaman in Cape Ann hat, which started out as a temporary response to the cancer treatment, began to take on a life of its own. Paul seemed older, starker, odder. His affinity for the land and sea and his penchant for the old ways were growing more and more apparent. He was going from town hero to town eccentric.

He exchanged his dress shirts and sports jackets for wrinkled work shirts that looked more as if they were recycled through the Salvation Army than ordered from L. L. Bean's. When his head began to sprout some fuzz, he invited Rena, Tony, and Gladys, and anyone else to feel the new fuzz and congratulate him. He soon realized he was also growing some new facial hair and he wasn't shaving it. He was getting positively grizzled.

The combination of the physical change and the intensified behavior—he was haunting the wharves now, chatting with kids about their catch, pulling in a line and throwing it out again—began to worry Rena a little. Not that his heightened determination and perseveration foretold anything specifically sinister, but his changing image required some change in Rena, and Rena didn't want to change.

"What do you think it is, Tony?" she asked.

It was Tony who had told her about Paul's hanging out at the wharves. He had cousins who were fishermen. They reported seeing Paul here and there, in odd places, looking for something.

"Captain Ahab, he is," Tony had said.

"What made you say that?"

"I don't know."

Tony was right. There was an Ahab-ness about Paul. A driven quality that did not seem quite as based in the here-and-now as Paul had always been.

On the subject of Paul, Ada said to Rena, "Don't you think there's a time in your life when you refocus yourself and let go of some stuff that used to seem important?"

"I don't know." Rena hadn't let much go lately that she could think of.

Ada continued, "Paul's got his personal life all taken care of. He's done what he has to do about his family, and he's concentrating on what's really important. Don't you think?"

"I don't know about his family..." Rena said. "What do you mean he's got his personal life all taken care of?"

"With Leslee finishing up college and Maria serious about a good guy—finally—he doesn't have to worry about anyone but Maureen and himself. When you get to that point, you look at life a bit differently."

Rena knew what Ada was talking about. Rena had been through all that with Ada—the year's separation from Phil and the wavering between wanting to be apart permanently and wanting to get back together. Rena had secretly wanted Ada to go on her own. Ada was spunky. Ada would start a new life, and it would be more satisfying than ever before. Rena could imagine Ada saying later that the split was the best thing that could have happened because it opened up new challenges which she had met, and by doing so, had reached a new level of happiness. Instead, a counselor had asked the couple to decide one thing: Did they have something between them that was worth saving or not? They decided they did, and they worked on their relationship, and they stayed together. It seemed to Rena they had not so much become happier with each other as they had accepted their level of happiness. They had settled.

"And have you found your real self?" Rena asked.

"I have a feeling of peace that I didn't have when I was younger. I look at things and judge them by how they fit my values now because I'm not busting my butt any more just to get by. I'm not rich, and I'm not famous, but I'm secure."

"What would you do if Trimark got to develop Wildwater and Trimark asked Felton's Interiors to decorate their lobby and all the rooms. That would change your life, wouldn't it?"

"It would never happen, first of all, but if it did, I would never touch it. I would never profit from Paul's failure. It's just a matter of solidarity among friends. That's what I mean by serving my values."

"I admire that," Rena said.

"You'd do the same," Ada said. "All of us who have been together as long as we have would feel the same. If Paul loses, you would never go to the resort to eat or take a favor from Trimark or whatever. None of us would."

The Board of Appeals had been studying the Trimark plan and the changes requested by the other boards. The Board of Appeals would take an official crack at it at the end of April.

Once you get by the Conservation Committee, the Board of Appeals is where the power is.

"And sons of bitches they can be, whether you agree or disagree with 'em," Paul said. (Clean-mouthed even in high school, Paul's new persona had begun to swear, not quite like a sailor, but a little saltier than before.)

"But you're so good with sons of bitches," Rena said. "I'm not worried."

Indeed, in the weeks leading up to the meeting Paul had tactfully but systematically sounded out each of the Board of Appeals' seven members to see which way they were inclined to vote.

First, he contacted Gil Gilaspie. You never knew which way Gil would go. The plumbing contractor, a Stonehaven High graduate, was traditional in some ways—he was an organic gardener, who had turned an old cobblestone quarry grout pile into a lush garden by plowing into the rocky land tons of compost, peat moss, and seaweed. He was also a boater and sometime fisherman. He lived in a nineteenth century home, but he had also built and erected geodesic domes in New Hampshire for a decade. He had a hippie bent that sometimes took a surprising turn. Paul didn't want any surprises this time.

So Paul had sorted it out with Gil ahead of time in the guise of a gardener's call—Rena had provided a handful of unusual miniature gladiola bulbs to take as an offering.

"Tell him to plant them right away. The tips are coming out. Not deep. Only an inch. Up against a wall or he'll have to stake them."

Gil was pleased with the bulbs. As for Trimark's plans, he said, "Someday something will be built on North Point. We know that. I say let someone build something there that is attractive and meets our requirements and be done with it or we will be fighting another industry or resort that isn't half as aesthetic as this one."

"So you're leaning towards allowing the development?"

"Trimark will make a blessing out of that narrow road, you wait and see," Gil said.

It seemed that Trimark had chosen, for a development outside of Denver, a piece of property with a steep ravine across it. Instead of overcoming the obstacle, they used it to guide the architecture. The resort buildings cascaded down the sides of the ravine. Gil Gilaspie had seen it himself.

Paul admitted to Rena he was impressed that Gil had looked into other developments of Trimark. It was a startlingly sensible way to come to a variance decision.

It turned out that Gil's daughter had been recently married in this Trimark resort in Colorado, and Gil had found it was the most pleasant place he'd ever been. The family had chosen the resort for its blend with nature, he said. They'd had a shaman bless the marriage, they had released doves, they had felt at one with nature, and it was a totally spiritual experience.

Paul knew better than to tamper with a spiritual experience.

"What were the chances," he said, his hands turned heavenward, "that a plumber from Stonehaven would have a daughter who would marry two thousand miles away in a resort in Colorado and that the same developer would just happen to want to build here? Why didn't she marry at home like everyone else?"

"Because she was marrying a Jew," Rena said, "and it got too complicated with the families and all. You know how..."

"It was a rhetorical question," Paul said.

Dick Turbidy was a second Board member that would likely vote for the variance.

"He'll vote his interests," Paul told Rena. Dick had moved here a decade ago from the Midwest and bought up property along Bay Road, scattered lots that were leased out. One was the property where Kirk's Auto Repair shop was built back into the hill on the inland side of the road, just a painted doorway and a couple of bays sticking out of a cliff of granite like the elf houses in Rena's childhood books or the mossed centerpieces at Doug and Girard's parties. Other properties were less distinguished but all were likely to rise in rental value because of the proximity of hundreds of hotel guests and condo residents.

"But that's not fair," Rena said. "Shouldn't Dick disqualify himself?"

Paul shrugged. "Dick's interests are just as valid as anyone else's. Everyone represents some interest or other. No, I'll have to think of something more important than lease income."

Not likely, Rena thought.

The third board member who was leaning toward supporting the variance was, to Rena's surprise, Alice Mahaffey. Alice was a housewife and Responsible Citizen. She was raising three kids, volunteered at the Library, worked on community affairs to keep neighborhoods good for families. Surely she should want to keep a resort out of Stonehaven. Paul assigned Rena to verify this supposition.

But Alice had seen the cars pass each other on the narrow North Point road in the demonstration Trimark had arranged. It didn't look hard to her. She didn't know why the ordinance required so much extra space anyway for such a short distance.

"Besides, they seem like nice people," Alice told Rena. "Why should we be more hostile to them than to Boogie Rilman, whose deck we allowed ten feet closer to his neighbor's line than permitted? Everyone likes Boogie so we voted yes for him, and now he sits and drinks beer in the very laps of the people next door. The Trimark resort isn't in anyone's lap. It's almost an island. It's not as if Trimark were refusing to devote more land to the road. There IS no more land."

Rena had nothing to say back. Alice was a very sensible person and exceptionally nice. All Rena could do was report back to Paul. Poor Paul. There was even worse news.

Leon Englebrook also planned to vote in favor of the variance. Leon was a crusty old lawyer who had spent thirty years litigating in the brass trimmed court rooms of Boston and who had semi-retired to his summer house in Stonehaven some fifteen years before. He was voting for the variance because, whether they liked it or not, the variance in question was the sort that had been allowed many times before in deference to the exigencies of the land and the difficulty of

200

doing any business following inlanders' rules on the ragged coast. Plus, Leon had just represented the Town in a horrific law suit which the town had lost, costing the town millions, to be paid by raising taxes. He could now see lawsuit written all over this impasse with Trimark.

"Costly if you win, and costly if you lose," Leon said. It could be easily demonstrated that the variances were denied not just because of the merits of the case but because of a general dislike for the personality of the project.

So that was four in favor of allowing the variance. A majority. There were also two firmly opposed.

Millicent Wright, an expert in seashells of the world, her septuagenarian skin weathered by the winds off the oceans of the world, was opposed to any development of the last wild headland in Stonehaven. She had long wanted the point to become a park, part of which would be a bird sanctuary and nesting grounds for a variety of seabirds whose tranquil habitats had all but disappeared. It was thought that Millicent would leave her considerable estate to that end so that the town could buy the point outright. But she was not dead yet, and previous inquiries had indicated the family who owned the point was not interested in selling anyway. But almost everything is for sale if the price is right and Trimark got the price right. Now the price was beyond even Millicent's means, dead or alive. But Millicent was enough of a conserver of every pebble of the sea coast that she would have opposed the granting of the variance if one sumac bush was moved or one bird rendered homeless. Her vote was certain.

Vincent "Sal" Salvatore was also opposed to granting the variances. He was raised a fisherman; he was still in the fish business as a broker, but he was out of his boat because his sacroiliac had gone bad. More than once he'd been seen walking home backwards, dragging his foot on the affected side; he hadn't been able to get aboard his boat. Sal said he'd rather stay out of the boat than skipper it as a cripple.

So he studied accounting and got into computers and was now a first rate businessman. But you can't get the sea out of the fisherman even though he loses his sea legs; Sal could be counted on to vote for the way of life that sustained his mother and father and brothers and now his nephews and their families. He would vote against allowing the variances because, apart from the merits of the case, he was against anyone who infringed on the fishermen's way of life.

"Well, there's two," Rena said cheerfully to Paul. Paul grumbled.

Four votes for the variance meant that, even if they won over the seventh, undecided vote, they'd lose. Rena had never seen Paul lose. She knew he'd think of something. He might lose a minor skirmish, but he'd win the war. Somehow.

Harriet Willingham was the undecided vote. She'd been a quiet housewife for forty-some years until two years before when her husband, a retired colonel, had died. Rena had known nothing of the Willinghams until she read the notice of the colonel's death in the *Gloucester Daily Times.* The obituary began: "Retired Army Colonel Harry Willingham despised double creases in his pants. In one of his final statements to his family, the colonel said, "If there are any double creases in my dress blues, I will get out of that coffin and haunt everyone." Rena, who was attracted to quirks wherever they might be found, was fascinated by a life from which this small detail was offered at the head of an obituary even before the man's World War II combat record and before his travels and civilian accomplishments. A bit of humor perhaps to open with? Perhaps, but the obituary went on to say that "Colonel Willingham's dedication to single creases made the dry cleaners a place for the children in the family to avoid." A son was quoted on the subject of the embarrassment over the constant wrangle with the cleaners. Three paragraphs altogether were devoted to the issue of creases which obviously loomed larger than one might guess in the life of the Willinghams.

Harriet Willingham had blossomed since the death of her husband. She went out into the community with the vigor of fresh troops. She'd volunteered for the beach cleanup and brought cole slaw to the workers' covered dish dinner; no small chore because the cabbage had not been bought pre-chopped. She had joined committees and written letters to the newspaper. She was a new woman. Rena figured Harriet would either make everyone toe the line as straight as her late husband's creases or she'd go around kicking the shins out of every rule she encountered. Rena had suggested her for the Board of Appeals just to see which.

It turned out, somewhat to Rena's disappointment, that Harriet Willingham went to neither extreme but was fair and reasonable. She often had more facts than anyone else and less bias. She was pragmatic, low-key and affable. Harriet dismissed all the peripheral reasons on both sides of the Wildwater issue and declared she would look at the law and at the variances and base her vote strictly on these.

"If you pressure the other sons of bitches, they just get more stubborn," Paul noted. "But Harriet will be influenced by reasonable arguments."

So there was nothing left to do but marshal these.

Paul studied the Trimark plans and made an ever-growing list of the sins of the development. He made calls to experts. He disseminated his findings almost daily. However, he could detect no headway. Indeed there was none.

The vote had been held on a day Paul had spent with his second family. "Call me if anything unexpected happens," he had told Rena.

When the vote was in, Harriet had swung to Paul's side and voted for denying the variances, but that made it three against granting the variances and four for allowing them. Rena didn't call Paul.

The next morning when Paul came in, he shrugged and said simply, "Plan B."

Rena knew that would be a Town Meeting, which could be called, but rarely was—only once in her memory—to override the decision of the Board of Appeals. The calling of the Town Meeting required only the signatures of twenty voters. Rena had a list of people she regularly called to make motions and second them, and so she got on the phone. The petition was soon complete, and the special Town Meeting was scheduled for the second Tuesday in May.

In the meantime, the effort by Trimark to collect rent from the fishermen on North Point was gaining a head of steam. The development company, having failed to come to an agreement with any of the fishermen, chained and padlocked the entrance to the harborside road one night at the end of April. Rick Talbot reportedly was the first man to arrive the next morning. He parked his truck on the shoulder, stepped over the chain and went about his business in his boat. Others followed and soon there was a jam of cars and trucks at the gate. The police were called to manage traffic through the bottleneck. Chief Giordano called in to Town Hall to ask Paul if they should tow the cars that were clearly parked in violation.

Rena could hear Paul's voice rising on the phone in the next room. She got up to see what was the matter. When he told her, she saw his eyes darting around the room. Though he slid his desk drawer shut and picked up his keys with the usual motions, his body was stiffened against pent up adrenaline. She followed him down the hall.

"Don't come," he told her.

She waited until he was out the front door before she gathered her things. He was going to do something rash. He could get into trouble. She wanted to be with him. There was no question of her obeying him.

By the time she got to the scene, the traffic was too backed up along Bay Road for her to get through. She parked it in a NO PARKING AT ANY TIME zone and hurried through the crowd.

When she got near the gate to the harbor, she could not get through the people. She could hear shouts and then a loud chopping noise.

"What's happening? What's happening?" she asked taller people.

A young man standing on a post said, "Paul Lawson is breaking off the padlock with a rock. He's pounding the hell out of it."

The banging noise stopped, there were cheers and then the crowd pressed forward and swept through the gate. She could see Paul striding up ahead of the crowd hurrying to the fish market. She hurried to catch him.

Behind her now there was some commotion. Apparently someone from Trimark had arrived and was calling to the police,

"Arrest these people. They're trespassing." And then, "Do your duty. These people are breaking the law." And then, "Who broke this padlock? This is vandalism."

Rena reached the market, a white board and batten building. It was padlocked, too. Paul was calling for another rock. His wild eyes and red face frightened Rena. Rick ran up with a hammer from his shed, pushed past Paul, and started flailing at the lock.

Then there were calls of "Coast Guard! Coast Guard!" They all looked out into the harbor and saw a Coast Guard cutter sliding into the harbor, frothing behind.

Rena ran to the edge of the pier; the sun glistened off the quartz in the granite. She shielded her eyes against the sun to watch the man from Trimark and another man go down to meet the boat. One offered papers to the officer in charge of the cutter. There was pointing and staring on the dock. The crowd by the market stared back, and the pounding on the padlock beat faster. Then the Coast Guard officer and a sailor came up to the market. Someone with a video camera had arrived, and a reporter started asking questions, which the officers ignored. They seemed to agree to clear the area and started herding the people back down the harbor lane.

"Let's all go home now," an officer called out. "This is something for the lawyers to solve." Most of the people moved back as the officers approached, arms outstretched. Paul stood by Rick who was breaking the lock, giving him the support of his presence, until the job was done.

Zach Harris came up to Paul. "They have a court order...they must have expected this.... we really do need to clear out, don't we..."

Then the Coast Guard officer turned to the fishermen. "This court order seems to be proper. This is private property, and you'll have to leave." The fishermen shuffled and muttered to each other. Then, instead of walking to the road toward their vehicles, they headed as a group to the water and scuttered into their boats. Motors started, engines hummed, outboards putted, and all the craft in the harbor turned to the ocean. The whole North Point Cove fleet gathered at the mouth of the harbor, and, merging like a marching band, they filed through the mouth of the harbor single file. The crowd looked after them silently while the American flag on the pier snapped in the wind.

Sal Salvatore limped up to Paul, "I'm staying here to see they don't take the fish from the locker."

Paul nodded and looked up at Rena, seeming to see her for the first time.

"I thought you were going to stay at Town Hall," Paul said sharply.

"It's a free country," she shrugged, and then, reflecting on the fact that he was, after all, her boss, she added, "I get a coffee break like everyone else."

Paul quickly began to play the struggle out in a different theater. He spent the afternoon on the phone with lawyers and agencies trying to get a strategy to establish the fishermen's rights to their traditional toehold at the edge the harbor.

By late afternoon, word came that Trimark was not going to let the fishermen land with their catch or use the fish houses and market. While people were milling around the harbor, customers were not; the market was locked up with a new padlock. Trimark representatives turned away boats from the pier. While they still could tie up in the harbor at their moorings, Trimark security men would not let them unload their catch. Boats circled; radios crackled; arrangements were made; blood boiled.

That day the fishermen scrambled to other harbors and sold fish to dealers in Gloucester. Some went all the way to the markets in Boston. Some hired trucks. Some unloaded their catch in dangerous rocky places where their wives had brought trucks to public landings or where friendly people offered docks.

The press came from Boston to record the efforts. Townspeople came down to watch. People offered help. Efforts on the fishermen's behalf took on a heroic cast like the escape from Dunkirk or the Berlin airlift. The people of Stonehaven did their ancestors proud.

As the weeks went by, however, the effort grew more difficult. The fishermen were losing money because the impractical methods of moving and marketing were costly. The public began to lose interest. The docking on public beaches and hauling of fish across residents' front yards became a nuisance. Everyone was tired of it. The Town quickly established that the right of public access to the water was there, because of the history, but the right of individuals to use the buildings on the land was another matter. Legal measures were slow in coming to fruition, if indeed there was any basis for success, but a legal fund was established and an official organization of fishermen was formed. Fishermen's groups from towns for miles around sent contributions. Rick Talbot organized a fundraising dory race. Rowing teams from New Hampshire and Maine as well as Massachusetts were recruited.

Trimark began to catch on to the power of sentiment and announced in early May that when the universal permit was granted for the building of Wildwater, the rim of land that supported the harbor would be opened free to the fishermen who had moorings there, and the market and shacks would be an integral part of the Wildwater experience. In truth, the quaintness of the harbor would be a major attraction for the resort, but business there was not of any value to Trimark until and unless the resort was permitted.

Trimark apparently counted on this promise to help get the permit. Paul counted otherwise.

"If we can defeat the resort," Paul figured, "the land will be put up for sale. The price will go down because of the limitations on building. A new owner will see the necessity for accommodating the fishermen. Or, better still, the fishermen or the town or somebody will be able to buy the harbor from them at a reasonable price and settle this matter forever. We just have to have the determination to do the project." The town supported the lobstermen but how to act on their behalf was open to debate. The Town Meeting, now called The Trimark Meeting, was fast approaching. Paul began to talk less and brood more. He was out a lot and no one knew where he was. He didn't want to discuss his plans, not even to Rena, whose main source of information began to be Rick Talbot.

The fishermen were forming the North Point Fishermen's Collective, a collective like the ones the lobstermen had in Maine, for the day when their market reopened. Even now they were cooperating to bring their catch to market. They were scheduling loading teams and sharing truck rentals. They rented a space where the minerals and shells shop had been the previous summer. There they began to sell lobsters to tourists to make up for their loss of direct sales on the Cove. They were becoming more savvy. In another effort to mollify the Town, Trimark announced shortly before the Town Meeting that they were going to present even more changes designed to meet the citizen's wishes. These were not yet revealed.

"They think curiosity might bring out more voters," Paul said. A large turnout generally favored the opposition because people would come whom Paul could not have personally contacted.

The Town Meeting was held at the high school in anticipation of a crowd of a thousand. Paul and Rena went early. They parked by the main door as usual right next to the principal's space. Paul opened the trunk of the Town car and took out a Styrofoam ice chest on which he balanced his brief case. Rena went ahead to unlock the door. She held the door open for Paul with her foot. He braced his back against the door and let it creak shut plaintively behind him.

"What's in the ice chest?" said Rena.

"The booze."

"At a Town Meeting!"

"For the celebration afterwards."

"You really think there's going to be a celebration?"

"SOME body's going to celebrate."

Rena shrugged and held open the door to the auditorium.

Paul set the ice chest down by the podium and mounted the wooden steps onto the stage. He disappeared behind the curtain and began playing with the light panel.

He found the house lights, the down front lights, the upstage lights, and the apron spots.

"Wish they had all those things when we were in high school," Rena said. She could have used some drama back in those days.

Paul dimmed the lights slowly and then brought them back up, dimmed them again and brought them up.

"Here, you try it."

"Okay. Don't mind if I do."

Rena tried each of the knobs and several speeds and she noted

208

how the shade of the red carpet changed as the light went down slowly as if she were adding black paint to red paint little by little to bring the brightness down.

"Neat," she said.

"Now I'm leaving," said Paul.

"Leaving?"

"Just for now. I'll be back. When I do come, I want you to be standing behind the curtain."

"Behind the curtain! I want to be up front basking in the light of your glory."

Paul didn't grin as she'd expected.

"Stand behind the curtain by the light control panel and watch me. When I give you the signal, slowly, sl-o-w-ly, dim the lights till they are off and only the light on the podium remains." He flicked the podium light on and off.

"Off. Okay. What is the signal? How will I know?"

"You will know."

"I'd feel better, Paul, if you'd tell me the signal."

"You'll know."

Rena rolled her eyes. Smug he was. It would serve him right if she didn't recognize the signal.

"Trust me."

Paul knew those were magic words. Rena trusted him.

The big meeting convened. Where was the villain, Mr. Leland Johns, this time? From behind stage, through the crack at the edge of the curtain, Rena sized up the crisp suited Trimark representatives at the square table to the left of the podium. She noted Mr. Weiss, the flunky who had been on North Point Cove pier the day of the lockout, and beside him the woman attorney. But again the archvillain was not present.

To Rena's astonishment, Lyndon Moore, who was designated to preside in Paul's place when Paul could not be present, took the podium. He must have been forewarned. She was miffed that Paul must have told Lyndon the plan, and she wanted to rush down and ask him what was going on. It couldn't be done without making a grand entrance on stage and a dramatic scene in front of an audience of hundreds. Besides, grave concern pushed aside her own disappointment. She was panicked that Paul had given up so much power by letting Lyndon preside.

Lyndon, acting as chair, called the meeting to order. In the driest voice possible and the dullest words, he gave a summary of the project, noting that the plans had been revised according to the demands of the various boards and the Board of Appeals had subsequently voted for approval of the permit. The Town Meeting had been called to consider reversing that decision based on only two areas of nonconformity. On these two matters, the citizens were going to decide whether or not to nix the project.

Trimark was allowed to show their new modifications to the plan. The first was represented by a large architect's rendering of the forty-five-foot high structure, not merely a corporate landmark, but a water tank whose exterior would closely resemble a light house. It would hold aloft a steady beacon light, but without the brightness of a true coastal sentinel. In addition, and here was a new wrinkle, it would hold the 450,000 gallons of water necessary to serve the entire resort without stressing the Town's precarious water storage. This was a major item for the town. But Rena was dismayed. Except for its shorter stature, this pseudo-light house cum water tank appeared like an authentic light house in every way, the more to displease her, for it trivialized the genuine light house which greeted her from Cormorant Island every clear morning, that had, for over a century, greeted and warned away sailors from the treacherous rocks where the Atlantic Ocean poured into the great Ipswitch Bay.

Rena wanted to leap from behind the curtain to protest, but fortunately her sentiments seemed adequately expressed by the murmurs of disapproval from the crowd.

Lyndon invited a motion and Charlie Bonneau rose to make the motion to overturn the Board of Appeals' earlier decision. John Henry seconded the motion as planned.

Lyndon called for discussion and recognized people with no observable bias. Solly Bryson said that while he did not find a bare water tank acceptable, he was utterly opposed to a fake lighthouse as a disguise. They would no more countenance a fake lighthouse on North Point than "an inflatable rubber whale in the harbor."

Lyndon recognized Gil Gilaspie who, to Rena's surprise,

favored allowing the fake light house.

"The citizens of Paris opposed the Eiffel Tower saying it was an eyesore," Gil observed.

Gil's flippant explanation boded poorly for the outcome. In fact, the lighthouse water tank was denied but by too close a margin for the comfort of some.

Before moving on to the second variance request, the final vote that stood between the Town and Trimark, Mr. Weiss gave a gracious little speech about cooperation and wanting to be part of the Stonehaven community.

"We appreciate your concerns about the lighthouse, and we accept your wishes," he said. In fact, Mr. Johns, the project manager for Wildwater as well as executive vice president of Trimark, would soon be, Mr. Weiss said, talking to the engineers about the possibility of using a quarry for storage as an alternative.

"Now that we have clearly heard the wishes of the Board, we will move to develop this quarry."

The speech was so ingratiating, so benign, it was as if the developers never expected to win the lighthouse vote. Maybe it was just a straw light house they planned to be knocked down so the Town would win something and feel victorious and less hell-bent to win the next vote. Rena turned instinctively to tell Paul this little insight before she remembered he was not by her side. She was behind a curtain, and he was nowhere in sight. Rena's muscles were tightening all over her body. She could feel a pain beginning in her neck. Would Paul come in time? Surely he would come and save this vote.

Next, Lyndon read the request for a variance on the width of the roadway. Trimark was asking to build its entrance roadway over the existing road on the narrow peninsula which was twenty-one feet narrower than the ordinance required for public establishments with more than twenty parking spaces.

Billy Elmore beat Charlie Bonneau to making the motion to deny the variance. Good old Billy. So Charlie was the second. And the discussion began.

The chair asked Rob Rollins to report on the public inspection. Since the first public hearing, the owners of property abutting the property at the point of entrance and other concerned citizens had inspected the site at Trimark's invitation. The situation was pretty much cut and dried, Rob said. Clearly the road to North Point was too narrow to meet the regulations. Clearly, also, cars could enter and leave at the same time with ease and comfort. These were just the facts.

But there had been more than just facts. Rena had been at the public inspection when it had broken into whispered reminiscences. A woman wearing a bandanna agreed; there had been no need for wide shoulders, curbs and gutters, she said, when carloads of picnickers and birdwatchers rolled easily onto North Point on mild weekends. Voices lowered as others recalled among themselves their teen years when they rumbled their hotrods through the stone gate laden with blankets and booze and carnal thoughts. The road had not been too narrow then. Then a wave of sadness had run over the group, as they realized their memories, these very memories that denied the need for a wider road, would ultimately promote the destruction of wild bushes, the obliteration of century old footpaths, and the defacing of bald rock. Mr. Weiss took the floor. A resort such as Wildwater, Mr. Weiss pointed out, did not have a rush hour. Traffic would be steady and light throughout the day. Fire trucks could negotiate the road as had been demonstrated in 1980 when the original inn went up in flames.

"Many of you remember," he said, holding up a giant photo of the old Hesperus Inn taken from the water with a bit of the narrow road showing. Rena recognized the photo from the collection at the little Hambidge Museum on Everett Street. Again, these guys had done their homework. Paul would have been impressed if he had not been so at odds with their intent—and if he were only here.

Mr. Weiss further offered that Trimark was willing to build, at considerable expense, an attractive granite bridge along the isthmus to widen the roadway to the required width, but, he reminded them, the Conservation Board did not want a new structure there and Trimark, like the Conservation Commission, wanted above all to retain intact the isthmus, the awesome natural feature that no engineer could rival.

Trimark struck a note of agreement here: building up the

isthmus to widen the road meant defying God and the tides and would require substantial structural engineering that would deface the natural spectacle worse than anything else Trimark had proposed.

Trimark was willing, Mr. Weiss declared, his voice soaring, followed by a silence that hung like fog. He was willing to do whatever the people wanted. In the hush that followed, his voice dropped low to add "except give up the resort."

This vote WAS the resort. It all boiled down to this. No one had to remind them.

And so, after a few cursory questions about the road itself, the public discussion turned to the merits of the resort in general.

Ray Wheatley talked about property tax increases, citing an area near Marblehead which was ruined by the development of a resort. Taxes had risen so that local people could not afford to live in houses their grandfathers had built. Rena was moved by this argument. People like her were going to be taxed out of their comfortable gray shingle houses which would be bought up by couples from Manhattan who thought the taxes were peanuts and would neglect to prune the lilacs or lime the hydrangeas, and let the tuberous rooted begonias in the front flower pots freeze to death.

Bob Turamina expressed the opinion that the property taxes Wildwater resort would be required to pay would be so great, tax rates for the rest of the town might actually decline as a result. People who lived and visited resorts like Wildwater, he reminded them, rarely send children to school locally or require public assistance or other town services in proportion to the taxes their property pays.

Leon stood to remind the assembly that while the whole resort might ride on the issue of the variance, they were to confine their discussion to the merits of the variance request.

But the citizens had done all they wanted with the subject of the entrance road.

"If there's no more discussion,..." Lyndon began.

Then Rick Talbot stood up, now the established leader of the lobstermen as well as Rena's attentive friend. Lyndon acknowledged Rick who shuffled his feet and cleared his throat, then spoke.

"Stonehaven is a fishing town, a lobster town. It's true we've overfished. There's not so many of us now whose living depends entirely on lobsters. But the character of our town depends on lobsters. If we have a thousand more live-in tourists lining the docks, we'll be living on a movie set."

Not really a metaphor, Rena noted; three movies already had been filmed in Stonehaven harbor, though not so identified. But good for Rick, speaking up like that.

"Are we going through the motions for the tourists, cartoons of our former selves....or are we true lobstermen making a living from the sea? Better the land be used, if it must be used, as a fishing science research company or a marine equipment industry. Something real."

Jimmy Herrick stood up. His family had been lobstermen, but he now made a good enough living in his barber shop.

"What you forget," Jimmy said, "is that we are already a fake lobstering town. We were once a true lobstering town, like Rick says, but when mechanization came we didn't go for it. When the big companies came calling, we wouldn't sign up. Why not, if we are a lobstering town? Because we already knew we're a tourist town, no longer a working lobsterman's town. We are running our lives for the tourists. We hide our plastic pots and mend our wooden ones for show, we have filled our old grog shop with souvenirs. We are faking the whole damn thing. Fake, fake, fake," he cried out, his hair sliding into his eyes.

Everyone in the room who was not already glued to his face turned to the voice of the man crying "Fake." Rena would never have believed the affable barber had such latent passion.

"I'm not fake," Rick cried at the realtor. "You may be fake...."

"You say "Fake", Mr. Herrick," said Tom Holmes, rising. "Maybe, maybe not. But before we stop Wildwater, we might ask ourselves who are we really–in today's world? Maybe it's time to realize we are a resort, we are not a fishing village. We haven't been for thirty years. We have great summer weather, an historic port, magnificent views. Maybe we should just have a modern hotel complex, build a convention center and forget the lobsters. FORGET THE LOBSTERS!" He wiped the air with his arm and sat down.

They were past the roadway, long past the variances. They were asking the basic question about the nature of progress. The unanswerable question with a thousand momentary answers, sharp clear answers at first, soon blurred beyond comprehension.

The underlying question swept over Rena, and it seemed the question of her life that she had not even asked for a long, long time since she had first found it uncomfortable. She broke out in sweat. She leaned against the back wall for support. She took a deep breath and counted backwards from ten to calm herself. Where was Paul when she needed him?

Then they saw him, gaunt and strange under the brim of the Cape Ann hat, a figure out of the darkest waterfront where Captain Ahab had ever signed on seamen. Out of nowhere–could he have been standing behind the flag?–Paul quietly glided up to the front. Lyndon faded to the side. Paul stood at the podium not saying anything, breathing audibly into the microphone, drawing his arrival out into palpable suspense.

"You kept a few pots when you were a boy, Ned," he finally said in a surprising relaxed, gentle way.

Ned Wilson nodded.

"How many lobsters did you take in a week?"

"Dozens. Sometimes two to a trap. They were fighting to get in. All summer."

"Sal?" Sal nodded, burly arms folded over his belly. Paul waited till he answered. "Same. Twenty, thirty a week."

"How big were yours, Zach?

"They were big. Didn't much have to take the measure of 'em."

"How many were too small to keep?"

"Not many."

Paul was quiet then, looked in the eye of each citizen in turn.

He turned to the row of Selectmen seated at their table beside him and included them with his eye. "When we were boys, lobsters were big. They were plentiful." Paul paused again, looking out over the audience in reverie. "When we were boys, we got up in the grayness of dawn."

Paul lifted his hand like a preacher. Rena knew this was the moment. She slowly dimmed the house lights, imperceptibly till only the reading light of the podium illuminated Paul's face. All Rena saw was the Cape Ann Hat back lighted, but she knew what the others saw: the hat brim like a bright circle over his ruddy face, his eyes gleaming.

"When light came early in the morning and shadows hugged you like your mother, when the chill of the air was sharp and silent, you went down to the wharf and slipped into your skiff. The slap of the waves, the sound of the lines flapping against wood, the jingle of fittings, the creak of the oarlocks as you pulled: these sounds were sharp and solid and certain. And your lobster boat tugged at its mooring."

Rena was mesmerized. Paul was not just sketching a scene, he was slathering the paint on with a palette knife.

"The way the motor caught, the way it chattered, the way it hummed when you picked up speed, you knew that motor like you now know your baby's cry. You turned the bow just so, you lined her up with the light at the end of the breakwater. You took her out with care. You could have taken her out with your eyes closed.... Couldn't you?"

He looked some of the men in the eye and some of their lips curled up in involuntary smiles.

"When you broke through the mouth of the harbor and opened the throttle.... Was there ever a day the bow lifting to the open ocean didn't give you joy?"

The crowd was silent. Paul looked them all, it seemed, in the eye, scanning the room from one side to the other. As he turned, Rena saw his face now beatific in a halo of light and realized she was seeing an orator, a poet even. She was seeing a future governor of the Commonwealth of Massachusetts.

"Then you caught sight of your first buoy, picked out that red stripe or that orange stripe or that blue stripe," Paul glanced at Rick and Tony and Raymond as he mentioned their principal colors. "You cut the engine back, circled the buoy, caught it with your hook. And you knew, KNEW, there was a lobster down there. You pulled up the line, hand over hand as our fathers and their fathers did."

216

Paul pulled at an imaginary line, leaning back against imaginary resistance. He pulled Rena in, pulled them all in.

"When the pot came up and the water poured out....." Paul reached dramatically down to his side as if to haul up the pot over the gunwale. "You could see him, green and mottled, he was big, proud and feisty..."

A shadow began to creep across the room, like an eclipse of the moon, first unnoticeable, then unmistakable.

"You pulled the lobster out with your hand behind his head. The claws were snapping at you and the tail flapping as he fought."

A dark shadow swept around the room like a claw pulling everyone into darkness. The people ducked as the shadow raced around their heads, enveloping them. And then in the aura of the reading light they saw the source of the shadow. In Paul's hand, flapping and clawing, was the grandfather of all lobsters. Gargantuan, primeval, surreal. Dripping, splattering, opening and closing its claws so the lamp light flashed through intermittently like the beacon light on Cormorant Island.

"Gawd," the crowd said collectively.

"Look! Because this may be the last time you see a real lobster brought in to North Point Cove. Watch him move because it may be your last chance to look a local catch in the eye."

The lobster's eyes rotated on stalks and all human eyes were on them.

"Oh, we'll have lobster to eat. More than ever. At Wildwater. They will bring them in here from Maine in big trucks. Bulk rates. They won't fool around with our small independent lobstermen."

Paul slung the lobster out on the table, slid him down the teakwood runway, scattering papers, spraying the Board of Selectmen with the cold waters of the Ipswitch Bay. The lobster deftly seized and crumpled a page of the Agenda. It snapped its claws around a microphone and its crustacean grasp was transformed into a grating sound that pinched the soul. People in the back of the room pushed forward to see it. Bigger than their lobster kettles at home, bigger than the wash tub.

"Big, yes, big," said Paul. "Like the ones you saw when you were a kid. The one you kept in a tub outside your back door for

217

your friends to admire? Kept it a few days before you sold it for money for a new bike tire, money for the prom.

"Those days are over. Soon, when our boys wake up to a gray dawn, they'll pull on their jeans, but not to rush down to the harbor and unloose their skiffs. Not to go to sea because its in their blood. They'll be going instead to Wildwater Resort." He paused and the subject at hand was recalled with an almost audible scraping and rearrangement of images in their brains.

"The resort will give our boys and girls other jobs...waiting tables, making beds, selling souvenirs.

"Our children will like those jobs at the hotel. They'll like the California pay and the 15% tips. But one day they'll wake to a gray dawn and hear the call of the sea and they'll turn away because Stonehaven will be just another town like all the other towns which have forgotten who they are.

"This lobster here we'll eat." The lobster squirmed in slow motion in Paul's hand. "Suck his claws, dip his tail meat in butter. Because there's no use in throwing him back for sentiment's sake. For we will no longer be a lobsterman's town; we'll no longer be a fishing town. We'll be a Disney World town, a luxury resort. Oh, yes, there will be a little show held twice daily at the harbor amphitheater where a replica lobster boat will be open for tours." There was a long silence before the wheezing of the lobster was audible. "Think what you're doing." He put the lobster down.

There was silence. The lobster clambered around the notebook of Minutes and was headed into Millicent's lap. Sal grasped the crustacean behind its head and held it up, but it wrested itself loose and fell to the table again amid gasps. Then Paul leapt to the top of the table, agile as a boy doing a lay-up.

Rena was inspired. She flicked on the spotlight and encircled Paul with it. This was bolder by far than the time Paul had organized the "Keep Stonehaven Free" parade to save the high school from closing, more powerful than any of his campaigns for office, more wonderful than when he had addressed the Cape Ann Task Force and was drafted immediately to be its first chairman. More intense than his fight against cancer. Crazier than Ahab.

Towering over the Board members, Paul made them flinch as

he suddenly swooped down to the table top as if stealing a basketball on the dribble, then scooped the lobster up in his hand, leapt off the table. "Now let them vote! Vote YES to deny the destruction of our way of life."

Lyndon appeared at the podium calling out, "All in favor, rise."

Rena reached for the light switch and brought up the house lights. The people stirred and looked around as if they were in a movie house and the movie just ended. They stood up in large numbers and Lyndon and the other Selectmen took sections and counted. They conferred briefly about the numbers while the crowd sat again.

"All opposed to the denial of the variances, please rise."

Some rose and were counted, but it was clear the motion had carried. "The ayes have it. The motion to overturn the decision of the Board of Appeals has carried."

The people rose and shuffled their feet, looking to catch another's eye. Gradually they turned to one another, and their opening murmur exploded into loud rehashing and congratulation.

The developers grimly gathered their portfolios and charts and skulked out. A *Gloucester Daily Times* reporter caught Paul. The other Board members gathered their papers and slipped into the crowd.

Leon put both hands on the Selectmen's table and shook his head. "It's gonna cost," he said.

Rena waited for Paul to get free. It took a long time for the reporter to let him go, longer for the crowd to let him go.

And when the last of them were straggling to the door, Rena said to Paul, "Can we go somewhere to celebrate? You've got the booze." She gestured to the ice cooler.

Paul looked at the cooler and back at her. Then Rena realized it was not for booze, was never for booze. It was for the lobster.

"Oh," she said, wiping her mistake from the air with her hand. "Can we celebrate anyway? I have some champagne at home in the fridge. I keep it for just such an occasion. Maybe you and Maureen..." She looked around, realizing for the first time Maureen wasn't there.

"No," said Paul. "And speaking of Maureen, could you call her and tell her everything went well and I'm going to Gloucester to have a few drinks with the guys to celebrate."

"Oh, then I can go, too."

"No, 'fraid not. Just guys."

Rena scowled. Paul put his hand on her shoulder and lowered his head close to hers.

"Karen's expecting me."

Paul turned to leave.

Rena said aloud, "Well, so much for the champagne." But nobody heard.

19

P.S. I Love You

Rena's garden seemed particularly bright and dense that summer. The poppies and portulacas played raucously over the rock garden. The petunias exploded out of their pots and the zinnias branched enthusiastically. Nasturtium leaves bobbed over orange and yellow blossoms like parasols over geisha girls. Only Aunt Amelia's perennial baby's breath, pink roses and slender stalks of coral bells maintained their bridal dignity for the silver bowl on the dining table.

The bus tours appreciated the splendor, pausing in front of Rena's house by the front flower beds as well as at her back alley where the bus stopped to give a side view of the part of the structure that was The Oldest House. She could see them peering down the alley, too, wondering what was behind the gray fence of tightly packed saplings. Only tendrils of escaping clematis hinted at lush gardens within, where in fact the garage opened, the lawnmower was stored, and the garbage cans stood.

Rena bought a green garbage can to serve as a rain barrel and placed it under her downspout in the back. She'd save the water for when there would be a watering ban later in the summer. Between her own pleasure and the bus tours, she needed to keep the garden at its peak as long as possible.

In June, Leslee graduated from college with much family fanfare. "She asked me not to wear my Cape Ann hat to the ceremony," Paul said.

"That's reasonable," Rena said. Paul's hair had grown back.

"And she said to either shave or grow a beard."

"And?"

"I guess I'll shave now that it's summer."

"Good choice." Paul was probably coming out of his Ahab phase now that he was one up on Trimark.

Both girls had their birthdays in June, and the Lawsons gave a joint birthday/graduation party on their deck. Maria stole the show by getting an engagement ring for her birthday. She and her guy were the center of attention. It was a really joyful celebration which Rena enjoyed. She could see Maureen going into high gear the moment the engagement was announced. Rena offered to give Maria a party before the wedding. Basically, she hadn't entertained but there was no reason why she couldn't; she would start looking into what was involved right now.

That summer letters came from Trimark declaring a lawsuit the developer was filing against the Town of Stonehaven, based on a long list of similar variances the Town had allowed and on Paul's personal rather than legal reasons for persuading the vote at the Town Meeting and for using his position unfairly in other ways.

Ada told Rena that she had heard that certain people had been interviewed by Trimark's legal team about what issues Paul had raised in his campaign to line up votes. Paul scoffed. "Politicians campaign for things and I'm a politician," he said.

Peter Winship, the head of the legal committee of the Board of Selectmen, called Rena at home one night and told her that he and his committee needed her to help keep Paul out of this.

"We don't need any duels between Paul and the developer,"

Peter said. "Let's leave this in the hands of the attorneys. We've called in one from Boston to help out. Winning legal battles is not like winning over ordinary people. Besides we think we're going to have to....", then he whispered the word..."settle."

Rena's shoulders dropped, and she slumped over the telephone.

"You need to just say as little as possible about this, keep Paul from getting riled. Just send the letters from Trimark to the Legal Committee's box. He doesn't even have to see them unless it's his name on the front. You know what I mean."

Keeping Paul out of it was like keeping a St. Bernard puppy out of the cat's food, and Rena was in the middle.

"I took great pains not to force the issue with the Board of Selectmen," Paul said. "I was persuasive, but, good God, I never threatened or promised. I only did what any self-respecting caretaker of the Town would do. I never once went before the Board of Appeals itself. I spoke at the Town Meeting only as a Town resident. I didn't preside, for crying out loud."

Rena held up her hand to halt him. "I know, I know."

Throughout the summer, they were on pins and needles. Paul had his say a few times to Peter and his committee. Rena did not egg him on, but he often got beyond her influence. I am not responsible for everything, Rena told herself, going with the outbreath.

Paul mercifully had the upcoming Granite Festival and ground breaking to think about. By Labor Day the air had turned crisp and, two nights later, there were early frost warnings. Rena covered the tuberous rooted begonias with linen dish towels and they got through fine.

There was a dance at the Art Association the Friday evening before the Granite Festival celebration. Rick Talbot asked Rena to go with him.

"Oooooh," Ada said, her voice rising and falling in mock titillation when she heard.

"Okay, have your fun," Rena responded.

The Festival itself was begun on Saturday morning when the first chunk of granite was ferried from the dock at Whale Bone Cove to Main Wharf. Freddy Bocock escorted it. He was the son of the foreman of the last commercial quarrying crew to operate. The town's most important quarries were on the hills above Bay Road between Boding Point and Dory Beach, and, though these were now water reservoirs, it was from the side of these quarries that the first, ceremonial chunk of granite was being carried. Freddy kept his hand on the block during the trip as if it were going to get away. It was Patty Patillo's boat; he was honored because the Patillos had been among those who manned the granite barges way back, but really because his teenaged son had been killed in a car wreck earlier in the summer and the Granite Festival committee wanted to do something to distract him.

Boat horns blew and people clapped as the Patty Whack came in the mouth of the harbor. P.S. was there on the pier with Karen. The little boy clapped solemnly like a grownup. Rena sighed. She remembered when he had first learned to patty cake. Rena saw them again at the parade. Karen was holding P.S. back by the straps on his overalls so he wouldn't step in the way of the marching band.

There were negotiations between the Town and Trimark all September and on into October. The Town simply didn't have the money to fight Trimark; victory was doubtful. They were lucky to have any bargaining chips at all, their counsel had said. Offers and counteroffers were daily news around Town Hall. Paul was abreast of everything but Peter and the other Selectmen made him agree not to participate in the negotiations personally. Concessions were made, mostly by Trimark, because in the end Trimark got the permit. What had begun in the drama of victory was nullified in a whimper of defeat. The Board of Selectmen signed off on it in a specially called meeting which Paul did not attend.

The very next Monday morning Trimark broke ground for Wildwater. Of course, under other circumstances, Paul would have been at the commencement of a new development taking a turn with the spade. The PR would have been big. As it was, the picture was on the front page of the *Gloucester Daily Times* and the story continued in the Stonehaven section. Tony held up the paper for Rena to see. Rena raised an eyebrow and nodded and no one mentioned the event to Paul, who spent the day at the Community Center construction site. When Rena went out for lunch she saw

Paul actually helping to guide a block of granite in a sling and position it on top of the foundation, which was beginning to emerge from the ground like a row of baby's teeth.

Construction in town for the Community Center went on in parallel, Wildwater following weeks behind. By the first week in October, the granite walls of Paul's project were up to the armpits. Heaters were set around the walls at night while the mortar set. It was above freezing in the daytime, and things were going well.

One morning, Rena, working at her desk, was aware that two police cars had turned from the police station down toward the wharf. She failed to hear them gun their engines up South Street so she knew they had turned left toward Dock Square. Knew but didn't consciously note. But when a faint siren whined from somewhere near the rotary broke into her consciousness, she did a mental check like a mother accounting for all her children and noted the two cars were down by Dock Square. She visualized the older patrol car, the Pontiac–Sgt. McCarty always pulled it out fastest–parked under the first elm with its wheels up on the curb. The Jeep Explorer–she remembered how the Board fought that purchase–would be parked at right angles to the curb so it could turn quickly in either direction. Long before the wail of the siren stammered along the alley cut-through to Broad Street where Main went one way, Rena knew someone at the construction site was hurt.

Paul had not come back from lunch and it flashed through Rena's mind that the person hurt could have been Paul. But, when she saw Rosa in Ciardi's sausage department running across the street, she knew the injured person was Italian because Rosa got the Italian news before she did. The radio at the fire station was chattering all the time if anyone could understand it, but Rosa would get the word quicker from the fish market which was closer to the scene.

"Who is it?" asked Rena when Rosa hit the door.

"One of the Lonfrillo brothers from Long Beach," Rosa said, "We don't know which one was on the job today."

Rena called The Tog Shop to get the full story.

The Times reporter showed up at Town Hall forty minutes later for a statement.

"A guy named Lonfrillo," said the reporter.

Rena nodded.

"Vince Lonfrillo. Long Beach, his license said. His leg is messed up pretty bad. Know him?"

Rena shrugged.

"They told me he was helping guide a block of granite when it slipped in the chain and fell on his leg."

"Actually, he'd stepped back to take a drink from his thermos when it fell," said Rena "or it would have crushed his whole body."

"How do you know this?"

"Sarah in the gallery over the Tog Shop was watching when it happened."

"Oh, okay. So the story is he's lucky a quirk of fate saved his life, not he's unlucky that a freak accident doomed his leg?"

"Right. It's good news." Rena smiled slightly. She almost could give the reporter the quote: the man would say; "God's hand pulled me back. He must have saved me for something important."

And whose hand dropped the rock on his leg, she wondered. God gets all the good PR.

"I'll open with that. Got this Sarah person's number?"

When the reporter left, Rena called the Town's insurance representative first and then the Town attorney. Paul had still not come in.

P.S. had started three-days-a-week preschool in Manchester this fall. Up till then, his grandmother had kept him at home.

"Isn't preschool risky?" Rena had asked Paul. "Don't you have to give the child's full name or bring a birth certificate or something?"

Paul nodded. "Thought of that. Karen swore P.S. was his real name. They said they'd seen odder names than that. The birth certificate doesn't come up till the fall after he's five. That's the date to worry about. We have some time."

A winter-like storm from the northeast signaled the end of Rena's garden. The weather cleared up on the weekend and Rena spent several hours pulling up the zinnias and tomato plants and putting them on the compost. She edged the beds. She'd cover them with mulch for the winter. She enjoyed this putting to bed almost as

226

much as the coming out in the spring. Tidying up after the outburst of summer flowers made her feel in control of the course of her life. She stopped and went out in the car to the nursery with soil still clinging to her knees and bought a small juniper and some perennials, also peat moss and bone meal. She came home and planted the juniper next to the stump of the one that had died the winter before and planted perennials around it for color until the small tree grew bigger. She tied up the raspberry bushes with strong cord.

By November, the outdoor fruit and vegetables stands at Ciardi's market had long been put up for the winter and Rosa no longer yelled out to passers-by from an open upstairs window before the market opened. She had to come out on the street to share the news. One day Rosa crossed the street and came over to Town Hall.

"You know that Lonfrillo man who was hurt in the construction site?" Rosa said.

"Yes."

"He's out of the hospital—big cast, traction, everything—he had no place to go. His mother's sick and his brothers—I don't know, they were too crowded. So guess who's taking care of him?"

"Ummh," Rena was good at guessing so she took the challenge seriously.

Rosa bugged her eyes impatiently at Rena to make her give up. "Oh, Okay, who?"

"Charlotte. Charlotte Heath. She's got him in a hospital bed right in her living room. Judy Madruga's boyfriend delivered it yesterday afternoon and SAW. She's got the guy completely in her power." The whole Town Hall gang had seamlessly knit a circle around Rosa.

"She always did like Italians, " said Charlene from Dog and Business Licenses, who lived a half block from Charlotte's street.

"Of course. We've got the moves," said Tony.

"Remember the summer she had every guy who worked at the fishing packing plant. Each one got two weeks."

"This one's got more than two weeks. He's got to stay in traction for six weeks and who knows how much therapy after that."

"That guy's gonna know the meaning of therapy."

"In the second world war, European farm families used to take wounded paratroopers into their homes," Rena began. The others looked blankly at Rena as if she were changing the subject. People can be so dense. "The family would feed the injured soldiers and nurse them back to health. It met a need. Charlotte is like one of those farm families. This guy is lucky to have a place to stay and..."

"Yeah, he's going to 'meet a need' too, I'll bet."

"Maybe so, but did you guys ever think she might just be helping the guy?"

Dana, new in data entry, and Charlene shuffled away from Rena, and she could hear their giggles all the way from Taxes.

Tony put his hand on Rena's shoulder. "Don't be so serious. Lighten up."

People had told Rena she analyzed things too much. She thought she   analyzed too little.

Ada offered some family celebration for Rena's Christmas and Rena accepted for Christmas Day dinner. It was good to get just one night of lighted tree and fruit cake; that was enough for Rena. Two of Ada's children were home. Nicole helped with the cooking and Philip said a blessing with a homemade line about the family. Rena could not help but think of how precarious that family unity had been and about how both of Charlotte's marriages had failed and about Paul's two families, and she wondered how she herself would have done if she'd had a family. She tried to fathom if she was happy or sad at that actual moment. Then there was the Amen and they toasted their togetherness, and she thought for that moment she was happy.

The day before New Years, Tony teased Rena again about "going with" Rick Talbot, the lobsterman.

Rena says, "I'm not going with him. I'm just going to the party with him."

Tony reminded her they had gone to the July 4th band concert this year.

"I met him there," Rena said.

"That was once this year. Then the Granite Festival dance. That makes twice this year. Now the New Years Eve party. How many years has that been? First once a year, now three times this year. I believe we have a statistical trend. At this rate you'll be lovers by the turn of the century." He raised a nonexistent glass to her: "Here's to the turn of the century."

On New Year's Eve, Rick scuffed along, grinding the thin crust of storm-blown sand into the pavement, and Rena crunched beside him, unaccustomed to dressy shoes. They scuffed and crunched their way down The Lane. They could hear the voices of other couples ahead in the dark, a car door closing somewhere, and wheels spinning in an icy parking space. Rick and Rena hurried on because the wind blew bitterly, snatching up the edges of her wool coat and sucking the warmth from her legs. When the worst gusts howled, she turned to Rick and they huddled for a second before pushing on. She leaned on his arm, keeping her eyes almost closed. Little tears crept out the corners and blew an icy path back to her ears.

The little fishing shack shops on either side of The Lane were dark now, closed for the night or for the winter, their corners and gables seemingrounded by dusk and the wind of a hundred winters.

The Squirrel's Nest, their hosts' gift shop, was just ahead, lit up in every window, like the stable in Bethlehem or the little village houses set in angel hair in the hardware store window, a haven of conviviality and warmth.

Rick knocked. Someone inside turned the knob sharply and opened the door to them. It was their host, Girard. He took Rena's arm with one hand and pulled her in, sweeping his lips across her cheek. With great economy of motion he put his other hand on Rick's shoulder and pulled him firmly in. With what seemed like a third hand, Girard shut the door behind Rick so abruptly that the fisherman was bumped forward into a sea of shoulders. Everyone shuffled a half step one way or the other to adjust. Then Girard shook Rick's hand while little cries of delight greeted their arrival.

Ada and Phil were there. Rena hugged Phil, then she and Ada kissed. When they met each other every week, they barely gave each other a wave of a hand before resuming their lifelong conversation, but tonight they did each other full honors. Paul and Maureen were there, of course, Maureen, slim in black, her usual chic accentuated with one freeform metallic silver stripe. Rena put her cheek to

Maureen's; she hugged Paul. She took Miriam's two hands in hers—
Miriam from The Potter's Wheel. She put her arm around Angie's
waist, and they squeezed hip to hip gleefully. She did a full bosom to
bosom with Molly Thuesen. Godawmighty, she was soft and warm.
Made you just want to stay there till spring. Rena looked
heavenward. Thank you, God, for these friends, she said to herself.
That was her most religious thought of the year.

The shop, which from a distance had seemed like the cozy
stable in Bethlehem was now seen to be a little pagan oasis, where
Christmas and the Nordic feasts collided. A long table was given
over to a fantasy of gray-green moss and lichened bark and peopled
with elves which Girard and his partner Doug collected. The little
porcelain squirrels for which the shop was named scampered among
Christmas balls. Constellations of miniature white lights hovered in
the rafters.

Someone pressed drinks into the hands of the latest arrivals.
More kisses were planted on cheeks as they were pulled forward into
the crowded shop. At every turn, belly scraped belly and dozens of
bony elbows poked into the soft flesh of arms. Pardon me's
lubricated the mechanics of circulation.

Then down the stairs from the couple's apartment came Doug,
bearing platters of thinly sliced flank steak, pink in the middle,
skewered into three or four loops on long wooden picks with
roasted peppers and chunks of sweet onions. Girard one-handed a
tray of French bread sopped in cheese and toasted to a greasy
perfection. Bowls of pilaf and smoked turkey followed, joining
mounds of crab dip and toast points, flatbrot and Havarti. And the
warm glow of whiskey, mostly on the rocks, competed with flutes of
gewürztraminer.

But the wassail preparation was the performance of the night.
No midnight champagne here. The huge wassail bowl was filled with
red wine sharpened with the juice and pulp of several oranges and
lemons. A cone of sugar was affixed on a pinion above it. Doug
gently poured brandy over the sugar and set it afire. Each year the
sudden conflagration seemed as much a surprise as the year before.

The melting sugar dripped into the drink below like the liquid
sand that children let slip through their fingers to make turrets and

230

minarets on sand castles. Caramelized sugar fell in dribbles and sometimes chunks as when sand castle walls give way.

Everyone breathed the sweetness of the wassail into their lungs and their hair and the wool of their clothes which they would carry happily into the New Year until the cleaners got a hold of it.

The sound of partying escalated and voices rose till the revelers were tipping their heads toward each other, cupping their hands, and lip reading in the din. The noise hushed and then rose to crescendo when Doug carried a large tray down the stairs, holding it overhead till the crowd parted. When they gave him room; the tray settled onto the table like a swan into water amid appreciative murmurs.

On the tray were dozens of stubby earthen cups. It was the creme brulee, the most delicate linen-white custard with the richest burnt amber topping in the world.

Doug and Girard were heavily into flaming. They had once set the kitchen on fire broiling the tops of their signature dessert. The guests had cheerfully put it out.

Rena's little silver spoon darted from custard to topping and back as she reveled in the alternation of tastes and textures.

"Are there seconds?" she asked, reaching for another cup.

"Ah! Ah!" Girard deftly flicked her greedy hand away with a linen napkin. "I'm saving that one for Nat. He's coming later. He was prepping for the lobster feast at the Harbor Master, said he'd be here before ten, but he's late..."

"Ooh," listeners murmured. They had not seemed to miss the proprietor of Marley's Lobster Shack, such a surfeit of good company there had been.

There were always those in the restaurants and inns who could not get away for their own personal social events, but on New Year's Eve only the big restaurants like the Harbor Master were open; the little coffee shops were closed, and their owners were already here celebrating with the inner circle of Stonehaven's shopkeepers and town leaders.

Rena was dipping a crisp little cookie into the whipped cream on her after-dinner coffee, when the door flew open. A cold blast whipped around her legs and she let her cookie break off into the coffee. A cheer went up. Rena turned. It was Nat at last. Arms reached out and pulled him in so the door could be closed behind him. There was always room for one more.

Nat sharply clapped his hands. "Hear ye, hear ye! " someone yelled on his behalf. A rum on the rocks materialized in front of Nat, but he waved it aside, needing full use of his hands to talk.

Someone whistled for silence and got it.

"Ya gotta hear this," Nat began. "I'm over at the Harbor Master. Mr. Leland Johns has all his Trimark honchos and their wives for dinner and their..." he drew the word out slowly in its three sneering syllables "...financiers.

"I'm in the kitchen cracking lobsters, but every time the kitchen door swings open I can see them. All coats and ties...." Nat unwrapped a woolen scarf from his neck showing his own open collar and triangle of undershirt. Girard took Nat's coat and hung it on the deer antlers with the other coats. Nat cleared himself a little more room for his narrative by planting his legs far apart.

"So Mr. Johns says, 'Bring us the wine list!'"

Gales of laughter swept the room at The Squirrels Nest.

"So Angelo says, 'We don't have a wine list.'"

Nat was mimicking the voices now and striking the poses. He drew himself up in full corporate stature and spoke the lines of Mr. Leland Johns:

"Well, I'm sure the house wine will do, bring us a carafe of red and one of white for starters."

This time the burst of laughter in the shop rang the rafters.

Nat was warming to his tale. "'Do we need rose'?' Johns is asking his people."

"Oh, we don't need rose'." Nat, in the persona of the Wildwater developer, waves away the imaginary rose' with an affected flip of the wrist.

The company at The Squirrel's Nest was shaking with hilarity.

"So Angelo says, We don't serve alcohol."

"What?" the guy fairly screams. "THEY are drinking wine." He waves his hand toward some people with a wine bottle on the table.

"'They brought their own wine, and we're pouring it,' Angelo says. 'This is the one night of the year we pour wine if you bring it.'"

The one night a year !' Johns says. His mouth is hanging open.

He's about to bust a gut. Everyone in the kitchen is crowded at the door. All the other customers stop eating to listen.

"And why is that?' Johns says. 'Why don't you serve liquor?'

"Stonehaven is a dry town, sir," Angelo says. Deadpan, he was; you should have seen him.

"Johns jumps up out of his seat! He comes toward us. I think he's going to pick us all up and throw us over the steam table. So I jump back."

Nat jumped back and Phil and Ada caught him just as he was about to elbow the remains of the lobster Newburg into the surrounding moss. "But he pushes through us, and we follow him into the kitchen. Then he gets real quiet. He lowers his head, and we all gather round."

Nat lowered his head, and Rena and all the others lowered their heads, too. Then to the huddle of transfixed listeners, Nat quoted Leland Johns in a stage whisper, "The town is dry?" We all suck in. "You mean there's a law?"

"It's a law...and...the people want it that way," Angelo says.

Johns glares at him so hard, and Angelo says, "Well, I personally would like to serve liquor, but I respect the consensus of the town..."

"Johns cuts Angelo off with a swipe of his hand." Nat illustrated by swinging his hand under Rena's nose, and she flinched.

"Johns is livid, I mean, for him this is a five-star cluster fuck. He says, "This is New Year's Eve. So where do I go to get something to drink? What's the quickest way to get champagne?"

"Everyone is struck dumb, but Angelo points up Front Street. He's looking sort of scared. We all had eyes like flounders by this time...." Nat went bug-eyed for effect. "Can... I... get... wine... in... the next town?" he asks like that, one word at a time.

"Angelo shakes his head. Then Eric had to get in on this. 'Rockport's dry," Eric says. "Only two towns in the whole state."

"Then where can I get some?"

Angelo points up the road again. He hardly dares say anything. Then Sam McGinnty jumps in and says, "I'll go to Gloucester and get you some..." Sammy smells money here and sure enough Johns peels off a bunch of twenties, must have been hundreds of dollars, and he starts to name some wines. Ol' Sammy never heard of 'em. You know...he's a Four Roses man. "I can't remember all that' Sam says," you are going to have to write it down.'

"I don't have time. I'm the host here. Don't you understand? Just tell the man wine and champagne," he says and peels off a couple more twenties.

"So Sam heads out, doesn't even take off his apron, and Mr. Johns straightens himself up and pastes on a smile and goes back to his table. These are pretty important people for him to make such a fuss...and then it's New Year's Eve.... Speaking of liquor, I'm overdue. Catch me up, guys."

The crowd sucked the storyteller in, and the rum reappeared, bobbing like flotsam across a sea of hands into Nat's hand. He was soon swept into an eddy that dropped him off gently in a backwater of smoked turkey and pilaf.

As the story ended, Rena looked around the room at all the faces to see how they took the tale. Everyone laughed from the beginning as if it were even funnier than it was, on account of the occasion, and the wine and the whiskey. Some were adding their own quips to the story:

"...their first sober New Year's Eve since grade school..." Rena heard someone say.

"They could drink birch beer..." Miriam said.

Rick waved invisible stemware under his nose and pronounced "accessible flavor with musky overtones...."

Rena laughed. She was surprised the lobsterman could come up with that. She looked for Paul and was disappointed to see that Paul was not laughing. The corner of his mouth on just one side was turning up in an expression of mild amusement like when he caught a joke but was enjoying someone else's reaction more than his own. The corner crept imperceptibly up, and then the other corner began to match it until he had a full-fledged grin and a sort of silly look in his eyes, the look of a quiet, happy drunk just before he keels over. Paul wasn't much of a drinker these days. He must have been drinking his whiskey straight even though he knew he shouldn't. She'd better check on him.

She went over to where Paul had pulled apart from the crowd.

He was leaning against a door frame leading into the Icelandic woolens room.

"Pretty funny about Leland Johns and Angelo, isn't it? Bet he felt foolish."

"It's not funny, not funny at all."

Rena looked up at Paul sharply. She thought it was funny. They thought it was funny," she gestured to the revelers.

"Rena, listen. Don't say anything to the others yet, but just listen. If Leland Johns didn't know Stonehaven was dry...and that does seem to be the case...he'd be planning on serving liquor at Wildwater. Of course, he is. Any resort would. Not only planning to ...counting on it. The whole issue of liquor...Johns knows it better than anyone...is that you make your profit on liquor...liquor with meals...liquor in the bar...liquor after dinner... that's the profit margin; hell, it's the debt service. That's the part that makes a place of entertainment possible. If he can't serve liquor at Wildwater, he can't have a resort. He's in deep shit. This isn't big, Rena, this is huge."

Rena sucked in with pleasure. "You mean...." Paul nodded. "You mean this may stop Wildwater?"

"Absolutely. Being dry means changing the whole concept. Mostly it changes their financial projections. Liquor is the whole enchilada."

"I can't believe they didn't know. I can't believe they didn't ask."

"I can. I never dreamed they didn't know, but now I see how it happened. When I go to statewide meetings, if the subject comes up, and I mention Stonehaven is dry, everybody hoots. They ask if horses still pull our fire trucks or if our women wear chastity belts. When you live here, you forget how novel it is to sell no liquor."

"No wonder Johns hit the ceiling. It wasn't just the champagne toast he was worried about."

"Exactly."

They looked into each other's eyes and grinned at their shared secret. Then Rena threw her arms around Paul and they hugged in jubilation. Instead of letting her go then, Paul began to rock her slowly as if they were dancing and Rena melted into him, savoring the feel of his arms on her shoulders for as long as it lasted. He slowly let her go.

When midnight came, Rena quickly gave Rick a peck on the mouth and took both of his hands firmly in hers so she could keep them down low between them until the serving of the wassail distracted him. She wanted to go home with the imprint of Paul's hug on her shoulders; she wanted nothing to supplant that.

20

Collision Course

It had been three weeks since Trimark discovered the major obstacle that denied the Wildwater project the green light. It was a critical one and, according to Mr. Leland Johns's comments in the G.D. Times, surely surmountable.

Mr. Johns did not seem to know how firmly committed Stonehaven was to selling no liquor either from package stores or by the drink. The policy was of long standing and had never been successfully challenged. It was not that the community believed in temperance. Far from it. Stonehaven residents bought their liquor by the bottle in Gloucester and served it in their homes. Teenagers had no trouble buying beer for their beach parties, and Stonehaven had its town drunk who had grown up at a beach party and never left.

From the beginning, the restaurants in town made their success mostly as lobster roll takeout places, tearooms, and sandwich shops for the busloads of tourists. By nightfall, most of the tourists had left. Those who filled the bed-and-breakfasts made do by pulling out a pint from the elastic rimmed side pocket of their suitcases and scuffing along the narrow halls to get their ice.

True, fine dining places like the Captain's Table, the Spyglass Inn, and the Harbor Master Restaurant, where Trimark first discovered the town was dry, could all have profited from a liquor license. But the prime locations of these restaurants along with their prime rib and lobster tails kept them filled to the gills seven days a week. They did well enough without liquor profits, and so it had been since Hannah Jumper made her mark. The several attempts to bring an end to the Town's prohibition had been hotly debated and soundly trounced.

But with so much at stake Trimark was determined, applying conciliation as well as pressure. The bars and lounges of Wildwater need not intrude on Old Town, Mr. Leland Johns explained carefully to the newspaper. North Point was at the very end of the town at the Rockport line. The developers wouldn't ask Stonehaven to change its way of life—just let Wildwater's guests continue theirs.

Paul insisted the Town would reject the measure as it always had, but he allowed, "It may be close."

Rena knew Paul would not give up without a fight and a creative one, at that. She wondered what he would do this time to top his performance with the lobster.

Theoretically, the Board of Selectmen could decide the fate of the petition. In fact, the first week of February when the Trimark petition came in, Paul polled the Board and then asked for a quick vote at the next regular weekly meeting. He wanted the defeat to go on record and, he told Rena, "There's always a slight chance we can get away with it."

In reality, in a town where it took the signatures of only twenty residents to throw the matter into a Town Meeting, there was no chance they'd get away with it. A petition to that effect was signed by the prerequisite twenty and delivered to Town Hall the next day. Rena put the issue on the agenda for the Town Meeting the last week in February.

Paul had seemed cheerful ever since New Year's Eve when the

tide had turned again in the Town's favor. The matter of the petition didn't seem to worry him as much as Rena had feared.

A couple weeks later, he went to Boston for his monthly scan. He took these opportunities to visit some wholesalers and do a little boating business for which he took a generous cash travel allowance out of Lawson's Marine. He spent the night in a modest hotel, usually not alone, and he sent Karen home with whatever money was left. That was one of the ways he spent time with her and also provided a little cash for her and his son. It was kind of a marvel to Rena how all this worked. Occasionally, she had played devil's advocate, suggesting all the things that could go wrong, but Paul had them all covered. It was as if his malignancy had its purpose in the grand plan.

On his return from this particular trip, however, he seemed subdued. The monthly multipurpose bivouac usually left him lighthearted for at least three days. She always thought one day Karen would start to press him for some resolution to what must be an uncertain limbo for her. And that would ruin the mood for Paul, wouldn't it?

On March 2, P.S. turned five. Paul managed once more to get to the family celebration. When he got the pictures back, instead of doling them out one by one so he could beam over each of them with Rena, he gave her the whole pack, and he went to the corner of his office with his head bowed. When she gave them back, he raised his head, and she saw his eyes full of tears.

"He's growing up too fast," Rena offered.

Paul acknowledged her effort but couldn't speak. Rena put the photos away in the drawer for him, locked it, and put the key in its hiding place lest he forget.

One Thursday in mid-March, Paul had P.S. for the whole day. He seemed to love playing father. About once a month, Paul went up to Manchester early in the morning and woke his son up. He stayed with him till bedtime "to soak up real life with him, to hold it close," he said. They might go fishing or visiting the firehouse or sitting on a wharf watching the boats unload in Magnolia Harbor where people were not likely to recognize Paul or P.S.. Sometimes he asked Rena for suggestions on what they could do. By searching various listings, Rena had become an expert on exhibits of marine arts, wildlife carvings, and historical recreations all over Cape Ann.

On this particular day of full time fathering, the day passed quietly at Town Hall. The clock in the hall ticked more loudly, the shadows seemed deeper than when Paul was there. And Rena sighed more often. It was not an unwelcome diversion when, about one-thirty, the phone rang.

It was Paul calling from his car. He was at the water tank on Thuesen Hill. Don't ask why. Don't say anything to anybody, just come, he said.

Rena strolled to the hall bulletin board, pretended to check something there, then when the hall was clear she slipped out the door. The creaking of the door closing could have been anyone going out. She hurried to Thuesen Hill. The road to the water tank was so steep it was frightening. For a second or two she could see only the sky. Then the ground leveled off and she saw Paul's car dwarfed by one leg of the water tank. The door was open and Paul sat with his legs outside. P.S. was throwing gravel by the handful at nothing in particular.

Rena pulled up beside Paul.

"What?" she said.

"Keep him for an hour or two, please."

"Keep him! Where?"

"Take him home with you. Take the rest of the day off."

"Paul, I can't go home. I didn't even tell anyone at Town Hall I was leaving. My computer is running; I'm in the middle of a letter."

"Call from my car phone.... Tell them you feel sick and went home. Some women's problem that came up quick."

"I'd need to pick up some stuff I'm working on. Will you keep him until I make some arrangements?"

Paul shook his head. "I have to go quick."

"Paul what is this? Why can't you just be a little late."

"I can't tell you."

"You can't tell me, but you're making me turn my day upside down.... You can't tell ME?"

"Look, I don't have time...Take him. Please, Rena, take him."

Paul was obviously agitated and P.S. got resistant. Paul almost forcibly put him in a seat belt in Rena's car and knelt down to kiss him goodbye. P.S. clung to his neck. Paul peeled off his little hands from his neck and held them out to Rena. Rena took the child's hands in hers and felt them relax.

"Paul, are you crazy? I'll have to take him back to Town Hall for a few minutes to get some stuff or I'll lose a whole day's work. Who will I say he is?"

"A friend's child who had to run out for an errand."

"What friend?"

"Rena, who would interrogate you when you tell them a simple thing like you're keeping a friend's child?"

"Women do."

"Make up something."

"Paul, this is a major imposition."

"I owe you one big," he said, hurrying to his car. "Oh," he called back. "Meet me back here at...say, five thirty."

Rena took her time getting back to the office. She parked in the far space in the lot behind Town Hall. She considered if she could leave P.S. in the car while she ran in. She wasn't sure what a five your old child does and doesn't do when he's alone.

"Can you stay here for a minute?"

"Nooo. My mother never leaves me. She says the car might start."

The car was absolutely flat in park, with the brake on, but Rena dared not buck the principle.

"Well, come along, I have to do a little chore inside. You be real quiet."

"Why do I have to be quiet?"

"Because people are working."

In the office, Rena gave a preemptive explanation as she hurried past her desk into Paul's office. "I'm keeping him for his mother. A friend of mine. From Saugus. In town for the day. Daughter of a friend of my mother's. Just for a little while."

Tony threw up his hands in defense, "Okay, okay, I'm not keeping your time sheet."

I must have said too much, Rena thought. She gave P.S. some blank paper and a black, a red, and a non-repro blue pencil and a stamp that said "Received" and the date. He sat on the floor beside her and began furiously stamping while Rena looked up a number and dialed. Then she noticed that there were "Received" marks on the floor where P.S. had missed the paper. She put down the phone, spit on her finger, and leaned over to be sure the ink would come off the floor.

"Well, who's this?" a voice behind her said.

Rena whirled around to face Maureen Lawson, smiling sweetly at P.S.

"Oh! Maureen! Oh, it's... I'm keeping an eye on him for a lady...She's a friend of...the daughter of a friend of my...." I'm saying too much again, she thought; she can see my face red. She leaned back in her chair and took a deep breath. Go with the outbreath.

When the breath was completely out, she started over. "Maureen. Hello. It's been a long time since you've been in. Time flies." Rena winced at her own cliche.

"Well, you know how it is." She glanced around the room, noticed the boy, and said, "Town Hall is always the same." Rena said nothing.

"Is Paul around?"

"No, he's out. He went to a meeting of the public relations committee in Gloucester. He won't be back till..." She glanced at her watch..."after you leave." She didn't mean to say it that way. "I mean, probably."

P.S. stood up suddenly and held his paper out to Maureen. "It's lobster pots," he said of the Received stamp marks which were outlined in a rectangle. "One, two, free, six, seven... thirteen. And here's a lobster."

"Yes," Maureen beamed. "Lobster pots. And what is your name."

Rena sucked in.

"P.S."

"Pee-ess?" she repeated then turned to Rena, "What is he saying?"

"Pee-ess, that's right, I think it's Italian or French or something."

"Oh. Like Pierre? Piesse?"

"I guess," Rena shrugged.

"Well, tell Paul I dropped in. I was just going to trade cars with him if were here, so he could get the oil changed and the snow tires off. But it can probably wait. Well, bye now. Bye, bye, Piesse."

Maureen slipped gracefully out the door, waving goodbye to Gladys and Tony as the heavy door swung shut.

Rena put her head in her hands for as long as she thought she could get away with it, then she picked P.S. up in her lap and hugged him out of gratitude for his not being called Paul Lawson Jr. and put him down again beside his paper and pencils.

Rena sorted out the papers she wanted to take and stuffed her Rolodex into her purse so she could work at home. She hated to lose control of her schedule.

"Now let's go for another ride," she said.

Rena soon discovered you can't actually work with a child in the house. P.S. asked myriad questions all the while picking up Aunt Amelia's knick knacks that she had forgotten she had.

"Better put that down," she said more often than she could stand it; so she gave up and just played with P.S.

By five o'clock she was heading back to the water tank to meet Paul. This time she parked her car on Green Street and walked up the scary part. They had plenty of time. Rena carried a sack of cans she been carrying around in the car to drop off at the recycling bin at the Library. At the top of the hill she set them up in a pyramid for P.S. to use as a target. This was a winner of an idea and P.S. demolished the stack with handfuls of gravel. Then he stacked them up again and repeated the whole process over and over while his little hands turned red from the cold. Rena watched with shoulders limp and emotions damped, her chin tucked down deep in her collar to keep her face out of the March wind.

Her mind wandered back to the scene with Maureen and the disruption of her day and that episode began to represent the whole question that had been bothering her lately about where was all this going for Paul and where was her own life leading...one seemed to bring on the other until she was in a funk she could only define as questioning the meaning of life. This would inevitably lead to a depression of several days whose only cure would be accomplishing a major chunk on her "to do" list. And here she was stuck under a water tank not free to do anything.

Then they heard Paul's car spewing gravel on the road.

"Why did you leave your car down there?" Paul asked.

"I was trying to kill some time. I couldn't get any work done," Rena said, opening the door only slightly to her rising resentment.

"Oh, I'm sorry."

"Sorry? You are crazy, Paul!" she almost screamed. "Crazy, crazy, crazy!" She wanted to hit him– Crazy, wham! Crazy, pow, Crazy, bop! But she could only do a little wham, pow, and bop in the air because P.S. was watching her curiously. "And I am crazy, crazy to let you do this to me."

She set up the cans again and then pulled Paul away from the game P.S. was playing.

"Paul, this child knows who he is. He's your son. He's five years old, bright for his age, and he can perfectly well tell the whole damn world who he is, nickname or not. You have got to fix this, Paul. You've got to tell Maureen or send the child away or something!"

"What happened?"

"Maureen came to the office. She asked him what his name....She played with the curls..." Rena's voice caught. "...on the back of his neck with her fingers."

"What did you tell her?"

"I didn't tell her anything Paul. It's not that. Oh, I acted pretty damn weird in front of the whole office but I didn't tell them anything."

"I'm sorry you had to go through this."

"You're sorry, sorry, sorry. You're going to be even sorrier when...."

"Sorry seems to be your favorite word today," he broke in. "Let's talk about this when you feel better." He whistled and P.S. gathered the cans in the bag and came running.

"I'll give you a ride down the hill."

"I'll walk."

"I want to see that your car starts okay."

"It's never given me any trouble." But Rena got in the back seat behind P.S.

They rode silently down the hill, except for P.S. saying "Dad? Dad?" When Paul said, "What, P.S.?," the boy said, "Dad? Dad?" all over again until Paul quit answering. And Rena could see that Paul could see that the dream of an untroubled double life was over.

"Rena," Paul finally said, as they stopped at her car, "this is my problem, not yours. I'm sorry I made it yours today. And I am especially sorry that I have troubled you and that you have been angry. Especially now."

"We'll talk about it later," Rena said. She appreciated Paul's apology, but she could not turn around on a dime. She got quickly out of the car.

"Don't forget your cans," P.S. called after her.

Paul didn't mention this episode the next day; in fact, he said very little about P.S. in the ensuing days. The chill on the subject of P.S. bothered Rena. She found she missed his news.

The day of the meeting, Paul asked Lyndon Moore to preside just like he did the day he won the crowd over with the giant lobster. Paul was so quiet she wondered what new drama he was concocting and not telling her about. She was a bit worried fearing she might have a role tonight, too, and she wasn't sure she could pull it off as well as she had that other night. She hoped Paul wasn't counting on her.

That evening, the crowd was heavy. Lyndon did the honors in his usual limp voice. He read an item on the agenda and paused. It sometimes seemed possible that he and they would fall asleep and wake again a hundred years hence, all in their places, before he asked for a motion. Then, slowly, slowly he asked for seconds and discussion and votes.

When it was finally time for the liquor zone vote, for which most of the people had come, the restlessness was pervasive. Those who had asked for the vote before Town Meeting, made the motion and the second without the presiding officer's nod. But Lyndon put the brakes on by introducing a small band of visitors from afar who wanted to participate in the discussion. Rena, by that time had forgotten all about the visitors.

A group in Tennessee, an anti-drinking contingent from the Bible belt, had read about the liquor issue in Stonehaven and had asked for a public audience. Ever since Rena heard of their venture, she had pictured them as the women in black bonnets on the upper right hand page in her high school American history book and she saw them sitting on hard wooden pews, stern, unadorned, running their fingers along the printing of weeks old, obscure newspapers, like the G.D. Times picking out the word liquor, seeking the communities that needed saving from the demon liquid. She saw them loading up wagons and hitching oxen, traveling through mountain passes on their mission to Stonehaven.

In fact, the Temperance women—that's not what they called themselves, their organization had some initials Rena couldn't remember and a toll-free number: 1-800-BE SOBER—were indistinguishable from the rest of the crowd.

The audience listened politely and quietly to the statistics on the consequences of drinking, the cautionary tales, and the Bible references. The guests' invitation for questions went unanswered.

Rena smiled at the ladies as she escorted them out into the hall. She still saw black bonnets like auras around their heads.

"Do you think our talk was well received?" the head bonnet asked.

"Oh, yes. Didn't you think so?" Rena said.

"They were very quiet. Usually there is approval from a friendly crowd and lively discussion when feelings are mixed. I couldn't quite read this crowd. Were these people for or against, do you think?"

"Oh. Uh, for what?"

"Were they for the limitation of alcohol sales or against? Were they drinkers or abstainers?"

"Oh, drinkers, but that means nothing. You see, you may not have realized but this dispute is not really about alcohol."

"Not about alcohol? Oh, yes, I'm quite sure it is. The paper said the vote was about granting a liquor license in a town that wants to keep liquor out..."

"Quite frankly," Rena interrupted, "no matter what the papers said, this vote is not about liquor sales."

"What is it about, then," said the big bonnet, as if wounded.

"It's about going out on a winter morning feeling the cold wind in your face. It's about picking blueberries on the headlands in summer. It's about knowing whose buoys are coming up to starboard by the colors of the stripes."

"But isn't liquor a part of this? Those who don't drink and don't want the young people..."

"It's not liquor, ladies. It's...," and all she could think of to say was, "... lobsters."

"Lobsters!" The woman pressed her hand against her chest and recoiled as if a lobster had pinched her tit.

"Not just lobsters. It's about life. It's about knowing who you really are."

The woman looked at her companions, and they looked at their notes as if someone might discover this was the wrong day or the wrong place. Maybe the liquor vote was in the other meeting room.

"Thank you for coming," Rena said and turned to open the way for them to the front door. But they turned back to the meeting room, and Rena let them go back in where they settled down on a bench to regroup and perhaps wait for the results.

Various people spoke on the issue. Carl Reinertsen said liquor would change the way he and all the other restaurant owners did business in an unpredictable way. They couldn't know all the repercussions. "Are there any other towns that have gone from dry to wet and could we look at what happened?"

No one replied because there were no other towns in Massachusetts that had gone from dry to wet in recent history. Paul had looked into that.

Ada Felton then stood to say that it was not just restaurant owners who worried. The whole way of life in the town was threatened. Did they want Front Street to end up like Main Street in Gloucester? Ada had that same businesslike voice Rena had first noticed when she had gone to Ada's shop.

"How? What is the big problem?" a man said. Rena didn't know him. He must have recently moved here. A number of people leaned toward him to tell him what the big problem was.

Mr. Weiss, who was once again doing the dirty work for Trimark, was recognized. He offered a compromise, he said. How about establishing a limited zone where liquor could be served–from North Point to the Gloucester line. The rest of Stonehaven could be dry. After all, there was a little store that sold beer in Lanesville "a few yards away. What's the difference?"

"Compromise, hell," Carl Reinertsen burst out at Mr. Weiss. "You pretend you're offering compromise. But you're really just saying, 'Let us roll in the dough and let those suckers serve donuts and coffee.'" Carl turned to the citizens. "I've never pushed for liquor, but if those bastards get liquor, I sure as hell want liquor."

A commotion broke out, and Lyndon eyed his gavel dolefully.

"Use it," Rena mentally called to him.

Some other people stood up, and people were pointing at Carl and pointing at the Trimark representative, and you couldn't tell what anyone was saying.

Rena looked at Lyndon again and saw he had picked up the gavel and was looking at it. He felt its heft and turned it over in his hand as if he were buying hardware. The crowd continued unruly.

Lyndon made a trial hammering motion and finally let the gavel fall. When nothing terrible happened, he struck again. The level of commotion fell to the level of whispering, and the people sat down.

Lyndon surveyed the quieted room as if undone by his own power, then pulled himself together and said, "We have to vote on the motion on the floor before we can vote on motions not yet made."

"Let him withdraw the first motion," someone called. But the crowd was impatient. Other voices called out "Vote, vote," and "Get it over with," and a murmur set in again and became a roar. Lyndon gaveled again with newfound zest.

When Paul stood up, the room fell instantly into a hush.

"Times change," he said, looking far out over the crowd. He let that truism lie in a big trough of silence that could only mean the granddaddy of all breakers was forming behind their backs.

"People change."

Rena actually turned and looked behind her to see what was looming.

"I've fought long and hard against any ruling that would allow Trimark to build. I'm not giving up now, and I'm not giving in. But I'm changing," Paul said.

Rena stopped breathing.

"It's hard to know what is the best of tradition, what to save and what to let go, what is progress and what is standing in the way of progress." Heads nodded.

"Through this whole affair, the management of Trimark has indicated a willingness to work with us. Each objection we have had they have tried to accommodate and at great expense, including some infrastructure that will benefit the Town. The fact that we were a dry town was one factor Trimark was not aware of. Should have known perhaps but didn't. Trimark exercised its option in good faith only to discover that a major source of raising money was gone."

Rena forced herself to take a breath. It was not easy. She heard Paul's conciliatory tone and was waiting for the turning of the oratorical tide which would crash all the harder for the lull that came before.

"Perhaps it's a sign," Paul continued, pausing now and taking a deep breath. Rena breathed in with him long and hard.

"It's a sign that the time when the prohibition of liquor was a viable condition of business is gone. I stand before you now to vote FOR the licensing of liquor sales in the Town of Stonehaven and I urge you to vote with me in the affirmative. Thank you."

Paul remained standing, looking out above the heads of the crowd as if to some other audience, more distant in time and place. The crowd sat in shocked silence.

Then a cry rang out: "Hear, hear!" And the crowd rose, rumbling as if the roof were falling in.

The sharp crack of the gavel resonated through the storm and the noise fell off like branches falling as groups, still on their feet, gave in to the call to order. "All in favor of rescinding the prohibition against liquor please stand," said Lyndon firmly.

Rena could not move; paralyzed by the conflict between the words she just heard and the memory of the game plan etched in the granite of a two-year campaign. It flashed through her mind that to make no decision was to remain standing—a vote for the affirmative—and the crowd was already standing. Could Paul have foreseen that? Did Lyndon realize that? What did Paul really want?

Maureen dropped to the seat, looked beseechingly at Rena and mouthed, "I don't understand."

Rena turned her palms heavenward as if to say "God only knows" and stayed on her feet. The selectmen from their seats were counting their sections and making their slashes on paper. Before Rena had definitively decided whether to sit or to remain standing, Lyndon was calling for those in favor to be seated and those opposed to rise. Rena sank to the chair in exhaustion. Maureen kept her seat, in effect abstaining. Who could blame her. Her eyes were repeating, "I don't understand. I don't understand."

And then it was over. Rena looked for the Trimark representative to see if he was gloating. She looked for Paul to see with what spirit he took the vote, to know how she should take it, but he was gone.

Maureen turned to Rena to ask her question aloud. Rena cut her off before she started: "Maureen, I don't know any more than you do. You could knock me over with a gull's feather."

"But you stood. You must have known something." Reason told Rena that she felt sorry for Maureen being blindsided by this move of Paul's in public, but in her gut she felt nothing but irritation.

"What difference does it make to you!" she felt like screaming, or even, with sarcasm, "I knew everything all along, Maureen; it was just a trick to humiliate you personally."

And finally, knowing where Paul's deed really hurt, she could say, "What about me? I have supported and campaigned and listened and talked and lived and breathed his goal and he has done this without a word to me."

But Rena did not say any of these things. She would not hurt the blameless. Maureen suddenly gave a little, "Oh!" as if someone had pinched her, and she fumbled with a piece of paper she was wringing in her hand.

"Paul handed this to me, just after...., just before...." She opened the paper and handed it to Rena. It simply said, "I'm going to the lake house to be by myself. I'll be home tomorrow."

Rena didn't blame Paul for escaping. The onslaught of people would press him beyond endurance. And she would be first in line. She knew the lake house from that one spring she and Billy and Paul and his cousin had gone up on a Saturday to open up the house, and Paul and the cousin had gone off and left her and Billy alone in the house. That's when they had gone to third base. Now Paul had left her out in left field.

She had half a mind to drive up to New Hampshire and confront him. Or console him. Or wring his neck. Not knowing which she would do was enough to make her drop the thought. Besides she didn't remember the way.

Nothing to do but leave. She could hear the sentence ring out above the others: "Where's Paul? Where's Paul?" Now it was the reporter's voice; now it was an angry voice, sometimes it was soft voices. She could hear Maureen saying pitiably, "I don't know. I really don't know." And, as the questioners caught up with Rena, she found herself repeating, "I don't know. I really don't know."

Rena was devastated, confused, angry, sad, frustrated. Crushed by what people would say, were already saying about Paul. For all the votes that had been cast by people standing–who knows how many of them were stunned into staying on their feet–how many voices now were castigating him, voices saying, "I can't believe it," thinking worse.

Rena herself didn't feel like being alone now. She wanted to talk about what had happened. She would run out into the parking lot and catch someone to invite home for dessert and coffee. Maureen would be the obvious one, but Rena wanted someone she could say anything to. She thought of catching Ada, but something stopped her. She wanted to talk to someone disinterested. No such person. Besides she didn't have any dessert anyway.

She gathered her folder, put on her coat and buttoned the collar across her mouth. It was cold and raw. What might be the last snowfall of the winter was still underfoot, crunchy from thawing days and freezing nights. The edges of scattered snow chunks were harsh as a knife blade. She was getting a headache in the front of her head–maybe sinus, maybe tension, she'd never known which–and she was glad to get home and glad now to have invited no guest. She looked for a sinus pill, among the bottles on the shelf over the glasses. She pushed aside the one that said, "No drowsiness formula," wishing there was one that said, "Drowsiness formula."

Here was one that said, "Do not operate machinery..." that would do.

She pulled her clothes off and went to bed without brushing her teeth. She lay curled up with her hands over her face, going over and over Paul's words and recreating the thought processes that might have led up to these words, the possible motivations. Each scenario had some logic, each one had some point that rendered it totally implausible. She was holding to logic now anyway and she drifted off to sleep.

And then the phone had rung and adrenaline had shot through her like a lightning strike. It was the call from the police station. Her heart pounded. The clock said 3:15. Her eyes smarted from opening them too early and the flesh around them seemed too tight. She pulled on sweat pants and boots and picked up the coat she had not hung up the night before and went out into the biting wind.

Then like some kind of illogical switch in a nightmare, in which the dreamer gets dumped into another time and another place without the courtesy of explanation or even the presence of mind to question, she had suddenly found herself picking money out of bushes, chasing hundred dollar bills across the rocks, while waves crashed around her on Boding Point. It might as well have been Alaska.

As she salvaged the bills, hundreds and twenties by the dozen, her hands stiffened with cold like Howard Blackburn's hands, frozen to the oars. Blackburn in the end lost all his fingers to frostbite and somehow later, in spite of his loss, became an expert at card tricks. Rena worried about her fingers and wondered if she would have the will to become expert at anything if all her fingers froze off. She thought she would. She was resourceful. She went on picking the bills.

Paul had been stricken early on a Tuesday night and by Wednesday evening it had been determined that the cause of his condition had not been the crash itself. Maureen had called Rena Thursday morning to say that the doctor in Boston told her the most recent brain scan had shown a serious and rapid regrowth of the tumor since the previous month's scan. The scans confirmed that the tumor was the probable cause of the accident.

"Why didn't I know about this tumor?" she cried to Rena. "Those scans had gotten routine; I assumed Paul would tell me if there was any change. But I was wrong."

"Maybe he didn't know. Maybe he never got the results," hoped Rena.

"He did," Maureen cried softly. "He told the doctor he didn't want us to know."

"I'm sure he was trying to spare you. It must have been a difficult decision."

"The doctor said Paul took a few days to decide whether to undergo additional surgery—it would be of only short term benefit at best. He decided to let nature take its course. Rena, I'm hurt that I didn't know," Maureen confided, her voice failing at the end.

Nature had taken its course swiftly.

They kept him sedated and then when they let him come up, he was confused, he slept a lot. Maureen and the girls waited by his side for him to get better, in spite of being offered no hope.

On Friday Maureen called Rena to come. Rena had been impatient for this moment. Now that the moment was here, it was useless. She sat with Paul and held his hand and he seemed to recognize her, seemed to respond to her by the movements of his hand on hers, but no coherent conversation was possible. Rena let the tears run down her face without bothering to wipe them. She kissed his face when she left for the first and last time.

When the call came, it was Paul's daughter Maria, and she didn't say anything, just choked on words enough for Rena to recognize her voice. Rena finally said, "Your father's gone." And Maria burst into sobs, and that's all there was to it.

For two days after Paul officially passed away, Rena was the soul of competency. She went straight into Paul's office and pushed the empty chair aside without actually looking at it. She found the key to the desk drawer where the photos and memorabilia of Karen and their son resided. She stacked the contents in a cardboard file box, secured it with its string latch and wrote on the side, "Rena's Auto Records," so much less intriguing a label than "Personal." She set the box under her purse at her desk to take home. Then she called Karen. The mother of Paul's child wouldn't have to read the news in the newspaper this time.

Rena went through papers, made calls, talked to Jim Cohen, the Town attorney, double-checking the procedures for the transfer of power. She took the bylaws to Lyndon, to reinforce her conclusion that he was to be acting Chairman until the Board met to elect a new one. Then she personally drove him to the bank and got his signature on file in case the treasurer were unavailable.

She ordered an impressive official arrangement of flowers to be sent by Town Hall staff and then for herself she chose a small live lilac bush. She picked up little white cards with their tiny little envelopes from the florist shop counter. She pulled from her purse the tiny Rubaiyat she had kept in her special room all these years. She opened it, and, pressing the pages back with her thumb, she copied onto the card:

Ah, Love! could not you and I with Fate conspire—
To grasp this sorry Scheme of Things entire,—
Would not we shatter it to bits—
and then Remould it nearer to our Heart's Desire!

She had to write that. Of course, she wouldn't send it. She looked at the words for a long time, and then she pushed the card deep into her purse. On another card she wrote: "With deepest sympathy, Rena." She could do no better; there was too much to say. She slipped it into its envelope, wrote, "To Maureen, Leslee, and Maria," on the outside and handed it to the florist.

She didn't want to go to the funeral home, yet she was compelled to as if she had been tied with a rope and pulled behind a twenty-five hp Evinrude. She went into the building leaning backward against the pull. But when she got to the corridor outside of the receiving rooms, the pull stopped and she floundered, looking for a way out. She hung by the door unable to enter. She struggled to arrange a compromise with herself. She wanted to know where the body lay in the room; she thought she might go in with her back to the casket and face Maureen and the girls, do what she had to do and leave. She might be able to do that. Her eyes didn't meet the eyes of people she knew, but when a stranger emerged from the room, she asked him where the body was. The person waved her hand toward the back of the room. And where was the family? Back there, too, with the casket. Impossible. She could not go to the casket, absolutely would not go to it.

She shook her head, saying to the stranger, "I can't go in." She wanted the stranger to take her in her arms and hold her and pat her and say it was going to be all right. Strangers are the best ones for that. But the stranger shrugged and said, "No need to go in. It doesn't even look like him." And if it had looked like him that would have been reason to go? She stared after the stranger, not comprehending the matter-of-fact way people did these duties. There was something they knew which she did not or vice versa.

She pressed against the wall waiting from some deliverance she knew was unlikely to come. Then she recognized for the first time little Paul at the end of the hall moving playfully, using his body as a toy, falling and jumping up, running his fingers along the wall. Beside him was Karen.

Rena walked slowly toward them, almost sliding along the wall. hardly able to hold herself up. She dropped to her knees near them. Karen seemed too grieved to react. Rena rummaged around in her purse and found a number of pennies, a ridiculous number, Paul had told her, for they weighted her purse down. She took them from her purse and stood them up in two stacks and lay a pencil across the top. Then she gathered them up again. She lay them out in a circle, rolling them into place with the pencil. Little Paul stopped and watched. She made a stair-step arrangement of pennies. He stepped closer and finally dropped to his knees beside her.

Finally, when she laid out another row, he put out his finger and pushed one into place. They did another design wordlessly. Then, as he took up her play on his own, she watched the perfect skin of his arms stretch and dimple as he moved. She reached out and touched the blonde wisps on the back of the neck and he let her. He put his hand on her knee to balance himself with no sense of knowing or not knowing her. She touched the soft skin. She admired the curl of his lashes, drinking in every detail. All the while Karen stared ahead. Tears flowed down Rena's cheeks though she was comforted by this play.

"The shiny ones are yours, " she finally said.

"And the not shiny ones are yours?" he said.

"Yes, and the ones lying down are dog's dishes and the ones standing on edge are wheels." She set two on edge and rolled them with her pencil.

"I want mine to be wheels." He turned them up on their edge but when he pushed them they fell over.

"When they fall over they are flat tires and you have to blow them up."

He looked up at her and waited and she waited and then he leaned down and blew on the pennies. Then he gathered them up and let them drop.

"And when they fall they are..." he watched some of them curl on down the hall where mourners coming and going did not seem to notice.

"And when they fall, they are crabs and you have to catch them."

Paul ran to pick them up.

"And if you catch them, you put them in the pot."

She held out her purse and he dropped them in. Then as if worried she would take them away, he took them out again.

"Let me do it again," he said, and let them spill out of his hand onto the carpet and roll away. Rena had never liked silly stories. This nonsense appeared from nowhere and she didn't stop it. She and little Paul played and, for a long time, she did not think of why she had come here. When she did, she gathered the pennies up and tucked them in little Paul's pocket. Then she kissed the top of his head and rose to go.

Karen seemed to notice Rena for the first time. She put her hand out to stop Rena.

"Stay with him for a minute while I go in," Karen asked.

Rena nodded and sat down again. She watched wide-eyed as Karen went into the room where Rena could not bring herself to go. She had to remind herself that it was all right. There was no reason why Karen Omwek of the class of 1959 shouldn't come to pay last respects to her classmate. There was more than one reason why P.S. should not go in.

When Karen returned, her face was wet but she was calm.

"Thank you for coming," Karen said to Rena, adding, "I have

no one to grieve with."

Rena squeezed Karen's shoulder and left before she might break down. Rena hadn't intended to ally herself solely with Karen and her son, but her cowardice, she had to confess, had kept her from giving her first attention to Paul's first family.

Rena arrived conspicuously late at the funeral, but Phil and Ada made room for her on the second pew behind the family. Maria was directly in front of her, stony white. Leslee was crying softly. While the Reverend Butler read a prayer, Rena prayed for the ceremony to be over. Rena felt the dull pain of grief rising from her chest but it stuck in her throat and she felt a dark hand squeezing her neck. As people spoke, she heard nothing, not the words of Reverend Butler, not the sniffling of children.

She did not turn to look at the casket. She knew about caskets, knew why they were made, knew they had nothing to do with the person who had died. She considered them a travesty, an empty box. The presence of the body, however hidden by the casket, had the opposite effect of that intended. It was as if to say the body was important; it was worth saving only they couldn't save it very well. No. If it had been worth saving, Paul would have kept it. He didn't want it anymore. He left it. He was gone. And why do they keep this thing and put it in a box and carry it around like an empty ice chest is carried up from the beach, heavy with the trash and empty bottles of the party. Drain it. Throw the ice away. Toss the bottles. Trash is trash.

The spirit is another thing. When the party is over, you leave the spirit of the thing in the rhythms of the sea, let the fragments of frivolity slip away into the tide, roll in the undertow, splash up again another day.

The grip around her throat tightened and Rena felt faint. The room spun. She sat with her hands to her throat and her eyes closed. Finally, after what seemed an eternity, she felt people touch her and she realized the funeral was over. Ada and Phil patted her shoulder as they left and other well-meaning hands reached out to her. She felt their kindness but did not look up.

When everyone else had gone, Rena lay down on the pew until her head stopped spinning. She breathed in deeply and went with the outbreath until the grip around her throat was loosened. She got up and walked gingerly to her car, concentrating painfully just to find her keys, to choose the right one for the ignition, to stop at the stop signs. She arrived late at the interment and parked her car on the road outside the cemetery instead of inside with the others. She walked through the gate and hung in the back, unwilling to see, unwilling to stay away. She did not walk with the others up the hill where Paul would be laid to rest. She knew the spot well, where bright ocher moss splotched the headstones of every generation of Lawsons from Captain Josiah Lawson and to Joan Sorrell Lawson, Paul's mother. But she did not want to see Paul's place among them. Instead, Rena turned to the great rock near the entrance where a graceful curve of sculpted indentations had been carved. She placed her feet carefully in these steps and ascended. From the top she could look down on the group gathered at the Lawson row and beyond to the Ipswitch Bay, still and silver in the afternoon gloom.

She left before the others turned around. She drove to West Beach and parked in the spot closest to the sea. She stared at the surf without summoning the language to encapsulate thoughts. Then she slept. When she woke with a neck so stiff it pained her to move, it was dark. She drove home and went directly to bed. The next day, Ada called Rena, and they commiserated. Ada was obviously weepy, and Rena comforted her.

Two days after the funeral, Rena called Karen to arrange a condolence call. She didn't know why she would go to see Karen before Maureen. Maybe it was to transfer the mementos of P.S.'s childhood safely into Karen's hands and out of her own first. Maybe because Maureen would always be there, while Karen and P.S, well, who knew what would happen to them now.

The duplex where Karen lived in Magnolia were built of driftwood-gray planks placed vertically in the contemporary manner, with two little green doorways darkened by dense ornamental cedars. Rena found number 136 and rang.

Karen came. She looked better perhaps than the evening of the visitation but not the Karen of the reunion either. Her eyes did not sparkle and her hair did not glisten. She was a little plumper than Rena remembered, less taut. Comfortable like a wife. She smiled softly, said "Come in."

Rena followed Karen, crunching over sisal rug, through the dark entry hall into a small living room. A country pine dining table glowed with light from double glass doors opening onto a patio. Rena's eyes squinted in the light. She set the box on the table and turned back to the shadows of the small room. A futon sofa, a dark brown mushroom-shaped velvet chair, some dhurri covered cushions, and a Mexican rug made the dimness cozy. Karen reached to the wall and turned a switch. A bright spot suddenly glowed in the shadows, catching her eye. Over a bookcase, Paul's face, illuminated as if by the same light that streamed in the windows, looked out of a canvas–not directly as if looking at the artist, not stiffly as if posing–but engagingly as if in conversation. The painting looked like an oil, more likely acrylic, still unframed with the edges of canvas loose towards the back.

Paul's face did not shock Rena. His presence seemed natural there. Still the effect of his image swelled in Rena, the memory of Paul in health rushed over her, breaking like a wave in her stomach and running over her limbs like water sweeping up the beach. The wave of emotion finally receded, leaving her breathless.

"You like it?"

"More than like. I'm blown away. You did it?"

"Yes."

"I thought you no longer did anything representational."

She shrugged. "There's a time for abstraction and there's a time to study every concrete thing more closely than you ever did before."

"When do you find the time to do your own work with teaching and taking care of P.S.?" Rena asked, cutting her eyes around for signs of the child.

"I don't have much time for my own work, especially in the day time when the light is good."

"The light is good here," Rena said gesturing to the light that flowed over Paul's face. "We did that in the early morning, before work, right there. She walked over and touched the pine table."

Rena could see now that the table was the same as the one Paul was leaning over in the picture, his arms straight, his hands flattened out as he leaned on the table, looking down at something or someone who wasn't there. The paint scudded off into bare canvas.

"Unfinished?"

"I'm going to put P.S. there, looking up from his cereal bowl with his spoon in his hand. P.S. actually had breakfast at that table, every morning before preschool, talking to Paul while I painted."

Rena's eyes widened. Of course. Paul visited with P.S. during his early morning fishing time. The hours he'd reserved for himself to tend his pots, the hours she'd marveled at his devotion to the trade of his forebears, he had secretly given instead to his son. Rena had no trouble believing that Paul could have known P.S. almost as well as either of his daughters by giving the boy his undivided attention for the first hour of every day.

"I'm glad I finished painting Paul first because..." Her voice broke and she turned to the window.

"I'm sorry you've lost Paul," Rena said.

"Thank you. I'm sorry you lost him, too. I know what good friends...."

"Thank you. We were."

"Let me get you some tea." While Karen was gone, Rena studied Paul's face. It was exactly as he was in life but there was something else. His face was untroubled but intent, engrossed as a child playing with toys, lost in immediacy. Rena looked at the space where little Paul would be and back at Paul, trying to comprehend how a man can have two families and both be real.

Karen came back with little cups of tea in Japanese rice cups. Rena looked in vain for lemon, and then tasting the tea, realized it was one of those awful herbal things that even lemon couldn't save. Surely Paul had not drunk this stuff.

"And where is P.S. now?"

"He's with Mother next door." She waved toward the other half of the duplex. "I couldn't have managed without Mother. I moved here to look after her, but it's turned out I need her more than she needs me. But she's thrilled to have a grandchild."

Rena nodded empathetically even though she couldn't imagine herself and her mother relying on each other.

They were quiet. Karen sipped tea and mused. Rena touched

her lips politely to the hot liquid and then set the cup down.

"Karen," Rena finally said, "before the accident, did you know the tumor had come back?"

"I had no idea. I didn't know about the tumor till I read it in the newspaper two days later."

Rena winced. The day of the accident it had never come into her mind to call Karen. She had taken care of everything so efficiently at the office, had been in close touch with Maureen and the girls—Karen had just not come into the picture. And so that evening, when Karen had called, distraught and helpless, having read of the accident in the newspaper, an icy sweep of realization had hit Rena that Karen had no way of knowing anything. Karen was no longer connected to Stonehaven Town Hall except through Rena. And then only when Rena thought of her.

"Nobody else knew either," Rena assured her. "I don't know whether he even knew himself."

"He couldn't have. He would've told me. I would've known."

Rena sighed lightly. It was she who should've known. She'd decided to go through every hour of those last few days in her mind and remember each conversation, each look and then she would know. She just hadn't had the heart to begin.

Rena and Karen said their good-byes. Rena went to her car, got behind the wheel, and circled the end of the cul de sac. As she headed out, she saw P.S. come around to the front of the house, stop and put his arm around the trunk of a small tree. She wished she had a picture of that, his serious face, his blonde hair finely spread over his forehead. She waved to him; he smiled and came to her car window. She looked at him a long time, wanting to say something memorable but not goodbye. She finally said, "Someday you'll want to come see me. I'll be waiting. Just call me."

"Okay."

And she drove away.

It began to rain lightly. Nevertheless, Rena felt a strong pull to return to Boding Point for the first time since Paul's death, maybe to walk through the horrible event again, maybe to sit and calm herself. Maybe to comb the bushes again. She didn't know. Within minutes, she found herself standing among the blueberry bushes on the headland. She began to part the bushes compulsively with her hands. Some of the missing bills might not have made it to the water, some may have been caught on briers or pounded deep into the undergrowth. As she ferreted about in the brush, she heard two boys walk up. She stood up quickly, looking as nonchalant as a woman can look standing in a blueberry thicket in a drizzle with no hat on. The boys stopped and regarded her curiously. She returned their stare, then looked away, flicking a blueberry bush dismissively.

"What are you looking for?" the taller boy asked.

Rena hesitated a trifle too long but was relieved to hear herself finally blurt out, "I'm looking for my hat." She gave her bare head, beaded with droplets, a convincing clutch.

"Let's find it," the shorter boy said to his friend, and they were soon whooping through the bushes.

"Oh, don't worry about it. Maybe it blew in the water," Rena called.

The boys looked in the direction the wind was blowing, crossed the point, and started down the other side toward Whalebone Cove, thwacking the bushes with a stick as they went.

When they were out of sight, Rena picked her way out of the brush and went toward the opposite side of the point, down to the water of Boding Cove. As she stood on the farthest rock she dared stand on, the cold wind slapped her face. The spray of the breakers ran down her cheeks like tears, and the retreat of the waves were an amplification of her sighs.

Then suddenly there was a voice right at her elbow.

"Lady, is this it?"

She turned so suddenly she almost spun off her rock. There before her were the boys, one holding up a dripping, sodden, shapeless object the color of the sand at the bottom of the bay. She squinted at it, and the boy obligingly opened it up for her to see better.

As recognition swept over Rena, she grew faint. She took the object from the boy's hand and, in the same motion, slipped to her knees. It was an oiled fisherman's hat. It was Paul's hat. Paul's Cape Ann hat.

"Yes, yes," she cried. Her eyes filled with tears, and she clutched the hat to her chest. "It's a miracle. Thank you, thank you, thank you."

"No problem," the boys said and turned away, the short one hurrying after the taller one. They went on toward the end of the point to pursue the business of boys. Rena could hear their voices blowing back to her.

"Was that lady weird or what?"

"It wasn't even a good hat."

"No kidding. It was a crappy hat."

Rena shook out the hat and rounded out the crown with her fist. Then she carried it to her car and drove home, sobbing the whole way, releasing the tears that had been stuck inside. In her driveway, still clutching the wheel, she bawled.

It was two days later that Rena and Maureen talked for the first time since the funeral. Rena wanted to pay a formal condolence call. She didn't want her sympathy for Maureen and the girls to go without saying just because they were good friends.

And there was something Rena wanted to know besides.

"The scan," Rena began, "the bad one...when did Paul get those results?"

Maureen shrugged. "I didn't ask. It doesn't matter now," she said.

But it mattered to Rena. Back at the office, she called the doctor's office and asked for the bookkeeper, explained she was handling Paul's insurance at Town Hall, and asked if she would look up some things for her so that she could spare Maureen dealing with anything. Rena was particularly interested in the bill for the consultation about the scan. Had that actually taken place, she asked, and, if so, when? March first. Rena sighed. He'd known. The day before P.S.'s birthday. That explained Paul's breaking down over the birthday pictures. That explained a lot. Maybe that explained everything.

The next morning, she woke before the alarm and turned it off. She lay in reverie, letting questions and answers roll around together as in a pinball machine until the sound of something falling into place woke her.

She got up and went down to her study. She slipped to her

knees and pulled the cardboard box out from under the daybed and straightened up its crushed sides. She pulled out the plastic bag stuffed with bills.

Kneeling, she dug the fingers of both hands deep into the box and into the bag, weighing the money with her hands, feeling its coolness. She rifled through it, noting the mix of hundreds and fifties and twenties. She picked up a fistful and spread it out like a too full canasta hand. She let it fall and picked the bills up again one by one.

A beam of light from the rising sun shone obliquely through the stained glass in the window and splayed out over her, staining her skin purple and blue and rose as she knelt by the box. She rubbed an old hundred between her thumb and forefinger just to savor its silken thinness. She rubbed and touched and rumpled and smoothed until the bills began to feel like holy cloth and she was performing a sacrament. Maybe Paul was trying to tell her something. Maybe now Paul meant for her to have the money as a reward for all she had done for him.

She gasped as she realized she'd let in the thought that had been lurking around the periphery of her mind like a feral dog waiting for a scrap: Should she give the money to Karen for P.S. or (she winced at the whisper of the words)–keep it herself.

Of course she wasn't going to keep it, but she could briefly engage the thought, couldn't she?

The inheritance of Aunt Amelia's house had relieved Rena of housing costs and kept her from having to get a better-paying job, but taxes had been rising, the roof needed replacing. When was the last time she took a real vacation and went somewhere? Maybe she could join one of those archeological digs they advertise–go to Peru, go to Kenya, go somewhere startling and life-changing, meet some new people.

On the other hand, P.S. did need the money; it was hard to raise a child on an art teacher's pay. And the aging grandmother wouldn't be able to keep P.S. forever. Would she want Paul's child to have to go to after-school day care so his mother could work fulltime? And what about college? Paul's child shouldn't have to do without. On top of that, Karen had a mortgage, Paul had said; her mother had always rented.

Rena sat up cross-legged on the daybed. She held her head in her hands and rocked as she dissected the issue. First, there had been no hint from Karen, no oblique questions about the car after the crash or where Paul had been, nor any hand-wringing silences at their first meetings. Paul would not have told Karen in advance that he was getting the money. He might have said, "Somehow I will get some money to help you." He might have said that, but he would not want Karen to know he'd commit a crime for her. No, Karen didn't know.

Well, it didn't really matter anyway since Paul intended that money for P.S., and that should settle it. If Paul sacrificed his integrity, it should be redeemed by this good deed. Otherwise the circumstance of his death would constitute an even greater tragedy than it already was. It was Rena's responsibility to do the right thing.

She went to the attic to find an old suitcase. The one she had in mind was tan, of some sort of woven material hardened with shellac, with a pair of brown stripes around it, her father's, the one she had taken to college.

She found it between the Christmas decorations and the summer slipcovers. She pushed the round buttons aside with her thumb to release the latches. The latch on one end popped open. The other didn't. Then she remembered it was not the suitcase's lack of style that relegated it to the attic; it was its broken latch. There was a trick to opening it. It was a trick Rena the college student had tolerated well but Rena the adult avoided, especially since she regularly forgot the trick and had to rediscover it each time. She tried unlatching them both simultaneously but that wasn't the trick. She tried lifting the latch with her fingers but it didn't budge. So she pushed the button to the side with one thumb and with the other hand pulled the latch open. That was it.

She didn't even remember what was in the suitcase, now that it was a storage box. She rummaged through it, pulling out some out-of-season shoes and a dressy hat she never wore and tossing them into the bottom of a garment bag.

She carried the emptied vintage suitcase to her room. She stacked the tidy bills from the box in the bottom of the suitcase and she dumped all the cash from the bag on top of that. She snapped the suitcase shut and carried it to her car. She set it in the trunk on top of her beach blanket. The trunk door thudded loudly, "End of Chapter." She had not delivered the money, but she had got it out of her house.

The next day at work, however, Rena's sense of closure was jarred open by a call from Karen. The bereaved young mother wanted Rena to come meet with her again.

"There's something I want from you." Those were Karen's exact words.

Well, here it was. She'd want the money. This demand of Karen's would verify the suspicion that Rena had been fending off. It would bring her face to face with the excruciating torment Paul must have faced in the vise between honor and obligation, between integrity and love. How rare, alas, is the clear choice between good and evil.

But no such problem tore Rena. If Paul had intended the money for Karen to raise his son, then she would have it.

When Rena arrived on Karen's doorstep on the appointed Saturday morning, she was struggling with the old suitcase.

Karen reached for it, but Rena stopped her.

"No, no. I can handle it."

They sat down on Karen's sofa. Rena barely glanced at the painting of Paul that presided over the den. Through the sliding glass door she could see P.S. digging in some sand. His grandmother sat in a folding lawn chair, watching him with an expression of contentment.

"A sand pile," Rena said. "I had almost forgotten they exist."

"Actually, we had a sand pile once and little Paul never played in it. That pile of sand there was for mixing concrete. Paul was going to pave a little track around the roses for P.S. to ride his Big Wheel. But now I guess it will always be a sand pile."

"He had a special concrete formula, I bet, something that was going to save the environment," Rena said.

"He did. How did you know?"

Rena chuckled. Karen would never know half as much as she knew about Paul.

"I came to see how you and P.S. were doing and...," she gestured toward the suitcase.

"That's very sweet of you. We're doing as well as can be expected. He doesn't really understand his Daddy's gone for good. He's used to Paul coming and going. I'm afraid he still expects Paul to come back."

Karen served some herbal tea again with thin Swedish crackers that Rena could have devoured all in one mouthful but nibbled with great discipline while thinking of what to say and what not to say. She wanted to come away from perhaps their last meeting with some sense of resolution.

"Are you bitter, Karen, for what happened?"

"No. You're only bitter if you think, 'Someone did this to me.' I did this to myself. Little Paul is a gift I unknowingly wanted and I take full responsibility."

"Well, Paul did his part."

Karen shook her head. "Don't try to take this from me: Knowing I am responsible—that's also a gift."

Rena smiled and bit into another flatbrot.

"Well, I know it isn't easy. It's not easy for me either, but I brought you something that should help." Rena got up and went to the suitcase. She bounced one end of it onto the sisal rug and began to push it across the room.

"Raising a child alone is not easy emotionally and..." She tipped the suitcase over on its side in front of Karen. Karen slipped to the edge of the sofa to watch.

"...it's not easy financially either," Rena went on. She flipped the lever beside the latch and looked up to catch the look on Karen's face when she lifted the top. But the lever didn't work. Rena had forgotten about that glitch again. She squared herself with the suitcase to perform the two necessary thumb moves at the same time.

"Well, financially, we're going to be okay," Karen said. "I've taken care of that."

Rena stood straight up almost straddling the prone suitcase.

"How did you take care of that?"

"Well, it just happened that right after I got pregnant I got an ad in the mail. Junk mail, you know. This ad talked about life insurance you could get without a medical exam. You know Paul told me he would give me money whenever he sold something big at the company and he did that. Well, it dawned on me, even then, that if anything happened to Paul there wouldn't be anyone, you know, who would help out like he would. I didn't in a million years think anything would happen to him, but the ad said, 'You think it won't happen....' and that's exactly what I was thinking. Like it was meant for me. So I took out a policy on his life."

"You took out a policy on his life?" Rena's heart was in her throat....If Paul had insurance, why did he...or maybe he didn't...and if not....

"Yes. I didn't tell him. It didn't seem like a nice thing to do. You know, like I was saying he was old and might die or something. Or I was too interested in money. So I didn't tell him."

"But how could you do that without his knowing?"

"Paul had almost never been sick until...., you know. I knew his doctor's name. I filled out the form. I...well, I signed his name just like his signature. It's not like it was cheating or anything. I didn't know he was going to get sick, and I made the payments."

Rena put her hand to her pounding heart. She felt like the pilot of a plane taking off and seeing the dials go crazy and having to decide whether it's too late to change course, whether to go up or to reverse the engines. Rena grabbed the suitcase by the handles and set it upright.

"So what's in the suitcase for me?"

Rena stared at the suitcase in disbelief as if it were a whale getting ready to swallow her. Then slowly like a zombie she reached her thumb for the latch button and pushed it to the side. The latch didn't open.

"Oh, this old suitcase. It must be a hundred years old." She shoved the button several times, as if frantic. She shook the suitcase fruitlessly.

"I'll just have to take it to the hardware store and let Charlie open it with a locksmith's tool."

"At least tell me what's in the suitcase."

"It's...just some...well, it's.... It's Paul's hat," she said. "I wanted you to have it."

"His hat! I never would have guessed! The suitcase looked so heavy. Oh, you were fooling me, dragging it in like that. How sweet of you!"

Rena pushed the suitcase toward the door trying to make the move look effortless.

"Oh, let me try it," Karen said, jumping up. "I bet I can open it. Paul always said I had mechanical ability."

Karen set her thumb firmly on the button and pushed it. Nothing happened. She stepped back and looked at the suitcase, her eyes cutting from one latch to the other, appraising the faulty mechanism.

"I know...maybe if I ..."

Rena saw the wheels of Karen's mechanical ability turning. She saw Karen's thumbs go up into position. It was now or never. Rena stepped between Karen and the recalcitrant suitcase.

"Karen, this is a sign...from ...you know...." –she tried to think of what people with futons and herbal tea would say– "...from higher worlds... that it's not good for me to give you the hat. It's a sign that I should keep it. Remember Paul's devotion to the Cape Ann hat? I was the one who said, 'Buy it, Paul, if you love it that much.' I was there when he brought it back to Town Hall. I was with Paul when he wore this hat–" she patted the side of the suitcase– "for the very first time. He wore it when his hair fell out. He wore it when he stood in front of the whole town and asked them to save our way of life. He wore it the last day...." Tears came into her eyes and her voice squeaked. "I loved that hat. I said I was giving it to you, but I have changed my mind."

Rena felt Karen staring at her, and she realized that her desperate lie had taken on the resonance of truth in mid-speech. She had been transported by passion for Paul articulated as clearly as if she had shouted it out. And that passion had equally brought her to a new state of certainty.

Rena jerked up the suitcase as if it had weighed no more than a feather and carried it to her car, Karen trailing behind.

She put the suitcase in the trunk and closed the door. She went around the car to get in.

"Wait," said Karen. "Come back inside. I asked you to come today because I needed something from you."

"Oh!" Rena remembered now. Yes, that's why she had brought the suitcase full of money in the first place. Now that she had woven the money into a hat and taken it back, what could Karen want? She turned back to the house with Karen. Any request the young mother made now would seem trivial.

"I want them to acknowledge Paul's son," Karen said.

"Who?"

"His family. P.S. was as much Paul's son as his daughters are his daughters."

"Yes, of course, but you can't expect them to look at it that way."

"Why not?"

"Karen, P.S. is Paul's illegitimate son. That is their way of thinking."

"That doesn't exist anymore."

"Maybe not, but it's a very basic concept. It doesn't change easily."

"I'm not asking for their money. I'm only asking them to accept that P.S. is Paul's son."

Rena would have welcomed even the herbal tea to give her pause, but she had to forge ahead.

"Don't you understand jealousy? Hurt? Righteous indignation?"

"Don't you understand pride? I'm proud to be Paul's..."

It gave Rena some small satisfaction to see Karen grope for a word.

"I'm proud to have Paul's son. P.S. is proud of his father, he has a right to be. You've seen them together. He has right to stand up and say I'm Paul Lawson's son. I'm Paul Lawson Jr."

"Maybe someday... but right now is not the time."

"Next Sunday."

"What about next Sunday?"

"Next Sunday at the dedication."

"WHAT at the dedication?" Rena held her breath.

"When they unveil the name, Paul S. Lawson, on the new community center. P.S. will be there. He has got to see that."

"Well, okay. He can see that."

"Up front."

"What are you saying?"

"I want him to stand up front with the rest of his family."

Rena put her hand over her face. *You are not responsible. You do not have to make this happen. You do not have to make it NOT happen. This is not your doing. She can't make you take responsibility.*

"Why are you telling ME this?" Rena finally said.

"Because you're the one who understands. And...I called Town Hall, and they said you're the one making the seating arrangements."

Rena's hand struck her breast with a thud. "Me?"

"You, because you already acknowledge P.S. as Paul's child. Now all I want is for the community to acknowledge him as Paul's son. So he can walk down Front Street and say, 'My father was the town's leading citizen for twenty years.' He can't have a living role model any more but he can have that. And someday he can take HIS son down Front Street and he can point to the name in stone. He can say, "That was your grandfather. Paul S. Lawson." Rena's eyes widened and her hand pressed her chest as if to hold back a gasp.

"None of this is the child's fault, Rena. HE shouldn't have to fight for acceptance."

"Couldn't he win acceptance by being a nice, ordinary citizen. Does he have to be the Chairman's son. I mean, being the son of the Chairman of a small town Board of Selectmen is not like being President."

"It is, in his small world. Paul is gone, his name in granite is the most tangible reminder...."

"There are scrapbooks, Karen, and photo albums. When he's old enough to understand, I'll talk to him about his father, tell him little stories. I promise."

Karen was shaking her head. "Now. While he is forming his identity. He's Paul's son. That must be acknowledged, not denied. Especially not on Sunday at the dedication."

"Sunday, you're going to spring this on Paul's family—in public? Maureen may have a heart attack! Think of how hurt she'd be. To have Paul's memory ruined. You can't do that."

"Of course, I won't spring it on her," Karen grumbled, seeming to search for an alternative she had not prepared. "But I could use a little help. I was hoping you could...prepare her a little bit. Or at least have some ideas about how to tell her gently."

"I'm fresh out of those ideas. You're on your own here."

"OK, I'll deal with it myself then. All you have to do is seat us on the dais in such a way that Paul's son is equal to his daughters. I want him to remember that."

How could this sweet, soft, bosomy woman be so tough? Artists are supposed to be unassertive, that is why they starve.

But then Rena saw that Karen was trembling. It was one thing not to fear; it was another thing entirely to fear and go ahead with resolve. Karen's recklessness gave Rena pause. Maybe this quivering determination was what got Karen through art school and into a job as a high school art teacher. It was a long way from chopping off fish heads in a sardine factory as her mother had done.

"If you just want P.S. to get a clear view of the unveiling, I could arrange a high...."

Karen was shaking her head.

"Look, Karen, I'll make you a deal. If you promise not to tell Maureen or anyone who P.S. is until after the dedication, I'll find some way to put you up front..."

Karen waited.

"...in chairs with the dignitaries."

Karen waited.

"...in chairs...near the family. But Karen you have to promise me you'll just say he's your son if anyone asks. Nothing more."

"For now," Karen agreed, then added wistfully, "The people will be congratulating Maureen and his girls and no one will be acknowledging us and our grief.

"That's right, Karen. That's the price you pay for having a child with a married man."

"I willingly pay the price. But little Paul shouldn't have to pay."

Little Paul? Since when was she calling him Little Paul?

"I don't know why I'm even discussing this with you." Rena got up and got her jacket and moved toward the door. She turned back and raised an eyebrow at Karen. "Remember, I seat you on the dais, you don't tell anything."

272

All the way home, Rena gave an imaginary speech to Karen, the one she should surely have given to her face: You have this harebrained idea you're going to get your lover's family to acknowledge your child and you think I'm going to arrange the seating for you. Well, you have another think coming. I'll do nothing of the sort. I'll just go right on as if nothing is amiss and you can settle it any way you want!

Rena was exhilarated by her anger, enjoyed her outburst–alone in her car–but in reality she was afraid to leave the matter to be settled any way Karen wanted.

What if Lyndon Moore, who was going to be the master of ceremonies, would say, "Rena, why is this woman sitting up here with her child next to Paul's family?"

She could say, "Maybe her child wants a better view."

And what if Maureen would say, "Rena, why didn't you tell me this child was Karen's?"

And she'd say, "Oh, that's right. I forgot you two had met."

And that was just if Karen didn't say a word. If she opened her mouth, Paul would be ruined. So that is why it fell to Rena to humor Karen, at least until the dedication was past, to keep things the way they were.

Rena awoke the next morning in mid-worry and sat up in bed, pulling the pillows up behind her. She thought getting all the way up in one jolt wouldn't be good for her today. From her bed she could see the ocean, silver as a knight's armor. Small waves were making unexpected explosions out of proportion to their gentle approach. The tide was strong, its force held down as if by a spring and then, at the last second, let loose.

Suddenly it hit her: this was all Paul's fault. He, in his misguided belief that she was to make all things smooth around him, had laid this mess at her feet. Well, she would just have a word with Paul S. Lawson.

She pulled her raincoat on over her pajamas, picked up her purse, and roared over to the cemetery. She jolted to a stop under the first elm. She marched up the hill to the Lawson section. Where else could she go to confront him?

This was the first time she had seen the grave up close, so she checked the name on the stone just to be sure. She did not read further as she wanted to be sure whatever laudatory phrases might be inscribed there would not soften the edge of her anger.

"Paul. Paul, you listen to me." She shook her finger at the too new sod. "Look at me. And do not WINK."

"You had your fun, you had your deep understanding, your acceptance of you just the way you are. Fine. You had your stolen nights, your borrowed days. You witnessed your son's birth. You cut the umbilical cord. Great. Yes, she is a warm, wonderful person. I'll take your word for it.

"You had all that. And then you LEFT. Left me to deal with this. You scoundrel, Paul, you son of a sailor, you wharf rat.

"Oh, yes, Miss Karen is willing to raise the child on her own. Oh, yes, you kicked in child support. We won't go into THAT now. Except to mention who had to harvest it from the blueberry bushes in the middle of the night. And it was a very cold night, Paul, very, v-e-r-y cold like this grave is going to be next winter.

"But orchestrate the dedication of the new community center with the mothers of your several children in attendance and be mistress of ceremonies to your son's coming out?

"This time you have crossed the line, Chairman Lawson."

She circled once around the grave, squinting her eyes at it as if she thought Paul might be cowering behind the head stone.

"Paul. Are you listening?" she shouted. "You are not getting out of this so easy. I am giving you twenty-four hours to solve this and get back to me.

"Don't worry, I will know the sign," she said, hand on hip. "It can take any form: it can be a light bulb in my mind, it can be a smoke signal rising from a burning bush, it can be written on stone tablets, but Paul, hear this: it had better include a completely legible seating plan."

She wheeled and marched down the hill snapping twigs and skidding on leaves. She jumped into her car and dug out, gouging troughs in the newly thawed mud.

21

He's My Daddy

Lyndon Moore had not disturbed a paper on Paul's desk in the two weeks since he had become the acting Chairman. He had gathered up some files a few days after the funeral and had paused in front of Rena at her desk. She had looked up at him, fixing him in the eye. "Shall I....?" he had started to ask, and then turned and headed for the work desk in the copy machine room, mumbling, "I'll just do it in here."

Rena herself did not go into Paul's office easily. She'd only been in Paul's office twice since his death. Now clearly she had to go back to do the right thing for Lyndon, who was just beginning to grasp the enormity of what Paul had been doing.

She took a deep breath and went in. She pulled the old blotter off Paul's desk, noted the phone numbers, names and trial spellings of words scribbled on it, hesitated, then balled it up and put it in the trash. During lunch break, she went to the General Store and bought a new blotter, a box of paper clips, and a clutch of new pencils and ballpoint pens. On impulse she picked up a ceramic mug with "The Boss" written on it and stuck the pencils in it. Passing by the grocery store, she was inspired to buy one rose, and she brought all this back and arranged it, putting the rose in a florist's vase saved from some previous occasion. Then she called Lyndon at his office at Cape Ann Box and Lumber.

"Lyndon, it's time you moved into the Chairman's office. I've got it ready for you. Thought you might like to do that this weekend when no one's around." Her voice didn't break at all.

"It won't be easy sitting in his chair."

"You'll do fine, Lyndon." This time her voice broke.

Now all the while Rena was clearing out Paul's office, she was looking for a sign from Paul, some little thing that would tell her what she should do about Karen and "little Paul" and Maureen and all that might happen at the dedication. She still expected him to take responsibility, if not here, from somewhere where he would presumably be more enlightened. But as much as she looked and listened, the sign never came.

Worrying about the dedication ceremony made it quite impossible for Rena to concentrate. Finally, she gave in and put away her work.

Rena cleared her desk and set out a legal pad and pencil. She would get to the heart of what was bothering her. She would see if the solution to the dilemma could possibly be as simple as a seating plan. It was not that she actually planned to seat Karen and little Paul on the dais, she simply wondered if seating plans had the power to control situations like this. She remembered when the participants of a Summit meeting during the Cold War had argued for days on the shape of the negotiating table. There was apparently something to positioning.

Obviously a dais would not do. She sketched a platform where Lyndon would sit, as master of ceremonies, along with their state legislator, who would be the speaker for the occasion, and maybe the architect; just below, and on the left, seats for the selectmen, and on the right, Paul's family. Maybe she could put the spouses of the selectmen on the front row of the audience and slip Karen in among them unnoticed. Rena held the sketch as far away as her arm could reach and tried to look at the configuration as a disinterested celebrant might look who was arriving at the scene. What she saw was a lopsided arrangement with too many selectmen and not enough family–Maureen, the girls, and Maureen's mother. Symmetry tolerates little disruption.

So she moved the aisle into an S shape to help confuse the issue of who is more important. Two chairs in the narrow section at the bottom, to the right of the aisle, were the lowest level of the configuration, barely elevated and almost indistinguishable from the public. Guess whose these would be, Rena thought.

If the family, meaning Maureen and the two girls were lined up along the curve of the S, with Maureen at the top and the two girls slightly lower, then Karen and little Paul even lower, then Maureen would end up three levels higher than Karen and separated from her by her two girls and yet they would be in a straight line of stair steps with the family. Potted ferns, randomly placed, could further confound the pattern. She made a note to get ferns.

She half thought that Karen would chicken-out and never show. The other half thought that she would think better of her demands and just sit quietly in the audience.

Rena proceeded nonetheless with her seating plan. She almost had to take a whip to the carpenter to get him to do as she said, so addicted was he to the conventional. She caught him evening up the unequal and matched the unmatchable when she didn't keep a close enough watch on him. She thought she should have perhaps hired a stage designer instead of an ordinary carpenter.

The Saturday of the dedication, Rena woke early. The sea was bright and choppy and the sun danced in celebration. She dressed in a navy dress with tiny white polka dots and hurried down to the dedication early to direct the placing of the chairs and to put names on the seats. As Tim, the Town Hall custodian, placed the chairs, Rena went a few rows back to squint at them. She came forward to adjust them. She closed her eyes and meditated a moment after each adjustment, saying under her breath, "Here's your last chance," and waiting for Paul to say "now you have it." But he never did and she finally had to be content with her own decisions.

When Tony arrived, he said, "Good grief, Rena, why didn't you just have a straight aisle like everyone else?"

"It's aesthetics, Tony. If you'll watch, you'll see it has a very pleasing effect."

Of course, the whole granite building had been visible for months but the inscription had been covered with a long cloth held up by strings at even intervals. Tony had rigged a release string that would let the cloth down little by little, revealing the writing underneath left to right.

"I've decided to stay at the back to have an overall view," Rena told Tony pointedly. She sat in one of the folding chairs by the entrance to the park and greeted people who came in.

"Oh, hello, Dick, when you're ready, just find your seat up on the platform. Your name is on the seat." She smiled brightly as if she were not worried sick.

All the chairs on the raised levels were marked except two. If Karen and little Paul came, Karen would surely spot them. And maybe it would seem to observers that the pair thoughtlessly sat in them not realizing they were part of the special guests' section. It might not be a big deal at all.

The Legion band began to play at one side while the platform filled. Suddenly Rena spotted Karen and P.S. coming in the other side. Karen, under a wide brimmed hat, was fresh and lovely in ecru coat dress trimmed with white. Paul was indeed adorable in navy blue short pants and high socks and a white shirt with navy vest and a peter pan collar. They were well turned out.

In spite of her decision to let nature take its course from here on in, Rena rushed forward to intercept them. She greeted Karen enthusiastically as if she hadn't seen her since the reunion and deliberately took her time with the pleasantries. She said to P.S., "My, don't you look wonderful."

And then Karen said, "Where are our seats?"

Rena breathed in a long breath and with the outflow she said, "Your seats are over there, on the FIRST level, see the two by the fern, right ON THE FRONT ROW." She marveled at how these words, "first" and "front" came out in place of the "lowest" and "last" of her secret intent. Suddenly, as Karen and her child headed to their seats without a word, there didn't seem to be any problem. It was as if she had unconsciously solved it. Or maybe Paul was working things out inside her. It was amazing how little her earlier crisis now seemed. Karen could sit on the platform with her child, and nobody would care. And then, by the end of this day, Rena's role would be over and whatever happened after that was not her affair.

Rena sat down in a seat with the audience and began an extra cheerful conversation with Beth Stone about the new plantings that had gone in the landscaping only this week.

The clock on the Congregational Church rang ten times and Lyndon began his welcome. The Reverend Butler read a few lines of scripture, and Father Monahan gave a blessing. Lyndon then introduced Cape Ann's congressman, and they settled in to the meat of the event. The congressman spoke of the progressiveness of Stonehaven's leadership. He listed the accomplishments of "our beloved long time Chairman" and all the words–courage, foresight, commitment– that Rena knew to be true of Paul from boyhood on. She let the tears run quietly down her face because she had realized they were less noticeable that way than if she mopped them. She tried to forget Karen and P.S. and focus on Paul's whole life and career achievement, but she couldn't help glancing to the two people on the front row.

P.S. kept lifting his legs straight and studying his shoes. Then he dropped his feet with a clunk and lifted them again with a scuffing sound. Rena saw Karen put her hand on his knee and pat it, whispering a soft admonishment. He was still then, looking up at some moths flickering in and out of the shade of the new building.

After the congressman's speech, the band played "Pomp and Circumstance" while Tony and Lyndon positioned themselves on either side of the inscription. Tony hung on to the string and Lyndon removed the microphone from its stand.

"Guests on the platform may all stand for the unveiling," Lyndon said. And they rose and turned their backs to the audience to better witness the dropping of the veil.

"I'm going to ask Maureen Lawson to do the honors." He made a welcoming gesture to Paul's widow and she graciously stepped up to join the new and officially elected Chairman. He took her elbow and steered her over to Tony who gave her the string and murmured last minute instructions.

"We dedicate this Community Center," Lyndon began, "to the memory of our long time and greatly loved Chairman." He paused and Maureen gave a light jerk on the string. Nothing happened and Rena could see Tony pantomiming a bigger jerk. Maureen put a little more muscle into her second try, and the veil dropped a few feet on the left to reveal the words, "Paul S. Lawson".

The crowd gave an "Aaah" of approval.

Maureen jerked again and the veil fell another few feet to reveal two more words: "Memorial Center."

The crowd murmured again.

A third jerk brought the remainder of the veil down, revealing the date.

The crowd applauded for a long time, more than a polite applause, a heartfelt long applause.

Well, Paul's son was seeing what his mother wanted him to see and remember. Rena saw him watch the unveiling, while pivoting on one foot. Then she saw him pointing and talking excitedly, but she couldn't hear his voice over the applause. When the applause died down, his clear high voice became intelligible.

"P! Mom, I see the letter P. A! See, Mom, A. U! See, it says Paul. That's me. Paul!"

Little Paul had stepped out into Rena's carefully planned aisle and was jumping up and down on his tiny little oxfords alternately pointing and jerking his mother's arm.

"And look! An L." His voice was getting even higher and louder.

People laughed pleasantly.

"L for Lawson. Paul Lawson. Mom, that's me!"

The whispers of people quietly asking each other, "Who is that?" became a rumble.

The speaker hesitated to go on.

"Paul Lawson! That's my name." He was pointing and jumping at the same time.

"No, no, honey. Paul Lawson was the Chairman," Leslee

Lawson said to him kindly. "That's his name up there."

"I know." the boy said almost frantically. "Paul Lawson died and went to heaven. He's my daddy."

Voices jumbled. Rena slumped down in the folding chair till her head rested on the chair back. She took a deep breath. *This is not my responsibility. This is not my responsibility.* Time passed, closing words were drowned out. Rena sunk in her chair through it all, going with the outbreath. When the crowd stood up to leave, Rena stood up and darted out.

22

Picking Up the Pieces

Rena turned off the ringers of her phones before she went to the side garden. There she stabbed the ground with her stainless steel trowel, scooped out dirt and plopped in gladiola bulbs. In front of them, she gouged out a trench and lined it with annual larkspur. She scattered zinnia seeds between the two rows for good measure.

In spite of exhaustion she did not sleep that night. She tried counting bedding plants and she tried concentrating on nothing but always came back to Little Paul and Karen and Maureen and she repeatedly advised herself, *This is not your responsibility.* Sunday she was still exhausted and had a headache. She stayed in bed till noon. She kept the ringers off all day and that night she took a dose and a half of Tylenol P.M. On Monday she slept late again and then called the office. Gladys answered and Rena told her she was sick and not to disturb her.

At noon the doorbell rang. Rena looked out the window and saw Tony's car.

"Well, I have to start somewhere," she said aloud to clear her groggy voice. She put on her robe and went to the door.

"Tony, it's you."

"We've been calling you. You weren't answering. I was actually worried."

"Who's 'we'?"

"Me and Lyndon and, well, Maureen....Rena, I've got to talk to you."

"What did Maureen say?"

"Gladys told her you were sick. She said you should be sick. Rena, we've got to know what's going on. Can I at least come in? You don't need to dress."

Rena agreed, better to begin with Tony than anyone else. She stepped aside and let him in. She motioned him to her kitchen table, and he spread his lunch out on the table and got himself some water.

"Now, Rena. Tell me about this child."

"I don't know anything. What did Maureen say?" She wanted to know how much, if any, room for innocence there was left to her.

"She said the child who proclaimed himself Paul Lawson Jr. at the dedication is the one you were keeping that day in the office. You must have known whose child it was and you lied to her."

"Oh. Well, I didn't lie. I said it was a friend's child. It was. What was I supposed to tell Maureen: Let me introduce you to Paul's child?"

"Paul's child! So it's true. How did that happen?"

"The same way it always does, Tony. The same way he got two girls."

"He got two girls with his wife. Who is this woman?"

"She went to school with Paul and me. And she's no shrinking violet. She wants her son to be accepted as Paul's son."

"Accepted! What does that mean?"

Rena shrugged. "Look it up in the dictionary."

"Boy, does she have balls. And why were you keeping the child for her the other day?"

"Not for her. For Paul."

"For Paul? I thought you said..."

Rena's headache was getting unbearable. She pressed the heel of her hand hard to her forehead and wondered if there was anything to be saved by not talking frankly to Tony. She certainly needed to talk to someone. She'd thought of a counselor of some kind. But Tony was here at hand and he was pressing.

"Okay. Tony. Look. I was keeping him for Paul. Paul had him for the day. He did that sometimes. Tony, he was a good father to that child. Also, he was under a huge amount of stress. I've checked on this: Paul had just found out a week before that the tumor had come back, that he didn't have a lot of time. He wanted to spend that time with his son. I don't know why he had to leave Little Paul with me, but something urgent came up, and he couldn't reach the child's mother. Hhe didn't know what else to do. I was stupid to bring him to the office. I just hated to leave my work so I stopped by there to get myself together...and wouldn't you know Maureen would come. What were the chances?"

"I guess it doesn't matter," Tony said. "Since the kid was going to introduce himself to the world anyway."

"Well, it matters because Maureen knows I knew about the child. I wish I were totally out of this picture."

"Why weren't you? Why did you get involved?"

"I don't know, Tony. You had to be there."

"How could he have been so stupid?"

Rena looked at Tony and sighed. How do you explain need, emptiness, passion, longing, love, growth, risk taking, blindness?

"It's a long story, Tony. But I'm not going to tell it to you. Paul had a six-year love affair, he had a baby with her, he was a good father to the boy, he died, and now everybody knows. That's it."

"I'm afraid you're in deep trouble."

"Me. Why me?"

"Because you knew. You even covered it up. If that's not trouble, I don't know what is. Maureen is going to have your head on a silver platter."

"Tony, listen to me!" Rena stood up the better to yell at him. "I didn't have an affair. I didn't have a baby. I didn't encourage him to have an affair. I didn't do anything. And I'm not in trouble!" Her head hurt so bad she wanted to throw up. She sat down again, holding her head.

Tony kept staring at her. Finally, she spoke again quietly.

"I kept a child for a dear friend in need when there wasn't time to do anything else. So I knew the child was a secret. Was I to turn the child out to play in the street? Was I to call Maureen? Was I to call the God Damn Times? It was not my business."

"Okay. If Maureen calls again, do I tell her to call you at home? Do I tell her what you told me? God, I feel like we need to put out a press release."

"Try 'no comment'. It's not your business either."

"I can't believe this. I can't believe you knew Paul had a son all this time.

Little Paul? That's what you call him, Little Paul?"

"They started out calling him P.S. for Paul Sorrell, but I guess when Paul died she started calling him Paul and naturally since he's little..."

"Paul Sorrel Lawson Junior? Paul gave the kid his whole name? My God, he had balls, too. Paul, of all people."

Tony finished his sandwich, shaking his head from time to time. Rena sat quietly by. Then he left and Rena swept across his place with a damp paper towel as if that would wipe the slate clean.

"What's the worst that could happen?" She asked herself out loud after Tony had retreated down the walkway to his car. She turned the ringer on the phone back on. Then she poured herself a glass of wine. One thing she had learned about "the fruitful grape" since she gave up drinking on a regular basis was that a little bit judiciously taken at the right moment will dull anxiety and whisper a low "So what?" in the ears. Better than prayer.

No call came that day, and, when she took some aspirin and went to bed, she fell mercifully asleep.

When Rena awoke, she could hear no surf. A rare calm had fallen on the sea. She, too, felt a strange calm. She had worried herself sick over this secret. Paul had worried himself into cancer probably although he wouldn't have admitted it. And now the secret was out and the sun still came up and the tide still came in and the world hadn't come to an end. Not yet anyway.

Rena went to work. A light headache was still with her but a sedative kept it at bay. No one disturbed her, and she did a remarkable number of items on her list and checked them off.

For lunch, she crossed the street to Ciardi's. "Good morning, Rosa." Rosa turned quickly away as if she had not heard. Her daughter, the middle one Rena thought, took her order.

When Rena's sandwich came, she took it toward the group of tables under a collage of patrons, famous and not so famous. She didn't see a free table but Mildred Huffines and Mrs. Northcutt, Stefan Northcutt's mother, seemed to have an extra chair. She took one step in their direction when she saw them glance at her, then look away, putting their heads close together. Then abruptly they got up and stuffed their paper plates in the trash and left without looking back her way. Rena stood in the middle of the store holding her plate and her drink, trying to look nonchalant. Seeing no lunch companion, she settled herself, as if she had intended to all along, at the recently vacated table. She hadn't seen the old "Let's pretend we don't see her" routine since junior high school. Rena's ears burned and she ate her sandwich quickly. She glanced around her. She knew almost all of these people. None of them met her eye.

Eating alone—she did that well. She had mastered the art of aloneness as an only child living with an aging aunt. The mantle of dignity had rarely been necessary in her forty-some years but Rena pulled it up now and covered herself with it, skimpily like a blanket a little too short.

Rena returned from lunch to find Tony and Janet from the tax department and Charlene from dog and business licenses and Paul's friend Charlie Bonneau gathered where the two halls crossed.

"I think it's terrific," she heard Tony say. "Guests can stroll out on the deck with all the boats..."

Maybe it was her imagination but she thought Tony stopped talking the moment he saw her.

"Hi, guys. How's it going?"

"Fine. And yourself?" Charlie said. The question seemed more formal than usual.

"Gotta go," Charlie said and left with a wave of his hand

toward the group.

"Okay. So...what's going on with all the boats," Rena asked.

Nobody answered as they cut their eyes around to each other.

"Tony, you were saying guests were going to stroll around the boats. Okay, so I'm not invited. Well, even Cinderella got the facts from her ugly sisters. What's up?"

"Maria Lawson's wedding reception. We were just saying..." The others drifted away, leaving Tony to respond. "...the Yacht Club was a great place for it, overlooking the harbor. Paul would have loved it."

Rena was shocked for an instant that she didn't know where the reception was going to be until she realized that without Paul she had no pipeline to the source for early information. "Oh, the wedding. The Yacht Club. That's great. Yes, Paul would be delighted. How did you know about it?"

"The invitation came yesterday."

"Oh. I'll probably get mine today."

The invitation did not come that day. Or the next or the next. Rena let a week go by. She practiced different scenarios and the next Monday she called Maureen. The answering machine was on and Rena left a message saying, "I hear the wedding invitations are out. I haven't got one yet, but, remember, I was planning to host a get-together for the out-of-town guests." Maureen did not return the call.

On Wednesday, Rena stopped Tony outside as he was leaving work.

"Tony, I haven't got my invitation to Maria's wedding."

"Hmm."

"Do you think it could be lost in the mail?"

Tony shrugged.

"Tony, do you think it's possible they didn't invite me?"

"Gosh, Rena, I don't know. There's that bad feeling about the child."

Rena squinted her eyes and opened her mouth wide to protest but Tony cut her off. "I know. I know. You asked me. I just said it's possible."

"It is not possible. Even if Maureen were mad, Maria would

have sent one. She and I were close."

The next day, Tony took Rena aside. "Rena, I asked around and the word is you're not invited because the Lawsons don't want to be reminded of the child at this time."

"I didn't have the child."

"That's what I said, I promise you, Rena. They said that's the way it was anyway."

"Who said?"

"I can't tell you. I did the best I could for you."

Rena called Ada at work. "Ada, I guess you got your invitation to Maria's wedding." There was a silence and then a short "yes."

"Well, did you know that I didn't?"

"Rena, I can't talk about this now."

"Oh. Okay. I'll call you tonight."

That evening, Phil answered the phone. "She's not feeling well."

"I'm sorry she's not feeling well. I'm not feeling well either."

"Oh. Well, I hope you'll feel better soon."

"Thank you."

On Saturday, the sea was green and the sky was heavy with clouds smearing into the yellow of dawn. Rena had gotten up earlier than usual to bake some cinnamon and raisin pinwheels for her coffee with Ada. It's hard to close the door on someone who's bearing goodies still warm from the oven.

She knocked and instead of going on in the unlatched door as she usually did, she waited outside. Eventually, Ada came.

"I'm sorry, Rena," she said through the cracked door and without a glance at the dish covered with a napkin in Rena's hand. "I'm just too upset to see you today."

"Ada," Rena pleaded, pushing the plate forward. "At least,...."

Ada pulled the door to.

Rena went home and ate three cinnamon pinwheels without knowing what they tasted like.

On Monday, Town Hall was quiet. Rena heard every chair squeak and every pencil fall. The only person to come by her desk the whole day was Gary Beatty. The Selectman strode by Rena, carrying some papers into the Chairman's office. She heard the papers slide into the in-basket and Gary blew out.

Rena was so surprised by his breezing in and out that she didn't call, "Hello, Gary," until he was going down the hall. She heard the door swing closed behind him.

Rena accomplished a lot of work that day which had piled up during the transition. That was a consolation.

On Tuesday, Rena picked up the G.D.Times and flipped by the headlines about septic tanks to the Stonehaven news. One of the items there was a notice of a called meeting of the Board of Selectmen "to discuss leadership issues" following Chairman Lawson's death.

Rena flashed with anger. She had always sent the notices of Board meetings to the paper and she didn't even know about this one.

She went straight in the Chairman's office and looked through the papers in his in-basket. There was a copy of the announcement of the called meeting. There was other mail addressed to the Chairman including an envelope from the Secretary of State's office marked "Renewal Notice" on the outside. She opened it and looked for the due date. It wasn't past but it was close.

She got Lyndon on the phone, called away from his production line.

"Lyndon, your mail has been sitting in your in-basket for days. One was a dated notice for renewing the Town's incorporation bond. I don't even see the mail addressed to the Board any more. All that stuff used to come through me so I could take care of it in a timely fashion.

"Rena, I can't be down at Town Hall all the time. I have a full time job. And, yes, you should get my mail and do what needs to be done. We need to make some basic changes now that Paul is gone, and that's why I called the meeting next Monday night."

"You called the meeting. Well. I'll be sure to be there."

"Just this once, it would be better if you weren't."

"Oh." Rena held the phone in her hand until she heard the machines on Lyndon's production line start up again.

On the afternoon of the rehearsal dinner, Rena called the Lawson's house hoping to get one of the girls. She got an answering machine instead.

"Maria, this is Rena," she said softly. "I wanted to wish you the very best for tomorrow—and..." she struggled to finish, "...forever."

She hung up before the tears came.

At 2:55 on the day of the wedding, Rena drove past the church and noted the cars parked on the curb. Right in front was a limo and beside it was Billy's car and Tony's car and Charlie Bonneau's Suburban and a Lexus coupe with a New York license plate. Maureen had family in New York. She circled the block and saw the back parking lot was full. A couple of ladies were running to the front in those tappy little steps people take when they are late and dressed in pumps. One woman clutched a wide brim hat to her head as she ran. Rena did not know them.

Rena parked behind the Town Hall, walked to the Yacht Club, wanting to get away from the church but unwilling to let the wedding be. She stepped onto the L-shaped granite wharf at 3:15 just as she supposed the bride was advancing down the aisle on the arm of...who? She realized she didn't know who. An uncle on Maureen's side, maybe.

"Paul, how could you let anyone but YOU take her down the aisle?" she asked out loud. "Maybe she's walking by herself." She hoped so. Nobody should replace Paul.

Rena paused for a moment like a tourist against the rail of the wharf, looking out over the little lobster boats at their moorings and the row of skiffs tied to the dock below. At the water's surface, the more-or-less rectangular chunks of granite stacked in more-or-less straight rows punctuated with slightly crooked wooden pilings met the wavering reflections of brightly colored boats and wiggly streaks of barn red, prosperous white, and winter gray from the buildings on the far side of the harbor. Even a shaky-handed artist could reproduce the inexactitude that was a large part of the town's charm. It was hard to tell where imperfect reality ended and perfect reflection began.

At 3:30, when Rena thought the young couple would be well into their vows in the church on the hill, she walked directly up to the yacht club, opened the gate and walked quickly across the club porch and down the steps to the dock where the skiffs were tied. She knew most of them by sight. Paul's skiff was close to the club in a slip virtually inherited. She walked down the dock in the narrow strip close to the water, playing a game, trying not to step over the line into the shade from the wharf.

When she heard the crunch of parking, the slamming of car doors, the people walking along on the wharf above her with tinkly voices, she knew the wedding was over and the guests were arriving at the reception. She coiled and uncoiled the end of the rope that held Paul's boat.

When she heard one more car grating on the gravel, and she heard cheers go up and then the footsteps grew fewer, she knew the wedding pictures had been taken and the wedding party had arrived.

A motor boat came in the harbor. "For some, life goes on," Rena thought. The boat's wake bobbed the skiffs one by one like chorus girls dipping in rapid succession. Rena was standing by Paul's boat still when the idea came to her in as clear a form as she had ever hoped Paul would send her. Take his boat out to sea. Of course, that was it. He would want her to have the use of it. Who was to use it otherwise on this day of days when all the Lawson's friends but one were eating little salmon sandwiches with no crust and drinking champagne from Gloucester.

"Thanks, Paul," she said half aloud.

She unhitched the boat, picked up the line coiled as neat as a snail shell, and stepped onto the bow. She checked for the life jacket under the bow, sat down on the seat and put the oars into the oar locks. She'd not rowed for decades, but today she'd pull the oars till she was exhausted, breathe in the healing air from Labrador.

She didn't row right by the club. She wasn't that crazy. She wasn't going to let the guests look down on her. She rowed directly to the shore on the far side and then followed the shore line along the outside edge of the harbor, staying a yard or so off the rocks that were the back yards of the houses on Beatty Hill Road. The rowing was not easy, but it felt good to exert herself, to spend her frustration in labor. As she neared the opening of the harbor that would take her out to sea, she could see the choppy surface, knew how hard it would be to keep off the rocks, but she exulted in her strength.

That strength did not last long and she stopped to rest. But the ocean was not restful; bobbing and slapping and pitching do not soothe the soul. What would soothe her though was the enveloping cold of the water. Rena knew what she would do. She took her shoes off. She pulled off her shorts and shirt. She lowered herself slowly off the bow holding tightly to the bow line. Her feet and legs were eager for the crisp cold water, but her waist was squeamish and her arms were appalled. She clung to the rope, partly dry, until her arms gave in. Then, she plunged into the cold and beat off the shock with strong, swift strokes.

When she became accustomed to the cold, she tread water and exulted. Pity the poor soul—his name is legion—who is not bold enough to take the first plunge, who does not know the cold Cape Ann water that washes away sin, that buoys the soul.

She dove for the joy of the ocean in her face. She opened her eyes under the water and saw nothing but quartz green light. Cold fingers parted her hair and massaged her scalp.

When at last the cold chilled her, she tried to hoist herself into the boat. She could never forget that motion, the scissoring legs, the arms' downward thrust, but Lord, it was harder than it used to be. She tried twice and failed.

What irony for her to die here and be together with Paul as they had been in life. "Stupid," she muttered to herself and gathered all her strength one more time, shoved the gunwale down with all her might and hauled herself over it. She lay draped over the gunwale for a few seconds, bottom up, resting. She could feel her wet panties stuck against her skin, transparent. Let the sea gulls look. Then she dragged herself all the way in the boat, drubbing her thighs red. She lay in the waning sun, letting her skin blow dry. She felt as much at peace as she ever had, impressed by her own exertion, lulled by the rise and fall of the boat.

When the sun was no longer warm, she began to shiver. She put on her clothes and rowed back inside the harbor, deeply satisfied by the long pulls on the oars.

She had no sooner passed the mouth of the harbor when she could plainly see a crowd of wedding guests all standing on the porch of the club, the bride's white bell of a skirt floating like a Portuguese man o' war. They were all looking down and someone was shouting: "It's gone. The skiff's gone." Groomsmen were running up and down the wharf.

Ohmygod. They see the skiff is not there. Why in hell do they care about the skiff at a time like this? For heaven's sake, let it wait. This is a wedding, guys, not an inventory.

She couldn't go rowing up now letting them see she borrowed the skiff, but what if they looked out in the harbor and noticed her coming. She headed quickly and quietly behind the Deborah Ann. She tied up on the back side of the small yacht and crawled out on her bow to where she could just peek around.

The crowd seemed confused and restless for an inordinate amount of time. Then, amid clattering and shouts, the groomsmen, like crabs with black legs, scuttered across the Yacht Club porch and disappeared on the other side of the wharf. Pretty soon a bright blue skiff with a crew of three emerged from the back side of the wharf and headed out into the harbor towards the big white yacht Beaucoup de Souci II, moored at the north edge.

The boarding party clambered aboard, whooping and hollering, and waved to the wedding party, and then set about getting the Beaucoup II going. Finally, they cast off and the engine chortled and guzzled and began its slow turn towards the Club. It was not a good docking. The pilot had too much champagne perhaps. The yacht creaked the outer pilings loudly and vibrated while the landlubbers among the guests squealed. Lines were snatched and knots were tied and everyone piled down at the boat. The groom lifted the bride into his arms and then looked at the boat, slowly rising and falling in the water. Then he put the bride down as everyone laughed. On his second try, he climbed onto the yacht and held his arms out to Maria while several groomsmen lifted her over the side to the waiting groom. Applause. Then, in a shower of rice, the Beaucoup II was off, leaving only an iridescent skim of engine oil beside the dock. The waving lasted until the boat burst through the mouth of the harbor, the bride and groom bracing to the first true ocean waves.

Rena had to wait behind the Deborah Ann till sundown to return the skiff. She shivered and grumbled. Time had never moved so slowly. When the shadows were long and the guests had left the porch for the warmth of the great room, she untied her line and rowed slowly, dipping quietly, squatting low. She secured the skiff carefully in Paul's slip and skulked back to her car.

Rena woke early the next day, feeling restless. Before churchgoers were lining the streets and well before the tour buses emptied their loads in the village, Rena was heading up the hill behind Cove Road in first gear. The road leveled off and Rena found herself without plan or explanation sitting in her car outside Charlotte's gate. The gate was, as Charlotte had complained in her petition for a variance, low enough for her to look over and see the darkness of Charlotte's windows. The dew had been heavy on Rena's windshield and drops broke through the arc made by her wipers and dribbled across her field of vision to the bottom of the glass. When a lamp light suddenly went on in Charlotte's living room, Rena sat up and began to think what explanation she'd give for being there.

Charlotte was wearing a man's shirt hanging out over her jeans and her hair was loose when she came to the door. She smiled and Rena heard the little tinkle in her voice.

"For crissakes, what are you doing here? How the hell are you? Jeez, it's been a hundred years."

Rena came in without answering. Charlotte was pulling her hair back and twisting it in a knot as she threw some newspapers onto the floor to make room on the sofa for Rena.

"Well, I was feeling kind of... You know, Paul's daughter got married yesterday."

"Yeah, I know. I saw the engagement in the paper."

"And I wasn't invited to the wedding...." A tear welled up in her eye and she tried to keep it from falling.

"F'crissakes. The jerks. Well, what are you gonna do."

Rena tried to start various sentences and couldn't. Her voice wouldn't do right.

"Just cry. It's okay. I still remember how I felt when Paul didn't invite me to his wedding."

Rena looked up abruptly. Paul hadn't invited Charlotte to his wedding? After all the good times they had at her house? Rena was shocked. As an aftershock, she realized she herself had not even missed Charlotte at the wedding. Rena did a quick appraisal: It must have been at the worst of Charlotte's drug stuff and the many men. But did Charlotte's behavior justify the snub?

"After all those years of being buddies," Charlotte went on, "he invited everyone in town and half of Cape Ann but not me. You know what I did on his wedding day?"

"What?" Rena sniffled more softly.

"I drove up to the quarries and I took off all my clothes and threw them in the water and jumped in after them. You know how the water changes your mood?"

"Yes!" Rena licked the tears from her lips and smiled. There is nothing more glorious than a shared crisis, the lightning strike of empathy that melts boundaries and solders soulmates together.

"I did that, too!" she cried.

"I came up out of the water feeling different," Charlotte said. "I got back in my car and drove around town buck naked. There wasn't a soul on the streets. They were all in wherever-it-was at Paul's wedding. A burglar could have ripped off the whole goddam town. The police cars were lined up at the station; I swear to God there wasn't a soul on duty. I went on up the street to Paul's house–his mother's old house–and I stopped and got out of my car and mooned the goddam house. Not a peep out of the neighbors. I felt like a queen."

Rena burst out laughing through her sniffles, at the image of Charlotte the queen. Rena pictured Queen Elizabeth II, her face not unlike Charlotte's own now that you mention it, wearing her pill box hat and nothing else, stepping out of the royal coach and displaying her royal behind to Paul Lawson's house–his parents' house. They both were gone now as if mooned off the face of the earth. There is something to be said for someone who can imagine herself a queen when left behind, uninvited to the royal ball.

Rena laughed and wept and didn't know which was which until she was exhausted. Charlotte had pulled out some tissues and Rena was using them by the fistful.

"So I got over it. Paul was a good guy, always, and he had his reasons." She looked at Rena sympathetically. "I'm sorry he died. Very sorry. Well, I know what you need. You want a joint?"

Rena shook her head. "I don't even know how to smoke."

"Oh, that's right. You never did. Well, it's not too late to learn."

Rena shook her head.

"I'll get you a drink." Charlotte stepped into the kitchen. Rena heard ice thunk into a glass. She heard the hiss of a broken seal and the gurgle of pouring liquid.

"You want some hooch in it?" Charlotte called.

"No thanks."

Charlotte handed her a root beer. Rena smiled. As a kid, it had been her favorite. It seemed that Charlotte had remembered that. Charlotte sat down and shoved an ottoman toward Rena with her foot.

"Put your feet up."

Rena sipped while Charlotte sat and dragged on her joint. The smell reminded her of the incense they used to burn while she and their crowd meditated. The scent itself brought a certain tranquility.

"Why don't you run in the next election for Paul's place?" Charlotte asked.

Rena shook her head.

"Why not? You know everything about it, you're as sharp as anyone in town, you'd be a shoo-in. That is, if this thing about Paul's child blows over."

"I'd hate running...I don't have the confidence...."

"Confidence! Hell, you're reeking with it."

Rena shook her head. "I have confidence when I have permission to take something over. Then I can do it. When someone says, this is your job. I have no confidence saying I should be the one. I need permission. If there's some kind of opponent saying I shouldn't be, I'd want to give up the first day. Running for office seems so presumptuous."

"Did it seem presumptuous for Paul to run?"

"No. It seemed natural."

"See there."

"I get your point."

"I think you should do it."

"Actually, how I feel is beside the point. I'd have to quit my job to be on the Board. I have to have my job. No, I'll keep on doing what I'm doing. I'm the only one who knows the nitty-gritty of running the Town now. I'll try to keep things the way they were."

Charlotte took another hit, and they both were transfixed by the smoke curling out across the beam of sun coming in the window.

Finally Charlotte said, "As long as things stay the way they were, you won't get over Paul."

"Get over Paul? Of course I won't get over Paul."

"Get over being in love with him, I mean."

"In love with Paul!"

"Of course. That's the problem."

"Since when have I been in love with Paul?" Rena felt hot in the face.

"Since grade school."

"God, Charlotte, I wasn't in love with anyone back then. And in high school there was Stefan—that was nothing—and then Billy. How could you say I was in love with Paul when there was Billy? It was always Billy."

"That was puppy love. Teenybopper love. But through it all, there was Paul. No wonder you never married."

"God, Charlotte, I've had boyfriends. It's not like....Well, they just never worked out. That's all."

"I know, I know," Charlotte soothed her.

They sat silent for a while, and Rena felt mounting irritability.

"So how come you could see this—my being in love—and no one else could?" Rena said bitterly.

"Now, now, don't get all hot and bothered. Here take a drag." Rena brushed the proffered joint aside. Charlotte went on: "I knew because I was so hungry for love myself, I could smell it. I knew that under all the necking with all the guys there wasn't anything real that would last. Not like you and Paul had. If I was ever jealous, it was of you and Paul."

"Me and Paul. No one ever linked us."

"Everyone linked you. Mr. and Mrs. Stonehaven High. You were a pair.

"But that's not romantic...even if it was true..."

"Romantic, schmantic. Whatever it was, it was real. And I bet Mrs. Lawson noted it a time or two."

"Oh, come on. Maureen always knew we were just friends."

"Why do they say just friends?, like it was something less than lovers. I wish I had one tenth the friends as I've had lovers. Oh, we were just lovers, I oughtta say."

"OK, then...suppose I agree I was in love with Paul. Was he ever in love with me?"

Charlotte smiled. "You know men. If it's not sex, it's not love." She shrugged again. "Paul was a great guy, for crissakes. But you did his legwork. He couldn't have run the town without you. You've been as important to the town as he was. Hell, he was no hero; he got himself into trouble and then he skipped out. Forget Paul. Do your own thing."

"I don't even know what my own thing is."

Charlotte lay back on the sofa pulling the smoke in slowly, letting it out slowly. Rena thought she had lost her to a cloud of reverie. Then suddenly, Charlotte sat up and said:

"Rena, when was the happiest time in your life? What you were doing when you felt truly happy?"

"The summer between junior and senior year in high school. The summer of the Rubaiyat."

Charlotte nodded. "The summer I broke my leg. Okay." And she lay back in the chair for the longest time as if that were the end of that. But Rena was mulling the subject over.

Finally, Rena said, "I had Billy so I felt safe and loved. I had the other guys, Paul and Whit and Ada and Lynne and they always included me in everything and made me feel liked. I could say anything I wanted. There was no one to say, 'you shouldn't think that' or 'that's not wise' like my Aunt Amelia would. If I said something silly, they would just laugh. There were no consequences, so no need for caution about what we said."

"Okay, what else?" Charlotte laughed a deep down laugh. "I got this routine from my shrink, so I know it's good."

"We had sun and water and laughing and petting above the waist. Well, okay, sometimes below the waist." Rena smiled. "That's about it."

"And also you had no responsibilities."

"Well, maybe I had no responsibilities, but that had nothing to do with it."

"Sure, it had a lot to do with it."

Rena was stung. If nothing else, she was responsible. She never shirked responsibility.

"What do you mean, Charlotte? If anyone was responsible, I was. My teachers always said, 'Rena's so responsible.' They wrote it on my goddam report card, Charlotte. I invented responsibility."

"Hey, I never said you weren't responsible."

"I know, but you said I was happy because I had no responsibilities."

"I just meant you—and I and all of us—had a house and food on the table and our clothes taken care of and a job we could quit anytime we wanted...no responsibilities. It was great."

"But why did you add "no responsibilities" to what I said, as if that were the main point?"

"I don't know. I didn't mean anything. But if you want to know the truth, that business about the teachers saying you were responsible—that meant you did what they said, how they said, when they said it. You did what you were told. Being good at taking orders is not responsibility. Responsibility is figuring out what you have to do all by yourself and doing it in spite of what some other people want and in spite of difficulties. Responsibility is carrying decisions on your shoulders. Responsibility is risking."

The word "risking" made Rena tingle.

"Now," Charlotte said, "I have made some stupid decisions and I have done some harmful things. I have risked and lived with the consequences—I still live with some of them—but I take care of myself and I am, at least now, responsible."

"And I'm not?"

"I never said that. Jeez, Rena, what's with you and responsibility? It's not a fighting word."

Rena was glum. Well, there was a world of difference between her and Charlotte. Always was. Why would she think of getting comfort from Charlotte anyway. She wanted to go back to her daybed. She opened her pocketbook up and rummaged for her keys.

"Anyway, I'm sorry I made you mad," Charlotte said suddenly. "I just said you should do your own thing and you said you don't know what your thing is and I was trying to figure out what made you happy, that's all. I shouldn't have put in my two-cents worth. I guess it was my problems talking, not yours. I'm sorry."

Rena curled one side of her mouth up in disgust, but Charlotte's apology softened her resolve to get up off Charlotte's sofa and go home.

"You're right," Rena said. "I don't even know what my own thing is and that's the first thing to find out. Maybe I should go to one of those...." She hunted for the term.

"Psychics," Charlotte finished for her.

"I was going to say, career counselors."

"Same difference," Charlotte said.

"Do you believe in psychics, Charlotte?"

"Not necessarily believe. But they do shake up your thinking. Make you see something as important that you might have missed."

"Oh." Rena was silent for a minute. Then she said, "So you know a psychic?"

Charlotte shrugged. "They're in the yellow pages."

"How do you know if one is any good," Rena heard herself say and wanted to kick herself for being so damn pragmatic. If you're going to shake up your thinking you don't need the resume of the shaker.

"You don't," said Charlotte. "You just go to one and see. Once a friend of mine told me to go to a certain one. I wasn't all that keen on it. She's a tarot reader. I already had a guy who reads palms—I'm a sucker for having my hand held. But I said okay, why not."

"And this tarot reader told you something useful?"

"She told me a young man would soon come into my life asking me to advise him about a health problem. I said, 'a young man?' To tell the truth it's been a long time since I knew any young men. Men, yes, young, no. But she insisted he was young. But why would anyone come to me about a health problem? I'm not a nurse."

"And a young man came?"

"It wasn't two days later that I got a call from my brother, you remember Greg? We're not close. We almost never speak. But he calls me up from New York and says his twenty year old son I barely know is coming to Boston and he's going to come down and visit me. And—get this—he says the son is going to ask me for advice about a health problem! I just about dropped my teeth. Then my brother says his son's concerned that he's had yeast infections and he's thinking of being circumcised and is going to ask me what I think. 'My God!' I said. What do I know about circumcision? Why doesn't he go to a penis doctor? Why me?"

Rena flashed her eyes to the side as if exchanging knowing glances with Whit or Ada or Spencer and she saw that Charlotte saw the glance and they both burst out laughing.

"Well, okay, so I've seen a few..." Charlotte said, and they both laughed a long untrammeled laugh Rena barely remembered from long ago, sitting on the pier, dangling legs in the sun, eating Cracker Jacks. Back then, circumcision would have been a juicy subject with which to regale friends, if only she had known anything about it.

"I'm sold," Rena said. "How do we hitch up with a psychic?"

Charlotte reached for the phone book. "The closest one is over in Rockport." She made the call.

"Nina—a gypsy, I'd think—and her daughter. She says they're booked up today except she thinks her four o'clock appointment tomorrow won't show. So how's four for you?"

"Wait. She has a four o'clock. I don't want to leave work early for nothing. How does she know her four o'clock won't show?"

They looked at each other and grinned in tandem.

23

Running, Hunting, Reaching

On Monday at quarter to four, Charlotte picked Rena up at Town Hall and they drove into Rockport. Rena didn't care who saw them. They lucked out and got a parking spot on T-Wharf, which stuck out into busy Rockport Harbor like an arrow pointing to the famous red fishing shack called Motif # 1. They walked back to Dock Square. The shop they were looking for was on the inside of the curve, across the street. A big sign announced "Psychic Readings" and in the window were prices: $30 for palm reading; $40 for the crystal ball.

Crystal pendants and freeform wind chimes dangled in the windows. Rena peered in the glass. In each corner of the front room were curtains printed with moons and suns pulled across like voting booths, but one was open. Rena could see a dark haired woman–Nina, she supposed–and a client. Nina was staring into a crystal ball, smoky lavender with an amethyst quartz base. The phone rang inside, and Nina took her client's hands and placed them on the ball and got up to answer the phone. The client sat obediently with her hands glued to the ball.

"I want the crystal ball," Charlotte said. "I've never tried that."

"I don't know," said Rena. It looked too much like Salisbury Beach to her. "You go first. I'll just walk around and...", she glanced at her watch, "... be back by four-forty-five." Charlotte went in and Rena crossed Dock Square to Bearskin Neck. She read the historical marker, as she did every year or two, about how the settler killed a bear on this rocky promontory. She examined the jewelry and pottery in the first few shops. At the Blacksmith's Shop, she took a left. On the left side of that road, there was a little restaurant with yellowed reviews posted on the window. The owner, Cutty O'Leary, was a descendant of one of the early settlers, the review said. Rena leaned to the window, holding her hand to her face to cut the glare. She could see right through the restaurant to the back window, which framed a view of the original Rockport harbor. The old harbor was small, only recently restored, and much less known than the larger one. A few skiffs tugged gently at their moorings.

"Excuse me," someone said and Rena turned around. A huge, pleasant-looking fellow stood there needing to get in the door. Rena jumped aside, and the man ducked his head to fit in the door.

"We're not open yet," the man explained, but come in and look around."

Rena was pulled in by his friendliness. All around, colorful fish were painted on aqua walls. It was like being inside an aquarium. Rena noticed a little card propped on the front table saying, "Tarot Reading by Debbie Coulter."

"Tell me about this," Rena said, gesturing to the card.

"Debbie. Yeah, she's great. She'll be along in a few minutes if you want to see her."

"I don't have time." Just then a blonde woman with yellow pig tails came in.

"Here's Debbie now," the man said.

Debbie was like a doll Rena had once, with yellow braids on either side of her head, bright blue eyes painted on. Debbie was older than her pigtails suggested. Rena instantly liked her.

"Do you have time to do a reading now?"

Debbie looked at her watch and nodded.

They sat at a table by the window. Debbie explained that she did numerology, Tarot cards, and astrology, all three. She showed Rena how the Tarot cards had numbers on them and astrology signs as well as mystical pictures. "So how could anyone do Tarot well without knowing numerology and astrology as well?"

First, she asked for Rena's birth date and scratched some numbers on a pad.

"Oh! A great destiny number," she said. Rena thought she heard genuine excitement. "An eleven. That means you see things in a different way from other people; you see more meaning in things; you want to do something memorable.

"You are a triple Capricorn but .... here. This is really interesting. A very mixed chart. I like that but it presents difficulties for you."

"One thing I've always wondered," interrupted Rena. "It doesn't seem to make sense that astrology is based on the date someone is born. It seems to me the time when you were conceived would be more important. That's when it all begins. And when you are born—well, for example–I was supposed to be born naturally on...I don't know the exact date...but my great aunt, who was a surgeon, delivered me by cesarean section before I was due. Didn't that accidentally change my horoscope from what it should have been?"

"No. That doesn't matter because there are no accidents. You were born when you were supposed to be."

Debbie was looking up Rena's numbers in a thick dog-eared book.

"Now, what I'm going to tell you are tendencies. You can go against them, but it takes effort. You are a triple Capricorn. A Capricorn holds things in. Doesn't like change. Security is the most important value for a Capricorn. A Capricorn is serious, has a certain presence, and retains a youthful appearance the longest. I can see you have these characteristics."

She looked up at Rena, and Rena nodded.

"Then here's a complexity," Debbie went on. "Your Mars is in Scorpio. Very passionate, intense, the most sexual. You want freedom. So you think like a Capricorn, but you desire more passion. While your Cap is cool and restrained, looking for a steady pay check, your Mars in Scorpio means you are happiest when you are pursuing something with intensity–the silver chalice, the lost cause, the next frontier. Your Mars in Scorpio means you are at your best when you have a mission. Especially a life or death mission." Debbie looked up Rena.

"Do you have a mission?" Rena shrugged. She had a to-do list. She wouldn't call it a mission. For twenty-five years, in fact, she'd served Paul's mission.

"Can you remember ever in your life being so caught up in something that nothing else mattered? Can you remember running, hunting, reaching, grabbing..." Debbie stretched her arm up to the ceiling and made grasping motions toward the old-style glass buoys that hung from nets on the ceiling. Her face mimicked desperation.

"Yes, yes, I remember once!"

"That's what you want to feel again."

Rena sat back in her chair, her face impassive but her pulse quickening. She remembered running, hunting, reaching, grabbing. The wind was cold on Boding Point that night but she had a mission. At first she'd thought of Paul and worried where the money had come from and then she had worried about what she would do with the money and what the consequences would be. Then she had realized that gathering the money immediately to protect him was the goal and listening to the questions, analyzing them, was a distraction. She gave herself over to the goal, turned her energy to the process. As her hands numbed in the March cold, she had been mesmerized by running, hunting, reaching, grabbing until she was taken over by the strange peace of single-minded purpose.

Just like Howard Blackburn. He must have cursed the storm, cried out to his ship, sobbed as his comrade behind him turned blue. He looked then forward, reckoned the miles he had rowed, yearned for the boom of waves against shore, longed for strong arms that would pull him out of the boat, wondered if he would be dead or alive. And finally he must have let all that go and lived only in the reach and pull of the oars until his efforts transcended pain. His hands frozen to the oars, he had persevered.

"Your birth date," Debbie said, running her finger along a line in her mammoth book, "gives you a Sagittarian modification. A Sag is a free spirit, open and frank. A Sag 'goes at it,' sometimes putting his foot in his mouth, sometimes contradicting himself, sometimes getting into trouble. A Sag likes fun and risk. If a Sag wanted to cross a river and there was no bridge, he'd grab a boat or he'd swim. If he wanted to learn about something, he wouldn't read a book, he'd write a book. If he wanted to drink with his buddies, and there was no bar, he'd open one."

"Open a bar?"

Debbie went on, "Yeah. Opening a bar would be risky, but an impetuous person, a gregarious person, as a Sag would be...."

"Open a bar," Rena repeated. It was a statement this time.

"It was just an example."

"I've never even thought of running a bar. They don't even allow bars where I...." Rena's heart pounded when she remembered Paul's vote to allow liquor in Stonehaven. She felt she was almost physically whirling around.

"It could be anything," Debbie said. "I just meant that if you felt like opening a bar, the Sag part of you would do that. But the Capricorn would worry about the risk. So there would be conflict."

"There would be conflict all right. But without conflict there is no growth."

Rena's heart was pounding, her mind grasping. A bar.

Debbie went on:

"Then your North node to the Moon is Libra. Libra traits are good for you. Libra sees all sides, seeks balances. It's through Libra that you will accept the contradiction of yourself."

"Well, let's say I did something risky now. Would the venture succeed? Would it pay?"

"That's the Capricorn in you talking," Debbie said without answering. "Now here you have three things in Taurus. Taurus is productive, sensuous, interested in objects. It doesn't concern itself with philosophy but objects, like buying a piece of pottery.

"So Capricorn with Libra for balance, Scorpio for passion, Sag for risk taking and fun, Taurus for acquiring. I really like mixed charts."

Rena was blown away. Here was her mixed chart, clicking into place. She suspended disbelief purposefully, effortlessly.

"As for the numbers," Debbie continued, "This year is a year three for you, a year of self-expression. That means that in all the challenges that arise this year, you should move towards self-expression. You'll have to manage the Capricorn to do it, and it won't be easy. But that is the way to growth."

Rena went out full of destiny. Crossing the Square, she could see Charlotte waiting by the gypsy's doorway. She wanted to run, leaving Charlotte on the sidewalk, so she could plunge headlong into her year of self-expression. "Sorry. I lost track of time," Rena said.

"Yeah, she's waiting for you."

"I'm not going."

"Not going? But we came for you."

"I found someone else," Rena said, pointing down Bearskin Neck, "and I've had my reading. Let's go." She pulled Charlotte back toward the car before the gypsy came out to summon her.

"So now you're finding your own psychic. You learn quick. How was it?" Charlotte said. They passed the ice cream stand and The Doll House and stopped at the corner of Broad Street to wait for a break in the traffic.

"It... I can't even talk about it."

They darted between two cars and threaded their way through tourists, who were stopped, four abreast, to take pictures of a gull on a post.

Open a bar. The most ludicrous idea. A bar. The thing Paul fought against. The thing Paul voted for. The thing Paul skipped out on. A bar. Wouldn't it be ironic if she opened a bar? *Wine, wine/Red wine! the nightingale cries to the rose,* she found herself saying, but she was picturing no nightingale and no rose, only the boys of the Rubaiyat calling out to a waitress.

"How about you? What did Nina tell you?"

"Same old same old."

"And what's that?"

"She sees a new man in my life. Handsome stranger."

"I'd take it," Rena said. "I've had it," Charlotte said.

"What else?" Rena asked when they reached the car.

"Also, I have an obstacle that is preventing me from resolving the issues in my life but, for a little more money, Nina could meditate this week, and next week she'd help me with it. But we came for you. What did your psychic say? You've gotta tell me something."

They got in the car, and Charlotte gunned the engine, blowing two tourists in the air behind them.

"She didn't predict anything–she's not that kind of reader–but like you said, it shook up my thinking."

While Charlotte eased out of her parking place into a stream of pedestrians, Rena debated about whether sharing her experience would dissipate its energy or the opposite. But if you were going to open a bar in a dry town, Charlotte would be the one to tell.

Rena swung around to Charlotte and pulled her knees up tight to her chest. "Charlotte, listen to this: A bar. Stonehaven can have a bar now. Right there in town. If there's one thing Stonehaven really needs, it's a bar. A place to gather and relax and loosen up, right in the middle of town. A sort of central meeting place." The words, "central meeting place," seemed radically new on her lips, yet somehow familiar.

"Damn right. Wouldn't have to drive to Gloucester for a brew. No more driving home stoned. Drink right in Stonehaven."

"Damn right, yourself. Running a bar sounds a lot like the Rubaiyat summer. You know, the time that made me really happy."

Screech, as Charlotte slammed the brakes.

"Yeah?"

"I'm gonna do it!"

Charlotte laughed a contagious laugh, and Rena began to giggle. Then she stopped.

"I'm serious," Rena said.

"I'm serious if you're serious."

"I don't know anything about bars."

"Well, I know a lot about bars. I know what makes a bar work. You know all about money and regulations and all that. And I can tell you everything else. Hell, you've already run a business."

"I have?"

"Yeah, the Town."

"Okay, I'll open a bar. I'll name it The Grog Shop, that's what the old bars were called back in the old days. Paul knew all about it, he had pictures....."

"Forget Paul. Forget the old days. Call it Thelma and Louise's."

They laughed, and the screech of Charlotte's tires as she spun out of the T-Wharf lot onto South Street for once felt appropriate.

"Of course, I don't have much money. A few thousand dollars of savings without going into my 401K," Rena said.

One of the lights on Cormorant Island is red, when you look head on, but if you catch its flash out of the corner of your eye it looks white. In just that way, looking head on, Rena saw herself with very little money, but out of the corner of her eye she saw a flash that looked like a suitcase under a bed, and it was full of money, Paul's money.

"Wouldn't the Town Hall crowd just die if I opened a bar?"

"If you don't, someone else will. The tourists will come in droves. You won't need the Town Hall crowd," Charlotte said.

"One weird thing is they can't ever say I crossed them," Rena said. "After all, it was Paul who voted for liquor."

"Why'd he do that anyway?"

Rena breathed in long and went with the outbreath. And then she said, "I guess he was a human being just like the rest of us. A hero sometimes but a bastard too. A goddam baldheaded bastard in a Cape Ann hat."

"But why'd he do it?"

Rena shrugged. "Your guess is as good as mine."

She came in to work on Tuesday morning with her resignation speech composed. Lyndon was fidgeting outside the door. Rena put her key in the lock, pushed the door in hard, and then pulled it back slightly to the exact position where the key worked. Lyndon followed her in.

"What's the occasion?" she asked, and then remembered the meeting the night before. The fact that the meeting had all but disappeared from her consciousness reinforced her decision. She hastened to begin her speech before the Chairman gave his.

"Listen," she said. "I have something to tell you."

"Don't you want to know what the Board did last night?"

Lyndon said. She shook her head. "It doesn't matter because I've made a decision. I want to do something different with my life."

"Good," said Lyndon.

Rena blinked.

"The Board has unanimously voted to hire a professional town manager. The job's getting too complicated for us part-timers."

"Oh! Good idea."

"We've appointed a search committee for the new Town Manager. Even so, I have a better idea."

Rena reached to pull out her own chair as she motioned for him to sit in the extra chair beside her desk.

Lyndon shook his head. "No, you come in here."

He turned toward the Chairman's office, stood by the door, and ushered her in. He waved her to the vinyl-covered chair. "Sit down. Sit down."

"No, no."

"Please."

Rena sat on the front edge of Paul's chair. In the moment of silence that followed, she ran her fingers lightly over the clean blotter, picked up the mug reading "The Boss," and set it down in a slightly different place.

"Rena, you could be...what I want...is...for you to be that Town Manager."

"Oh, Lyndon!"

"I mean it. Sit back, Rena, let me talk."

Rena moved back from the edge of the seat slightly, still ramrod straight.

"Rena, you know everything about the job. The transition would be smooth as butter. Nothing would fall between the cracks."

"But, Lyndon...."

He wiped her protest from the air with his hand.

"Sure you have some weak areas. Utilities, for example, but that's what consultants are for. We'll send you to management workshops whenever you need. I'm not only counting on your past performance and experience, but I see your potential."

Rena smiled and settled into the valley of stretched vinyl that was the seat of town government. No one had talked to her like this before, not lately anyway.

"I think we could double your salary. We know something about the pay scale of town managers."

Rena did the multiplication instantly and smiled to herself.

"You say 'we' know something about the pay scale.... We. That's you and the rest of the council?"

"Yes, well, we talked about the pay and...."

"Lyndon, they've been very, very cool to me since...."

Lyndon nodded quickly. "There's been some hostility. I recognize that, Rena. I never did see they had any cause to blame you. It's just that everyone feels terrible for Paul and for Maureen and for the girls. That...business has devastated the town. And they don't know where else to put their disappointment."

Rena put her head forward, lifted her reading glasses on their chain, put them on, and, having nothing to read, took them off and rubbed her eyes.

"But Rena, they'll come around. They'll do what's best for the town. Soon as the decision is made, they'll be pleased with themselves. Soon as they're pleased with themselves, they'll be happy with you."

He moved toward her and patted her on the shoulder.

"You just sit here a while and think about it. Get used to the idea. This would be your office, your desk. I'm not here enough to use it. It's only right you should have it."

He turned to go. Then he turned back.

"Rena, Paul would have wanted you in his place."

Rena shot to her feet. Her heart beat; her limbs tingled. She wanted to run, to run and kick off her shoes, to run on the beach, on a long beach whose distant rocks moved on and on to give her endless room.

"I..." her voice came out higher than she expected. She started again: "Lyndon, I have other plans."

Lyndon stared at her. She almost pushed him out of the way.

"Tell the search committee to begin the search," she said, passing him in the door.

She fled to her own desk. "And Lyndon, listen. Please accept my resignation as Town Clerk."

Rena returned to her own desk. She pulled out a drawer as if she were going to clean out her things. She stopped and looked up at his face, like an owl stunned by the light. Poor Lyndon. This would only make his job harder for him. "I'm grateful for your offer," she said, forcing herself to sit down and gently close the drawer. "Really. But no."

"I'm so sorry to hear you say that. But you haven't had time to consider the matter properly. I hope you'll think it over."

"I will, Lyndon." She smiled graciously at him as he turned to go. Then she let the smile drop off her face like a lead sinker.

She took a deep breath and went to find Tony. She didn't want him to hear from anyone else. She took him outside under the poplar tree and told him.

"What!" Tony grimaced. His dismay moved her.

"It's time to move on, Tony."

"First Paul, then you. Times are gonna be tough."

"I'll be here for a few weeks. I'll get someone to replace me."

"No one can replace you, Rena."

"Sure, I know that, Tony," she grinned. "Actually, they're going to hire a Town Manager."

"What! Nobody tells me anything."

"I'm telling you. They just voted on it last night."

"It could take months to get a Town Manager. And it's gonna be chaos around here if the Town Manager doesn't have you to get him straight."

"I know, but he'll have Gladys to help him."

They both laughed heartily at that.

"They'll have a new Town Clerk before I leave."

"Rena," Tony leaned close and said softly. "Did they fire you?"

"No. Honest to god, no. In fact, Lyndon offered me the job as Town Manager."

Tony went bug-eyed. "And you didn't take it! Whew. I need a drink."

"Too bad there's not a bar around the corner," Rena said.

They went in the door together, and Rena's eyes met Gladys's, and Rena knew she had to finish the job.

"Gladys, I want you to know that I just turned in my

resignation to the Board. They'll be hiring my replacement, and you will be a key part of the transition."

"I knew something was going on when you and Tony went outside," Gladys said. She beamed at her own astuteness. "Can I apply for your job?"

Of all the things Rena might have guessed Gladys would say, that was not one.

"Gladys,..." she began and, after an indecent pause, "Of course you can. But Gladys, among other things, the job requires a lot of computer work. Word processing and spreadsheets and all kinds of stuff. You always said you'd leave if you had to work on any program different from that old one you use. You told me you refused to touch a mouse."

"A person can change."

Rena stopped dead. A person can change—Yes! Rena was counting on it for herself. But for Gladys? Pu-lease. You learn to count on things, you build around them. Rena had counted on Gladys's rigidity just as much as she had counted on Paul's integrity. Each had its place. Losing one was a tragedy, the thought of disturbing the other was godawful annoying.

Rena looked at Tony and saw he had his face turned to avoid dangerous eye contact.

The thought that there was the slightest chance that she would have to spend her last weeks at Town Hall teaching Gladys to use a new computer program made her stomach churn.

"We'll talk about it."

Rena went into the bathroom and laughed then cried quietly—quick ups and downs made her weepy—then dipped a paper towel in water and wiped her face. She could see there was going to be a lot of going with the outbreath in the next few weeks.

24

Fear vs Exhilaration

The first thing to do: Get a place. Provide a setting for the adventure. Rena picked up the phone book to look up Collins Realty. And then stopped. If she told Susan Collins she was looking for space, she'd have to tell her about the bar, and then the secret would be out. That pulse that was beating in her limbs took a dive, turning into a cold lump in her stomach at the thought of confronting Stonehaven with its first bar. She felt more fear than she had felt years ago marching for civil rights. Back then, there had been courage in numbers. Today she was alone. To match her fear, she felt more exhilaration than in her dreams of discovering ruins of a lost civilization on the Yucatan. It was going to be that way, wasn't it? Fear against exhilaration. That's what Debbie Coulter had said. She'd better get used to it.

On successive lunch hours over the next couple of weeks, Rena and Susan looked at the properties for lease. Besides the feel of the place, she had to consider where to position the bar and whether the single bathroom could be expanded to two. She took notes on the square footage and the price, and its present use, since change of use required special permission, something she was unlikely to get.

She looked at a sandwich shop on Front Street where Bay Road split off. It was across the street from the waterfront stores. What it had was a restaurant permit. What it didn't have was windows. The rear of the building was jammed into the hillside, and it shared side walls with a gallery and a sportswear store. No wonder the restaurant had failed; it had no view, and it was dark and gloomy.

She considered a too-small space over a bait shop and a too large space by the depot. She looked at a too expensive place on the Lane and a too out-of-the-way place behind a garage.

Leasing the old Oddfellows hall finally seemed the best option. When Rena asked Susan to pursue it, the moment had come to tell Susan her real purpose.

"A bar," Rena said over the phone, controlling her breath and trying to soften the word.

"What?"

"A bar," Rena said, letting the B explode.

"Oooh." Carolyn drew the syllable out. "Well. I'll see what I can do."

Within hours, she had her answer and not from Susan.

At quarter to five that afternoon, the chief Oddfellow himself called Rena at work to say that under no circumstances would the fellowship lease their building for a bar.

"A pub," Rena said.

"By whatever name," he countered, "there's never been a drinking place in Stonehaven and for a good reason."

"The reason was there was a law against it, but now the law has changed and..."

"Young lady, you'll rue the day you ever thought of a bar in Stonehaven."

A shiver of fear ran up the back of her neck which she quelled by reminding herself, no hurdles leapt, no victory won.

On her lunch hour next day, Rena passed by Lawson's Marine and glanced away but not before her eye caught a notice on the door. She walked on, but curiosity soon got the better of her, and she turned back.

The sign said, "For Lease," and it also had Collins Realty and a number under it.

How long had that been there? She'd walked by here every day. And why didn't Susan tell her? In fact, why didn't Susan tell her before the sign went up, as soon as she knew. Because this place, the site of Lawson's Marine, was twice as wide as the other stores, right on the harbor with the absolutely best view in the whole town. It was heart-poundingly perfect.

She looked for a pay phone. She scarcely knew where one was, having never been without a friendly phone before in Stonehaven. She fumbled with her purse and tried twice to get the quarter to go in right before she made the call successfully.

"Susan," she began when she got the realtor to the phone. "Lawson's Marine. There's a sign saying for lease."

"Oh, yes. Yes. We just put it two days ago."

"Susan, it's perfect. It's perfect. Why didn't you tell me?"

"Oh. Well," Susan sputtered. "Rena, you know that's Maureen Lawson's property and, well, I wasn't sure...." Rena slammed the phone on the hook.

Moments later she dialed Susan again. "Sorry, this pay phone isn't working right. What were you saying...?"

"I was saying, if you're interested, I'll see what I can do."

Rena hurried back to Lawson's and pulled open the door. The place was in upheaval, as if they were moving out. No one was around. She rushed out the front door, to the corner of the building, and down the path to the back. Someone would be out there; that's where the action was, where boats pulled up to be serviced. Engines guzzled at the dock below as they started up. The rich fuel smell was the satisfying scent of men with purpose, heady even now to Rena.

Sure enough, there was Paul's long time manager, Dave McWhorter, working on an outboard, starting, adjusting, starting again. When he wiped his hands on a rag and stuffed it in his back pocket, Rena stepped down on the wharf.

"Good morning, Dave."

"Morning."

"What's up?"

"Nothing much."

"The store's for lease."

"Yup."

"Are you moving out?"

"Not if I can help it."

"But how can you stay if the store's for lease?"

In this arduous manner, Rena determined that Paul's dealership was for sale. His girls weren't interested in it. Dave couldn't buy it, mainly because the building, which was part of the business which Paul's grandfather had started, was on such prime property Dave couldn't afford the lease."

"Any takers on the business?"

"Nope."

"Any nibbles?"

"None they're telling me about."

"Have you figured out what you're going to do?"

"Not yet."

"Well, you and I have something in common then."

Dave might be among those who were mad at Rena, but she chose to attribute his curt replies to the taciturn nature of many who worked by the sea. After all, he sounded not unlike the young Stefan Northcutt in full courtship. She decided to continue accordingly.

Soon she and Dave were concocting a "just supposing" deal with Rena doing most of the supposing, whereby Maureen would continue to own the building. Peter would buy the marine inventory left after the end-of-season sale and consolidate the marine motor business into the lower dockside level of the building where the lease might be affordable.

"It could work," Dave said.

Lawson's Marine took up all that room on both levels because it was there, but many an Evinrude dealership operated out of spaces the size of Lawson's lower level alone. That would leave the upstairs for her bar–though she didn't mention the word to Dave. In the daytime, her patrons could look out over the bustle of the people on the wharf and the real working boats in the harbor. At night they could see the lights that marked the mouth of the harbor and the lights from the windows of the houses all along the harbor. It was too fantastic!

Rena knew the idea of her leasing from Maureen was problematic, but she went fatalistically on.

She called Susan back and explained her idea of splitting the building with Dave. Susan soon arrived, and they looked the space over together. Susan agreed to approach Maureen and point out the advantages of leasing to two lessors in order to keep the faithful manager in business.

"And remember, Susan, Paul voted for allowing liquor licenses. He must have decided it would be good for the town in the long run. Remind her of that, Susan, but don't say I said so."

Susan nodded knowingly.

Rena had plunged so pell-mell into this opportunity that she hadn't taken time to call Charlotte.

When she did, Charlotte said, "Best location in the whole goddam town, no question." Then she added, "Problem is you still haven't quit following Paul around!"

"For God's sakes, Charlotte. I looked everywhere else before I looked here. From a convenience store to an attic over the bait shop. You're beginning to tick me off with this theme of yours. I'm over Paul, Charlotte. Get it through your head."

"I'll get it through my head when I quit seeing the signs."

"There are new signs up all over the place, Charlotte. You just don't read them."

"And another thing," Charlotte said, "you'd be paying so much for a view. You don't need a view."

"It would be damn nice!"

"Look, Rena. Let me tell you about bars. They're dark places with no windows. They're cozy. They're safe. They're places to forget where you are. Places to turn to your friend or, even better, turn to a stranger and be someone different from who you are in the daylight. If you had a view, you'd pull the curtains over it at four o'clock. So why pay for a view?"

Rena sighed. She called Susan and left a message on her machine: "Thanks, but let's just forget about Lawson's Marine."

Saturday afternoon Rena snuggled into her day bed, stacked the pillows under her head, tucking the mohair close around her neck even though the room was warm. She let her mind drift.

Her mind slid to Sunday night suppers. Fish chowder with the solid comfort of potato chunks, flaky cod, and hot milk. Served with popovers. Ah, yes, popovers. Crispy on the outside, hollow on the inside, the soft egg-rich lining dipped in melted butter.

She called Charlotte.

"I've been thinking about pub food and I've got this wonderful idea...."

"Whoa. Rena, a pub is not about food. Food is the last thing you need to worry about."

"Oh, I know. I've been thinking about the drinks, too. I'd want a large selection of foreign beers..."

"Hunh," Charlotte scoffed. "Rena, I know what we need to do. We need to go to a bar. A real bar. A successful, down-to-earth, Honest-to-God bar. I know you've been in bars before, but this time let's notice the important stuff."

Charlotte began running through bars she knew. One was too rough, one was not lively enough, one was not a real bar, one she had been thrown out of.

"How about Blackburn's?" Rena said. The mention of the Gloucester hero's name made her fingers tingle. "I take an interest in Howard Blackburn."

"Oh, if you take an interest in Howard Blackburn, then you don't want to go to Blackburn's. That place has his name but Howard Blackburn's real bar is a couple blocks away. It's called Halibut Point."

"What do you mean, Howard Blackburn's real bar? I didn't know he had a bar; I thought he was a fisherman."

"Sure he was. He froze his fingers off rowing to shore when his fishing boat sunk, so he opened a bar."

"How do you know this?" Rena's pulse quickened. It was as if Howard Blackburn were haunting her.

"If it has to do with bars, I know it."

On Friday, Rena and Charlotte parked in front of a pawn shop on Front Street and crossed the road. Rena viewed with new eyes the store front she had seen many times before without noticing.

Sure enough, it's sign said, "Halibut Point."

The bar was dark as Charlotte had said. Cozy, not gloomy. No windows except at the narrow front. A bar on one side lined with eleven stools, a patron on each one, eight tables for two on the other. Green Formica with wood trim. No tablecloths. Captain's chairs. Ships models and stuffed game fish on one wall. Peanut shells on the floor.

Pitchers hung from metal racks above bottles of liquor. The "Drink of the Week" was described on a blackboard over the bar. Nobody was drinking it.

"Bar or table?" the waitress asked.

Rena chose a table. She didn't know what to do with herself at a bar.

"You get to meet people better at the bar," Charlotte said.

"Next time. I need to take this slowly."

There was only one table free. Rena sat against the wall under a framed document listing "persons comprising the crew of the U.S.S. Seal." A harried but cordial waitress came at length and took a drink order.

"I see you have a large selection of imported beer. What kind of beer do you sell the most?" Rena asked.

"Draft."

"What kind of bottled beer do you sell the most?"

"Bud." Charlotte turned her hands out to the side as if to say I told you so.

Rena ordered a Bud.

The waitress whirled away, then returned to plunk some salsa and chips on the table.

While Charlotte dug into the munchies, Rena looked the clientele over. A family of six had put three tables together for dinner, but they were leaving. People coming in from work waited for their tables to be wiped clean. A woman with very long black hair, black pants and top, and an extravagant black shawl was accompanied by a longhaired blonde guy. A few coats and ties. The row of feet on the rungs of the bar stools were overwhelmingly shod in athletic shoes. Two very old ladies had the table to the right. A youngish couple had the table to the left.

"My kind of people," Rena said. "This is what I want for my bar."

"Yeah, the after-work crowd. Earlier, the instead-of-work crowd. Later the one-for-the-road crowd. You have to learn to love them all."

"So far so good."

The beer came. Rena tipped the bottle up. The first long tingly swig of beer was almost as soul-washing as salt water in the hair. Like going with the outbreath only colder—and surer.

She picked up the menu. On the back she read about the man who had run his bar in this very room:

Blackburn's dory was an open boat flung off the sinking schooner Grace L. Fears into a storm in the winter of 1883. The dory was without water, food, or provisions of any kind. Blackburn had rowed without sleep for five days and five nights arriving on a beach in Nova Scotia with his fingers frozen solid to the oars. His mate had died from cold and want.

After being taken in by a kind family in Nova Scotia and nursed back to health, Blackburn returned to Gloucester in 1891, a hero. The townspeople raised $500 for him, and he opened a cigar store.

Soon after, the menu narrative went on, he made a daring single-handed voyage across the Atlantic to Lisbon, Portugal, in the Gloucester-built sloop, The Great Republic. Blackburn set a new solo record for the voyage—thirty-nine days. The vessel was on display in the Cape Ann Historical Association Museum.

And here was Blackburn's photograph, one hand behind his hip and the other tucked under his lapel like Napoleon, an affectation that served a fingerless man well.

After his record-breaking feat, the printed history continued, Blackburn returned to his cigar store. There he had begun to serve liquor two years before he got a pouring license. It seems he'd got into a little trouble for moonshine trafficking and, hero or not, the license was not a foregone conclusion.

"That trouble was called Prohibition," Charlotte said.

"I'm starting a bar on the heels of Prohibition, too, Charlotte, and my license isn't a foregone conclusion either."

"Pssh!"

"What?"

"Liquor licenses are always inside jobs anyway. And who is more inside than you?"

"Maybe you don't realize how things have been turned inside out."

But Rena remembered that, when she had gotten back with Lyndon after she had supposedly mulled over his offer, she had been gracious and he had been most gracious. He had told her, moreover, that if there was anything he could do to help her with her next position, to call him.

She had also designed a form for the application for liquor licenses and had provided a stack and delivered them to Gladys with an explanation for their use. She took a few for her own use, of course, without Gladys being any the wiser.

"Actually, Charlotte, I think maybe I can get Lyndon to get my license approved by the Board and without too much publicity."

"Lyndon? I thought he was sort of a wimp."

"He hates confrontation. So I think he'll find a way to do this quietly. He may be the perfect man for the job."

Rena and Charlotte mused over their beer for a few minutes. Then Rena struck up a conversation with the couple next to them. They were from Bristol, New Hampshire, celebrating their anniversary, taking a few days away from the kids. He sold used computer parts to the Pacific Rim; he could do it from anywhere. She took care of their three kids; the oldest wanted to be a psychiatrist. One thing Rena knew. People would talk to her, tell her their life story. Charlotte smiled knowingly and lit up a cigarette.

Cigarettes. That was going to be a problem owning a bar.

"Is it possible to have no smoking in a bar?"

"Not possible."

Rena winced. She'd have to leave the bar to someone else in the wee hours when the smoke hung heaviest. "Charlotte, you are going to do this bar with me, aren't you?"

"Hey, this is your thing."

"Charlotte! I need your help."

"Listen, kiddo, don't ever take on anything you can't handle alone."

"But you said, 'Name the bar Thelma and Louise's." I thought..."

"Listen, you couldn't get a license with my name on the application. I got caught once back in the early seventies with more than the limit of pot, so you're on your own here."

Rena felt like Howard Blackburn must have felt when he turned around and saw the man behind him in the dory was dead.

"What!"

"Well, okay, I'll help. I could use the tips....," Charlotte said mischievously, "...now that I'm not dealing any more."

25

Hanging the Goddam Cape Ann

Hat

Rena went to Gloucester for a Small Business Administration workshop to write a business plan. She'd learn to run a bar the same way she'd learned the Town's business, by serious study. She came home, estimated her expenses, and added them all up, but she couldn't make it work. She cried, then she stared at the new liquor license she'd posted on the wall of her Rubaiyat room. Then she started her plan all over again. She cut out some things, wrote it out again, and took it back to an SBA volunteer for advice. Then she repeated the whole process until her assigned mentor said she had it right.

Finally, when she'd figured out what kind of rent she could

afford, she called Susan Collins.

"Is the place on Front Street at Bay still available? The small one off the water. The dark, gloomy one. That's the one I need."

When the lease came through, Rena was as shocked as she was ecstatic. Before the deal was signed, however, Susan told her the owner wanted a certified check. "I'll do him one better," Rena said, "I'll give him cash."

Rena bounced out of bed every morning and drove into work. She took unexpected pleasure in putting her affairs at Town Hall in order, attaching stick-on notes to documents as instructions to her successor, doing things "for the last time." She raided the Town's supply fund for the price of an evening computer course for Gladys; it was not her problem whether the course "took" or not.

In the evenings, she wrote lists, drew sketches, went through catalogues and price lists, and outlined questions to ask vendors.

On weekends, Rena swept and washed and painted right behind the vacating tenants. When the old cash register went out the door, she was right behind with a measuring tape.

Once she took a weekday off and drove to New Hampshire to a place that sold used restaurant furnishings. There she set up a row of bar stools, sat in each one, looked at the row from the back, and finally chose nine of almost even height and legs blackened with age. She bought seven dark booths with little hooks on the ends for coats. The wood on the back of the seats was rubbed raw at hip level. She was happy that her bar would look well used as if not-too-careful people belonged there. She also bought some freestanding tables and a flotilla of captain's chairs.

Charlotte came by often and told her what this bar in Gloucester did and that one in Hyde Park did. Charlotte was an encyclopedia of bars.

"You must have a phone for the customers," Charlotte said. "Being able to make a call is crucial in a bar. The phone must be a little bit away from the counter so it won't be too noisy to talk, but it must be close enough so you can keep an eye on your coat. It helps if local calls are free." Charlotte's word on that was gospel to Rena, and she ordered a big black wall phone. "When they first come in a bar, people like to be able to see what kind of a place it is, what kind of people are here, before they commit," Charlotte went on. "But the people in the bars don't like to be looked over by every Joe who comes in off the street, so you need a divider here to separate the lookers from the drinkers.

Rena called information in Boston for The Wrecking Bar where she had spent more than one idle Saturday afternoon many years before. It was still there on a side street off Dot Ave.

Within the week, Rena was driving through St. Margaret's Parish looking for a familiar gateway. There it was. A pair of English iron gates, a mass of interlocking black curlicues, loomed in front of her like the entrance to *The Secret Garden*.

She drove in and parked. Swinging the heavy door open as she remembered how strong he was for one so wiry. There it was—a jumble of disembodied pieces of architecture. She began systematically touring the rooms, scrutinizing everything, twirling the wooden wall paper rollers, handling the glass doorknobs, running her fingers over the acanthus leaf pediments. This was almost as good as brushing off the dirt from fragments of pottery at an archeological dig.

She found herself almost breathy with anticipation, and she wondered how much was eagerness to discover treasure for her pub and how much was from being again in the dusty alcoves where she and had glided, touched, kissed a former lover. She pushed on to the back room and fairly gasped when she found the rows of etched glass doors, different ones, no doubt, but still the same. Quickly, and without hesitation, she committed herself to buying two small etched pub windows, one saying BAR and the other SALOON, as if they had been waiting all these years for her.

She hurried to the basement rooms, where she found the very place beside the furnace where she had given pleasure on the rattan porch glider. She could not imagine she had ever done such a thing in such a brief and tenuous moment of privacy. She paused a moment and pictured him, sprawled limply, dark hair curling around his neck and spilling over the rattan, zipper bursting. She felt a twinge of wanting. She slapped the divan that had taken the porch glider's place. A cloud of dust rose from the cushions. Same dust, she thought. She chose some objects to put on ledges and hang on walls of her pub: a case of wooden spools from an old woolen mill, $175; a chemist's scale in a glass and mahogany cabinet, $125; and an English toy horse of paper mâché on wheels, $250. A ship's wheel, though too shiny to have ever been on the high seas and a bit trite besides, seemed a must for the tourists at $200. Ditto for the brass coat of arms for $175, most stereotypical with lions and crowns and the motto, "L'union fait la force." More to her taste was a lovely fragment of a carved screen from a carrousel for $120. She had to have it. She found an old stair rail, a simple pine handrail with balusters and a walnut newel post with turned segments as big as hams. She was sure she could use it to separate the entry area of the bar from the back—the lookers from the drinkers, as Charlotte had advised.

The lady at the cash register seemed startled when Rena pulled out a wad of cash to pay for her purchases and shipping charges. But the sale was made, and Rena filled out the shipping address with pride and tucked the receipt away carefully.

The carpenter, the flooring refinisher, the electrician all took their pieces from the money under the daybed. The industrial ovens, refrigeration, and dishwashers, though bought used, set her back a chunk. Adding an extra bathroom for women was not cheap.

Nevertheless Rena took the plunge and hired a cook.

"This is not a restaurant. This is a bar," Charlotte reminded her more than once. "This is not gourmet, this is merely satisfying."

Rena was grateful for the distinction.

Rena and Charlotte went over the glassware together. She ran an ad for an experienced bartender and also called the school of bartending in Boston in case they had to settle for a recent graduate.

"If he can provide the hustle, I can provide the experience," Charlotte said.

"Or she," said Rena, heady with her own power.

All the while, Rena had been reading books about English pubs. Long ago, one book said, people agreed to meet "at the sign of the Black Bull" or "at the sign of the Rose and Crown" because most people couldn't read and they needed to identify the pub by the image of a black bull or of a rose and crown painted on a sign.

The idea appealed to Rena.

"What do you think would be a good object for the name, Charlotte," Rena said.

"Just call it 'The Bar on Front Street.' That's what people will call it anyway."

"I may have to do that for now because we need to be getting out some publicity. Forty-two Front Street."

"Fine."

But Rena had a better idea.

The tables and chairs arrived at last. Setting them out was perhaps the most exciting thing Rena had done yet. She bought permanent press table cloths and planned, for the time being, to take them home every night to wash in her own washer. Lord knows, living by herself, she had kept her machine underemployed. She also put the old woolen mill spools on the tables as candle holders.

Then Rena addressed invitations to the grand opening. She invited everyone she had ever worked with at Town Hall, all the selectmen, all the town's vendors, and all her neighbors on Dory Beach Hill. She sent a notice to all the shopkeepers and landlords in town and an invitation to all her old paperboys aged twenty one and over, all the artists who had ever invited her to a show opening, everyone who had ever cut her hair or repaired her car or unclogged her drain. She left an invitation in her box for her mailman. She sent a notice to the newspapers and to the tour company that ran the bus by the Oldest House on Cape Ann. She had asked Donna the Diligent for her old reunion list of everyone from Stonehaven High class of 1955 through 1959, and Donna had given her all their addresses on a disk. She printed out address labels on the computer at Town Hall while she still could.

Opening night would be like the wedding she never had, Rena thought, sitting cross-legged on her day bed with all her old address books in her lap. The thought of a wedding reminded her of her mother. Rena added her to the list.

She took out an ad in the G. D. Times. One free mug of beer for all comers, it said.

Monday, Tuesday and Wednesday, three days in a row, she, the new cook and Charlotte cooked and served lunch and evening fare for a small crowd. They baked popovers by the bushel, cooked buckets of chowder, dozens of greasy burgers, and tossed a hamper of salad. Rena invited the assisted-living home in Essex to send a bus load of ambulatory patients to shake down the restaurant. She hoped no one would see them and take this for her clientele. She treated Boy Scout Troop 12 to hot dogs and tonic after their weekly meeting. They were equally inappropriate clientele but honest critics and a good place to dispose of food. During all of this, she took notes on omissions and glitches and tried to solve them.

Thursday, on the afternoon of the grand opening, Rena was trying the outside lights for the umpteenth time and turning the neon "Pabst" in the window on and off. The mounting for a sign had been hung over the door that morning. Charlotte stopped under the empty mounting and pointed up and cleared her throat to bring Rena's attention to the neglected detail.

"Oh, that. The man from the sign company is coming to hang it at five o'clock." Rena looked at her watch.

"A sign would help," Charlotte said.

At quarter after five, Ernie from the sign company arrived with the sign wrapped in brown paper. He set it down, and Rena and Charlotte watched while he tore off the brown paper and looked up at Rena for approval.

"The Cape Ann Hat?" Charlotte read. "What's a Cape Ann Hat?"

"You know, the hat that the Cape Ann fishermen wore."

"You mean the yellow thing like on the statue in Gloucester?" She put her hands behind her head to outline the shape of the brim dipping in the back.

"No, that's not the Cape Ann hat. That's a sou'wester."

Rena pulled a box out from the mop closet.

"What's that?"

Something I ordered from one of those companies that bronze baby shoes."

"Oh, my god, not baby shoes."

Rena pulled a carton out from under a table, opened it, and pulled back the tissue. There was a brown object, amorphous in shape, every wrinkle petrified. Charlotte gawked, then ran her fingers over it. When it did not give to her touch, she tugged at it, thumped it, and tried to bend it.

"It's a frigging hat in bronze," Charlotte said.

"Acrylic, actually. Space age bronze."

Charlotte held her palms up in bewilderment. "I give up."

"It's the Cape Ann hat, the real Cape Ann hat. The one Paul wore."

"Paul wore! I thought you said you were over Paul. How many times do we have to go through this? This bar is not a memorial to Paul Lawson or I don't want any part of it. Jesus Christ. Why not use the sou'wester from the frigging statue? Everybody knows that. Every kid with a yellow raincoat. Everyone who ever ate a Gorton's fish stick. Nobody but nobody knows the goddam Cape Ann hat."

"Fine, Charlotte," Rena said with mock sweetness. "When you look at the sign, you can think of the sou'wester; when the tourists see the sign, they can think of the sou'wester, or the Fisherman's monument, or Gorton's fishsticks, or whatever they want. But people who know will recognize the Cape Ann hat."

"Yeah, there were two of 'em, and now one of 'em's dead."

"And I'm over him!"

Ernie looked worried. "Is the sign okay?"

"It's fine," Rena said.

Rena took Charlotte's arm roughly and pulled her inside. Then she spun Charlotte around so their noses almost met.

"Now stop it." Rena gave Charlotte a shake. "I'll even admit to you that I was in love with Paul—if you will concede I'm finally turning this to my advantage. The skills I learned at Town Hall I am using now for my benefit. By his vote for liquor, he's giving me my due. And I am taking it, by God. When I put that hat on that bracket out there, that means that from here on Paul Lawson is working for me!"

Rena lifted the hat and put it rakishly on her head, even though it weighed as much as a pitcher of beer, and struck a sassy pose. Then she jerked the stepladder out the door and climbed it. She took the hat off her head and set it on the bracket.

In the late afternoon, Rena and Charlotte went home to bathe and change clothes for the evening's activities. Rena manicured her nails, and put lavender scent in the tub, and treated herself to a lingering soak.

She wondered what Howard Blackburn had done in the hours before he opened his bar. He didn't soak in a bath of lavender water, she was sure. And he didn't manicure his nails. Rena winced at her own bad joke. The fingerless old salt probably smoked a cigar and played his card tricks. It gave Rena satisfaction that a man of Blackburn's heroism had found opening a bar worthy of his efforts and determination.

Of course, the former fisherman had already proved himself in his fight for life on the North Atlantic. Rena felt cheated on that score. How scattered and trivial by comparison are the usual demands of life, how hard to be a hero, how hard to find an arena for dramatic effort.

But here was her chance. The goal would be clear. Survive. Make it. Succeed. Every shred of her being would pull in one direction.

Then she thought of the money left in the suitcase. That unearned money would diminish her effort by dulling the challenge of her new venture. With money to fall back on, there would be no moment when she would overcome, when she would prove herself greater than she'd ever dreamed, when she'd know she had triumphed. Paul's money would take away full responsibility, in the sense that Charlotte had once defined the word.

Rena had freely used the money for startup expenses for the bar. She was now debt free. But she would use no more of it, not for operating expenses nor food for her own table. She would toil and sweat and sacrifice before she would ever touch this money. Oh, she would be tempted but never would fall back on that.

She pulled herself out of the lavender water and was dressed to go by the time the last bath water gurgled down the drain. She went down and pulled out the remainder of Paul's money that was still in the suitcase, and she counted it, every last bill.

She sat down at Aunt Amelia's antique desk and drafted a letter to the nursing school of Deaconess Hospital which had years before taken over Aunt Amelia's beloved New England Hospital. In this letter, she committed to donate $51,380, the exact sum of the contents of the suitcase—to endow an annual scholarship for one promising nursing student from Cape Ann. Aunt Amelia had been devoted to the nurses, the ones who made patient care ultimately possible. A few thousand dollar scholarship every year would keep one nursing student in school.

Rena would honor the determination and ambition of her great aunt who went out into the working world at the turn of the century and became an independent woman. If, by giving Rena the means to her present comfort, Aunt Amelia had encouraged a certain dependence, that had surely not been her intention. Amelia Douglas's example of a woman choosing a difficult field and persisting was beginning to take hold.

Rena wrote the letter by hand, addressed and stamped it, put it in her purse and went to the Grand Opening.

Charlotte was already there. She came out front to greet Rena, in fact, before Rena even got to the door.

"It works, Rena," Charlotte said. "Yes, it's right. I admit it now. This hat, this frigging Cape Ann hat, looks like the average Joe just hung it up there and came in for a brew."

Rena looked up at the hat and the sign and down again at the antique door etched with scrolls and the word, "Saloon." She examined her new beer glasses decorated with the name and logo of the bar. It they're stolen, they say, it's the same as advertising. All the large effort and small details had come together, and she was proud.

"And, Rena, I take it all back about Paul. I concede you've turned this whole thing to your advantage. Rena, you can't lose."

Rena only glanced quickly at Charlotte's face for fear she'd cry. At 8:05 Rena was looking at her watch. Charlotte was sitting at the bar bantering with the cook. Rena sighed loudly, and Charlotte looked around.

Rena grimaced at her.

"Nobody comes at eight o'clock," Charlotte said. "Nobody wants to be first. It doesn't mean anything."

Rena broke open a popover in the warming oven to see that it wasn't drying out.

At twelve minutes after eight, the door opened and a stranger poked his head in and swept the empty room with his eyes. Rena smiled at him. "Good evening," she said, and then looked down to polish the already glassy bar so as not to put the visitor on the spot.

"Nobody in here," he said to someone behind him. The door was propped open by the man's shoulder for a full minute, it seemed. Rena went with the outbreath. Then they left. Rena sighed.

"Don't worry," Charlotte said. "A bar has two peaks, the before-dinner crowd and the after-dinner crowd. The after crowd doesn't get going till nine."

Rena turned her back to Charlotte to hide the tears she feared were coming. But she got a grip. She brought a dozen more glasses from the kitchen and put them upside down on a linen towel.

Rena heard an occasional car pass by. She tried not to hold her breath when it slowed for the turn. She tried not to let her heart sink when its sound faded. She couldn't realistically have expected the Town Hall crowd, she reminded herself, or the class of fifty-nine or any of Paul and Maureen's friends which included all of her own. She had known that when she stuck the labels on their invitations. But it hurt.

By nine fifteen there was no one. Rena turned her back to the bar and the tears swelled. She let them come, let her face contort, and cried like silent rain.

Then, blindly, she reached for her purse and, without explanation, stepped out into the night. She crossed the street and went down a block to the mailbox. She pulled the letter to the nursing school out of her purse, pulled down the mail door and poised the letter over the dark gulf of no return. She waited for a feeling of peace, a sign that this was right, a message of hope. But no feeling of peace swept over her, no sign, no hope. And so, in the midstream of pure terror, she dropped the letter.

When she stepped back inside the bar, she heard the tones of the phone behind the bar beeping out a little tune. Then Charlotte's voice was tinkling. Rena could hear her voice, talking, giggling; she couldn't hear the words. Rena couldn't have giggled if her life depended on it. Her vocal chords, tight for hours, now lay spent in her throat like seaweed stranded on the beach.

The cook muttered softly to himself. Charlotte's voice bounced along, high and flighty with cascades of mirth. She's probably a little manic, Rena diagnosed; that would explain a lot.

Rena stood, her back nearly numb, grooved by the edge of the bar she was leaning on. This went on for she didn't know how many quarter hour rings of the clock.

Then a motorcycle passed outside, snorted, then went on smoothly—or did it die? It could have been just outside the door. A car crunched gravel somewhere close by. Voices. Someone yelled. "F'crissakes. take up two spaces, will ya?" Then laughter. A commotion, you could call it, Rena thought glumly. The door opened, and the commotion was on her doorstep. A bunch of strangers. Charlotte laughed.

"No bikes allowed inside," Charlotte joked. "You guys were quick."

"We laid rubber, babe."

One of them whooped, one of them picked Charlotte up and carried her a few steps before putting her giggling on a bar stool. "Let it hang," a third prescribed.

They bellied up to the bar and ordered draft. New arrivals piled in behind the first. The newcomers stood behind the first row at the bar.

"There are tables..." Rena said waving to the rows of dark polished table tops and the blur of spindles of empty captain's chairs.

"They can see there are tables," Charlotte admonished her. "Relax."

By ten thirty the place was murmuring. Half the tables were taken. One table was telling stories of other nights in other bars, and the waitress and Charlotte were scurrying. Rena stepped outside the front door and looked at a flotilla of cars lining the sidewalks. Five Harleys were parked perpendicular in front of the door, illegally, like skiffs tied up at a dock. She looked at the sign on an easel ... "Grand opening," it said in old English lettering. And under it, hand lettered, $2 was crossed out and above it was written $1 beer. Rena rushed inside.

"Charlotte, the sign outside says dollar beer!"

"Well, yeah, this is the grand opening, isn't it?"

"I know, but the invitations said 'Free Beer' for the grand opening."

334

"So who has an invitation? Not these guys."

Rena thought a minute. "So what about the two dollar sign that was crossed out? The first guys had to pay two dollars?"

"No, no, no. It's been like that all along. You know. Looks like a bargain. Hell, they've been paying three dollars for a beer in Gloucester. Don't worry. It's going to be all right."

Rena started to sniffle again, this time with relief. She ducked her head on Charlotte's shoulder. "Thank you is all I can say. But tomorrow the place will be empty again."

"Maybe. But there's a lot of tomorrows. It will build. I guarantee the townies will come around. They need a bar too much to stay away."

Rena posted herself at the door again, assuming body language she thought suggested confidence, her arms open, her foot resting on the bottom rung of a stool.

The door swung open and couple of guys came in. Rena glanced hopefully their way. No, nobody she knew. "Welcome to the Cape Ann Hat," said Rena brightly. She was grateful the men allowed her to show them to a table; they were the first to sit in her captain's chairs, the first to even look at a menu. She was thrilled but tried not to show it.

The door swung open again. Rena turned around.

A middle aged man and his wife. Rena did not recognize the woman at all, but the man's face with its square jaw on the thick football player neck seemed familiar. She couldn't think who. More and more lately people looked familiar when they weren't. Maybe she had met all the types of faces and figures there were in the world. There were no new types. She showed the pair to their table and gave them menus. The waitress fairly pounced.

She could hear the couple asking the waitress questions. She had to hold herself back from rushing over to answer them. She did not relax until she saw the basket of popovers steaming on their table.

A few more of Charlotte's crowd came, a few left. The gathering at the bar went from pathetic to raucous to respectable to hard core. Rena was too shaken to measure passing time.

As the couple—the ordinary couple, the only couple—was

leaving, the man said to Rena, "Nice place you've got here."

Rena shrugged her thanks.

The man seemed to catch her feeling. "It'll build," he said kindly. "It takes time. I know. I've sweated through a few opening nights, myself. By the way," he said leaning confidentially toward her. "Thanks for taking the heat off me by serving the first liquor in Stonehaven."

Rena was puzzled, then embarrassed.

"I'm Leland Johns. That's my development–Wildwater–over on the point."

"Oh! Mr. Johns."

"Leland. And this is my wife, Beth."

"I'm Rena ...." They shook hands, and he headed for the cash register. Rena stood dumbfounded. Her first colleague in her new world and it had to be the enemy.

"Leland!" she called after him. "It's on the house."

The developer turned back. "Thanks. Nice of you. I'll return the favor when my place opens."

When the last of the bikers left, Rena talked Charlotte into leaving the cleanup for Saturday morning, and she went home and slept as if drugged. She was clearly going to have to become a night person to run this bar.

Saturday morning Rena was lying groggily in bed as if she had always been a night person. The phone rang. She hurriedly pulled together swirling images into some kind of reality and picked up the phone.

The caller was a woman from Cape Ann Tours, the ones who drove the buses by The Oldest House in Stonehaven. The general manager had seen the mention of Forty-Two Front Street opening in the paper. Did she want to talk about making the pub a possible stop at the end of the tour, a place for their clients to gather after shopping on The Lane? Was the place big enough, was it suitable, the woman wanted to know.

They'd expect a special discount coupon, of course. Of course. Rena tried to keep her voice cool and businesslike. When she hung up the phone, she beat her pillow with her fists in joy until wisps of feathers floated off the bed and disappeared into the pattern of the oriental rug.

By noon, Rena was sitting alone at the bar. The room was empty. The rhythm of a wire whip creaming chowder in the kitchen was the comforting sound of emerging routine. Rena was scratching a pad with a pencil, figuring how much a bus load of tourists would bring her. She was thinking of offering a free slice of quiche with the purchase of one drink. Eggs were cheap, and quiche was chic. Maybe real men don't eat it, but have you ever seen a tour bus full of men?

Also, the full impact of Rena's gift to Deaconess Hospital was beginning to hit her. So what would she do? Hand them a suitcase of cash?

She began to mull over the implications of cash and the possibility of getting a check or perhaps a money order. She wondered which type of transaction would attract the least attention from, say, the IRS. She wondered if the amount were sufficient to generate a press release from the nursing school and what repercussions that would have. These and other questions added a cold mass in her stomach to the general chill from the risk to which she was so unaccustomed. She thought deeply and jotted her thoughts down on paper then crossed them out. Finally, she looked at her watch, went to the phone in the back, and made an appointment.

"I was wondering," Rena said, as she tried not to squirm in the leather chair in the Trimark executive offices, "if you could help me with something."

"Certainly, I'll help, if I can," said Mr. Leland Johns.

"I want to give a gift to the Deaconess Hospital for a nursing student scholarship in the name of my great aunt."

Rena supposed the developer nodded.

"My great aunt was a pioneer surgeon in Boston. She saved blue babies among other things, before blood typing was done. She had a soft spot in her heart for the nurses."

"That's interesting...."

"At the end of every day, I have put in a box every one dollar bill I have left in my wallet. I've saved them over the years. It's amazing how they eventually mount up. This is the money I'm giving. I've informed the hospital of the gift just yesterday.

Leland Johns raised his eyebrows.

"There's only one thing I'm concerned about. It's in cash...in a cardboard box–a canned dog food box, to be exact. Now I don't want to be in the newspaper as some old eccentric who handed a small fortune to a hospital in a dog food box!"

Leland laughed.

"Of course, I could put the money in the bank. But I've heard the bank takes note of large deposits and informs the IRS. I certainly don't want to be audited. Oh, my accounts are in order, but I don't want the IRS to be on my case."

"I understand."

"I wanted to ask your advice, since you are more experienced in accounting and finance than I. How do you think I could handle this best?"

"How much money are we talking about?"

"A little over fifty thousand. There used to be more but...some of it got away."

Leland Johns's *face* said nothing but Rena thought she heard the synapses of his brain crackling.

"What exactly do you want me to do?"

"I was thinking maybe if I gave you the money, Trimark could write a check to the hospital in honor of Dr. Amelia Douglas. Of course, that $50,000 might seem like petty cash to you." She tilted her head in a coquettish way, but Leland Johns was pokerfaced.

"The donation would help with taxes, wouldn't it? You get a tax break, my great aunt gets her scholarship, and I get the box out of my house."

She was quiet now, reading Leland Johns reading her.

Finally he said, "Wouldn't you want your name on the gift? After all, you were the one who saved the money and you were the one who wrote the letter to the hospital."

"It's enough to have my aunt's name on it...and it would be nice to have the pleasure of presenting the gift to the nursing student, but couldn't I do that anyway as Dr. Douglas's niece? As for the letter, how will we explain that?"

She turned the question to him, made it his problem, to see if he would buy into it.

"If you were on our board.... No, then the board would have to approve the gift. Too complicated.... I have it. How would it suit you to be the liaison between Wildwater and the Town of Stonehaven?"

"I'm afraid I couldn't be much of a liaison because almost no one in town is speaking to me."

"No one in town is speaking to us either, so it's a perfect fit."

They both laughed.

"Give me a day or two to work this out," the executive vice president said. "I have to talk to some people."

"I'll be waiting to hear from you, then," Rena said, handing Leland Johns her new card with her name in bold under the sign of the Cape Ann Hat.

She stepped outside on the sidewalk and fairly clicked her heels together. The brilliance of her scheme dazzled her. Her currency problem was solved.

As she drove down the line toward Stonehaven, she exulted. She was making an honest man, well, an almost-honest man, of whichever man—or men—might need redemption. And she was rid of the money. Evening came.

"Day Two," Rena said.

"But who's counting?" Charlotte said.

Patrons trickled in; the door squeaked shut behind them. Rena watched their faces. They looked all around the room once and then up at the ceiling and, as if concluding it was not a trap, they settled down on a stool or chair. Rena no longer felt it necessary to force feed them. She greeted them, she passed by again after they were served, she asked if they needed anything.

"How did you hear about this place?" she asked a few. An ad in the *Gloucester Daily Times*, they said. The power of advertising was modest but observable, as was her progress. She became comfortable with her guests, however few or many.

A palpable calm overtook her. She had stopped thinking of success or even of tomorrow. She moved from door to bar to tables and back without a ripple, becalmed like a tidepool after the tide has passed, thinking neither of the wave to come nor the one receding, completely absorbed in the lifespan of the moment, sharpened into crystal focus.

It was one in the morning before the place cleared. One of the bikers from the night before had come back and was nursing a scotch at the bar. Now he was standing forehead to forehead with Charlotte over the bar. He finally turned to go, and Charlotte came out from behind the bar to see him out, his arm around her, her hand under the back of his shirt.

"Go on, Charlotte. I'm in the mood to do the cleanup on my own." The cook put the food away, Rena swept the floor, the waitress wiped off the counter and loaded the dishwasher. As the last glass was going in, Rena said, "I'll take that." She wrapped it in a napkin and put it in her purse.

Sunday morning Rena's phone rang all too early. Rena knocked the phone off its cradle and picked it up to hear Charlotte's voice already reading, "'The newly opened Cape Ann Hat, the first bar to test the previously dry waters of Stonehaven, has charm, and the popovers are worth the trip.' Isn't that incredible? Congratulations!"

"What are you talking about?"

"In the paper this morning. A review—well, okay, three sentences—on the 'Cape Ann Places and Faces' page, under 'Stonehaven Sightings,' first item."

"The paper? The G.D. Times? Oh. Read it to me again."

"The newly opened Cape Ann Hat, the first bar...." Rena jumped to her knees in bed to listen better.

"And get this: 'The crowd was sparse on opening night, but hurry before the tourists take it over.' Cool or what?"

Rena was silent a second, processing the "sparse" and then jubilant. "Hurry? Hurry? Hurry before the tourists take it over!" She was bouncing on the bed like a child when she was seized with a sudden puzzlement.

"Charlotte, since when have you been getting up at 6 a.m. to read the paper."

"I picked it up on the stands on my way home this morning. I thought you'd want to hear about it right away."

"On your way home this morning!"

"Yes, mother. Just because you were snug in your bed all night, doesn't mean the rest of us can't have a little fun." Charlotte's unfettered laugh made Rena chuckle and then sigh. It was going to be hard for her to play the free spirit. With Charlotte as her sidekick, she was afraid she'd always be the old fogy by comparison.

Rena was wide awake now. It was fully light, but most of the world was still asleep. The sea was gray, sun-tipped wavelets bobbing lazily. Rena couldn't hear them hit the shore at all. It was a gentle morning, a morning to lie in bed after a hard night. The kind of morning she imagined Howard Blackburn woke to, lying in bed covered with a down comforter, after being plucked from the surf on the beach of Nova Scotia at dusk the day before.

Though the story of the man who froze his fingers off had long ago seemed like a ghost story or a cautionary tale to frighten a small child into wearing her mittens, he had suddenly become a person to her, beckoning with the stub of a finger, offering her some advice. From the first prickling of fingers in the cold on Boding Point the day of Paul's accident to the day she heard of Blackburn's own bar, Rena had felt a connection. And when she read how he had opened an illicit saloon and won his way to respectability, she was infatuated. Howard Blackburn. So what if he was just a symbol. You take your inspiration where you can get it. Symbols give meaning to life's prosaic jumble of concrete events, whether it is the sea or the flowers or the words of Omar Khayyam or Our Lady of Good Voyage or a stack of lobster pots. Some are for Omar and some are for Our Lady. Some are for the lobster pots and some are against. Each is a magnet that pulls the objects around it into a pattern that centers effort. You know it when you feel it, and Rena felt it. You can't go against the gut. The gut is more powerful than the mind. You can argue the mind around, but you can't convince the gut.

Rena pulled on some jeans and a sweatshirt and drove over to the cemetery. She made her way up the hill through the grass, wiping a green swath through the silver dew, soaking her tennis shoes. She stopped in front of Paul's grave. Two angels adorned the top corners of his headstone, the kinds of ornaments, she thought, that would be known in later years for their missing heads. She had begun to get the hang of this grave thing. She was carrying a beer glass with its new white lettering: The Cape Ann Hat. She assumed an exaggerated thespian stance, lifted her glass to Paul, and recited out loud:

And when thyself with shining foot shall pass
Among the guests star-scattered on the grass
And in thy joyous errand reach the spot
Where I made one—turn down an empty glass.

Rena turned the glass over and placed it on the headstone, cocked over one of the angels. The thick curved bottom of the glass shrunk the cherub's body, widened its eyes in surprise, and curled the corners of its pious mouth. Rena walked away, taking no care to follow the cleared path of her arrival, tossing the dewdrops of a new path off the ends of her toes.

THE END

www.ingramcontent.com/pod-product-compliance
Lightning Source LLC
Chambersburg PA
CBHW022205010726
47493CB00002B/416